The Old Man in the Park

The Old Man in the Park

FRAN MIRABELLE

Charleston, SC
www.PalmettoPublishing.com

The Old Man in the Park

First Edition

Paperback ISBN: 978-1-63837-184-7
eBook ISBN: 978-1-63837-185-4

DEDICATION

1971 Rocky Mountain Oysters

This book is dedicated to the Rocky Mountain Oysters, an extraordinary collection of talented athletes, scholars, jokers, tough guys, and most of all, friends. They were my inspiration for writing the book. It is my distinct honor and pleasure to have been a teammate of those boys.

It is difficult for me to fathom that 2021 marks the 50th anniversary of our championship season and that the time has gone by so quickly. On a better note, at this writing, all team members are still alive. I just wonder if any of us can still shoot a basketball without pulling a muscle.

CONTENTS

ACKNOWLEDGEMENT

A lthough most of what is included herein never happened, a few of the accounts and descriptions actually occurred in one form or another. Literary license allows me to alter, change, modify, amend, vary, transform, rework, adjust and revise the narrative to adapt to the situation being described. The characters herein are generally composites of people I've met through the years, and of course, the names were changed to protect the guilty parties. Seriously, my life experiences have largely been filled with decent, interesting, and talented people. At the forefront of those sentiments are my family (especially my wife and parents) and my friends.

CHAPTER 1
Family Ties

The persistent buzzing woke Jordan Marsh from his restless sleep. Through half-open eyes, he looked at the clock radio on the nightstand next to his bed. It read 3:18 a.m. Jordan realized immediately that it wasn't time to get up, but rather the call he had been dreading. He fumbled for the knob on the lamp by the clock radio and was finally able to rotate it two clicks and get some light into the bedroom. Gaining his senses he located his cell phone and quickly checked the screen for the identity of the caller.

Jordan answered with his standard greeting, "Hello, this is Jordan Marsh," although his voice was anything but in *standard* mode. Instead, it belied the fact that he had just been awakened. His voice was rather raspy and low-pitched. He silently wished for the glass of water that he usually kept on the night stand beside the bed, but had forgotten the night before.

The voice on the other end of the phone replied, "I'm sorry to have awakened you, Mr. Marsh, this is night shift supervising nurse, Mary Starling. You had better come to the center fairly soon." She gently added, "Your father began slipping since you left last night and may be only hours from passing. Of course, these situations are difficult to predict, so it still may be several hours. At any rate, I just wanted you to be informed."

Jordan asked her a few questions relative to his father's condition, breathing, and pain level. Nurse Starling responded that Thomas Marsh, Jordan's dad, was resting more or less comfortably, but his breathing had become shallower. He was now running a low-grade fever. She further explained that it was likely due to the onset of an infection, possibly pneumonia since his father had been bedridden for some time. Morphine had been administered in small doses periodically to keep him as comfortable as possible. Jordan assured her he would be there within the hour. She then mentioned, "It would be a good idea to notify others in Thomas's family." Jordan assured her that he would, thanked her, and ended the call.

His conversation with nurse Starling lasted less than two minutes, but by now Jordan was thinking clearly, fully awake, and alert despite having had only a few hours of sleep, albeit a restless, dream-filled sleep. As the adrenaline kicked in, he quickly made his way to the bathroom and washed up as much as possible, then got dressed. Knowing full well that he had to call his sister, he decided to do that while making the half-hour ride. At that time of the morning, there wouldn't be many other vehicles on the road, but he still wanted to be heading to the Mercy Hospice facility quickly, just in case.

By 3:30 a.m. Jordan was backing out of his driveway and on the phone to his sister, Jackie. Jordan apologized for calling so early, then explained the urgency of the situation. He quickly filled her in regarding the nature of the phone call from the hospice facility. Jackie understood and told Jordan she was half expecting the call. She, too, had not been fully asleep figuring her father's condition may turn for the worst.

Jackie wondered aloud, "Maybe one of us should have spent the night at the hospice center with Dad."

Jordan reassured her, "The medical staff didn't think anything was imminent when we left last night." That was around 11:00 p.m. Jordan further reminded Jackie, "The nurses urged us to go home and get some rest." Besides, he explained, "They are the experts in these situations and have seen many similar cases." Jackie understood, but being close to her father, she still felt a little bit of abandonment.

Jordan suggested that Jackie take care of her family first, then get to the hospice center as soon as it was practical. He would be there in a few minutes, assess the situation, and get back to her. She agreed that it was a good plan, but wanted to be called immediately if there was any further worsening of their father's condition. Jordan reassured her that he would.

Jackie was married to Richard Cardel, and the couple had two children, Richie, Jr., and Amanda. Both children were still of school age, so some of Jackie's family responsibilities centered around getting them up (and ready) for school, making lunches, and getting them to and from school. Richard had worked as a certified financial planner (CFP) for a local investment firm for five years before branching out on his own in partnership with another broker. Jackie was a stay-at-home wife and mother but had finished college. She hoped to resume her career once her children were old enough to more or less fend for themselves during those after-school hours when no parent was home until the workday was finished and the commute completed.

Jackie and Richard met at college in their sophomore year. She pursued business while he studied finance. They both graduated college in four years. Richard went on to graduate school and obtained his MBA while Jackie pursued law school finishing in three years with her Juris Doctorate. Because of their backgrounds, it was only natural that Thomas Marsh's financial affairs were handled by Jackie and Richard, but in reality, it fell mostly to Richard, since he was the CFP. Jordan had no problem with his sister and brother-in-law handling their dad's finances after Thomas took ill. Besides Jordan's education, background, and interests were not remotely related to handling tax returns, investments, Medicare regulations, and the many medical billing statements related to Thomas's declining health. Also, Richard handled Jordan's retirement portfolio, as well.

Jackie and Richard dated for several years before deciding to marry in their late twenties. They both started entry-level jobs in their fields after their schooling was completed and began the progression up their respective corporate ladders. They decided to wait to have children, but by their mid-thirties, they realized it was now, or never. As Jordan would later say, once they decided to have kids, Jackie popped out two in rapid-fire succession. They also decided that Jackie would take time off from her career to stay home with Richie, Jr., and Amanda, who were now ten and nine, respectively.

Jordan was godfather to both his nephew and niece and loved them as if they were his children. He made time to see them in many of their school programs and sports activities. Jordan particularly enjoyed watching Richie, Jr. play T-Ball and basketball even though at times those athletic endeavors deteriorated into a game of *everyone chase the ball* instead of each tyke staying in his or her assigned area. Of course, if baseball and basketball were a calamity, soccer was the ultimate scrum, but Jordan always got a laugh out of watching the kids run around and have fun.

Jordan further enjoyed playing with his nephew and niece. When his work schedule allowed, he would drop by their house to play catch or shoot hoops with Richie. Amanda was more interested in music than sports, but Jordan dutifully listened to and encouraged her to play her piano pieces for him. By all accounts, Jordan was an ideal uncle.

It was natural for Jordan to be more interested in sports. At an early age, he played every sport he could in its season. Thomas was a supportive parent but to a point. He always wanted Jordan to be a scholar first and an athlete second. Jordan understood quite well where his father was coming from, especially because he knew if he didn't do well with his studies, his sports life would be curtailed, and that edict came from the top: Jordan's mother, Vivian.

Vivian Marsh was an excellent mother to Jordan and Jackie. She raised them to be caring, loving, and honest people who always knew right from wrong, especially from her and Thomas's perspective. Vivian was raised by strict parents, who expected her to complete her chores and homework before even asking to go outside and play. During her formative years, she learned how to cook and bake from her mother. Vivian's mother also taught her and her sisters how to sew, knit, and quilt. By the time she was in high school, Vivian was already a well-trained, old-school homemaker. It was no surprise that she was always at the top of her class in any home economics project.

During her teen years, Vivian was discouraged from dating by her parents. At first, it didn't bother her, but after meeting Thomas at a high school dance her feelings changed. For the better part of the school year, Vivian and Thomas would meet at the Saturday evening school dances. Even though they never left the dances together or went on a formal date, they considered themselves going steady. Finally, Vivian got up the nerve to ask her mother if she could invite Thomas to meet her and her father. This was mostly due to the school year coming to an end, and Vivian not wanting to miss out on seeing Thomas throughout summer vacation.

Initially, her mother said "no", citing her age as being too young, which at the time was 16. Of course, Vivian persisted, and with the help of her sisters, she was eventually allowed to have Thomas visit her on weekends with her parents as chaperones. They continued their courtship over the next year with dates and house visits, but always under the scrutiny of her parents. Over time Thomas was becoming increasingly less satisfied with that arrangement but figured it was probably better that way than making an issue of it. At least, he figured, he was getting to see Vivian and, ever the gentleman, would work within the system outlined by Vivian's parents.

Thomas was a year older than Vivian and a charter member of the baby boomer generation, who were now getting ready to graduate. He was also in the process of deciding his future. He knew that full-time college was out of the question since he wasn't from a wealthy family, but he hoped to pick up some night classes at the local community college in perhaps plumbing or auto mechanics. In the meantime, he could try to find work as an apprentice at one of the local shops in town. That was all well and good, but there was one more unknown hanging over Thomas, and that unknown would affect the rest of Thomas's life.

His senior year was filled with the usual fun and frivolity, dances and parties, a prom and graduation ceremony. It was 1964 and times were changing across the country. Unfortunately, shortly after graduation Thomas (like all-male American 18-year-olds at the time) was now eligible for the military draft, having lost his high school deferment upon graduation. Doubly unfortunate, and naturally unknown at the time, the United States would greatly escalate its involvement in the Vietnam War in early 1965.

Thomas, the ever dutiful soul that he was, had signed up for the draft right after his eighteenth birthday, as was required by law. He now had a decision to make: get a job and wait for his draft notice or bite the bullet and enlist. If he enlisted, he could have his choice of the services, but likely that meant a longer period of service. He recalled meeting with an Army recruiter during a school visit when he was a junior. Now, he wished he had paid more attention to what he was told about the military, service options, opportunities to travel, job training, and the like.

Having graduated in June, he weighed his options for a few weeks while hanging out with friends, doing odd jobs, seeing Vivian, and playing American Legion baseball for the local post. As it turned out, Thomas was an excellent high school baseball player in particular, and generally a fine athlete. He was a good enough baseball player to make the semi-pro team in town. What kept him from being looked at seriously by area scouts were his slight build and lack of a strong throwing arm. When Jordan began playing sports it was obvious to Thomas where Jordan got his athletic ability.

By the eighth grade, Jordan had realized a second love, sports being the first. He found that he enjoyed reading, and not just the sports section of the local newspaper.

After a class assignment involving a book report of his choosing from a list of 19th century American authors aroused his interest, he started reading some of the other great literary classics. He found himself reading more and more books, and well beyond those which were required for his classes. The more he read, the more he began to appreciate the writing styles of the various authors like Nathaniel Hawthrone, Ernest Hemingway, Edgar Allan Poe, Herman Melville, and Mark Twain. Even foreign writers, such as Leo Tolstoy, Charles Dickens, Anton Chekhov, and Sir Arthur Conan Doyle piqued his interest. He realized that his newfound interest was different from those of his peers, which resulted in a reluctance to discuss his latest readings with them. Of course, that didn't stop them from wondering why Jordan always seemed to ace his literature classes. Jordan not only did well in literature, but he was also an all-around excellent student finishing in the top ten of his graduating class, in addition to being an officer in the National Honor Society. This delighted Vivian much more than his sporting acumen.

Like his father, Jordan was a pretty good athlete, and like his father, he excelled in baseball. Jordan was built bigger and stronger than his father, perhaps because of better nutrition during his growing years, or perhaps because he inherited some of the genes from his mother's side of the family. By the time he graduated high school he stood six feet tall and weighed 175 pounds. Jordan did inherit his father's same dark brown hair and blue eyes. He could have easily been a three-sport star in high school if he chose. Instead, he concentrated more on academics than sports, playing just baseball for his high school team. After high school, he didn't grow much, but that was fine with him since he was not interested in pursuing playing sports at the collegiate level, even baseball. He did, however, stay active by playing some intramural sports for his fraternity, since sports were still an interest of his, just not as much as they once were.

One of Thomas Marsh's proudest epiphanies was that he knew Jordan was better than he was at the early stage of their respective athletic lives. There was good reason for it, though. Thomas practiced with Jordan in all sports, but Thomas knew the most about baseball, so naturally, Jordan got the best instruction there. It wasn't only advice as to how to hold the bat, or how to throw without putting too much strain on his arm, but Thomas was able to instruct Jordan in situational baseball, the finer aspects. That is, where to position himself defensively depending on the batter; where to throw the ball if it were hit to him depending on how many men were on base, which bases and how many outs there were; what pitch to look for from the pitcher in certain counts; not to mention batting stance; base running techniques; and the various types of slides.

Jordan started to play Little League at eight years of age. Immediately, he was elevated to play with the nine and ten-year-olds. It was obvious to the coaches that he was a class above his eight-year-old counterparts. This continued for Jordan throughout Little League resulting in him being named the player of the year when he was twelve. His hitting and fielding resembled that of a kid with natural ability rather than one who was mechanically completing each sports movement in fielding, throwing, or batting.

In early August of Jordan's last season and during his team's All-Star competition, Jordan completed two rare feats. In a game against their archrivals, Jordan was playing shortstop. It was the bottom of the sixth (and last regulation) inning. Jordan's team was clinging to a one-run lead. They were in the field with no outs and the bases loaded. As the batter hit a line drive to Jordan's left, he instinctively raced toward the ball, two quick steps later he snared it on the run, and in one fluid movement stepped on second base to force the runner who had started for third. Without breaking stride he kept right on running toward the baserunner from first base, who was now running at him. He tagged him for out number three to end (and save) the game. Jordan's swift and effortless movement caught the umpires a little off guard, and it took them a few seconds to realize that he had just completed an unassisted triple play to end the game in the most dramatic fashion.

His team's next game was the semi-final in district play. Jordan was considered a decent pitcher, but on this All-Star team, he was the number two starter. As the game progressed into the late innings, neither team had scored. What was particularly interesting was that Jordan was pitching a no-hitter. Further of note was the rule that no pitcher could pitch more than six innings in a Little League game. After striking out the side in the top of the sixth inning completing his pitching day where he had recorded 16 of the 18 outs via strikeouts, Jordan knew his pitching day was complete. As fate would have it,

Jordan was due to bat third in the bottom of the sixth inning. Both teammates ahead of him struck out without so much as fouling off a pitch. Jordan then stepped up and hit the first pitch over the centerfield fence for a game-winning home run.

From that point, it was assumed that Jordan would be the next superstar baseball player, at least by his father. However, after Little League, there was no organized baseball until high school or American Legion. In those few years, Jordan's interest migrated more toward literature than baseball. His obvious athletic talent and ability to outshine his competitors were rapidly dwindling, despite playing mostly sandlot sports. By high school he was still an above-average player, but no longer was he the best on the team, and this disappointed Thomas.

During his junior year in high school, Jordan began looking at colleges. He had begun to consider pursuing a career in journalism and by his senior year, he was sure that was his destiny. He would find an excellent liberal arts school to work toward his journalism major and a minor in English Literature. By the time he graduated he had not only written scores of articles for the college newspaper but was named the paper's editor in his senior year. Having enjoyed the opportunity, it solidified in his mind that journalism was his future.

Jordan pulled into the hospice parking lot just before 4:00 a.m., then quickly parked and locked his vehicle. The ride over had been uneventful, as expected, and it had provided him the opportunity to talk with his sister. He knew he still had another call to make. This one would be to his Aunt Pat, Thomas's sister, but that could wait until a later hour, and after Jordan had seen his father and talked with the hospice staff. He now hurried up the sidewalk into the hospice center, signed in at the reception desk, and took the elevator to the third floor where Thomas's room was located.

Thomas shared a room with another man. Their beds were separated by a curtain. Jordan entered the room quietly to not disturb either his father or the other patient, although that was unlikely since both were in that comatose state that precedes death. He used the time to assess his father's physical condition. Sliding into a chair bedside he observed that Thomas was still breathing, but as nurse Starling had stated earlier, it was less regular and shallower than he had noticed the night before.

Jordan also took the time to say a short prayer, although he wasn't a particularly religious person. It just seemed the right thing for him to do at the time. His only hope and prayer were that his father was not feeling any pain. He then placed the back of his left hand on his father's forehand to feel for warmth. Although not burning up, Jordan could detect a slight increase in his father's body temperature. He next felt for Thomas's pulse, but not being medically trained, it was difficult to find. He, therefore, looked at Thomas's neck and was able to see a faint throbbing motion. His final observation about his father's condition was one that many people exhibit shortly before passing. Thomas's color had faded from a normal flesh tone to an ashy gray.

By now it was a few minutes past four. Jordan knew he should check in with the nurse's station and particularly with the supervisor if she had the time to speak with him. Once at the nurse's station, he explained who he was and inquired if nurse Starling was available. The nurse at the desk explained, "She's with another patient, but I'll ask her to see you at her earliest convenience." She then recommended, "You may want to return to your father's room and wait there because it'll be more comfortable. Also, it will allow you to have some quiet time with your father, and perhaps you can even catch a nap because, frankly, you look very tired."

Jordan thanked her and returned to his father's room which was only about five or six doors from the nurse's station. Once there he tried to get comfortable moving a chair near the wall so he could rest his head backward, close his eyes, and let his mind wander to happier times.

He began thinking of a few things he wished he had talked over with his dad. For some reason, the first thought that popped into his head was Thomas's service in Army. Jordan knew that his father had been drafted within a year after graduating high school. He also knew that he served in Vietnam during the ramping up of hostilities there. What he never found out, although he had asked a time or two, were the details about Thomas's military service. He knew he could likely find out some general information through Army records, but he had hoped for specifics, such as where he served, with whom, in what battles he fought, and most importantly what it was like to be on patrol where there were snakes, bugs, booby traps, not to mention the chance of being shot at any moment. Through other accounts and movies, Jordan had learned of drug activity and rampant alcohol consumption during soldiers' downtime. Having never served, Jordan was naturally curious. Sadly, he realized that his father's accounts were now lost. What he never understood was why his father didn't want to share his experiences. This was not uncommon, however, since many combat veterans choose not to relive those details.

As those thoughts slipped to other remembrances, Jordan's mind next moved to his mother. His first thought was of her death and how much he missed her. Having passed away unexpectedly and suddenly two years prior due to a stroke, she was now, once again, foremost in his thoughts. Vivian was just 70 when she died, young by 21st century standards. By all accounts, she was a special person, devoted to her husband, children, and two grandchildren. Like Jordan, she wasn't an especially religious person, certainly couldn't recite biblical chapter and verse, but she was very much a kind, sweet soul, who never spoke harshly of anyone. During quiet times, such as these, Jordan's thoughts often drifted toward his mother, her very kind nature, and the fact that she was taken from their family so suddenly and much too soon.

Vivian never had a formal occupation, although her skills as a seamstress allowed her to supplement the family's income through her sewing. Jordan recalled that Vivian was so capable with the needle, thread, and sewing machine, not to mention knitting needles, that she was easily able to make all of her own and Jackie's dresses, even prom and wedding attire. When she and Thomas were first married, Vivian knitted several pairs of socks for Thomas (winter wear), not to mention sweaters and scarfs. They were such high quality that Thomas was able to wear many throughout their marriage. She often completed several dozen sewing projects over the winter months so that when spring arrived, she was able to hock her wares at flea and farmer's markets in the surrounding area. After her grandchildren were born, she turned her attention and sewing expertise toward making them clothes, and of course, babysitting, when needed.

Jordan's thoughts then returned to his father and something that his Aunt Pat had mentioned to him. Shortly after his mother's funeral, his aunt told him, "Keep an eye on your father and his health, now that your mother's gone." She continued, "Often it happens when one spouse passes away, the other seems to give up on living and declines rapidly." This was certainly the case for Thomas. Several years prior he started having unexplained medical issues. He had always been athletic and healthy, but by his mid-50s some irregular test results started showing up on his annual wellness exams. At first, no conclusive diagnosis was made, but eventually, it was determined that his exposure to chemicals from his military duty, possibly Agent Orange (the herbicide and chemical defoliant in wide spread use in Vietnam in the 1960s), was the likely cause of his ailments. Over time Thomas's medical problems worsened, despite many trips to the local VA hospital for treatment. Now, fifteen years later, they were taking his life.

Jordan recalled what the hospital generalist explained to him and Jackie right before Thomas was sent to the hospice center, "Your father's organs are shutting down.

His lungs, kidneys, liver, and heart are shot. He doesn't have much time left. He should spend his last few days in hospice care where they can keep him comfortable and out of pain." Jordan wasn't sure if that suggestion was made out of compassion for his father, or rather the hospital just trying to free up a bed and not wanting Thomas to die under their care. Somewhat cynical, he knew that hospitals were businesses, care-giving businesses, of course, but businesses nonetheless. On the other hand, he was astute enough to know that hospitals were in the business of treating people to get better; however, when patients were deemed beyond help, the best course of *treatment* was hospice care. It was a slippery slope, indeed, and Jordan wasn't envious of their jobs making those life-and-death judgment calls.

It was only a few days after arriving at the hospice center that Thomas was on the verge of death. To Jordan's relief, at least, he could see that Thomas was comfortable. Jordan took the opportunity to whisper in his dad's ear, "I don't know if you can hear me, Dad, but if you can, please know that I love you. I realize this is a little late for me to be telling you this, but I appreciated everything that you did for me along the way and all the wonderful times you made for our family." He continued, "One more thing, Dad, and I really have no right asking you this, but if you can hang on a little while longer, Jackie will be here soon, and I'm sure Aunt Pat would like to be here to say good-bye."

Shortly thereafter, nurse Starling peeked into the room and introduced herself to Jordan. Jordan sprang to his feet and introduced himself. For some reason, he was expecting an older person and was pleasantly surprised to see someone he figured to be close to his age. She gently suggested, "Why don't we move to the family meeting area for a consultation?" He agreed and followed her down the hall and around a corner to a nicely appointed lounge. At that time of the morning, there was no one else there, so they could have a private conversation. Once seated, she explained, "Predicting end of life timelines is an inexact science. It could be a few hours or several. Each patient is different, and we try to learn a little from each to help with the next one." Jordan instantly noticed her very compassionate tone and caring words. She continued, "I'm sure you noticed that your father's condition has worsened since yesterday. Please know that we are keeping him as comfortable as possible. We only administer a small puff of morphine when he becomes restless. This won't necessarily accelerate his passing. It just keeps him calm and hopefully out of any discomfort."

Jordan nodded so that nurse Starling could see that he was understanding what she was telling him. She then asked if Jordan had any questions for her. Jordan thought for a second, then mentioned, "I noticed my dad's skin tone was more grayish and less pink. Is that normal?"

She explained, "That's very normal in these situations. You may have also noticed that your father's hands and feet were getting a bit cooler. This, too, is normal."

That reminded Jordan of touching his dad's forehead, so he then mentioned, "But, my dad's forehead felt a little warm, and you mentioned an infection when we spoke on the phone earlier and possibly pneumonia?"

She acknowledged that she recalled the conversation and reiterated, "Again, very common observations at this stage. It wasn't unusual for a dying person to feel warm around the head, for example, but cool at the extremities since the heart was probably not able to pump the blood very well."

He apologized for being out of his element and not knowing anything about what to expect. He mentioned that the only other person in his life that had died was his mother, but she had passed suddenly, so this was all new to him.

Nurse Starling quickly made him feel at ease, "It's not a problem asking me anything. That's why I'm here. If anyone on our staff can be of any further assistance, please don't hesitate to ask." Turning to her clipboard, she then directed a few questions to Jordan relative to the information he and his sister provided when they checked Thomas into the hospice center. She needed to verify that the undertaker they designated was still the one they wanted to be notified when the time came. She also wanted to be sure that Jackie was correctly listed as power of attorney. Jordan acknowledged that she was. Next, she asked if the chaplain on duty when Thomas passed should be called bedside for a family prayer. Jordan nodded approvingly.

Finally, she said, "Included in the chaplain's duties, we have an excellent grief counseling service here at Mercy. Patients of any denomination and their family members are not only welcome to participate but encouraged to do so." Jordan again nodded that he understood, said that he would pass along the information to his family, and thanked her for her time and kind demeanor.

Having covered the administrative matters, medical discussion, and conveyed the counseling services opportunity, nurse Starling asked, "Is there anything I can get for you right now? Would you like a drink, snack, pillow, or blanket?" Jordan assured her that he was fine and didn't need anything. She then suggested that he return to his father's room and perhaps catch a little rest while he could. He agreed that it was a good idea, but that he needed to call his sister first. Nurse Starling then offered that he could stay in the lounge to make his call, and if he felt it to be more comfortable there, he could use the sofa for a nap. At that point, she departed, but not before letting Jordan know that she would check on him and Thomas again before her shift ended at 7:00 a.m.

Since it was still very early, Jordan didn't want to call his sister just in case she was able to fall back to sleep. Instead, he sent her a short text, "R U awake?" In seconds a reply arrived on his phone letting him know that she was. Jordan then made the call to her even though he had no new information to convey. He just knew that Jackie would appreciate hearing from him rather than receiving a text. Jordan quickly filled her in about the discussion he had with nurse Starling explaining that it was a wait-and-see situation. He further explained that there was no normal, so predicting the exact number of hours their dad had left was just not possible. Jordan then asked what she was going to do with Richie and Amanda regarding school. Jackie said that she was going to get them ready and send them and that she and Richard would probably get to the hospice center around 9:00 a.m. Jordan was fine with that and mentioned that he had whispered in Thomas's ear about hanging on until she and Aunt Pat got there.

Jackie thanked him for that and said, "If I can get there earlier, I will."

Jordan replied, "Do what you need to do for your family, I have this covered, just be safe."

Jordan knew it was still much too early to call his Aunt Pat, so he decided to set an alarm on his phone for 7:00 a.m. and call her then. That way it would give him a chance to catch a couple of hours of sleep. He was now walking back to his father's room and already thinking of the next several items on his agenda. He knew that before he could rest his eyes, or hopefully catch a nap, he should leave a message for his editor that he would not be able to see him for their scheduled meeting that morning. His editor was aware of Jordan's situation regarding his father's imminent passing, so it wouldn't come as a surprise. Jordan also knew that his usual column would be missing from his paper's next edition. He felt bad about it but realized that there wasn't much he could do about it, either.

After college Jordan and a friend decided to take the summer months off before earnestly looking for employment. They used the time to travel, see some sports stadiums, national parks and take in several concerts at various venues around the country, finally getting to see some of their favorite performers. Jordan had saved some money by working throughout his college days at the university book store and writing freelance articles. He was fortunate to have had several of those articles published in major magazines and Sunday newspaper special sections. Of particular note was an essay he was able to cobble together through research and personal interviews about the professional baseball's Negro League. Unfortunately, by the mid-1990s when Jordan was writing the story, many of the Negro League stars had already passed on. However, he was able to interview a few by phone to get their accounts as to their plight. He came away understanding, and his article reflected it, that the Negro League stars were just as good as those of the Major Leagues, but many never got the chance at the big league level.

Another of his stories centered on the Battle of Gettysburg during the Civil War. He became very interested in that battle in particular and the war in general after taking a family vacation there shortly after his Little League playing days had concluded. He recalled his family taking a battlefield tour and being fascinated by the tour guide's vivid accounts, the details of the battle, how the fighting had spilled into the town, the positioning of the North and South forces, Pickett's ill-fated charge, and the amount of dead and wounded during the three-day battle. Jordan astutely tied the Battle of Gettysburg to another one in Vicksburg, Mississippi at approximately the same time. Both were Northern victories that changed the course of the Civil War, and of course, the history of the country. As a human interest sidelight, it didn't hurt that Jordan and Jackie were able to complete their Junior Ranger requirements, get their badges, and have their pictures taken with a National Park Ranger's hat atop their heads. This only served to further Jordan's interest in researching and writing, not to mention visiting the country's national parks.

From there his family continued north to Williamsport, Pennsylvania, in time for the Little League World Series in August. Eventually, Jordan would get around to writing about that experience, as well, but with an added storyline. Through his research, for that project, he realized that even when kids are involved, adults will sometimes find a way to foul the process. He found more than one instance where older-aged kids were able to play beyond the maximum age. Some had altered birth certificates. Some kids from foreign countries had suspect credentials. Also, some jurisdictions encompassed larger than allowed areas making the talent pool competitively unfair. He concluded his article on a positive note with the observation that children from all over the world, who often couldn't communicate with one another verbally, were able to compete and have fun; and in the end, they all shook hands and moved on, hopefully, better for the opportunity to have met and competed.

Jordan figured correctly that those published works would be viewed favorably on his resume when the time came for him to seek career employment. He also knew that he didn't have a large window of opportunity, so he continued to write just enough to keep himself in the game, so to speak, while having as much fun as possible during his downtime after four years of studying, exam taking, working and writing. In the fall after graduating and having his summer of fun, Jordan put together an impressive resume and sent it to several newspapers and magazines. He was delighted to receive multiple offers for employment very quickly. After careful consideration, he decided to accept a position with a large metropolitan area publication in New York, one that had published some of his previous freelance work. He thought it would be a good opportunity for him to learn the journalism ropes at a large newspaper. He also knew that if/when he decided to move on, this also would be a fine resume builder, especially if he did well, and he was determined to do well.

Back in his father's room, Jordan did another cursory check of his dad's condition. Thomas didn't appear to be any different than when Jordan left with nurse Starling so that was comforting, at least as comforting as it could be under the circumstances. Jordan decided to try to get some sleep since his father looked to be peaceful. He knew that by later in the day everything was likely to change and not for the better. He knew he had to be functional at that time, and a bit of rest now would go a long way toward helping him be ready and clear-headed later. Once again, he sat in the chair alongside his father's bed and leaned his head against the wall.

Before nodding off Jordan recalled a story his father had told him about how his mother and father were married. Jordan knew there was some resistance from Vivian's parents, but he was surprised to learn that there was an absolute forbiddance the first few times the idea of their getting married was offered to them. Thomas explained that Vivian's parents were very strict and wanted Vivian to wait until she was older. To Vivian, it seemed that she was always told to wait until she was older, no matter her age, or the subject. Jordan was very aware of the strict nature of his maternal grandparents. As a young boy, he never really warmed up to them. They weren't cuddly, hugging, kissing grandparents, but more the type to want the visiting grandkids to be quiet, not touch anything, sit still during meals, eat what was in front of them, and then go outside to play as soon as dinner was finished, no matter the time of year or weather conditions. Needless to say, those visits to Grandma and Grandpa Schultz's house were few and far between, and that suited Jordan and Jackie just fine. Thomas was just as happy to have those visits spaced out, but he hid it well. Vivian, while wishing the situation to be different and her parents to be more hospitable, understood it for what it was. She, therefore, didn't push for her family to visit her parents, only succumbing to major holidays and birthdays.

The irony of the situation and the very great testament to Thomas's kind nature came later in his and Vivian's married life. During their elder years, Vivian's parents became needy due to the usual medical issues that often come with advancing years and a nutritionally poor ethnic diet. Also, they had a lifetime of hard work that saw both working in factories during the day and gardening in the evenings during the spring and summer months. The constant manual labor had taken its toll on both. By their early 70s, they were unable to maintain either their yard or garden, but of course, they wanted both to be the way they had kept them in the past. As what usually happens, the children get tasked or asked to help out. In Vivian's case, it was only going to be her, since her sisters were no longer living in the area. Thomas being the kind, giving soul immediately stepped up and took the burden off Vivian. He offered a plan whereby he would take care of the yard and garden if she would entertain her parents inside the house, or at least her mother. It was a good plan, but he knew his father-in-law would insist on being outside to supervise his work. That didn't work well when Thomas was cutting grass, because it was difficult keeping an eye on him and keeping the lawn-mower moving in straight lines. Thomas came to be able to tolerate his father-in-law while they were in the garden together. He sat him in a lawn chair while he did the hoeing, planting, weeding, and watering always under the watchful eye of his father-in-law, and the occasional, 'That's not the way I'd do that' comment.

Throughout the years the great unspoken sore point for Vivian's parents was the circumstances surrounding Thomas and Vivian's marriage. After she finished high school and right before Thomas was to report for his army physical and induction, they gave an ultimatum to her parents. Since Vivian was by then 18, and no longer needed parental consent to get married, either her parents blessed their marriage or Vivian and Thomas were going to elope. They tried to reason with her parents. From a romantic point of view, they offered their deep love for one another. From a realistic point of view with Thomas going into the army it was smart because Vivian would then be his dependent and acquire certain benefits, not to mention a death benefit in case Thomas became a battlefield fatality. Her parents wanted them to wait to see if they still felt the same way about each other when Thomas's military stint was over. Thomas and Vivian persisted, and at the eleventh hour, her parents relented. They were married in a very simple ceremony without much fanfare and no honeymoon. Having passed his induction physical already, Thomas was required to report the next day for basic training. He got married in the morning and was on the road to Fort Benning, Georgia that afternoon. While their marriage got off to a rocky start with her parents, it was never an issue between Vivian and Thomas. They remained loyal to each other and happily married until Vivian's sudden and untimely death just two years after their golden wedding anniversary.

Jordan was finally able to doze off around 5:00 a.m. and stayed sleeping until his phone alarm went off at 7:00 a.m. While asleep he dreamt of some of the better times in his life when he was younger without the burdens of work deadlines or the worries of an aging (and now dying) parent. His dreams drifted from his youth and the fun activities associated with school and sports to his dating life in high school and college. For the last several years he had been having one recurring dream sequence of his only real girlfriend, their dating, engagement, wedding, and married life. It was a fun ride, as he liked to say until it wasn't anymore.

Jordan married Kathryn O'Mara when they were both in their mid-20s and after dating for four years. They met in college on a blind date arranged by a mutual friend. While it wasn't love at first sight, there was certainly a spark. They continued to see each other pretty much exclusively throughout their first year of dating, then decided on a steady relationship. After graduation and their summer of fun touring the countries' ball parks, national parks, and concert venues, they both got jobs. Jordan's decision to move north to New York resulted in Kathryn also applying for employment there. It wasn't a problem for her to find work in the education field as an elementary teacher, especially in an urban area.

They were together for nine years, married for five. Unfortunately for them, the romantic spark began to diminish over time and problems crept in. Jordan's work kept him away from home more than either one of them liked, but as a sports writer, it was his job to interview players after games, and many of those games didn't end until late. Of course, Jordan's workday wasn't over when the game was, since he then had to interview players and construct a storyline for his column, not to mention write it in time to make a deadline for the morning edition of the paper. The easy games were his city teams' home games. When those teams were on the road, he was expected to travel with the teams and report on the games.

Kathryn, or Katie, as Jordan liked to call her, had a schedule that required her to be up early and at school by 7:30 a.m. Jordan was a night owl. Katie was growing lonely not seeing him and being marooned in their city apartment. He was leaving for work many days when she was coming home, and he would get home in the early morning hours well after she was asleep. Weekends weren't a given that he would be home, either, as that was when many ball games were scheduled. Finally, she decided after a few years that the big city life wasn't for them, or at least not for them with their current jobs.

Kathryn discussed with Jordan the idea of finding a different line of work. He immediately balked. Writing, and sports journalism, in particular, were not only his passion but now his occupation. He was doing well in his job, had developed an interesting writing style and a large readership, not to mention winning some awards for his work, all in his first few years. She understood and moved the discussion to the back burner – for a while. After a few more months, of course, the loneliness and resentment surfaced again, and then again a few months after that. This recurring pattern was frustrating both. Kathryn had some valid points. She offered that many nights they had opportunities to go out with other couples she knew through her work, but Jordan could not make many of them. She was also off work during the summer months, but Jordan was working. So, the disjointed work schedules were becoming an issue.

As with any relationship that is struggling, it's not just one parameter. Additionally, there was the larger problem of Jordan wanting children and Kathryn not wanting any part of motherhood. The irony was perplexing to Jordan. Here was an elementary school teacher who enjoyed teaching kids, but didn't want children of her own. Further confusing Jordan was the fact that Kathryn O'Mara was Irish Catholic. Traditionally, that ethnic/religious demographic had large families, and Katie, herself, had two brothers, two sisters, and many cousins. However, this was a new age where the old traditions often weren't followed. Even if Jordan wanted kids, he understood that it took two wanting the same thing to make that happen, and he also understood that it was likely not going to happen.

The final straw for Jordan occurred when Kathryn developed a relationship with a work colleague. Over time he sensed an escalation in Katie's coolness toward him. At first, he tried to ignore it, but after a year, it became more than he was willing to live with. He finally summoned up the nerve to ask for a discussion, then was shocked to learn that Katie was in a relationship and had been for the last year. What floored him was that Katie was involved with another woman, not a man. He had no idea, and it left him stunned.

Shortly thereafter, they mutually decided to get a divorce. Jordan was in no way interested in trying to seek counseling, or reconcile since he felt betrayed. Kathryn, on the other hand, didn't seem to know what she wanted.

Jordan considered her the consummate *me* person, spoiled rotten and always needy. She thought of herself first, last, and all places in between. When Jordan would get overly frustrated with her self-centeredness, he often began singing a few lines from the Wallflower's song "The Difference" to her. He deemed them very appropriate in describing her, so he'd begin singing, "You always said that you needed some, but you always had more than anyone. The only difference that I see, is you are exactly the same as you used to be." Needless to say, Kathryn didn't like the mirror being held up to her.

In the end, though, she still had feelings for Jordan, but she was also missing something in their relationship that she was now getting elsewhere. Ultimately, she agreed to a divorce arrangement whereby she would collect a small amount of alimony since Jordan had a higher-paying job.

Within a few months, Jordan decided that he no later wanted to be in the same city with his soon-to-be ex-wife, even though the likelihood of them crossing paths was remote. Besides, it was costly enough living in a New York City apartment with two salaries, let alone one, and with the added expense of soon having to pay alimony, it was going to quickly become cost-prohibitive. Kathryn had moved out of their apartment and into her partner's in Brooklyn, nearer to where they both worked.

As much as he hated to leave New York and getting to see and write about all the teams there, Jordan was now in the process of putting out some feelers for employment closer to his hometown. About the same time that their divorce was finalized Jordan was very pleased to land a sports writing job back in his hometown. The divorce hit his parents very hard since they very much loved Katie like their own daughter. But, on a brighter note was the return of their son. Jordan took up residency with his parents for a few months until he got settled both emotionally and financially. Also, he was beginning to sense that there was a change in his father's health, so he rationalized his moving back home as there being a reason for everything in life.

By now it was 7:15 a.m., and Jordan had gotten a cup of coffee at the refreshment area near the nurses' station. He needed just a few sips to get going and become clear thinking before calling his Aunt Pat. Once on the phone with her, he immediately identified himself, "Hello, Aunt Pat, this is Jordan. Sorry to be calling you so early. Did I wake you?"

She replied, "No, honey, I've been up for a little while. How's your father doing?"

Jordan continued, "Well, that's why I'm calling. I got a call in the middle of the night that his condition was declining, so I rushed right over. As it turns out, he's resting comfortably, but it may only be a few hours."

"I'm so sorry to hear that, Jordan," she said. "He has suffered so much lately, and you know that he pretty much gave up on living once your mother passed. There was not much anyone could do for him medically. I know that you and Jackie took great care of your dad, especially these last two years, and for that dedication and the honor you showed him, you both should be proud."

"Thank you for the kind words, and yes, I know you were right on the money giving me a heads-up concerning how my mom's passing would likely affect my dad. Also, you are correct in that he has suffered. As harsh as it may seem, he will be better off passing quietly and quickly. It's not like he's going to recover or even come out of his coma," he concluded.

"Well, you are being realistic," she said, "and I know you have had some time to get adjusted to not having your father around. It's a different situation than your mother's passing for sure. I don't know which is better, dying suddenly or lingering. I'd guess from the family's perspective your father's long decline has given everyone time to understand that he wasn't going to recover, so ironically, we can accept our loved one's passing a little easier. Like many difficult times in life, there is a process that we go through to get to acceptance."

Jordan knew his aunt to be a special woman that always spoke with a rare combination of compassion, strength, honesty, and pragmatism. This time was no different. What amazed him was that it was her brother dying, someone, she had known longer than Jordan had. He knew that she had to be hurting, as well, yet she was trying her best to comfort and console him. Jordan then mentioned, "I know you wanted to see your brother once more, so that's the reason for this update. The staff here feels that my dad is probably not going to live through the day, but they were cautious reminding me that end-of-life estimation wasn't an exact science."

She thanked Jordan and concluded their conversation, "Your uncle and I will be there as soon as we can. Until then, try to get some rest, honey."

A few minutes after he finished his conversation with his aunt, nurse Starling popped her head in the door. "How's your father? Any change?" She asked.

Jordan got up out of gentlemanly respect when she entered the room and answered, "I haven't noticed any change, but if you have time, please check him over. Sorry to ask that of you since your shift is over."

"Oh, I'm fine," she said. "We often are here awhile after the end of our shift. We need to make our reports for the next shift, anyway." She then listened to Thomas's heart, took his pulse, and felt his forehead for any fever. "Hmmm," she said. "That's interesting."

"What's interesting?" Jordan asked.

"Well, your father seems to have rallied a bit. His heart sounds a little stronger, he looks like some color has returned to his face, and he's not as warm as he was three hours ago." She then suggested, "He may be waiting for someone. Sometimes when they feel that someone is coming, they'll hold on for them."

Jordan then mentioned, "I did whisper in my dad's ear a few hours ago that if he could hang on a little longer, my sister and aunt were coming later."

"OK, that's probably why he's rallying," she concluded. "Even though they are in a comatose state, and it looks like they aren't with us, they can often still hear. Hearing is the last of the senses to go."

"Wow, I didn't know that. Perhaps I should not have said anything to him," he said.

"No, you did the right thing. Your father's time will come when he's ready. I don't think it will be much beyond today, though. We've seen this scenario before, many times," she reassured him. "If there's nothing else, I guess I'll be on my way. It's been a pleasure meeting you and your family. I just wish it could have been under different, better circumstances."

"Me, too," Jordan reassured her. "I want to thank you and your staff here at Mercy for the fine care you provided my dad."

"You are more than welcome," she said and then departed.

Jordan once again took a seat in his chair against the wall and slowly sipped his coffee. He began to wonder about the staff that serviced hospice centers. In particular, he wondered how they were able to do the jobs they did day after day. Dealing with death daily must be quite exhausting, he thought. Yet, they kept coming to work showing a great deal of care for their patients and compassion to the patients' families. The burnout rate in their profession had to be exponentially higher than other lines of work. Even nurses in hospitals, who see their fair share of death, don't have the situation where they know no one is getting out of there alive. He reasoned that those nurses had their share of success stories, and he thought, hopefully, more successes than failures. All of a sudden he realized that his job was a piece of cake, relatively speaking, except for the occasional looming deadline when he had no solid storyline.

Since his father was resting comfortably and now apparently waiting for his sister and daughter, Jordan figured it might not be a bad idea to close his eyes and see if he could catch another nap before the rest of the family arrived. He expected Jackie in an hour, or so, and his aunt sometime thereafter. Before drifting off, his mind went to nurse Starling. He recalled that they were about the same age and that she was attractive with ash-blond hair and blue eyes. He also noticed that she was physically fit. His final thought before falling asleep was whether or not she was married. He hadn't seen a wedding ring, but he knew that she could still be married.

Ever the punctual one, Jackie arrived in Thomas's room precisely at 9:00 a.m. after dropping her two kids at their elementary school just before their starting time of 8:30 a.m. While at the school, she decided to see their principal letting her know the family situation regarding Richie and Amanda's grandfather. Mostly, Jackie wanted her to know that Richie and Amanda may have to miss a day or two of school depending on services for their grandfather. Mrs. Marchand, the principal, naturally understood and told Jackie not to worry about the school work. It could easily be made up because both her children were excellent students. She then offered her sympathies to Jackie, and Jackie thanked her before departing.

Once in Thomas's room, Jackie tried to be quiet to not awaken Jordan. She knew that he hadn't gotten a lot of sleep, but then again neither did she. After a quick check of her dad, she sat down and started to look through her purse for a pencil. She figured to pass some time by working the crossword puzzle that she had started the night before. About that time Jordan opened his eyes, "Oh, you're here." He said. "How long have you been here? What time is it, anyway? He continued.

"Just a few minutes passed nine." She answered. "I got here right at nine. I would have been here earlier, but I decided to stop in the school to talk with the kids' principal."

"Everything okay at school with them?" Jordan asked.

"Oh, yeah, everything is fine. I just wanted to let Mrs. Marchand know that the kids may have to miss a day or two depending on the wake and funeral arrangements. She said it would be no problem."

"That reminds me, the supervisory nurse asked me if we were still good with Granatelli's Funeral Home," he continued, "she was just double-checking her paperwork and wanted to be sure we hadn't changed our minds. I told her that we were good with Granatelli's."

"Still good by me. I see no reason to switch now. They did a nice job with mom's viewing, funeral, and burial, and they have ample parking and are not too far from the church and cemetery." She then added, "I recall that they were a bit pricey, but then again, I'm guessing they are all about the same.

"Yeah, no doubt," said Jordan. "I guess you can't even die without it costing a small fortune these days."

Jackie then interjected, "You know we'll have to go to the funeral home and select a casket for dad, as we did for mom, and make a few other decisions. I can call them in an hour, or so, just to give them a heads-up that we plan to use them to wake and bury dad, and to see what they have available as far as dates. Hopefully, it'll work out with them."

"Fine by me, but if you prefer, I'll do it," Jordan offered. "Just let me know."

"Nope, I'll take care of it," she concluded.

Then Jordan asked, "Where's Richard?"

"He had a client meeting later this morning that he had to prepare for and then a conference call after that, so I'm not sure he'll make it to see dad in time," Jackie stated matter-of-factly and with a slight bit of contempt.

"Dad's not *his* father, so no big deal," Jordan said.

"Yeah, well, dad's been very good to him, to all of us. The least he could do is honor him by showing up to say 'good-bye'," Jackie snapped.

"This dying stuff isn't for everyone. We all handle it differently. He may not be able to take it," Jordan countered.

"Nice of you to try to defend him," she blurted out. "It's not a matter of not being able to handle it."

"I'm not defending him. I'm just pointing out that we are all different, and besides, he has work responsibilities," Jordan replied. "Remember, that's what pays the bills."

"Let's just drop it," Jackie suggested, and Jordan was only too happy to oblige.

He apologized by saying, "OK, no problem. Sorry to have brought up a touchy subject." He then continued, "I've been sitting here for some time now, dozing off and on, so if you don't mind, I'm going to take a walk, stretch my legs, maybe get some fresh air, and give you some time alone with Dad. I won't be long. Are you okay with that?"

She nodded and said, "Go and take a break. You look like you could use one."

"Call me if things go south. You know what I mean," he said as he got up to leave.

"OK, see you later," she said.

Before departing, he added, "I talked with Aunt Pat a couple of hours ago. She said she and Uncle Charlie would be here as soon as they could. So, expect them any time now." He then headed for the door, walked down the hallway, took a left after the nurse's station, stopped to use the restroom, then got on the elevator. Jordan wasn't sure where he was going. He just knew after being there for the better part of five hours, he needed to get out of his father's room for a few minutes. He took the elevator to the ground floor, checked out at the reception desk, and decided to go outside to get some fresh air.

CHAPTER 2
Chance Encounter

It was a beautiful early May morning. Jordan thought of the many days like this that he and his father played catch, tossed a football, or shot baskets some 30 to 40 years prior, and well before his father started showing signs of slowing down. He silently longed for one more opportunity to do any one of those fun things again with his dad.

Outside the hospice center and across the parking area Jordan noticed that there was an inviting park. It was across the street from the hospice facility and on the main street that led into town. Jordan could see that the park had a large open area and a tree-lined path with walkers and joggers that encircled the open space in the middle of the park. Spaced out along the path were benches. In a different city, they might be the same benches where the homeless population would spend the night, but not here in Middleboro.

Jordan decided to take a walk across the parking lot toward the park after stopping at his car and depositing his jacket. The night before, he needed the jacket, but now it was already 70 degrees, sunny with very comfortable, low humidity air. As he crossed the street and entered the park, he figured that was as good a place as any, and better than most, for his walk to help clear his head and stretch his legs. He thought to himself, 'How did I miss this park the previous couple of days when I was visiting my dad across the street?' He surmised that he was focused on getting to see his dad and didn't take the opportunity to look around outside. When leaving, it was night, he figured, and being emotionally drained and just plain tired, his focus was on getting home and getting to sleep.

Before entering the path around the park Jordan decided to see which direction dominated the flow of walkers and joggers. Some were moving clockwise, others counter-clockwise. He then figured counter-clockwise was for him. The path was wide enough to handle the traffic in both directions, and at that time of day, there wasn't an abundance of pedestrians, anyway. Jordan noticed one person riding a bike, but the path was only about a mile in circumference, so biking was hardly worthwhile, he thought. Mostly, the bike traffic would only be small children, who would be there with their parents.

As Jordan started his leisurely stroll, he checked his watch. He didn't want to be gone too long and leave his sister alone for a great length of time. He noticed that it was half-past nine, so he figured he would try to return in an hour. When he got to the far side of the park, he spied a coffee shop across the street that ran parallel to the street on which the Mercy Hospice was located. He had not eaten, so he decided to check it out, but not until he made another revolution around the perimeter of the park. Once he had gotten something to eat and drink, he figured he could just cut across the park to save a few minutes and get back to see his dad, sister, and perhaps his aunt and uncle by then.

When Jordan had just about completed his first loop around the park, a jogger coming toward him slowed and waved. He wasn't expecting to see anyone he knew and was frankly in a bit of a daze. He stopped and stared for a second or two, then realized that he recognized the face, but couldn't immediately place it.

"Hi, Mr. Marsh, it's Mary Starling, the nurse from the hospice center," she reintroduced herself as she took her headphones out of her ears.

"Oh, hi," Jordan replied, having been caught off guard. He continued, "I thought you would be long gone by now."

"Well, usually I am, but sometimes I need to release some stress, and I find a jog around the park is a good way to accomplish that," she stated.

"I understand completely. You have a tough job. I don't know how you handle it every day," he sympathized.

"I do get some days off, so I use them to re-charge my batteries in addition to the running," she said.

"Great, good for you," he said.

Not missing a beat, she said, "I'm almost finished with my run. Have you had breakfast yet, if not, and you have the time, are you interested in grabbing a bite, perhaps at Perk Place?"

Jordan hesitated for a second, then asked, "Sure, where is it?"

Pointing to the other side of the park, she said, "It's right over there."

Jordan, a little embarrassed, said, "Oh, I saw it on my first trip around the park, but didn't notice the name. I was going to stop there in a few minutes for something to eat before heading back to my dad's room. So, yes, that would be fine. You finish your run, and I'll finish my walk. Whoever gets there first can grab a table. Is outside good for you?"

"Perfect, see you there in a few minutes," she said.

Jordan knew his time was limited, but he wanted to spend a few minutes with Mary since he was now very intrigued that she asked him to join her for breakfast. He figured that he should text his sister and let her know that he might be a little later than originally planned. He sent, "Ran into someone I know. Going to grab coffee and breakfast. Call if any change in dad's condition."

Immediately, a text came back from Jackie. "No problem. No change. No Aunt Pat yet. Stay as long as you like."

Jordan replied, "Thx, won't be too long."

Jordan, now out of his walking daze, had a purpose in his step. He made it to the other side of the park in a few minutes by cutting across the open space. Once at the coffee shop he waited for Mary to get there. She arrived a minute or two later by completing her last lap around the park.

As soon as she caught her breath, Jordan jumped right in and said, "First off, we have to get something straight, please call me Jordan, no more Mr. Marsh."

"OK, Jordan it is," she said with a smile and extending her hand. "Please call me Mary."

He took her hand and gently shook it. It was a bit sweaty, but he didn't make her feel self-conscience about it. She apologized nonetheless for the dampness and her appearance after her run, but she knew there wasn't much she could do about it. He countered with, "Well, I'm sure I'm not a pretty sight, unshaven, red-eyed and God only knows what my hair looks like." They both laughed and agreed to not pass too harsh judgment on one another.

"Where would you like to sit?" he asked. She pointed to a table with two chairs under the coffee shop's awning so they could enjoy their breakfast in the shade. He said, "You sit and hold the table, I'll grab us something to eat and drink. Just tell me what you would like."

"That's very kind of you, but you don't have to do that," she said.

He countered, "I know I don't, but I would like to, anyway, to show my gratitude for your excellent care of my dad."

"Well, thank you, but again, it isn't necessary," she said. "However, if you insist, I usually have a chia tea and a cinnamon raisin bagel, no butter or sour cream. Just let them know it's for Mary from Mercy. They should know my order by now, if not, just wave to me, and I'll pop my head inside the door."

"OK," he said, then went inside, got in line to order, and perused the large boards above the ordering station and the glass-enclosed bakery case. After a minute or two, he decided on a blueberry muffin and coffee, but it took a few more minutes until it was his turn to order. In those extra minutes, he looked outside to see what Mary was doing and noticed her checking her cell and then texting. Jordan took a glance around the coffee shop and noticed a few tables along the wall, a business executive in a gray suit about his age, a group of teenagers in line ahead of him goofing around like teenagers usually do, and an older gentleman holding a cane. The old man was dressed in a designer golf shirt, creased khaki slacks, and button-down, old-fashioned golf hat. He wondered why the teenagers weren't in school since it was the middle of the week and not a holiday, but it wasn't any of his business.

Once the orders were ready, Jordan decided to make two trips outside. He made sure to get Mary's order first and deliver it to her, then went back inside to pick up his. On the way back inside the coffee shop he noticed the older man was approaching the door to come outside. Jordan saw that the elderly gentleman didn't have a free hand. He had his cane in his right hand and a beverage in the other. So, naturally, Jordan held the door for him and invited him to exit before he entered. About that time two of the teenagers bolted past the old man and quick-stepped out the door that Jordan was holding, never saying a word, just laughing. The old man stopped suddenly but was in no danger of being bumped or falling. He then exited as Jordan held the door for him and gave his appreciation, "You, sir, are a gentleman, thank you."

Jordan responded, "Thanks, but I wish those two boys had a little more respect for you."

"No big deal, my young friend," he said. "I'm old and have nowhere special to be, they're young and in a hurry to get anywhere. It's just the way it is."

While that exchange was happening, Mary saw the near-collision at the door, and as the two boys ran past her, she yelled, "Hey, you almost ran into that man, slow down!"

They turned, laughed, and one of them made a crude gesture, which, fortunately, she didn't see, and since Jordan by then was back inside the coffee shop getting his breakfast, he didn't see, either. However, the old man did and shook his head in disgust. He ambled to the curb and waited there for the "walk" sign to flash, then proceeded to the park where he found an empty bench in the shade.

By now Jordan was back outside with his breakfast. Mary asked, "Do you mind if I freshen up a bit. I'll only be a minute, providing no one is in the restroom ahead of me.

Jordan said, "No problem, take your time. I'll be here when you get back."

While she was gone, Jordan took the opportunity to look around the park across the street. He noticed a gathering of young mothers to his left; some of which had kids in strollers, some with small children running around playing, and others with babies either in their arms or in papoose carriers. In another area, he saw two college-aged guys throwing a baseball back and forth near a rough cut out of a ball field. Farther away were a bunch of boys and girls playing Frisbee. They looked to be about the same age as the kids in the coffee shop. He, also, noticed the elderly gentleman he met on the way out of the coffee shop. He was sitting on a park bench in the shade and talking on his cell phone. Jordan thought it was pretty interesting that the old man had what appeared to be a smartphone, and he was using it at his age, which he figured to be around 80.

"OK, I'm back. Sorry for running off, but I just had to wash up a little and make myself as presentable as possible," Mary said upon her return.

"It's not a problem. It gave me some time to look around and notice how beautiful this park is," he said.

"I come here often after a tough shift. The running trail is nice because it's close to my work, usually not crowded when I run, and mostly flat." She continued, "I take it that you're not from around here?"

"I live about 30 minutes away on the other side of town," Jordan responded.

"Oh, you're not that far. Do you have anything like this where you live?" She inquired.

"No, not really," he said.

"Well, then, when you get over this way, you should make the opportunity to enjoy what the park and this end of town have to offer," she said.

"I certainly will," he replied. Then added, "How are your bagel and tea?"

Mary was almost finished with the bagel, and said, "It must've been good, I think I ate it in record time. I'm not sure when I ate last. We had a rough night."

"I hope it wasn't my dad that caused it," Jordan offered.

"Oh, no! It wasn't your dad, it was two other patients. Both were on the same glide path and passed before my shift ended. We could have used some extra help, but one of our staff was off with a family emergency. It never fails, the worst nights are when we are short-staffed."

"Wow, and you still found time to call me, talk to me when I got there and stopped in again before you left," he said commending her.

"Of course, we do what we have to, Jordan. I was sorry to have had to make that phone call, but it's part of the job," she said.

"Well, sorry for your rough night." He said, "You must be exhausted by now."

"I will be when I get home, but I'm good for now." She added, "I'm still running on adrenaline. Those two boys got me angry. I'll shower, then jump in bed and probably be out before my head hits the pillow."

"Indeed, they were rude." He continued, "Not to change the subject and not to be too personal, but how does your schedule play into your family life? I always wondered how people, who work the night shift, function in a world that is a day driven for work and night driven for sleep."

"It's not too personal. You get used to it after about a year. Then, it becomes your normal. As far as family life, that's easy, it's just me at home. Why do you ask?" She inquired with a sly grin.

Jordan was now turning red and quickly retreated, "That was rude of me. I'm sorry to have put you on the spot. I wasn't prying."

"Jordan, I'm teasing you," she responded. "I'm perfectly fine with the question. I'll be honest with you, though. I was married for 15 years. I have a son. He's 24 now, graduated college two years ago, got a job out-of-state, and he only visits me when his live-in girl-friend lets him. That boy is whipped, already."

Jordan was now rocked back on his heels, so to speak. One innocent question had elicited much more informa-tion than he wanted or needed. He chalked it up to Mary being tired, and perhaps a little more forthcoming with her personal life than she normally might be. He could only imagine what she would say if she had had a couple of drinks. After a brief silence, he said, "Well, again, sorry for that, not sure what I can say to make you feel better . . . kids will be kids?"

"I'm the one who should apologize," she said. "You don't need to hear any of that stuff. After all, your dad is in the process of passing on and you have enough to think about in that regard. You just wanted some down-time from sitting bedside while waiting, and I toss some of my issues on the table."

"Hey, no problem," he said, "but really if you would feel better talking about it, I can be a good listener, if you give me an opportunity."

"Perhaps another time, but now that you know a little about me, what are you willing to share about Mr. Jordan Marsh?" She asked turning the tables on Jordan.

"What do you want to know? My life's an open book," he began. "I was married, but only for a few years. We divorced. Never had any kids, but I wanted them. My wife didn't. That was part of the reason we divorced."

Mary quickly interjected, "Did you ever re-marry?"

"Nope!" Jordan said. "Never found another woman I wanted to settle down with, and frankly, I wasn't looking. The first time was a bit traumatic."

"In what way, if you don't mind me asking?" Mary inquired.

"Well," he started slowly, "What would you say if I told you that my wife was having an affair while we were married?"

"First, I'd say, 'I'm sorry,' then I guess I'd say, 'That's not that unusual these days.'"

Jordan interjected, "With a man, perhaps not, but my wife found a new partner with her teaching aide, who was a woman. At first, it damaged my ego, but I eventually got over it by understanding that she needed to be happy, and if that was with another woman and not having kids with me, then so be it."

"OK then, I guess you could say, we both have had some interesting times in our lives," she concluded.

"Again, not to pry, but you said you were married for 15 years. You made it a lot longer than I did. How did it end?" He inquired.

"Divorce, like you," she said. "My ex-husband not only had a roving eye, but he had the extra added attraction of being physically abusive," she added cleverly. "It didn't start that way but built up over time. In the beginning, it was only verbal abuse, but then it grew into physical abuse, as well. I was 20 when we got married, and likely too young and naive. He was a couple of years older and certainly more 'experienced'," she said making quote marks in the air. "I was in nursing school at the time, my last year. We had some good years, in the beginning, then things started going downhill. I hung in for another 10 years thinking it would get better, it never did. I guess I mostly stayed for our son."

Jordan was once again taken aback, he tried to console her, "That's not a good situation to be in, at all, I'm sorry for your troubles, you didn't deserve that, no woman does. Were you ever seriously hurt?"

"No, not seriously hurt, just slapped around a lot. The worst part was that it often happened in front of our son. I just hope he doesn't end up like his father," she concluded.

"Well, you mentioned nursing school, have you always been a hospice nurse?" Jordan asked, trying to change the subject and lighten the mood.

"Nice move," she said, "trying to get off a tough subject? No, I started my nursing career at a hospital. Worked there for many years. After my divorce and after my son went off to college, I decided on hospice care nursing. I started at the bottom and worked my way up. There's a high burnout rate in hospice nursing, so the attrition helped me move up the ladder quickly. Who knows, I may still go back into nursing at a hospital. That's the good part about nursing. It's portable. You can pick up a job pretty much anywhere if you decide to move."

"I never thought about that," Jordan said, "but you seem so good at what you do, why would you want to move on?"

"I have no plans to move on, at least right now," she told him. "So, what's your line of work, if you don't mind me asking?" She again tried to get back to finding more out about him.

"I'm a writer," Jordan said. "I write for the local paper. I'm a sportswriter. Many years ago, when I was married, my wife and I moved up north, and I wrote for a larger metropolitan newspaper. It took most of my time in the evenings and weekends, which was another reason that led to our divorce."

"Hey, I read your column in the local newspaper from time to time. So, you're that Jordan Marsh. Sorry, I didn't put your name with the sportswriter Jordan Marsh."

"No problem, probably better that you didn't," he said, "but I'm curious, you read the sports section?"

"I do sometimes," she said, "I've always been a bit of a jock. As you can see, I run. Many years ago in a previous life, I was quite the tomboy."

"Really?" Jordan said. "Besides running, any other forms of exercise?"

"I take yoga classes, mostly for the mental health aspects, and I have a gym membership, so I get my exercise regularly. I took self-defense classes some time ago. How about you?" she asked. "You look like you keep yourself in pretty good shape."

"Back up the truck for a second. You know self-defense?" He asked.

"I haven't trained in a long time, but I know enough to protect myself. Honestly, I started taking it after my ex-husband started to get physically abusive. One day I had had enough. He came at me, and I blocked his slap, then put him in a hold and dropped him to the floor. I could have hurt him, but it's not my nature, and of course, I didn't want my son to see that. My ex-husband is much larger than I am, but my training neutralized him in a few seconds. That's the last time he hit me. Of course, it led to him asking for a divorce. I guess he knew he could no longer control me, so he wanted out. We had shared custody of our son until he went off to college."

"Well, the more I find out about you, the more interesting a person you become," he said with a smile.

Jordan worked his way back to her reference of his physical condition, "You mentioned being in shape, but I'm probably not in as good a shape as you," he replied. "As you said, exercising is a great stress reducer. I don't have that much free time now, but after we get my father's affairs settled, I'll get back to running and exercising."

She jumped on that, "You run?"

"Yes, I run when I can," he answered, "but probably not as much as you. I may get in three or four miles twice a week."

"We are right about the same distance," she said, then mentioned, "you should try to get down here sometime when things settle down for you, and maybe we can have a run together."

"I'd like that," he said, then glanced at his watch. It read 10:15.

"Don't let me keep you if you have to get back," Mary offered.

"I'm good," Jordan replied, "I've got a few minutes. I told my sister that I would try to be back by ten-thirty, and it's only a ten-minute walk at most. I'll send her a quick text to see how things are going. Please excuse me for just a minute."

"Go ahead," she said, "that's most important right now."

Jordan then texted Jackie, "How are things there?"

Her text came back quickly, "All fine here. A. Pat and U. Charlie just arrived."

"OK, will be back in 15," came Jordan's reply.

While Jordan was texting his sister, Mary noticed a small commotion in the park where the kids had been playing Frisbee. She pointed it out to Jordan. It was difficult to ascertain the nature of the problem, but they could see that it involved a large policeman and what looked to be the two boys that ran out of the coffee shop nearly knocking over the old man. They didn't leave their table, but they could barely hear the nature of the conversation. The policeman was pointing a finger at the two boys and scolding them loudly. Mary and Jordan didn't know what the two boys had done to warrant the reprimand, but they were pretty sure it was somehow deserved, based on their experience.

Jordan stood up and said, "I want to thank you for making this time pass so quickly. I can't tell you how much I enjoyed our conversation and you spending time with me after your long, tiring night. It was a treat I wasn't expecting."

Mary replied, "Believe me, it was mutual. I needed someone to talk with, also. I usually don't open up to anyone unless I feel very comfortable around them, and for some reason, I feel pretty comfortable around you, Jordan."

"Well, thanks," he said as he started to leave. Then he stopped, turned around, and asked, "Would you be interested in meeting again sometime, maybe for dinner some evening on one of your nights off?"

"Absolutely," she said, "I thought you were going to run off, and I would never see you again," she said with a wry smile on her face and a little bit of devil in her eye.

"How can I reach you?" Jordan asked.

"Give me your phone," she said. Jordan obliged her, and she typed in her contact information.

"Thanks, I'll be in touch, I promised," he said, as he departed.

"You better," she shot back as he darted across the street. "I didn't invest all this time with you for nothing." She laughed as she said it, then cleaned up their breakfast trash, and collected her belongings before heading for her car and then home for some well-deserved rest.

On his way across the park, Jordan saw the old man that was in the coffee shop sitting on the park bench. He knew he didn't have much time to spend with him, but he wanted to say, 'hello', nonetheless. "Excuse, me, sir," he started the conversation. "Unfortunately, I don't have a lot of time, but I wanted to make sure you are okay after almost getting run over at the coffee shop by those two boys."

"I'm fine and thank you for asking," the old man said. "It would take more than getting bumped into to keep me from enjoying this beautiful day."

Jordan then said, "Well, I'm glad you are okay. I just wanted to be sure. It looks like those kids had another run-in with that policeman. I wonder what that's all about. Well, it's none of my business, so I'll be on my way and leave you to enjoy your day."

The old man waved, and Jordan hightailed it across the park toward the hospice center.

Once back at Mercy, he quickly checked in at the reception desk, briskly walked to the elevator, and took it to the third floor. By now, he knew the routine by heart. As soon as he got to his father's room, he immediately went to his Aunt Pat and gave her a kiss and a big hug, he then shook Uncle Charlie's hand, and asked how they were both doing.

"Just fine," Aunt Pat answered, "and before your uncle says anything to the contrary, he's doing fine, also." Ever the glib one, she knew how to keep the atmosphere light-hearted without being disrespectful.

Jackie and Jordan laughed, and Jordan turned to his uncle and said, "Glad you are doing so well, Uncle Charlie. You look great, as usual."

"Not bad, I guess, for an old man, or so I'm told," was his reply in obvious reference to his wife's comment.

Jordan then asked, "I guess there has been no change in dad's condition since I left?"

"No, not much," Jackie replied.

"The nurse told me that dad may have rallied a bit when I told him that you were coming to see him. So, however that works, he's trying to hang in there." Jordan then offered, "But she cautioned that it's only temporary."

"We're very glad we had a chance to see him before he passes," Pat said.

"Of course," Jackie replied.

They made small talk among themselves for the next hour, Aunt Pat asking how Jackie's children and husband were doing, and Jackie asking her aunt about her and Uncle Charlie's health and social life with their friends.

Jordan mostly talked with his uncle. They had a common interest in sports, so most of their conversation revolved around their favorite team's chance of winning a championship that year. The Yankees, Jordan's team, as was his father's team, always had a chance to get to the World Series, or so it seemed. Uncle Charlie followed mostly National League teams. His favorite was the Pirates since he grew up in a small town in western Pennsylvania. His team's chances weren't as good and hadn't been good for a long while.

The longer their conversation stayed on baseball Charlie inevitably got around to the 1960 World Series. In that legendary Fall Classic, the Pirates beat the Yankees four games to three. The Yankees, however, outscored the Pirates 55-27 over the seven games. The seventh and final game was a classic in itself. The Pirates won it, 10-9, on a walk-off home run by Bill Mazeroski in the bottom of the ninth inning after both teams had traded the lead throughout the game.

Charlie's roundabout reasoning for bringing up the 1960 World Series, beyond rubbing it in a little that his Pirates had beaten Jordan's Yankees, was that he thought it would be a great storyline for one of Jordan's articles. From Jordan's point of view, it was something that happened long before he was born, and it was a sporting event that he had no direct knowledge of, not to mention that it was his beloved Yankees that took the loss. Jordan did learn of that World Series and many others before he was born from his father's vivid recollections, so he kept the idea of an article, or series of articles, about them in the back of his mind. He just wasn't sure how many of his readers would care about a World Series that happened almost 70 years ago.

Charlie was an avid fisherman, so eventually, the conversations with Jordan got around to his stream, lake, and deep-sea fishing. Jordan, not being a fisherman, hung in there with the many fish stories, particularly the ones about Charlie's big catches. The upside for Jordan was that he got to enjoy some of his uncle's fishing prowess. He, Jackie, her family, Vivian, and Thomas would get together once a year in the late summer at Aunt Pat's and Uncle Charlie's house for a fish fry and picnic. The fish were always outstanding, as was the rest of the fare. It was an event that everyone looked forward to attending and kept the Marsh family as close as any other and closer than most. Even after Vivian passed away, the tradition continued until Thomas got too sick to attend. During the conversation at Thomas's bedside, they made a pact to reinstitute the tradition of the annual summer fish fry as long as Uncle Charlie was still fishing and catching those wonderful tasting fish.

On her 15-minute drive home Mary had time to reflect on her unexpected, yet very pleasant chance encounter. She first marveled that she had met someone she perceived to be a kind, attractive, eligible bachelor her age, who had a job and was intelligent, as well. She knew it was only 30 minutes of getting to know him, and she did most of the talking, but she liked what she had seen and experienced, so far. That was a plus in her mind. She knew it was difficult meeting someone with one of those qualities, let alone all of them.

Next, she thought about perhaps sharing too much of her personal information. She wasn't sure she had done the right thing in that regard, but since it was already done, there was no taking it back. She figured, if she had said too much and scared Jordan away, it would be a lesson learned. But, if he called, and they were able to set up a dinner date, she made a mental note to try to let him do more talking. She thought perhaps she could think up a few questions that would get him to talk more about himself. Also, she made another mental note to read some of his columns in an attempt to be more familiar with his work and more knowledgeable of sports in general. She had always been a good student in school, so learning a few sports terms, or better yet, understanding what they meant, should go a long way with impressing Jordan. The internet, she thought, could help with the learning curve.

As she turned onto the entrance ramp to the highway, she changed the radio station to find more lively music in the hope of keeping herself awake on the rest of the drive home. She was also hoping that the caffeine in her chai tea, that she was still sipping and no longer hot, would help with staying alert. Being the beautiful day that it was, she had dropped the top on her convertible and was enjoying the wind in her hair and the sun on her face. At that moment she felt very content and blessed, and her past problems were no longer big issues.

Mary made it home in record time. On the days when she took the time to jog in the park, she noticed that the usual morning rush hour traffic was greatly diminished by the time she was driving home. Also, today, it was even later with less traffic since she had taken the time for breakfast at the coffee shop with Jordan. She parked her car in the driveway, closed the convertible top, and hustled to her front door, all the time hoping that her neighbor wouldn't see her and want to engage her in conversation since she was pretty tired by now. It wasn't because she didn't like the man next door, but he often was clueless about the fact that she worked nights and was trying to get to bed as soon as possible when she got home. It was bad enough that she sometimes had to endure the noise from his lawnmower or weed eater while she was trying to sleep.

She made it inside unnoticed, quickly undressed, jumped into the shower, and turned the water to as hot a setting as she could stand. After a good run and after working where she was on her feet most of the night, the only thing that helped ease the aches and pains was a long, hot shower. She stood under it for a few minutes before washing her hair and bathing. Once finished, she dried her shoulder-length hair, styled it enough to make it presentable for work that night, then jumped into bed for a solid eight hours of well-deserved rest.

Back at the hospice center, Jordan suggested that since it was almost noon, and if anyone was hungry, he could suggest a nice coffee shop across the park. He told his sister, aunt, and uncle that he was good to stay with his dad if they wanted to take a break. Thomas's condition was unchanged, and since nothing seemed imminent, it might be a good time to eat something. He described where the coffee shop was and mentioned that it was only a short walk. Aunt Pat thought Jordan's suggestion was a good idea and spoke up, "Yes, let's take a break, I'll treat everyone to lunch. Jordan, we can bring something back for you, if you would like."

"I'm good for now, Aunt Pat," he said, "I just had a muffin and coffee."

"Are you sure?" She persisted. "You are going to be hungry in an hour. How about I bring you a sandwich if they have one there?"

"That would be fine." He said. "I would appreciate it. You are always thinking of us, Aunt Pat. You know, we consider you our second mother. Now, you and Uncle Charlie are going to become our surrogate parents." He said it with a laugh but was only half-joking.

The three of them departed, and Jackie doubled back to tell Jordan, "We won't be too long. Call me if there's any change."

"You know I will," Jordan replied.

Now having some time to quietly reflect on his morning's happenchance meeting with Mary, he inwardly smiled. He found himself to be ultimately conflicted. Here, in front of him, was the man who, along with his mother, raised him. Not only did he raise him, but he taught him so much. He loved the man dearly, and now he was dying. Yet, his thoughts were on his meeting Mary and the nice time, albeit short, that they spent together. He finally rationalized it by considering a couple of factors. One, he had spent a considerable amount of time at his father's bedside already and was there now. He had only been gone an hour and just to take a break. Two, he knew there was nothing he could do for his father, anymore. Finally, he was going to have to move on with his life sooner or later, so why not think about Mary as someone he might enjoy spending more time with.

Around 1:00 p.m. Jackie, Aunt Pat, and Uncle Charlie returned. Jordan was still bedside with his dad. Aunt Pat asked, "Any change?"

Jordan replied, "Maybe . . ." and left the sentence unfinished.

Jackie inquired, "What do you mean, 'maybe'?"

Jordan continued, "A nurse came in a few minutes ago to check on Dad. She said his fever seemed to be returning, and his breathing was shallower, again. I think his color is more grayish, also. What do you think?"

Aunt Pat chimed in, "I think you're right, honey. Tommy does look like some of the color has left his face. It may not be long now." Tommy was the nickname she used for her little brother almost from birth. Pat was a couple of years older than Thomas, who was now 73, but she was in much better health. Of course, she didn't have the life experiences that Thomas did, so her relatively good health was not surprising.

Jackie then offered, "Well, I guess we should all hang close by."

"Probably a good idea, all things being considered," Jordan concluded.

Not much conversation of consequence was spoken for the next hour, as all eyes cautiously surveilled Thomas. About 2:15 Richard arrived, much to the delight of Jackie. He immediately asked, "How's Thomas doing?"

Everyone deferred to Jackie, and she answered, "Not well, it appears to be just a matter of time now, perhaps within the hour. I'm glad you were able to get here," she said. Her previous contempt for Richard for not being there had suddenly vanished. She waved him out into the hallway and continued privately now, "I'm glad you made it in time. I hope your meeting and teleconference went well."

"Yes, well enough, I think. I guess they'll keep me on for another week," he said with a nervous laugh.

"What are you going to do, fire yourself?" was her reply. She did, however, notice that he was a bit on edge.

"No I guess not, just making a joke, probably not the right time for that," he said, then changed the subject. "What do you want to do about the kids and school? I can get them so you can be here with your dad, or if you like, I can ask my parents to pick them up around four."

Jackie, always the most organized adult in the room, quickly decided, "I'd rather you get the kids, take them home, let them change out of their school clothes, and get them something to eat if they are hungry. There are plenty of leftovers in the fridge, just heat whatever they will eat. After that, they can either play outside for an hour or do homework first. Just make sure their homework gets done, please. I don't want to have to deal with that tonight and thank you. It's much appreciated."

Richard knew better than to offer any adjustments to the plan that Jackie had just laid out, especially at this trying time. He nodded acceptance, if not approval, then rightly said, "I'll handle it."

She backed off a little, and said, "I know you will, sweetie, sorry to be so terse. It's just a bad time, as you know. Please understand that I do appreciate you taking time off from work to be here." She kissed him on the cheek, then they walked back inside Thomas's room.

Richard knew he had an hour to wait, so he gravitated toward Jordan and Charlie. They were making small talk, mostly about sports, but politics did creep into the conversation on occasion. Neither Jordan nor Charlie had strong political leanings; however, Richard, being in the financial business, was more conservative by nature. He adhered to the motto that 'the business of America is the business of America'. He voted for any candidate that favored businesses, lower taxes, and a free market. As far as Richard was concerned, as long as the stock market was on the rise, all was right with the country. He couldn't care less about any rise in violent crime, public education (his kids went to private school, of course), women's rights, systemic racism, poverty, or any other social issue.

The irony was that Jackie was very much a liberal-minded free spirit. Of course, she knew which side the bread was buttered and that Richard was their only breadwinner. However, her desire for fairness and justice kept her from 'going over to the dark side', as she liked to say. When she was lawyering, she worked on many progressive issues and fully intended to get back to them as soon as her kids were in high school. It wasn't an issue between Richard and Jackie, but it was something they were both aware of, and Richard also knew, which side the bread was buttered.

Once with Charlie and Jordan, Richard tried to fit in, but he was out of his element when they were talking sports. Richard knew the basics, but he had a tenuous time conversing in depth. He knew which major league teams belonged in which leagues, but he couldn't say which ones were the better teams in any given year. He was better with football, but not nearly on the same level as either Jordan or Charlie.

Jordan realized this. Therefore, to not make Richard feel uncomfortable, or leave him out of the conversation, he tried to ask some questions about finance, not that he knew, or even cared that much about it. He just knew that it would be a subject that Richard was comfortable discussing. Jordan began, "How's the market doing today, Richard?" Jordan knew the New York Stock Exchange usually closed at four, so he knew enough not to ask about closing numbers. More importantly, he knew that he should learn more about investing since his retirement hinged predominantly on the stock market's performance.

Richard seized on the opportunity, "When I left the office about an hour ago, the indexes were up about one percent across the board. The NASDAQ was doing slightly better than the S&P 500 and the Dow, but you know, things can change quickly depending on world events.

Remember, the market doesn't like surprises, so turmoil anywhere in the world could upset the apple cart."

Jordan tried to sound interested, "What are the year-to-date numbers looking like?"

Richard was quick to respond, knowing that information as well as he knew his kids' names. "All three major indices are up about 15%, but what scares me a little is the day-to-day volatility. Additionally, some economists are worried about a possible inversion of the yield curve, which historically has led to a recession." Having realized that he had just blown both Jordan and Charlie away with too detailed information, he backed off. "Sorry, I sometimes get carried away when talking shop."

"No problem," Jordan said. "I should make an appointment with you someday and review my portfolio. I have neglected doing it because I trust you, first and foremost, to do the right kind of investing for me, but also because I don't have the interest in it that I should."

"I won't discuss any details about your portfolio here, but suffice to say that you are not overly exposed to risk," Richard confided. "Of course, because of that, you won't have huge returns. They will be modest, steady, and over time, your retirement account should be sufficient for you to retire, as planned, in about 20 years."

Jordan nodded and thanked him, then changed the subject to ask about Richie, Jr., and Amanda. Richard replied, "They're fine and growing like weeds, but kids do that. As far as I know, they are doing well in school, too."

Jordan apologized for not seeing them recently. Richard replied, "Not to worry, you have had your hands full here the last few weeks."

They continued making small talk until it was time for Richard to leave and get his children at school. Richard said his goodbyes to all, including Thomas. He left a bit choked up, and Jackie walked with him to the elevator.

Shortly before 5:30 p.m., Thomas Marsh took his last breath. His family had gathered around his bed. Also, the day supervising nurse and the Mercy Hospice chaplain were there. They all joined in a prayer led by the chaplain. The supervising nurse called the death at 5:27 p.m. She then suggested that she leave for a few minutes so the family could have some time alone with Thomas. She asked if they wanted the chaplain to stay. They agreed that it was a good idea. He offered a series of prayers that Catholic priests confer on the dead. The Marsh family lowered their heads and listened as the priest prayed, even though they weren't Catholic.

After several minutes the chaplain concluded his prayer service and asked the family if there was anything further he could do for them. They thanked him for his time and the prayers and said that nothing further was needed. At that point, he bid them farewell, left his business card, and offered grief counseling services, if need be.

There were teary eyes all around by now. Jordan did his very best to hold it together, mostly because he knew he was supposed to be a strong figure in these situations. He figured that his grief could surface later when he was alone and out of sight of his family.

What would stay with Jackie and Jordan for the rest of their lives was the vision of their father on his death bed. They may not have realized it at the time, but when they had their quiet moments that vision would come back to them and still be very vivid. It certainly was a disturbing vision and unlike the last vision of their mother who died suddenly while appearing to be the picture of health.

The nurse re-entered Thomas's room to let the family know that she had contacted their funeral director. She said, "They promised to be here within the hour. You are more than welcome to stay with Thomas until they arrive if you like. If you decide not to stay, that's OK, too, we'll handle everything."

Jordan spoke up and said, "Why don't you three head home. I'll stay with dad until the undertaker's people get here. You've all had long days."

Jackie balked, "You've had a longer day than me. You should go. I can stay."

"No!" He countered. "You have two kids who are missing you. Go see them. I'll be fine. Besides, it'll give me some alone time with dad."

He then turned to his aunt and uncle. "Please drive safely. Thank you for coming and being with Jackie and me during this very difficult time. One of us will be in touch regarding the funeral arrangements, as soon as we know what they are." He then turned to Jackie and said, "I'll call you tomorrow morning, and we'll go to the funeral home to make whatever arrangements we need."

Jackie agreed, "Okay, call me when you get up. I'll call them to see when they can see us."

They then said their tearful goodbyes and left, leaving Jordan alone with his dad. After he was sure he was alone, he turned toward his dad and cried. He stroked his dad's forehead which was no longer warm. He rubbed his shoulder like his father had done to him many times when he sensed that Jordan was struggling. Most recently, it was when Vivian died. Jordan felt bad that he was being consoled by his father when he should've been the one to console his dad. But, he just knew that was the way his father wanted it. He protected his kids to his dying day.

CHAPTER 3
The Meeting in the Park

Jordan waited for the funeral home staff to arrive and remove Thomas's body. He asked them to be gentle, but then caught himself and apologized, "I'm sorry, I guess you hear that a lot, even though the people you are transporting are dead and can't feel anything."

The older of the two men from the funeral home assured Jordan that it was all right. "We've heard that, and more, before," he said. "Rest easy, sir, we've never dropped anyone and certainly haven't ever lost anyone in my 15 years doing this job, and we aren't going to jeopardize our record tonight."

"Good to hear," Jordan said. "If you don't mind, I'll just hang with you until you are finished strapping my dad in, then follow you downstairs to your transport vehicle."

"Suit yourself, sir," the older man said.

It took the two funeral home employees less than five minutes to secure Thomas's body. Once ready to leave, Jordan did a quick check around the room to be sure that he and his family had not left anything behind. He did notice an old newspaper and pencil, but he figured no one was going to be looking for them. Also, he spied the sandwich that his Aunt Pat had brought him from the coffee shop. He knew it was probably not good to eat, anymore, despite feeling hungry, so he tossed it in the trash can along with the paper and pencil. He then checked all the drawers and closets but found nothing. By then the two men had Thomas's body at the service elevator and were waiting for Jordan. "Thanks!" Jordan said, "Sorry to keep you waiting. I just needed to check the room for anything left behind."

They understood because they had seen it all before. "No problem, sir. So far, it's been an easy day. We'll take your dad back to the funeral home and wait for the next call. We're in no rush."

The elevator stopped at the loading area in the back of the hospice center where the funeral home's van was parked. They loaded Thomas's body into the van, passed along condolences to Jordan, and were off.

Jordan had an empty feeling in the pit of his stomach, but it wasn't from not eating.

The ride to his house was a blur for Jordan. He did his best to concentrate, but his mind wasn't on the road. Rather, it was on his dad laying in the back of a van, then laying on a table at the funeral home. He didn't want to think of his dad's plight, but he couldn't help himself. He knew that eventually his father would be embalmed and then put in storage until the viewing.

It was still daylight when Jordan pulled into his driveway. He knew he had driven home from the hospice center on autopilot and hoped that he had not unconsciously run any red traffic signals. Once out of his car he noticed his neighbor across the street was cutting his grass. The neighbor was walking behind a self-propelled lawnmower while his wife was edging and trimming. Both waved to Jordan, who returned the wave. The wife put down her edger and started walking toward Jordan. As she reached the sidewalk on Jordan's side of the street, she asked how Jordan's father was doing. They had been having regular conversations regarding Thomas's condition, so it wasn't a surprise when Jordan told her that his dad had just passed away.

"I'm so sorry, Jordan," she said. "You have our deepest sympathy. Is there anything we can do for you? Do you need anything?"

"No, but thank you just the same, Agatha," he replied.

Agatha was almost Thomas's age. Her husband, Andy, was a year or two older. Both were retired. They also knew Thomas, who made frequent visits to Jordan's house to help him with whatever project Jordan might need handyman assistance. Thomas was quite the handyman, but unlike his athletic ability, the Mr. Fix-it gene did not pass to Jordan. Jordan was always grateful for the help his father was able to provide, in addition to the time, he could spend with his dad.

Agatha continued, "I know your dad was sick for a long time. He fought the good fight as long as he could. About the only consolation is that he is no longer suffering and now he's with Vivian."

Not being overly spiritual, Jordan sighed, "I guess that's true. I know it's a good way to think about it, but honestly, Agatha, I'm going to miss him an awful lot."

"Well, honey, anytime you're feeling down and need to talk with somebody, just walk across the street and knock on our door." Agatha then offered, "I can always brew a pot of coffee, and we can talk as long as you want."

"That's very kind of you, Agatha. Who knows, I may take you up on that," he said.

Agatha functioned well as the neighborhood biddy but in a good way. She knew pretty much everything that was happening on the street. Probably because she liked to be outside in her yard as much as she could be, and that allowed her to see people and interact with them. She and Andy kept their yard in pristine condition. That was their hobby. Jordan would tell them that they set the standard for everyone else, and no other yard even came close to looking as nice as theirs. He also liked to tell them that he felt very lucky to live right across the street, so he could enjoy seeing the product of all their hard work.

Agatha realized that she may be keeping Jordan from getting in his house and getting something to eat, so she said, "I'm going to let you get to the rest of your evening. I'm sure you must be very tired and hungry." Then she offered, "That reminds me, did you eat? We have leftovers, chicken and vegetables, and some dessert. I'll bring you a plate."

"I don't want to trouble you, Agatha, I'm fine," he said, but he had no idea what he would eat.

"Don't be silly. It won't take me a minute. You go inside, and I'll be right over with a plate. It's no bother. Listen to your elders," she chided him with a smile.

"Okay, okay," Jordan said. Besides, he knew he had nothing in his refrigerator, it would take too long to go back out and pick something up, and best of all, Agatha was a great cook. So, for Jordan, it was another lucky chance event on a dark day that would forever be in his memory.

Before going inside Jordan walked to his mailbox and picked up his mail. As he walked back to his house, he scanned the handful of postal *treats*. He could see that it was mostly junk mail. There were, what looked to be, two bills in the pile. As usual, he thought. The last piece of mail was an envelope with no return address. There appeared to be a letter inside.

Jordan unlocked the door, entered his house, turned off his alarm, then tossed the mail on the kitchen table and figured he would get to it in a few minutes. He walked to the closet and hung up his jacket, then looked for the remote to turn on the television. He didn't care what was on the TV. He just wanted there to be something to distract him. If he were lucky, there might be a good ball game to watch.

He figured he should wash up since Agatha would likely be right over with his dinner, so he made a beeline for the bathroom. While there he made a quick assessment of how he looked. He noticed his two-day-old beard, which all of a sudden had more white in it than he remembered. He saw that his eyes were bloodshot and under both were puffy bags large enough, he thought, to accommodate the clothes for a weekend vacation. He rationalized that it had been a rough stretch of days with little solid sleep, so what could he expect?

The knock at the front door was Agatha with Jordan's dinner. She had two aluminum foil-wrapped plates in her hands. When Jordan opened the door, Agatha said, "Here you go, honey, this one is the chicken and veggies. It's breaded and baked, so it's good for you, and I know you keep yourself in good shape, so you must be watching what you eat. Andy likes his chicken fried, but this way is better, so that's the way I like to make it. Besides, he will thank me when he gets his blood pressure and cholesterol checked." She handed Jordan the first plate, then added, "I took a few extra minutes to heat it, so you don't have to." She then handed Jordan the other plate, "This one is dessert. It's a surprise. I hope you enjoy it."

Jordan replied, "I know I will, Agatha. You know I think you're the best cook in the neighborhood. I've never had a bad meal of yours. You should have one of those cooking shows on the Food Network," he said only half-jokingly.

She broke into a big smile, and said, "Well, you enjoy them, honey. It does my heart good to be able to bring you dinner, especially tonight."

"I can't thank you enough," Jordan said. "I know I will love it all, every bite. Thanks, again."

Agatha then left and went back to her yard to finish her edging and trimming. By now, Andy was finished with the grass cutting. He saw her coming back across the street and asked, "How much more do you have to do?"

"I'm almost finished. Go inside and take your shower," she suggested. "Besides, I know just where I stopped."

"OK, if you don't need me, I'll get cleaned up so I can watch the game later," Andy said.

⫸ ⫷

Back across the street, Jordan was devouring Agatha's breaded chicken, carrots and peas, and potatoes. He couldn't believe how good it all tasted, but then again, he reminded himself that it was Agatha's cooking, which was always great. She had some special recipes to turn ordinary breaded chicken breasts into culinary delights. They were fork tender and as tasty as any chicken he'd ever had in an expensive restaurant. Even the vegetables were perfectly cooked and seasoned. But then again, he was so hungry that a TV dinner would probably have tasted delicious.

After he was finished with Agatha's care package dinner, he figured to wait before having his dessert. He didn't want to spoil the surprise by looking under the foil, so he just placed it on the counter. He figured his best option now was to take a hot shower and get into something comfortable.

The shower felt so good to Jordan that he just stood under the hot water for several extra minutes trying to wash away all the grime, exhaustion, and heartache of the last few days. After the bathroom got so steamed that he could no longer see himself in the mirror, Jordan decided that he had had enough time under the shower. He quickly dried himself, then wiped the mirror. He had forgotten to turn on the exhaust fan before getting into the shower, so now everything was very moist. He waited a few minutes for the mirror to clear, then decided it might be a good idea to run his razor over his stubbly beard. He wasn't going to fuss about it. He just wanted to get it to the 90% level. If he missed a spot here or there, no big deal. It wasn't like he was going to be seeing anyone else that evening, or so he hoped. It was going to be him, the TV, and Agatha's dessert.

By now it was just after 8:00 p.m. Jordan checked the TV and immediately tuned in to ESPN to see which game they were broadcasting. The game between the Cardinals and Cubs had just begun, so he knew he could doubleback to that game if nothing else suited him. His local baseball market carried both the Orioles and Nationals. He knew that many times when one of those teams was on the road, the other would be home. That was the best of all worlds for a local baseball fan because you could probably watch one game early in the evening and the other later, especially when the traveling team was on the West Coast.

As it turned out this night, the Orioles were at home against his Yankees. It was already the fourth inning with the O's holding a 1-0 lead. He knew it was early, so he didn't worry since the Yanks had the better team and myriad home run hitters, and at Camden Yards lately the Yanks were feasting on Oriole pitching. He decided to leave that game on for an inning or two. At the commercial breaks, he would jump over to ESPN to keep track of the Cubs/Cards rivalry.

After about 30 minutes of a slow-moving game with no change in the score, Jordan suddenly remembered that he still had Agatha's dessert to enjoy. While on his way to the kitchen he noticed his unopened mail on the table. That letter now intrigued him, so he took it off the top of the pile and tossed it near where he would sit to eat his dessert. He figured to read it while having Agatha's wonderful whatever-it-was. Jordan decided to pour himself a glass of milk, and before unwrapping his dessert, he thought about what it could be. His first guess was probably cookies, and if so, he hoped they would be his favorite, chocolate chip. His next guess was a piece of Agatha's state fair blue ribbon-winning chocolate cake. However, when he unwrapped the foil, he saw the biggest piece of lemon meringue pie he could imagine. It could easily have fed two people, and of course, it was his favorite pie, and Agatha knew it.

Jordan sat at his kitchen table and took a forkful of the pie. It was as delicious as he imagined it would be. He then started opening the letter. Once out of the envelope, he unfolded the pages and noticed that the handwriting looked vaguely familiar. It started, "Dear Jordan, I know it has been a long time since we communicated, so I thought this was a good way to let you know what is happening in my life."

At that point, Jordan recognized the handwriting, and his heart sank. He quickly flipped over the letter to the last page and saw that it was signed 'All my love, Katie'. The next forkful of pie went down Jordan's throat like a rock. All of a sudden he had lost his appetite. He decided to push away the pie for the time being and got up from the table with the letter and his milk. He figured it best to sit in his recliner, turn the volume to mute on the TV, and see what his ex-wife wanted. Since their divorce, her only communication with Jordan was when she wanted something. He figured this time to be no different.

The last time Jordan saw Katie was at his mother's funeral. She had stayed close with Jordan's sister, so she was notified when Vivian died. To Kathryn's credit, she made the four-plus hour drive from New York to pay her respects. Of course, at some point, she cornered Jordan, who wanted nothing to do with her, and tried to steer clear of any confrontation. He recalled vividly the conversation she started by asking, "So, how are you doing? Are you seeing anyone?"

Jordan was guarded and coyly replied, "I see a lot of people every day."

"You know what I mean, Jordan. Are you dating anyone?" Kathryn shot back.

"Nope," he said, then added, "You cured me. Besides, do you think this is the time or place to have this conversation?"

"Well, I still care about you. Don't you know that?" she replied.

"All I know about you, Kathryn, is that you only seem to get in touch with me when you want something," he said bitterly, then asked, "so what is it?"

She replied, "Now that you mention it, I could use a bump in my alimony."

Jordan did everything he could to not yell at her, which would have been completely out of character for him. He answered, "No way, you are lucky I haven't gone back to court to have your monthly alimony stipend reduced since you are living with Veronica, and, I'm sure, your household income far exceeds mine. What's it been, Katie, 15 years of alimony payments?"

"Yeah, something like that," she replied only half embarrassed to admit it.

Before turning and leaving Jordan concluded the conversation with, "Go to court. See what happens. I'm sure you will lose what you have, once the judge finds out you are co-habituating with Veronica and have been for many years. Who knows, maybe you should be paying me alimony?"

Now back to the letter in his hand, he read on. The first page was nothing more than small talk about her nearly concluded school year and how she wasn't enjoying the kids she had, nor her new principal. The next page acknowledged some of the problems they had had over their married life and how sorry she was for her part in them. That surprised Jordan since it was so unlike Katie to acknowledge anything negative about herself.

By page three Kathryn got to the gist of her letter. It started rather innocently, 'Well, the school year is almost over, only a few weeks to go, and then I'm free for the summer. I've been thinking about traveling around the country again like we did after we graduated college, and I was wondering if you would be free to join me for some of it.' Jordan did everything he could to not rip the letter in shreds right there, but he continued reading it until the end. He felt that once again Kathryn was trying to use him to get something for herself, probably pay for her vacation. He also wondered what had become of Veronica. Was she still in the picture, or had she and Kathryn parted ways?

The final paragraph dropped the bombshell on Jordan. Kathryn was planning on moving back to their hometown sometime after her school year ended. Now, Jordan was perplexed, confused, and a bit worried. There was no mention of Veronica joining her or any mention of Veronica at all in Kathryn's letter. Jordan couldn't shake that thought. What would it be like to have Katie back in Middleboro? After all, he had left a great job in the Big Apple to get away from her, but here she was turning up in his life once again, and just when he had finally met someone he was seriously considering seeing.

The penultimate sentence was the clincher. It read, 'So, I was wondering if I could spend a couple of months at your place when I get back to Middleboro, you know, until I find a place of my own?' Jordan almost levitated off his recliner. He knew Kathryn had more Gaul (gall) than Julius Caesar, as he liked to tell her, not that he figured she understood the reference; but, this was too much, even for her. She cavalierly concluded her letter with, 'Let me know what you think. All my love, Katie.'

Jordan knew it was too much to deal with now, especially after the day he'd had. It had been a roller coaster ride through hell with a side trip or two to heaven. He recalled being awakened at an early hour because his father was nearing death. Then he unexpectedly met Mary in the park for breakfast. They seemed to hit it off very well and made tentative plans to meet again. Next, he had to watch as his father took his last breath, and his heart was broken. That was followed by Agatha's exceptionally kind offer of dinner and dessert, and then the final gut punch: Kathryn's letter.

At that point, Jordan decided to turn off the TV and go to bed. The Yankees would have to handle the Orioles without him, he thought. By this time he had lost track of the score, anyway, and honestly, he couldn't care less about it, now. He needed a good night's sleep, so getting to bed early was a good idea. He knew that at some point the next day he and Jackie would get together to meet with the funeral director about Thomas' arrangements. He figured to talk over Kathryn's letter with her and get her insights.

Jordan awoke the next morning around 7:00 a.m. He had gotten a solid night's sleep, which he desperately needed. He felt great and was ready to tackle a new day's set of problems. It was too early to check with his sister, so he realized that for the first time in several weeks he had a block of time for himself. He decided to go for a run, something he hadn't done in several weeks. So, this would be a nice way to start his day, he thought, and besides, it was supposed to be great running weather.

After washing up quickly he changed from his pajamas to his running clothes, grabbed his wallet, keys, phone, and water before heading out the door to his car. He briefly thought about running in his neighborhood, which he did many times when his schedule was tight, but today he had some free time, so he was heading back to the other side of Middleboro to the park across the street from the hospice center.

Despite the early rush hour traffic, Jordan made it there in less than 30 minutes and parked on the street across from the hospice center. He quickly got ready for his run with a three-minute stretching routine, then put in his earphones, tuned in to his favorite music, and was on the path shortly after eight. He wasn't sure just how far he would run. He figured he would let his body dictate that, but he was smart enough to realize that since he had not been running at all for several weeks, he should take it very easy the first time back at it.

After a few laps around the park, Jordan was starting to feel his lungs burn and his legs weakening. His GPS runner's watch told him that he had run just over three miles but in a rather pedestrian (for him) 30 minutes. He knew that was to be expected. He was also hoping to get a couple more laps in before calling it quits, but discretion being the better part of valor, he figured to run another half lap to the side of the park where Perk Place was, so he could get some coffee and perhaps breakfast.

He made it to the coffee shop in a few minutes, no worse for the wear. Once there, he decided to take a minute or two to cool down, stretch and catch his breath. He sat at one of the empty outside tables, checked his phone, and took a few deep breaths of the clean, cool air. Once he felt like he could breathe normally again, he went inside to see what he might like to have for breakfast.

Jordan scanned the overhead menu boards and the display case before finally settling on a hearty bowl of oatmeal with raisins and nuts and a mild roast coffee to which he would add a little half and half. He paid for his breakfast and left a nice tip for the workers hustling to accommodate the steady flow of patrons heading to work, school or just hanging out for a few minutes.

The table outside where he stopped to rest was still available, so Jordan sat there again. It gave him an excellent view of the park. He wondered if he might see Mary this morning, but knew that would be too much to hope for, and besides, he would not want her to think he was a stalker. He figured if he had not seen her by now, she was probably already home.

He was slowly eating his oatmeal because it was still steaming hot. His coffee was at the right temperature so he savored each sip while slowly scanning the park. Eventually, he spied a familiar figure sitting on the same bench as the day before. Despite being only able to see the back of his head, Jordan recognized the old-time golf cap the man was wearing. It had to be the same elderly gentleman that he had briefly spoken with the day before.

At that point, Jordan had a decision to make. He could either continue to eat his oatmeal and sip his coffee or make an attempt to talk with the old-timer and perhaps make his day a little happier. He decided on the latter. By now his oatmeal had cooled just enough for him to finish it without burning his mouth, and he accomplished that quickly, saving his coffee for sipping with the old man if he would have him as company.

Before heading over to see him, Jordan decided to check inside to see if the staff knew the old man, and more importantly what his drink of choice might be. He pointed him out to them, and they were only too happy to oblige. Kyle, the barista who had originally waited on Jordan said, "Oh, that's Mr. Nick. He comes in here almost every morning. We know his drink."

Jordan then said, "Has he been in yet this morning to order?"

Kyle checked with the other baristas, and none could remember waiting on Nick. He told Jordan, "Sometimes, he sits out there on his bench for a little while before coming in to order."

"Well, please make his drink. I'd like to buy it for him today," he said.

They happily made Nick's drink with special care, and Jordan asked to have his topped off, then paid for both drinks before thanking and tipping them, again very generously. He proceeded out of the coffee shop with drinks in both hands and headed straight for Nick.

Once there, he approached cautiously. He started the conversation by saying, "Excuse me, are you, Nick?"

"Yes, I am," came the old man's reply.

"Hi, I'm Jordan. I talked with you briefly yesterday," he said.

"Yes, I remember you. You held the door for me at the coffee shop, then stopped to talk for a minute before going into the hospice center," was Nick's very accurate recollection.

"You have excellent recall," said Jordan. "I hope I'm half as sharp as you when I'm your age. By the way, I took the liberty of getting your drink for you today. I hope that's all right. The folks at the coffee shop knew it, so I wanted you to have it."

"That's very kind of you, Jordan, but you didn't have to do that," he said.

Jordan replied, "I know, but I wanted to."

"Thank you, young man," Nick said, then continued, "you are welcome to sit and chat for a while if you have the time."

"Sure," Jordan said taking a seat on the other end of the bench.

Nick took a sip of his drink and started the conversation by saying, "You know Jordan, I sit here almost every day, and hardly anyone even notices me, let alone stops to talk. It's no big deal. I don't mind being alone and just sitting here watching people, but I do wonder at times if people are just going through the motions of life and not enjoying themselves."

Jordan, somewhat surprised and wondering where the conversation was going, replied, "Well, perhaps most of those people are in a hurry, and they just don't have the time."

"Perhaps," came Nick's comment, "but I see the same folks day after day, and none of them so much as even look around to enjoy this beautiful park. Most have their eyes glued to their phones. Many of the young mothers don't even watch their kids."

"Well, I guess that's their loss, the part about not taking the time to enjoy life," Jordan countered.

"But, you did, Jordan, and not only today but yesterday, as well," he said, then continued, "You have that old-fashioned respect for your elders. I don't mean that derogatorily but with admiration . . . and, I haven't forgotten that yesterday you saw me with my hands full, held the door for me, and waved me through. Those gestures are in short supply in today's society."

"I just do those things because that's the way I was raised," came Jordan's answer to the unasked question.

"Then, you had great parents," Nick said.

"I did, indeed," Jordan said, "but you said 'had'. How did you know that they had passed on?"

Nick recovered quickly, "Oh, just a slip of the tongue. Although, now I suspect you were visiting one of them yesterday at the hospice center."

"I was, my dad. He passed around 5:30 last evening," Jordan lamented.

"You have my deepest sympathies, Jordan," came Nick's reply. "I'm very sorry to hear that."

"We were very close," said Jordan. "I loved him more than anything else in the world. Of course, I loved my mother that way, too. She passed away two years ago. So, I guess in some weird way that makes my sister and me orphans."

"That's one way to look at it, I guess, even if it is not the traditional way one is considered an orphan," Nick offered with a smile.

"We will be all right once we get through the viewing and funeral. Then, I guess we'll have to deal with his estate, not that it will be much to divide, and then sell the house," Jordan blurted out.

"I'm sure you can handle it," was Nick's response.

"My sister will handle it. She's a lawyer and has a business background. She has been managing his affairs, paying his bills, and so on," offered Jordan.

"It sounds like you have it covered. It's just that . . ." Nick stopped short.

"Just that, what?" Jordan asked.

"Not my place to interject or interfere," Nick replied. "You hardly know me, and I should not offer unsolicited advice."

"No problem, I'll solicit some," came Jordan's response. "You seem pretty astute, and I'm sure your life's experiences run much deeper than mine."

"Well, what I was going to say, and don't take this the wrong way, money does strange things to people. I don't know your sister, so this may be totally off base. Does your father have a will?"

"Yes, there's a will," Jordan replied. "Why do you ask?"

"Well, that's good, at least his wishes for his estate are spelled out," Nick said.

"Sounds like you may have had a bad experience in this regard," Jordan said.

Nick then offered, "A very close friend of mine ran into some trouble regarding a will. As it turned out, there was a second, and later dated will. The first will had the heirs, the deceased's children, all receiving equal shares in his estate. The second will, which was suspected to have been coerced on this poor woman's death bed had only two children sharing in the estate. There were five children. This occurred back in 1940 when, unfortunately, things like that were somewhat commonplace, at least where I grew up. I'm sure your situation will be fine and all above board."

Jordan's jaw dropped, "What happened, what was the outcome?"

"It went to probate court. My friend had a priest testify for his and his siblings' side because the priest had heard the woman's confession and given her Last Rights. After the confession she told him that the two oldest children forced her to sign a new will earlier in the day that they drew up," Nick said, visibly upset and shaking his head.

Jordan quickly asked, "What was the outcome, the verdict of the trial?"

"The judge ruled that the later will was legal, and it had to be followed." He continued, "That's the way it was back then."

Jordan asked, "You mean the priest's testimony didn't matter?"

"Apparently not," Nick said, then concluded, "That's why I say that money does strange things to people. I'm sure it wasn't the only occurrence like that."

"If you don't mind me asking," Jordan said, then inquired, "where was this?"

"Northeastern Pennsylvania," Nick stated, "Although back then, I'm sure, it could have happened anywhere. The laws were not as good as they are now. Well, I hope they are better now, anyway."

Jordan then asked, "That's where you grew up?"

"Yes, good old Northeastern Pennsylvania, hard coal country," he affirmed, then asked, "How about you, Jordan? Where did you grow up?"

"Here in Middleboro," Jordan replied. I went to the town's schools and played sports here. I did go away to college, then got a job in New York, got married, divorced, and moved back here. That's my life in a nutshell."

"Okay, you gave me the abridged version, but there must be more," Nick said.

"I can elaborate," he replied, "I just don't want to bore you."

"I guarantee that you won't bore me, and even if I doze off while you are talking to me, I won't be out long, just keep talking," Nick said with a little laugh.

"Good one, Nick, but you are as sharp as a tack, quick-witted; and, I think there's a lot more about you that I should get to know," Jordan said.

"Well, I do have lots of interesting stories, not about me necessarily, but about people I've known over the years," was Nick's reply. "I don't mind sharing them."

Jordan then said, "I know we've only been talking for a few minutes, but I find you fascinating and extremely perceptive. Do you think we can meet here again sometime?" I would love to interview you for a project I'm contemplating."

"If you can indulge the ramblings of an old man, I'll be glad to talk with you, any time," he said. "But, I'm guessing by now you have somewhere else to be, so don't let me keep you."

Jordan checked his watch, "I'm good for now, but I do have to call my sister to see when we are meeting at the funeral home."

"Why don't you do that, to be on the safe side with your timeline," Nick offered.

Jordan then rang up his sister since she was likely back home after dropping Amanda and Richie at school. She picked up quickly, and Jordan jumped right in, "Hi Jack, what's the plan for seeing the funeral director today?"

"Nothing yet. I called him, but he wasn't there. He's supposed to call me back. I'll let you know the time when I know it. What are you up to today?"

He replied, "I went back to the park across from the hospice center, ran for about 30 minutes, stopped at that coffee shop for breakfast, and now I'm talking with this delightful elderly gentleman, named Nick. I was just wondering when I should head back home to get cleaned up before meeting you at the funeral home."

"Well, okay, but no word yet. How long will you need once he calls me back?" She asked.

"Give me 90 minutes to get home, shower, and get there," he said, but if he has to shoehorn us in, then I can just go straight there in my running clothes."

"Well, dear brother, I've smelled you after one of your athletic endeavors, and I vote that you go home first and shower," vetoing his plan with a laugh.

"Good to hear you laugh," he said. "How did you sleep last night?"

"Like a log," she said.

"Yeah, me, too," Jordan replied. "It must have been our bodies letting us know that we had pushed them to the brink."

"Yes, probably so," she said, then concluded with, "I'll let you know something when I hear from Granatelli's. Go back and talk with your friend. That park is getting to be quite the place for you to meet people. By the way, who did you run into at the park yesterday?"

Jordan deftly deflected the question, "Oh, no one you know."

"OK, don't want to talk about it, huh? You can tell me whenever you are ready," she replied.

"Well, there's one thing I need to discuss with you later today, but not that, so let me get back to my new friend," he said. "Talk with you later, bye."

Jordan turned to Nick and said, "Sorry to interrupt our conversation. I'm good until she calls me back."

"Great!" Nick said. "You mentioned that you played sports. I've followed sports all my life."

Jordan unwittingly bit, "Yes, I played Little League, then some in high school, intramural sports in college between studying and work." Of course, he was more interested in Nick's story, so he tried pivoting back to Nick. "Did you play sports growing up in Pennsylvania?" He asked.

"I played a little, mostly what you might call 'sand-lot' because when I was growing up, there just weren't many organized sports for boys and none for girls," Nick replied.

"I guess I should have figured that, but never thought of it," Jordan said. "That might be a good idea for a column of mine. By the way, I write a sports column for the Middleboro Ledger," Jordan offered.

"I know who you are, young man," Nick conceded. "I read your column all the time."

Jordan was now flabbergasted, and asked, "How do you know that?"

"Well, I like sports; I like to read about sports, among other things; and I get the local newspaper, so even though the picture they run in the paper atop your column is a bit dated, I'm not blind. I put all the evidence together and figured it out. It wasn't difficult, besides, you write a little like you speak, believe it, or not."

"I write as I speak?" Jordan asked surprised, "in what way?"

"Let's just say some of the words you use and the phraseology," Nick answered, "and we should leave it at that."

Jordan was beyond fascinated at this point and becoming a little intimidated by this extremely insightful gentleman. He decided to dive a little deeper, "May I ask what you did for a living, Nick?"

"How long do you have?" came Nick's smiling reply.

"Why?" Jordan asked.

"Because I've done a lot of things, most of which you couldn't care less about, but suffice to say that I ran a business for years. It was pretty boring stuff, but I made enough to live. The cost of living there is much more reasonable than Middleboro or many other places."

Ever the curious soul, due mostly to his journalistic nature, Jordan pressed on, "What type of business did you own?"

"I didn't say 'I owned the business', I said, 'I ran a business'. I ran it for someone else." Nick was keeping his personal information a little close-holed now, and Jordan was sensing it might be time to move on to another topic. Perhaps sometime later on Nick would feel comfortable enough around Jordan to tell him more, but not likely today.

He started down a new avenue of conversation, "Nick, are you married, do you have any kids, grandkids?"

"No, I have never been married. I could have married anyone I pleased, but I guess I never pleased any woman enough for her to want to marry me," he said laughing and with a twinkle in his eye. "After a while, I was a confirmed bachelor. I dated here and there, but nothing ever materialized."

Jordan felt bad now, he apologized by offering, "I'm sorry if I brought up a touchy subject." He figured that he was zero for two on topics Nick wanted to talk about.

But Nick was gracious, "Not at all," he said. "It's just the way life unfolds sometimes. I'm not sorry, so don't you be. Just remember, not everyone is lonely when they are alone."

Jordan was awed by this gentle old man's intellect. "How prophetic," he said.

"Well, it's not an original thought," he replied, "I read it somewhere and adopted it."

"You are one cool dude, Nick," Jordan said, then tried for a non-personal topic, "You said that you followed sports your whole life."

"Yes, I have," he said. "I've followed baseball, for example, since Babe Ruth's days of playing for the Yankees."

By now Jordan was realizing that sitting with him was a treasure trove of information, and not just about sports, but sports were a great starting point to keep the conversation going. He thought for a second or two, then asked, "What was the greatest game you ever saw?"

Nick mused the question for a few seconds, then asked, "Which sport?"

"Any sport," he said. "We can get into specific sports, later."

"Well, certainly there were some historic seventh games of World Series that stand out, most recently in 2001 when it looked like the Yankees had it won with Rivera pitching the ninth to close it out, and Arizona rallied to win it. Back in 1960, it was the Yankees losing a wild seventh game to Pittsburgh, 10-9, so that one stands out, as well. I know you are a Yankees fan, so how about the 2003 seventh game of the ALCS when Aaron Boone hit a walk-off homer in the 11th inning to beat the Red Sox?" He asked with a big grin. "Also, I recall in 1991 the Twins beat the Braves, four games to three. All the games were won by the home team, and all were close, except one. The Twins won the seventh game, 1-0."

"Hey, how do you know I'm a Yankees fan?" he asked.

"I told you I read your column," came Nick's reply.

"Wait, you picked up that I'm a Yankees fan from my column?" he asked. "I try very hard to keep that a secret down here in O's and Nats country."

"What can I say, 'try harder', it creeps into your articles every once in a while," Nick replied. "OK, they are some of pro baseball's games of note. There are so many others. Pro basketball had some great series and games between the old Philadelphia Warriors with Wilt Chamberlain and the Boston Celtics with Bill Russell and company," Nick stated. "And of course, lately, there have been some outstanding Super Bowls. My favorite recently was Super Bowl LII when the Eagles beat the Patriots with a late score."

"That's pretty good recall off the top of your head," Jordan said.

"Thanks, but the best three games I have ever seen in person occurred back in 1971. They were part of a Rotary Club basketball tournament for high school teams. Not everyone might think they were the best games, but for me, they were my favorites."

"What happened that made them your favorites?" Jordan asked.

"Well, Jordy, can I call you, Jordy?" Nick asked. "You see, you remind me of a fella that used to work for me, call Gordon. I called him, Gordy, so don't be upset if I slip sometime and call you, Gordy, by mistake."

"Sure, why not, no one else does, so you can have that as my special nickname, get it, Nick name," he said realizing he had just made a bad pun.

"I got it, very good. It's nice to see that you can still make a joke at this sorrowful time," Nick said laughing out loud. "I'll be glad to tell you all about those three games, but first you will need some background information, and that will take a few of these sessions to do it the justice it deserves. You asked what made them my personal favorites. Without giving too much away, I can tell you that they were all played with ferocious intensity by young men who got nothing out of it except the thrill of competing and the desire to win. No one paid them a dime, and all three games were barn burners among four teams that badly wanted to win. Finally, I had a stake in those games, which made them special to me."

"It's okay with me if it's okay with you," Jordan said, "and by the way, this is a better therapy session for me than sitting down with a shrink, and it's free." He added with a laugh.

Nick then began a new topic, he mused, "I'm also guessing that you, like every other writer, is looking for an idea for a book."

"Well, it had crossed my mind a time or two," was Jordan's reply, "and honestly, that's the 'project' I mentioned a few minutes ago."

"OK, then, the next time we meet bring a notepad and something to write with, or a recorder, whatever you like. I will refresh my memory in the meantime, you know, organize my thoughts, and we can start the story. As I said, it may take a few sessions. Of course, my ramblings may take a few side streets, you know, tangential topics. Are you good with all of that?" Nick asked.

"Good with it? I'd love it," he said excitedly, "but you will have to let me buy you your favorite drink, just to keep your whistle wet. By the way, is your coffee the way you like it?"

"Yes, Jordy, it's perfect, and thank you," he replied.

All of a sudden Jordan had a flash of the blinding obvious. He recalled Nick talking about remembering Babe Ruth. He knew from his sports research that Babe Ruth finished playing in the 1930s, and that was at least 80 years ago, so if Nick remembered him playing, how old was Nick, anyway, he mused. He figured a nice way to inquire, "Nick, you mentioned that you remembered when Babe Ruth played. When was that, and did you ever get to see him play, or was it only from listening on the radio?"

"I got to see him at the end of his career for the Yanks in 1934 in New York. My Uncle Al took me. By that time The Babe was pretty much finished, but he did hit a home run in that game," Nick said with a broad smile, "and that's when I became a Yankees fan. Yankee Stadium was majestic. It was like a palace or a cathedral to an 11-year-old."

"So, we, at least, have that in common," Jordan said, then added, "I have to ask, but you don't have to tell me, how old you are."

"I don't mind telling you that I just turned 96 last month, he said, "I was born in 1923."

Jordan couldn't believe his ears or eyes at this point, "Nick, you're 96 years old?" He said incredulously. "You don't even look like your 80. You look fantastic."

"Well, thanks," he said, "I get that a lot. I guess I got a good set of genes from my parents, although, and unfortunately, neither lived to see their old age. My father died when I was a little boy, and my mother passed away at the beginning of my senior year in high school."

"Oh, I'm sorry to hear that, Nick," Jordan said.

"My father worked in the mines, as did a lot of men in that area during those years." Nick continued, "It was difficult work, but it was work. The mine owners paid the workers just enough to live, but certainly not lavishly. Most of the money they earned in pay went right back to the mine owners, who just happened to own the company stores, where the miners spent their wages to get the commodities they needed to live."

"Almost sounds like a form of slavery," Jordan said, "You know, the miner worked for the mine owner, and in return, he got food, clothing, and a place to live."

"I guess you could look at it that way, but the miner was free to work elsewhere if he wanted. It's just that there were not many other opportunities for an unskilled laborer back there at that time," Nick concluded.

Jordan then asked, "If you don't mind me asking, how did your father die, and how old was he? He must have been young."

"I don't mind talking about it," Nick replied, "My dad was only 39. He died in a mine accident. They were common. The saddest part was that his fellow miners just carried him home and deposited him on the front porch. My poor mother had to deal with it. I was only four at the time, too young to remember him. My oldest brother, James, who was only 13, had to quit school and find work to support our family."

"That's an incredible story," Jordan said dumbfounded.

"Believe it, or not, it wasn't that unusual," Nick said. "It happened more than you might think, and certainly more than it should have. The worst part was that the mining company had no obligation to take care of the family. Over time, working conditions in the mines improved; you know, better safety equipment and better mining practices, but it was too late for my dad and others like him, who experienced the same fate. There was also a long-range effect of working in the mines. Have you ever heard of Black Lung Disease?"

Jordan replied, "No, what is it?"

"It's a lung ailment caused by inhaling coal dust for many years," Nick answered, "and many miners were afflicted with it, which prematurely caused their deaths."

"How ironic, my dad served in Vietnam and ended up with many ailments resulting from being exposed to Agent Orange," Jordan shared.

"Well, that's very unfortunate, as well," Nick said.

"Yes, indeed, but what happened to your family after your father died?" Jordan asked.

"My mother was an incredibly tough woman," he began, "she was bound and determined to keep us all together, but there was only a little money coming in from a small government subsistence check and my brother's job. So, when things got dicey, I was sometimes farmed out to a neighbor, or my mother's sister, and her husband, my Aunt Bonnie, and Uncle Al. Don't get me wrong, they were great people, and I loved them very much, but they weren't my mom and dad if you know what I mean, and I think you do."

"Yes, I do know, but I cannot wrap my head around what you have shared with me this morning," Jordan confessed.

"Too much information to handle, or too much sad information?" Nick asked.

"Both, I guess," said Jordan, "but it helps me put things in their proper perspective. I realize now, that no matter how bad things may seem, or how difficult your situation may be, just talk to someone else, and you will quickly realize that you will want to keep your own issues. For instance, I had my parents for 45 years. They died young, for certain, especially by today's standards, but yours died so much sooner. I cannot imagine never to have known my dad, like you."

"Well, Jordy, that's why I wanted to share that part of my life with you today. It's not to diminish your feelings, or tell you that you don't have the right to grieve, but to realize that everyone goes through it at some point. Yes, your parents died too early in your life, but no matter when they pass away, you will always want one more year, one more month, one more week, one more day with them. It's just the way it is when you love them, and they love you. The heart wants what it wants, and it's perfectly fine to miss them every day."

Jordan knew that he had just been given a tremendous life lesson, and he didn't miss the message being delivered. Unfortunately, his time with Nick was running short, and he knew it was probably better that he get going. He also realized that he had been given the great gift of meeting Nick, the old man in the park that no one else seemed to notice. He began to stand up and said, "Nick, I don't know how to thank you. That was the best couple of bucks I ever spent," he said jokingly. "Before I go, how can I reach you?"

Nick took out his phone and said, "What's your number? I'll text you a quick message, then you'll have my number. Call me anytime, Jordy, with anything you want to discuss or any problem you have. If I can help, I gladly will."

Jordan recited his number to Nick, who then sent him the following text, "Dear Jordy, this has been one of the best mornings of my life. Thank you for spending the time with me. I hope to see you again, soon. Your friend, Nick."

Jordan said he got it, thanked Nick again, gave him a friendly pat on the shoulder, then turned and walked toward his car across the open field in the park. On his way, he decided to read Nick's message. After he read it, his eyes teared up. He turned around to look for Nick, but by then Nick was gone.

CHAPTER 4
Struggles

Jordan's phone rang as he was getting to his car. He could see that it was Jackie calling. He answered, "Hi Jack, what's up?"

She replied, "I just heard from Mr. Granatelli. He can see us at noon if that works for you."

"I'll make it work," was Jordan's answer. "That'll give me just enough time to get home, shower, and get to the funeral home. Do we need to bring anything with us?"

"I don't think so," she answered. "Like what? What were you thinking?"

"Not sure, did we bring any info when mom died?" He asked.

"No, but we'll need to provide some details regarding what we want in the obituary," she responded.

"Okay, I guess we can do that," he concluded. "I'll see you there at noon."

Jordan knew he had ample time, but he didn't want to be late, so he drove directly home. While driving, he decided to call his editor to let him know that his father had indeed passed away the day before and that he could be available later in the day after he met with the funeral director.

His editor told him that it wouldn't be necessary and that he should take a few days off. Jordan appreciated that but wanted to finish one story he was working on. He explained to his editor that writing his column was therapeutic, and besides, he had some time available to work on it now, rather than later.

His editor agreed to hold some space in the next day's paper for Jordan's column, but he asked Jordan to let him know as soon as possible if he wasn't going to be able to meet the deadline for publication. Jordan assured him that he would be fine, but if something unforeseen came up, he would call immediately.

About the time he was ending his call with his editor Jordan noticed flashing lights behind him and heard a police siren blaring. He pulled over to the side of the road anticipating the police cruiser passing him by. To his surprise the police car parked behind him. Jordan was now concerned that he might have been speeding or had a broken taillight, or maybe even gone through a red traffic signal.

Jordan knew enough not to get out of his car and to do exactly what the policeman told him when he approached. When he arrived at Jordan's driver's side door, he asked Jordan if he knew why he was stopped. Jordan replied, "I don't think I was speeding, was I?"

The policeman replied, "No, not speeding, but you were using your cell phone, and not in a hands-free manner. We have been directed to crack down on offenders.

So, unfortunately, I have to cite you. May I see your license and registration, sir?"

Jordan explained to the officer that he had to reach into his glove compartment to get his registration and into the center console for his wallet which contained his license. The officer understood and directed him that it was all right to do so. Jordan handed over both, and the officer took them back to his patrol car to run a check on him.

While he was gone, Jordan tried to calm his nerves since he knew that there was always a possibility that something could go wrong during a traffic stop. He was a little upset, also, because this was the last thing he needed at this time, and besides, he thought, it was such a minor infraction. His day had been going so well, he thought, but now a glitch had occurred. As he sat in his vehicle waiting for the patrolman to return, he thought that the roller-coaster day of emotional swings that occurred yesterday was starting to happen all over again. He wondered whether today was going to be a 'stairway to heaven' or a 'highway to hell'. He finally concluded that it would likely be a little of both, like many other days, and that was just the way life unfolded.

The officer returned fairly quickly after running Jordan's license through the police traffic check system. "Good news," he said. "You have no prior traffic stops, a clean record, and no warrants out for your arrest."

"Well, that's all good news," Jordan said. "So, am I free to go with just a warning?"

"I wish it could be, but 'no,'" was the officer's reply. "I have to cite you. It's not a big deal. You won't have to go to court. It'll just be a fine. There are no points against your driving record, so that's good."

"OK, do what you have to do," was Jordan's answer. "I have an appointment at noon, so I don't have the time to argue about it, not that I suppose it would do any good, anyway."

"No, sorry to say, it wouldn't," he said. Then he asked Jordan to sign a form that he was cited, not necessarily that he was admitting guilt. Jordan complied, then was back on his way home. He put the citation in his console and tried to forget about it.

Five minutes later his phone was ringing again. He knew better than to pick it up. He let it go to his inbox figuring that whatever it was, it could wait. Besides, he was almost home, anyway.

As he turned onto his street he could see a police car in front of his house and a crowd that had gathered across the street in Agatha's and Andy's driveway. He figured 'what could this be? He pulled into his driveway and could hear his house alarm blaring. The alarm monitoring company must have called the police, he thought. Then he realized that the call he had received on his cell was probably them calling him to let him know that his alarm had been triggered.

He pulled into his driveway, went to the police officer, and identified himself as the homeowner. The policeman explained that he had not yet gone into his house, but the rear door looked to have been breached, and he was waiting for a backup unit before entering the house. It arrived a few minutes later, and to Jordan's surprise, it was the same cop that had just given him the traffic summons. They exchanged pleasantries, and the policeman said, "Man, this just isn't your day, is it?"

Jordan knew it to be a rhetorical question, so he didn't answer. He was told to wait outside, preferably across the street as one police officer would go around back while the other waited in the front. In all likelihood, the perpetrator would be long gone, but they had to check nonetheless.

While across the street with his neighbors he was greeted with many condolences regarding his father's passing. All of his neighbors knew Jordan as a kind, gentle and quiet person. They also told him how sorry they were regarding the apparent break-in, especially at this unfortunate time.

A few minutes later, the officer that entered through the rear door called the other officer in the front of the house to let him know that all was clear, no suspect was found. He signaled to Jordan to come across the street and explained that Jordan could now enter his house to see if anything had been taken. Jordan was hoping that the burglar was scared off by the alarm before he could take anything.

His house hadn't been ransacked very much, just a few drawers opened and dumped on the floor in his bedroom. The police theorized that the alarm for that door must have been on a delay, so it didn't immediately frighten the burglar or burglars away. Jordan confirmed that the back door was a delayed alarm, probably 30 seconds. He then looked around to see what he might determine to be missing. He had his wallet, money, and credit card with him, so that was a good thing. His television was still on the wall, so that wasn't taken. There were no other valuables in his house, except for his computer, which he usually left on the desk in his study. When he checked the study, there was no computer. His heart sunk. That was where all of his work, his columns, were kept.

He told the policemen that the only item he could think of that was missing was his computer. They made their report and told Jordan that if anything else was determined to be missing, then he should call the police station. They explained that the computer would likely be fenced at a pawn shop, so if he were so inclined, he could check them in the area. They would put out a message, but mostly no pawn shop owner would pay any attention to it. They left their contact information with him and passed along some advice regarding how to secure the back door until he could get it properly fixed. Jordan immediately thought of his dad, who would know how to fix it without too much trouble, but alas, that was no longer an option, although he had another one across the street.

When the police left, Jordan went across the street to let his neighbors know that the only item that had been taken was his computer. They again told him how sorry they were and mentioned that before he got home the policeman had asked them if they saw anyone in Jordan's house or anyone leaving it in a hurry. No one did.

Jordan knew Tom Johnson was a handyman, and that he might be available to fix his back door. As soon as Jordan mentioned the break-in point was his back door, Tom immediately volunteered to take care of it. Jordan didn't necessarily want to bother Tom with it, but he had little choice. I was going to ask you if you had the time to look at it, and of course, I want to pay you for your time.

Tom was adamant, "Jordan, you aren't paying me. I want to help out any way I can, especially in your time of need. Let's take a look at the damage. At worst you may need a new door. If that's the case, I'll get it, install it, paint it, and let you know what it costs."

Tom, his wife, Juanita, and their two children were the only African American family on Jordan's street when the subsection was developed. The children, a boy and girl, were both grown now and living on their own out-of-state. They were original owners and had lived there for twenty years. Tom was an Army veteran, now retired. He and Juanita bought in the development when Tom retired and just before Juanita was eligible for retirement. While in the army, Tom rose to the rank of master sergeant and was the highest-ranking NCO on his last post. He had served in the first Gulf War and was highly decorated, although one would never hear it from him.

Once at the back of the house, Tom did a quick assessment of the damage to Jordan's rear door. He said, "It doesn't look too bad. I think they just jimmied the lock with a pry bar or big screwdriver. There's some damage to the door frame, but I can fix it in an hour, then I can paint it. I know you must have things to do today, so why don't you go and do want you need to do, and let me handle this. If I need any help, I can get Andy or one of the other neighbors."

Jordan said, "I don't know how to thank you, Tom. I know you and my dad were kindred spirits being army vets, fix-it guys, and even sharing the same first name. Here's my key, please lock it when you are finished, and again thank you very much."

Jordan suddenly realized that he had two phone calls to make. First, he needed to inform his boss that he wasn't going to be able to finish his column in time for the next edition of the paper. Due to the circumstances, he was sure his boss would understand since they had a great working relationship. His boss knew that Jordan wouldn't miss a deadline unless the situation was out of his control. Besides, he knew that Jordan wasn't just the best writer in his department, but the best the newspaper had.

After Jordan called his boss, he called Jackie to let her know that he could still make it to Granatelli's, but he would be a few minutes late due to the break-in at his house. He didn't go into any detail because time didn't permit it, so he told her he would explain when he saw her later.

She was horrified when he told her and tried to talk him out of meeting her. He wouldn't have any of it. He explained, "I'll be there, just give me a few extra minutes. I still need to shower. Tom Johnson is going to fix the door while I'm out, so that's taken care of. I don't have much else to worry about except trying to get my computer back. It had all my work on it." They agreed to end the call and talk about it after meeting at Granatelli's.

Now hustling to get showered, dressed, and out the door in ten minutes, Jordan was in overdrive. He figured it would take twenty minutes to get to the funeral home. It was now 11:35 a.m., so if all went well, he would only be about five minutes late, which he could live with considering the traffic stop and his home being burglarized. The way the day was now going, he knew that he had better adhere to the speed limit on the way to meet Jackie at the funeral home. He didn't need a third problem to deal with before noon.

All went pretty smoothly at the funeral home. Mr. Granatelli met them and directed Jackie and Jordan through the process of flower, casket, and attire selections. They provided some details regarding Thomas's life which would be included in his obituary. As a final matter, Mr. Granatelli told them that he could work them in for a viewing on Friday evening and the funeral/burial on Saturday, which suited both.

On the way out of the funeral home, Jackie asked Jordan what had happened at his house. He began to explain, then suggested that they meet somewhere for lunch, and he would fill her in regarding his morning and 'something else', as he put it, meaning Kathryn's letter. They agreed to meet at the coffee shop by the park since it was only five minutes away, and they could likely sit outside and enjoy the beautiful day.

Jackie followed Jordan to Perk Place, and it being early afternoon, they were both able to find parking on the street very near the coffee shop. They found a nice table under the awning and out of the midday sun. Jordan asked her what she might like before going inside and ordering. Both decided on sandwiches. Jackie liked a chicken salad sandwich while Jordan opted for turkey and cheese on whole wheat. Both had water to wash down their sandwiches.

Almost immediately as Jordan returned with the lunches, Jackie said, "So, tell me about your morning."

"Not good, well, let me correct that," Jordan began. "The first part was great. I met this elderly man, named Nick. I met him yesterday and saw him again today. So, I decided to buy him his favorite drink and strike up a conversation. Let me tell you, Jack, he is delightful, smart, sharp, witty, and any other positive attribute you want to add. Additionally, there's something mysterious about him. I can't put my finger on it, but I'm hoping to find out more about him and maybe write a story about it."

"That all sounds great, but what happened to make your morning go downhill?" She asked.

He started, "On the way home from here after meeting Nick, I called my boss at the paper to tell him that I planned on having an article ready for tomorrow's newspaper. Unfortunately, I was driving at the time. A cop saw me on my cell and stopped me. He said that he had to cite me, so I got a ticket for that, problem number one, although not a big issue, but I will likely get fined."

He continued, "As I'm turning onto my street, I see a lot of people, my neighbors, hanging out in Andy and Agatha's driveway across the street from my house, and of course, a policeman is standing in my front yard. By now I can hear my alarm blaring to beat the band. I assume, correctly, that I've been broken into, problem number two."

"What did they take?" Jackie asked.

"The only thing I can determine, so far, is my computer," Jordan responded.

"How's that going to affect your work?" She inquired.

He replied, "It's going to affect it greatly. All my work was stored on it. My boss said I can stop by the office and get another one, but that one had my half-finished next column on it, not to mention some other projects I was working on."

"I know it's too late now, but you do know about backing up your work," she offered.

"Yes, I know about archiving and backing up my computer. Once again, I get to learn a hard lesson," he said now quite annoyed at himself.

By then they were just about finished with their sandwiches and slowly sipping on their drinks. Jordan then said, "If those two problems weren't enough . . ." he left it hanging for dramatic effect.

"Yes, what?" Jackie asked.

"Last evening, after that horrendous day we had, I get my mail, and what do you think is in it waiting for me?" Jordan asked.

"What?" Jackie asked back.

"A letter from Kathryn, of all things," he said.

"A letter from Kathryn?" She repeated it back to him in question form. "What does she want?"

"Exactly!" Jordan said raising his voice a little, obviously getting madder by the minute. "She always wants something. Now, she wants me to take a vacation with her this summer, but the kicker is that she is planning on moving back to Middleboro, and, wait for it, wants to move in with me for a few months until she gets settled here."

"What?" Jackie asked in an excited tone and half choking on the last bite of her sandwich.

"You can't make this stuff up, I guess," was Jordan's answer. "Normally, I would try to help anyone, and family of course, but Katie is a real user. So, I'm not sure if she got in my house, I could get her to leave. Also, I'm wondering what happened to Veronica, her live-in partner."

"Yeah, good question," was Jackie's comeback.

"By your reaction, I'm guessing that you didn't know anything about any of this?" Jordan tried to ask nonconfrontationally.

"No, why do you think that I might know something about Kathryn? She asked.

"Well, I know that you and Katie stay in touch," Jordan said. "Two years ago you let her know that Mom died, and she showed up for the viewing to pay her respects, and of course, she asked for more alimony."

"She did what?" Jackie yelled, "At mom's viewing?"

"Oh yeah, didn't I mention that?" Jordan asked.

"No, I think I would have remembered it if you had told me," Jackie said.

"It's water under the bridge now," Jordan said. "Besides, I told her 'no', and if she pressed it, I'd take her to court and ask the judge to look into her marital status considering that she and Veronica had been living together for at least ten years, you know, common law marriage. I never heard another word from her after that, until yesterday's mail."

"You may have grounds there with the common law marriage," Jackie mused, then asked, "What are you going to do?"

"For now, just let it be," he said. "I don't plan on dealing with her until after dad's funeral, and maybe not until after we settle everything with the estate. That reminds me, what are we going to do with the homestead?"

"I always assumed that we would sell it after we cleaned out the stuff we wanted," was her reply.

"Good, we're thinking alike on that," Jordan said.

"You know that you are only putting off the inevitable," Jackie said. "At some point, you will have to deal with her."

"You are probably right," he said. "But for now I can push it off for a few days. I don't want her moving in with me."

At that point, they decided to conclude lunch and go back to their respective homes. Jackie had some things to take care of for her family, not the least of which, was planning dinner. Jordan was pretty much free for the rest of the day, so he thought about stopping off at his office to get another computer and try to resurrect his story.

As he was walking to his car he noticed the familiar figure of Nick sitting on his favorite park bench. He thought it a bit unusual that Nick was back there, but Jordan didn't know Nick's schedule, so perhaps that wasn't so unusual. At any rate, he decided to stop by to say, 'hello' and see what Nick might be up to for the rest of the day.

"Hi Nick," Jordan began the conversation.

"Jordy, nice to see you again," came Nick's reply. "Did you get to the undertaker's?"

"Eventually," Jordan said.

"What's that mean?" Nick asked detecting perhaps a problem for Jordan.

Jordan then went into a lengthy discourse about the rest of his day from the time he left Nick until he met him again. He provided as much detail as he thought Nick might want to hear.

Nick then said, "Oh, Jordy, that's a shame." He then nonchalantly asked if Jordan remembered the officer who gave him the ticket. Jordan recalled that the name on the officer's badge was Wolfowitz, and Jordan mentioned that he was one of the two policemen that investigated the break-in at his house.

Nick then asked in an off-hand way, "I was thinking about replacing my computer. Is yours a new one, and if you don't mind me asking, who is the manufacturer?"

Jordan thought for a second or two, then answered, "It's a Sony VAIO laptop. It has everything I need to do my job: ample storage and speed. It contains all my work projects, so I'm at a great loss without it."

Jordan's despair was obvious to Nick, who realized that the computer must have contained some important work.

Nick sympathized with Jordan and told him how sorry he was for all the trouble that had come his way, especially now while he was trying to deal with his father's passing. He concluded that part of their conversation with, "Who knows, it may turn up. The police sometimes find them." He then asked, "Did everything go well with the undertaker?"

"Yes, it did," Jordan replied. "Mr. Granatelli handled everything professionally and efficiently."

"Excellent, Alfonso is a good man. I'm glad you are using him to wake and bury your father. He'll take care of everything," Nick said.

Jordan was curious, "Do you know Mr. Granatelli?"

"I do," Nick replied, "and I've been to several services at his business for people I knew, or who have had family waked there, and they have all been very happy with his service."

Jordan figured that was enough of a positive endorsement, and besides, he knew that he shouldn't try to probe too much into Nick's affairs, who he knew, or what he did. He figured that Nick would tell him what he needed to know when the time was right. Pivoting to a sports-related topic, Jordan asked if Nick followed boxing.

"Boxing? Yes, of course, but it was a better sport years ago," came Nick's reply. Then he elaborated, "Years ago, the boxers actually boxed. Today, too many fighters hold and dance. If you get five minutes of actual boxing in a 10-rounder, that's a lot."

"What about those mixed martial arts?" Jordan asked.

"You mean street fighting? That's what I call it. I'm not a fan," was Nick's reply.

"Who were some of the better fighters back in the 1940s and 1950s?" Jordan asked.

Nick thought for a moment, then said, "During that time all weight divisions had great fighters. The heavyweights, like Joe Louis, Jersey Joe Walcott, Rocky Marciano, Ezzard Charles, and Billy Conn, who was a light heavyweight, reigned supreme. However, some of the lighter-weight fighters were great, as well. Tony Zale, Rocky Graziano, Jake LaMotta, Sugar Ray Robinson, Marcel Cerdan, Sandy Sadler, and of course, Willie Pep were exceptional boxers. Those guys fought smart and could hit. I couldn't tell you any of today's boxers. I've lost interest in it. The last era that I followed was the 1980s and early 1990s when Sugar Ray Leonard, Tommy Hearns, Roberto Duran, Marvelous Marvin Hagler, and Wilfredo Benitez were fighting each other. Of course, my favorite was Smokin' Joe Frazier. He was a Pennsylvania guy, actually a Philly guy, like Rocky Balboa," he said with a laugh. "I didn't like Ali because of his antics but realized that he was just doing it for the hype. He and Frazier fought three spectacular fights, and when Ali defeated George Foreman, I knew he was a great fighter. But, like so many before him, he hung around too long, and in the end, he embarrassed himself a little bit, at least in my estimation."

Jordan replied, "That's pretty good recall off the top of your head." Then he asked, "Did you get to see any local fights where you lived?"

"We had a Catholic Youth Center, or CYC, in Scranton where we would go to see some fights from time to time."

"Any good fighters come out of your area?" Jordan asked.

"None that you've ever heard of," was Nick's reply, "but I recall a kid back there named Ronnie Rudzinski. He was the stereotypical Eastern European-looking guy: chiseled features, blond hair, never smiled. Think Ivan Drago in *Rocky IV*, except smaller. I loved to watch him fight because he was a brawler. He didn't care how many shots he took to get his licks in. He never took a step backward in the ring, always moving forward.

Ruddy, as he was nicknamed, threw punches from all directions. He was perpetual motion, always swinging. That said, in one fight he pulls a reversal. I recall that he let his opponent beat on him for five rounds. It was a six-rounder. Ruddy's face was a bloody pulp, but he wouldn't let the referee stop the fight. By the sixth round, the other guy is arm weary and dead tired. Ruddy knocked him out in 30 seconds. He wasn't a big kid, either, I think he was fighting lightweight, probably 132 pounds. Sometimes, he would go up a weight class, or two, just to get on the card that night and get a paycheck. His family was poor, so whatever money he was able to bring home, and however he could get it, was needed for his mother to run their household."

"Whatever became of him?" Jordan asked.

"It's a sad story, sorry to say. After a while, I had to stop going to see him fight because the pounding he was taking wasn't a pretty sight. I tried talking him out of boxing, but he wouldn't listen to me, or anyone else, a hard head. Unfortunately for him, his head wasn't hard enough to withstand the constant shots he was taking. In the beginning, I backed him with a sponsorship, then I had to pull out hoping it would get him to quick fighting. I did it for his own good. It didn't matter. He was one of those guys with a Napoleon complex. If someone looked at him the wrong way, or what he thought was the wrong way, he'd say 'Whadya you lookin' at, buddy', then, of course, the fight was on. He ended up with dementia, not surprisingly, and eventually passed away, much too young."

"I guess boxing is pretty brutal," Jordan mused.

"I think it has gotten better over the years. In the depression and war years, I'm talking about the 1930s and 1940s now, it was pretty brutal, especially in the many small-town arenas. Guys were fighting for next to nothing and getting their brains beaten out. I'm just surprised that more were not killed. Did you ever see the movie, *The Quiet Man*, with John Wayne and Maureen O'Hara?" Nick asked.

"No, I haven't," Jordan answered.

"There's a scene in that movie that shows what boxing was like back then. I won't give it away in case you want to see it sometime. It's not really a boxing movie, it's a love story, so watch it with Mary some night," Nick suggested.

"Hey, how do you know about Mary?" Jordan asked.

"I know a lot of things that happen around town that no one thinks I know. It's like Yogi Berra said, 'You can learn a lot by watching'," Nick said, then added, "two other movies on boxing that better depict 'the sweet science' at that time are *Raging Bull* and *The Harder They Fall*. Robert DeNiro played Jake LaMotta in *Raging Bull* and won an Oscar for his portrayal. Humphrey Bogart starred in *The Harder They Fall* as a sports reporter, like you. It was Bogey's final film, a bit of trivia."

"Again, I have to say, how much you impress me with your recall, especially right off the top of your head," Jordan said.

"Don't be too impressed. I just enjoy talking about those subjects. I lived through a lot of it, so the memories are ingrained because I experienced them first hand, and of course, I was interested in them," Nick countered. "It's like education and learning. Most students will do well in a subject that they like and are interested in, but a good teacher can present the material to the students in a manner that's interesting and makes them all want to learn. That's the trick. It's not much different than your writing. You have to find a way to present your articles in a unique, interesting way so that your readership will want to, not only finish the article but continue to read your work again and again. The same goes for an artist, I would think."

"What a perspective!" Jordan concluded. "You see things so clearly and explain them so well."

"Thanks, but it's just the voice of age and experience," Nick replied.

Jordan saw a chance to segue to a new topic. He began, "You mentioned teaching. My ex-wife is a teacher in New York. However, she's planning on moving back to Middleboro this summer."

"I see a potential problem arising for you," was Nick's very astute observation. "What are you going to do about that, if anything?"

"I know I cannot stop her from moving back here, but it may be uncomfortable if she thinks we can rekindle our relationship after all these years."

"Do you think that's what she's fishing for?" Nick asked.

"Not sure, she's a bit of a user, correction, she's a big-time user, one of the very best overachieving 'me' people you would ever have the misfortune to meet," Jordan said, then added, "For example, she wants to move in with me for a few months until she finds a place of her own. I'm guessing it'll be more than a few months, or she'll not want to leave at all once she gets in my house.

Now, here's the best part. She left me for another woman. So, I'm not sure if she is a lesbian or bi-sexual, or what."

Surprisingly not shocked by Jordan's disclosure, Nick calmly said, "You have some time to figure it out. I'm sure in the end you will make the right decision, the one that your parents taught you to make. I'm guessing that you're torn between wanting to help on the one hand and not wanting to get trapped in a relationship on the other hand that would be in direct conflict with you establishing one with Mary. Just remember, the perfect solution for everyone involved doesn't exist. So, something has to give, but also remember, the 100% solution for one person can't, or shall I say, shouldn't be the 0% solution for the other. Usually, there's some middle ground for compromise."

Jordan then added, "I'm not sure where it's going with Mary. We've only met once. We seemed to hit it off pretty well, and I like what I've experienced, so far. She is smart, kind, witty, and attractive. I have to get through this weekend with my dad's viewing and funeral, then I can think about calling her. Now, entering and complicating the picture is Kathryn, that's my ex-wife."

"Let me give you another bit of wisdom I read somewhere a long time ago," Nick began. "Problems are solved one of three ways. First, the problem somehow goes away. Second, you go away from the problem. Third, you solve the problem. Now, it's unlikely that the problem is going to disappear, although sometimes problems do just vanish, but unlikely, as I said. I doubt you are going to leave, that is, run away and hide from this situation. That leaves, solving the problem the very best way you can. It may require you taking a hard line and standing up to your ex-wife and telling her that she can no longer come to you for lodging, money, a relationship, or whatever if that's what you want. First, figure out what *you* want. Next, list all of your options for accomplishing your objective. It's alright to seek advice, kind of like what's going on here. Finally, you have to decide on a course of action and implement it. There's one more part to the process. Sometimes, you don't like any of the options you have before you. In that case, you have to create another option. That's where it gets difficult. It's called 'thinking outside the box'. Now, all that said, and it's a lot to absorb, I don't want to come across as preaching, so let's leave it there."

"Wow, you've given me a great deal of good advice, and I don't take it as preaching. I cannot thank you enough. I'll think over what you have said and implement a plan that, I hope, will cause minimal angst or heartache for all concerned," Jordan said, then added, "just out of curiosity, how do you know so much, I mean, how are you so good with ideas and problem-solving?"

Nick hesitated for a few seconds, then began, "Remember yesterday when I said I ran a business?" Jordan nodded in the affirmative, then Nick continued, "I don't like to talk too much about it, but I'll let you in on a little secret of mine."

Jordan inched closer as if he was going to be read onto a top-secret military project. Nick continued, "My job was a facilitator, or in layman's terms, a fixer. When people would have a problem, they would go to my boss. My boss would assess the situation, determine whether or not he wanted to get involved, and if he was inclined to help the person, he would contact me. I had great latitude concerning the methods or approaches I used to solve the problem. There was only one other person that worked with me. That was the young man that reminded me of you. That was Gordon, or Gordy, as I liked to call him. He was my assistant. Gordon had a special 'skill set'. I, also, had a skill set, different from Gordon's, that I learned in the Army during the war that provided me with the credentials and experience to accomplish a great many and varied assignments. You need to know one last thing. I never broke the law in solving any of the problems that were handed to me, although at times I hit the guardrails pretty hard. Fortunately, a little 'friendly persuasion' went a long way. I made it clear to my employer that I didn't want to be involved in any illegal activity. If that was required, then he needed to find someone else. Thankfully, he understood. So, that's my background in problem-solving."

Jordan's jaw dropped, but he was able to ask, "You don't have to answer, but I have to ask, was your boss a mobster?"

"Here's the politically correct answer, 'I have no direct knowledge of that', okay?" Was Nick's reply. "To ease your mind, I did jobs like talk to school board members when a needy kid just graduating college would need a job as a teacher, or if a small business owner was having a problem getting a certain license, I would take care of it. Sometimes, there would be a neighborly dispute that Gordon would settle. You get the picture?"

"Oh, I get the picture, all right," Jordan responded. "Your boss was like a Godfather."

"Well, let's just say, he tried to help people with their problems when they felt all other avenues had been used up," was Nick's coy reply.

Jordan then looked at his watch and said, "This is fascinating, but once again, it's time for me to leave you, Nick." He then concluded by saying, "Nick, it's been great talking with you. You brightened my day, again." As he got up to depart, he added, "I'm not sure when I'll see you again, but hopefully soon. I have to stop by the paper to pick up another computer and see how much of my work I can resurrect, then we have my dad's wake, funeral, and burial."

"No problem, I'll see you when you have time," was Nick's reply. "Please be careful on your way home, no more tickets," he said smiling.

Jordan walked back to his car near Perk Place and rode home with a smile on his face despite all the struggles that he was enduring and those that lay ahead for him.

CHAPTER 5
Life Goes on

As much as Jordan would have liked the remainder of his evening to have been uneventful, it wasn't to be. Fortunately for him, it was in a good way, mostly. He had time to sit, relax and enjoy the rest of Agatha's lemon meringue pie, which he made short work of. He then decided to re-read Kathryn's letter to make sure he wasn't overreacting to her suggestions of a joint vacation and her moving in. He was still pretty sure he didn't want any part of her working her way back into his life, but he remembered what his parents had always told him regarding difficult situations or decisions – think them through before acting on impulse. He would honor them by giving it the proper amount of time to make his decision.

Jordan also knew that he should get started drafting the eulogy for his father. He had a few ideas, and he wanted to write them down before he forgot them. The computer that he picked up at work was similar to the one that was stolen, so the learning curve wouldn't be too steep. He began the process by listing his father's interactions with other people in his life. He figured that was a good way to start, then elaborate on each. He didn't want the eulogy to run more than three minutes, four tops. He knew he could talk for an hour about how much his father meant to him alone.

Before he got started, he remembered his back door. He was sure Tom had gotten it fixed, otherwise, he would have heard from him. He put down his laptop and went to his back door. From the inside, it looked like nothing had happened to it. He opened it and checked the frame. It looked perfect. He figured that Tom must have replaced the entire piece of wood where the lock entered the door frame. He made a mental note to thank Tom the next day and get him a gift card to the local Ace hardware store, where he knew Tom liked to shop, as did his dad.

As Jordan was about to sit back down in his recliner and begin work on his dad's eulogy, a knock came at his front door. He put his new computer down and went to the door. To his surprise, it was officer Wolfowitz. He re-introduced himself to Jordan and said, "Sir, first off, I'm very sorry about the traffic stop and subsequent citation this morning. I should have used better discretion. After all, you had a clean driving record. I should've given you a warning. My chief would also like to apologize for any inconvenience we may have caused you during your troubling time. Please consider it just a warning. No further legal notification will be coming your way. Also, on behalf of the entire Middleboro Police Department, please accept our deepest condolences regarding your father's passing."

Jordan was dumbfounded and barely got out, "Thank you, I appreciate it," then he added, "for both."

Officer Wolfowitz continued, "Finally, we were able to recover your computer this afternoon. As we expected, it was hocked at one of the local pawn shops." He then handed it to Jordan saying, "Here it is, I hope it's okay."

"How were you able to find it so fast?" Jordan asked.

"I'm not at liberty to say, exactly. Let it suffice that, the case is still pending, so we are not able to discuss ongoing investigations," he said with a wink.

Jordan knew better than to look a gift horse in the mouth. About all, he could think to say was, "Thank you, again. You have no idea how much information this computer contains that I need to do my work."

Wolfowitz then said, "Sir, if there's nothing else, I'll be going. I hope we can meet again on a non-police matter. By the way, I enjoy your columns."

Jordan smiled and said, "Name it, I owe you a drink or two."

Wolfowitz smiled and waved goodbye as he walked down Jordan's driveway and back to his patrol car.

As soon as Jordan was back inside his house, his phone rang. It was Agatha from across the street. She was just checking to see if everything was all right since she saw the police car in front of Jordan's house. Jordan assured her everything was fine and told her that the policeman had just returned his computer that had been stolen earlier in the day. Also, he told her how much he enjoyed her dinner from the night before and that he had just finished the pie. He then asked her if she wanted him to bring the plates back. She said that it wasn't necessary, but if he wanted to talk, that would be fine. Jordan knew that it was the right thing to do since she was likely looking for someone with which to chat. Andy was likely either napping or watching a ball game. So, he agreed to bring the dishes back, but only stay a few minutes because he had some work to do. She told Jordan she would put the coffee on and made sure he knew it was decaf. Jordan knew he would probably need the high octane variety.

Two hours later Jordan was trying to figure a way to extricate himself from a very talkative Agatha. She covered a lot of ground in two hours from her son-in-law being a lazy, alcoholic bum to the grandkids not visiting enough to the high price of groceries to the political climate in the country to the break-in at Jordan's house to Jordan's father's passing to her and Andy's medical histories to some gossip she had just heard about the new neighbors down the street to climate change, and much more.

Jordan was doing everything he could to keep up with the conversation and stay awake. Finally, he was able to get a word in edgewise and let her know about the viewing and funeral arrangements. Since he had at least four cups of coffee by now, he knew it was bathroom time, as well.

He finally just stood up, told Agatha how much he enjoyed the time they had spent together, even though it was one of those little white lies people tell, to not hurt someone's feelings. He concluded with, "I still need to get some work done on my father's eulogy." He knew she would understand that, as he made for the door checking to see if Andy was still awake watching the game, so he could say 'good-bye'. He wasn't, so he asked Agatha to tell him he was sorry that he missed talking with him, as he left.

Back home now, Jordan was exhausted. All the energy he had stored up to get started on his dad's eulogy had been spent trying to converse with Agatha. He figured he would just write an outline of what he had thought about, so far and accomplished that in about 20 minutes. He knew it was too late to do much more, so he jumped in the shower, then went to bed.

The next morning dawned overcast and humid, but Jordan wanted to get a run in before working on his dad's eulogy and then finishing the article he had started, which he figured could run in the next day's paper. He thought the best course of action to complete what he wanted was to take his computer with him. If he was lucky, he could get his run finished, grab a quick bite for breakfast, then find a quiet spot to work, maybe the library, which was near the park. He knew he would be sweaty after his run, so he remembered to bring a wet towel (to wash up a little) and a clean shirt. At least, that was his plan.

He got to the park a little after 8:00 a.m. It wasn't too hot yet, but the humidity was fierce. Jordan thought that an even-paced 30-minute run would be good enough. He had liked yesterday's run and wanted to build on it. He was determined to work himself back into good physical shape, so why not start with two good days of running?

The pre-run stretching didn't take long. Jordan knew that the humid air was his friend in that regard. He also knew it would not be his friend while he was running. He cued some music on his phone and put his earphones in, but before he could take off, he heard a familiar voice calling to him from behind, "Hey, Jordan, wait up," came the call. It was Mary. Jordan was surprised, and pleasantly so.

"Mary, nice to see you," he said. "Have you been running long?"

"Nope, just started," she replied.

"May I join you?" He inquired.

"Sure," she replied, "If you can keep up."

Jordan thought for a second that he may be embarrassed if he couldn't run at the same pace as Mary, but said, "I'll give it a try. If I'm too slow for you, just keep going."

"Jordan, I'm kidding," she said. "Get your rear in gear, and let's get going."

They started at a moderate pace, which was fine with Jordan. He was wondering how long she might consider running, so he asked, "What was your plan for how long you wanted to run?"

"If I get in 30 minutes that will be good, "she said.

"Excellent!" Jordan replied. "We're on the same wavelength." He then took out his earphone on her side, so he could hear her while they talked and ran side by side. Mary did the same.

"Is this your first time running the park?" She inquired.

"I was here yesterday for the first time. It was beautiful, so I decided to come back. See, I listened to you and took your advice about running here," he said trying to curry favor with her.

"You're such a suck-up," she said.

"Guilty, as charged," he answered, then they both laughed.

The rest of their run was spliced with polite conversations about their jobs, the weather, and their plans for the rest of the day. They finished three laps around the park in slightly less than 30 minutes, so they decided to run another half lap to end up at Perk Place coffee shop. During the run, they had mutually agreed on breakfast there. Mary had some time before an appointment, but she would need to get home first to shower and change. She told Jordan, "I can hang for about 30 minutes, but need to leave by nine."

Jordan replied, "That's fine. I've got some things I need to get done today, as well."

Once at the coffee shop, Mary said, "You got the last breakfast, please let me get this one."

"Okay, but I get the one after that," he replied.

"What are you having today," she asked.

"How about turkey sausage and egg breakfast sandwich and coffee?" He offered.

"Sounds good. I'll be right back," she said.

While she was inside ordering breakfast for both, Jordan took the same table where they had sat the first time they met. He could see the entire park from his vantage point and enjoyed the vista. Not much was happening at that time of the morning in the park, probably because it wasn't as nice as the previous two days had been. The humidity had resulted in both Mary and Jordan soaking through their shirts despite them being made of a material that provides ultimate wicking. As soon as Mary was back with their breakfasts, he offered her first opportunity to use the restroom, which she appreciated. She was back to the table quickly so Jordan could then freshen up before they got down to enjoying their breakfasts and each other's company.

"I see you changed your shirt," she noticed.

"Yeah, I figured the humidity would be tough today, so I remembered to bring a fresh one," he replied. "I'm planning on going to the library to work after breakfast, so I didn't want to stink up the place too much."

"Why not work from home or your office?" She asked.

"I find it too distracting sometimes, and I need to work on my dad's eulogy and finish a column that I started," he said. "The library is a quiet place and no one bothers you with a phone call, or knocks on your door, or drops by to shoot the breeze. You know what I mean, I'm sure."

"Yes, I understand," she said. "How far along are you on your dad's eulogy?" She asked.

"I've got an outline, so I just need to fill in the details," he answered. "It's like writing a column in some sense, I guess."

"I suppose so, but this one must be difficult for you. I know how close you were with your father," she said.

"We were very close," he said. "I was close with my mom, as well, but since my dad and I were both guys, you know, we had more in common."

"Do people tell you that you look like your dad?" She asked.

"Yes, I get that all the time, especially when he was younger," Jordan said. "You only saw him at his worst. I wish you had a chance to know him and my mom when they were alive," he lamented. "I think you would have enjoyed them."

"I'm sure I would have," she said, "especially if they were anything like you."

"Stop, you are going to make me blush," he said. "That reminds me, are your parents alive?" He asked.

"My dad is still alive," she replied. "He's in his mid-seventies. My mom passed away in her early fifties of breast cancer. I had only been married for a few years. She did get to enjoy my son, her only grandchild before she passed. It was sad. She was first diagnosed in her late thirties. She had a lumpectomy, then 39 radiation treatments. The tumor came back some years later, so more surgery. They took the whole breast that time. She underwent chemo treatments for many months. Eventually, her cancer metastasized. She fought a good fight for 15 years."

"I'm so sorry to hear that," Jordan said trying to console her. "I thought my mom died too soon, but your story makes me realize that I was very lucky to have her as long as I did. It's interesting, we tend to think our situation is so bad until we talk with someone else. Then, we realize that it could always be worse."

"It could, for sure," she added, "it could have been my son who got sick. That would have devastated me. So, I try to keep a positive attitude. Even when I was going through problems with my ex-husband, I tried to look for a positive outcome. Sure, I was down, depressed for a long time, but I worked to get over it; and for you, this too shall pass. Remember, life goes on, whether you want it to, or not. So, you have to make the very best of it that you can while you are going through the hardship."

"Thanks for the pep talk," he interjected. "It seems that I come here to this park and coffee shop, and I come away with great bits of wisdom and sound philosophical thoughts. The last two days I've met this elderly man named Nick. He has helped me get through this tough time, also. By the way, do you know who I am talking about?"

"No, not particularly," she replied, "why?"

"Well, somehow he knew your name, and that we had been together here," Jordan replied.

"He knew my name?" She asked.

"Yes, he mentioned you and me," Jordan replied.

"Did you ask how he knew my name?" Mary asked.

"No, he's a bit secretive with what he's willing to tell me, so far," Jordan said.

"Well, I guess, I'd like to know how he knows me. It's not like he was a patient of mine at the hospice center and escaped," she said laughing.

"He's the elderly man that comes into this coffee shop regularly and usually takes his drink over to that bench," Jordan said turning and pointing to Nick's favorite spot. Then, he added, "Hey, there he is. I don't know how he got there, but he wasn't there when we arrived. I checked."

Mary replied, "Oh, I've seen him in the coffee shop and on the bench. I didn't know his name was Nick."

"If you still have a few minutes, would you like to meet him?" Jordan suggested.

"Sure, I have the time," was her reply.

They quickly finished their breakfasts and cleaned up their table before walking over to where Nick was sitting. Jordan took a wide swing so Nick could see him before he said anything because he didn't want to startle him. "Hi, Nick, how are you doing today?" was Jordan's greeting.

"Just fine, Jordy," was Nick's reply, "and this is Mary if I remember correctly from the coffee shop." As he was speaking, he used his cane to get up and tip his hat at her.

"Hi, sir, yes, I'm Mary," she replied, "So, that's how you know me, from the coffee shop?"

"Well, they call out the names of the people whose drinks are ready, and I just happen to remember the names of the pretty women," Nick debonairly responded.

"Oh, you old charmer, Nick," Jordan said.

"I call 'em the way I see 'em, Jordy," was Nick's reply.

"Well, thank you, Nick," Mary said, "but after our run today, I must be an awful sight."

"Not at all," Nick countered. "Do you have time to sit and indulge the ramblings of an old man?"

Mary answered, "Sorry, but I have to get going. I have an appointment later this morning, and I still have to drive home and shower first. So, I'll pass, but I want a raincheck to get to talk with you." She then extended her hand to shake Nick's.

He politely raised her hand to his lips and kissed it. Then added, "I'm here most days unless the weather is bad, then I hang out in the coffee shop. Either way, wherever you see me, please come over to chat. It will be the highlight of my day, to be sure."

Mary then departed. Jordan asked, "Nick, did you get your drink, yet?"

"No, but I can get it," he said.

Jordan quickly countered, "Don't be silly, it will only take me a minute to run over there, order your drink, and get back here. Don't run off on me, now."

"Don't worry, my running days are over, and thank you, again," he said.

While Jordan was gone, Nick took the time to survey the park. He thought to himself about the time 25 years ago when he proposed the idea of a park in Middleboro to the city council and their adamant initial refusal to seriously consider his idea. They cited the expense to purchase the land and maintain it among other excuses, such as the liability. He explained that he would take care of getting the land. Over time he was able to convince one council person after another to accept his idea. Those that did not want to listen to him met with an election challenge and subsequent defeat the next time they ran for re-election. Their opponents were well-financed by an anonymous donor. Finally, Nick gained unanimous city council acceptance and signed over the land to the city of Middleboro. Nick had two stipulations: the park was never to be linked to him in any way, and he wanted it named, 'Parc de Gisele', which was French for Gisele's Park.

Jordan returned with Nick's drink, just the way he liked it, and Nick thanked him again. Nick asked, "Do you have some time to talk?"

"Sure, what's on your mind?" Jordan asked.

"Nothing in particular. We can just chat about different things and see what comes up if you don't mind," Nick replied.

"Mind? Are you kidding? I love these sessions, although once again I didn't bring anything to record our conversation, so don't say anything too profound, okay?" Jordan said jokingly.

"I doubt much of what I say is that profound, Jordy," was Nick counter.

"Don't kid yourself. I find your conversation as valuable as I did talking with my father," he told Nick.

"That's nice to hear," Nick replied. "Speaking of your dad, I saw his obituary in the paper this morning. It was very nice. It covered his service during Vietnam and his membership in the American Legion, coaching, his work, his hobbies, along with mentioning his family and all of his great accomplishments."

"My dad was special to me and my sister," Jordan said. "I wish every kid had a dad like mine."

"Sadly, there are too many kids today that don't even have one good parent. It seems to be a lost art raising a child. Don't get me wrong, there are still good parents out there, but they seem to be in short supply. My observation, and admittedly, it's a small sample, is that the kids are allowed to do pretty much what they want with no consequences. For example, I was sitting here last week, and I saw a four or five-year-old screaming and hitting his mother. I just watched to see what it was all about and how this young mother was going to handle the situation. As it turned out, the kid wanted ice cream, and the mother wanted him to have his lunch first. Mind you it was eleven o'clock in the morning. Guess who won out? The kid! See acquiesced and took him over there to that ice cream parlor across the street next to Perk Place. I know I'm an old man with old-time views and opinions, but when the inmates are running the asylum, you are in for trouble."

"I know what you are talking about," Jordan chimed in. "I'm often made to feel that my opinions about kid's behavior are neither warranted nor appreciated, since I don't have any kids of my own. I'm told that I couldn't possibly know what I am talking about. But, I contend, that since I am an unbiased, objective observer, my opinions are very valid."

"Well, some parents can't be objective when it concerns their kids. I cannot imagine how difficult it must be for teachers who have to deal with undisciplined students," Nick offered, then added, "and their parents."

"Not trying to change the subject, but I was thinking about your family," Jordan mentioned. "Do you have nieces or nephews?" He asked.

"Yes, several," came Nick's reply. "In fact when we get around to talking about those high school basketball games that I mentioned to you, I'll tell you about one of my nephews. He played in those games. He was an excellent all-around athlete and still is."

"Really?" Jordan said, somewhat surprised. "Whose kid was he?"

"My brother, Joe's," came Nick's reply. "His best sport was baseball. He was a good hitter with the ability to play multiple positions. He wasn't big enough for football, but when he would play on the sandlot with the football players, he was their equal, at least. Basketball was his worst sport of the three, but he was still pretty good. Later in life, he played softball; tennis; tried his hand at ice hockey, water, and snow skiing; ran marathons, and ended up being a decent golfer. He even won a few local races in his age category and some golf tournaments. His finest attributes were his hand/eye coordination and his competitiveness. It didn't hurt that he was usually the quickest and fastest guy in the game. There's a distinction there that I'm sure you know. He was even drafted to run track for one meet during his senior year in high school because one of his school's sprinters had an injury. He didn't win, but he didn't finish last, either. He rationalized that he had baseball speed, which was usually only 30-40 yards at a time. At any rate, I'll tell you more about him when the time comes."

"Great," Jordan said. "About these games, where were they played?"

"As I mentioned, they were part of a Rotary Club basketball tournament back where I lived before relocating here. The format was single elimination. There were three games with the lower-ranked team having to play at the higher-ranked team's home court. Therefore, number 4 played at number 3 on Thursday evening. The winner played the number 2 ranked team on their court on Friday night, and the winner of that game played the number 1 ranked team on their home court on Saturday night. The Rotary Club reaped all the profits," Nick said. "As you know, the high school sports seasons run into each other, that is, football starts in early September and runs into basketball which goes into March about the time baseball and track are starting. So, the players often had to work around other sports to participate in the basketball tournament."

"So, are you going to tell me more, or do I have to wait to hear the rest of the story?" Jordan eagerly asked.

"It'll be a better story if I tell it over a period of time," he began, "not that I want to tease you, but because there are several backstories."

"Wow," said Jordan, "sounds like a murder mystery."

"No murder, but other high crimes and misdemeanors," Nick said with a laugh.

"Sounds fascinating, and who would've thought that a high school basketball tournament could produce so much intrigue and mystery?" Jordan mused.

"I can share a little more without ruining anything," Nick began. "Three of the four teams represented the area's high schools: the James Everson Academy Jesters, a private school populated mostly by students from upper-income families; the Weston Acheson War Eagles; and the Preston Acheson Paladins. The latter two were public schools named after two prominent brothers dating back to Revolutionary War days. Those two school's athletic rivalry was a bitter one, as was the rivalry between the two brothers. Legend has it that while the brothers were of British lineage, Weston decided to fight on the side of the Colonists. Preston, on the other hand, was older and loyal to the British Crown. Additionally, the brothers vied for the hand of the same fair maiden. So, as was the rivalry two hundred plus years ago, the two schools renewed it in the 20th century."

Nick continued, "Now, the fourth team in the tournament was the winner of the local YMCA basketball league for high school teams. Mostly, that team was just a fill-in to allow the Rotary Club to have one more game night and fatten their proceeds. The YMCA winner was always seeded fourth. They had no home court anyway unless you consider the YMCA their home court, but that wasn't realistic since it had no seating for spectators. Back in 1971, James Everson Academy got the third seed mainly because they had a smaller school enrollment and played a weaker schedule in the private school league. Preston Acheson was the second seed because it had lost two of its three games against Weston Acheson that year. The last of those three games was the league championship in which Weston Acheson held the ball for nearly all of the fourth quarter after blowing a big lead and letting Preston Acheson tie the game. This was before shot clocks and three-point shots. The momentum had swung to Preston Acheson, so the Weston Acheson coach, Sylvester "Cyclone" Buzinski had his team pull the ball out near half-court and sit for the last shot. I'll give you more details on that later."

Nick offered a little more, "That final team, the one on which my nephew played, was comprised of ten seniors from Weston Acheson, mostly football players. The five starters had all played basketball together in ninth and tenth grades. The reason that they didn't try out for the varsity team was coach Buzinski. He was a recent hire from another school with a fantastic winning record. Unfortunately, he was a nasty man with a vile temperament and quickly irritated some players. He was Bobby Knight before it was fashionable, so to speak. So, now you know a little of the backstory."

"You have me hooked," Jordan said. "I have the basic idea in my head, and I can't wait to hear how it all played out."

"You will, Jordy, give it its proper stage," Nick said waving his arm eloquently like an Elizabethan actor, then he added with a smile, "I know you are tied up the next two days, and the next day is Sunday, so why don't we plan on meeting again on Monday morning right here unless it's raining, then we can meet inside at Perk Place.

"That works for me," Jordan said, "around this time of morning?"

"That's fine unless you want to sleep in. Just text me, or call," he said.

"I do have to go soon and get started on finishing up two writing assignments, but before I go, have you heard anything about the scandal brewing in baseball regarding the Astros and their sign-stealing?" Jordan inquired.

"Just a few bits here and there," Nick replied, "why, what have you heard?"

"Well, there are rumors that they've been using electronic means to signal their hitters what pitch is coming," he offered. "My sources say that it's about to erupt into a big mess for them. Also, there's talk that the Red Sox may be involved. What do you think about all that?"

Nick began, "Well, if true, it's bad for baseball. Sign stealing has always been part of the game, but not with electronic means. It's alright to notice that a pitcher is tipping his pitches, or a catcher has a tendency to call mostly fastballs with a runner on first, but if they are spying using TV cameras or other means not within the rules, then the commissioner's office needs to 'go nuclear' on them." He concluded, "Isn't it ironic that 100 years ago we had the Black Sox Scandal? Now we have this. My guess, and it's only a guess, is that the baseball players will find a way to take care of it, you know, police their own game. I wouldn't want to be an Astros hitter if this turns out to be a situation where they cheated. If the commissioner is worth his salt, he'll strip them of all titles they won while cheating. Time will tell, though."

"You're right, time will tell," Jordan concluded. "Well, Nick I'm going to be on my way to the library to write my dad's eulogy, then finish a story for tomorrow's edition. Until we meet again, be safe, my friend."

Nick nodded and added, "You, too, Jordy!"

Jordan got about 20 yards away and stopped dead in his tracks, turned, and ran back to Nick. He blurted out, "I forgot to mention that I got my computer back last night. The same cop that gave me the ticket brought it to me at my house, and guess what, he said my ticket was taken care of, too. Funny, how things can look so bad one minute, then turn out great, the next. Today, I get to run and have breakfast with Mary, then get to talk with you. I'm living large."

Nick smiled wistfully, then said, "Sometimes, things just work out. I like to see good things happen to good people."

Jordan thanked him for the kind words, then remembered that his father had just passed away, and added, "Somehow, I shouldn't feel this happy two days after my father died."

"It's okay, be happy when you can. Remember, life goes on. You will have your down moments, and that's okay, too," came Nick's sage advice. "Just don't let them drag you down for too long. Now, hit the road and get your work done. Glad your computer was returned and your ticket squashed."

A few minutes later Jordan arrived at the library. It was still relatively early, despite some unexpected, but pleasant diversions. He felt good that his day had started with some exercise, breakfast with Mary, and time talking with Nick. He knew that it was time to knuckle down and get to what he needed to get done.

After entering the front door and walking up a flight of stairs, he found a quiet booth in the back of the library where he figured there would be no distractions. Initially, he thought about getting right to his dad's eulogy but rationalized that he had more time for that task than he did for finishing his column, so he shifted gears and opened the half-finished column on cheating in sports.

His question to Nick on that subject a few minutes earlier gave him some additional ideas. He decided to pursue the angle of pushing for the baseball commissioner's office to be more responsible for investigating the allegations and the handing down of justified punishment if found to be warranted. Also, he liked what Nick had said about the players taking matters into their own hands. He decided to plant that seed, as well. If nothing else, it might deter the next team, who might be thinking of doing something similar, to reconsider it. Finally, he addressed the issue that the suspected cheating, if found to be true, likely cost some other players awards and other teams championships, not to mention the loss of significant playoff money. Jordan knew that since his column was syndicated in many papers nationwide, his message would not fall on deaf ears.

Jordan finished up his column by noon, read it over again, made a few editorial corrections, and checked his notes to be sure his sources were accurately quoted. He then emailed it to his editor, who he was sure would not only like it but appreciate the fact that he had gotten it finished in time for the next morning's print run. As always, in the email to his boss, he attached a note that said, 'Change anything you don't like, no problem. Jordan'. He knew that his boss rarely changed anything he wrote, but he wanted to give him the option, just in case, as a courtesy.

Jordan decided to take a few minutes to look out the window and give his short-range vision a rest by gazing at the lake and trees across the library parking lot. There he saw what looked to be a father and his son fishing. It reminded him of the time his dad took him fishing at Jenny Lake. Jordan wasn't particularly interested in fishing, but since his dad was, Jordan decided to give it a try. After puncturing his finger with a fish hook in the first half-hour and not liking watching the fish fight to get off the hook, he pretty much decided that fishing wasn't going to be something he would ever enjoy. He figured to leave the baiting, catching, and cleaning fish to someone, anyone, else, like his dad in times past, and now his Uncle Charlie.

CHAPTER 6
Heaven Bound

Friday dawned hot, humid, and overcast. Thunderstorms were forecast for later in the day, which could impact Thomas Marsh's viewing that evening. Jordan had an idea that the wake could bring a large crowd because his mother's did two years ago. He knew his father had many friends from his work and the organizations to which he belonged, not to mention all of his neighbors. Also, Jordan's friends and those of Jackie and Richard would likely result in a waiting line to see him and Jackie to pay their respects.

Since Thomas's wake wasn't until the evening, Jordan had most of the day to get done some of the chores he had set aside for himself. He had finished his father's eulogy but wanted to take some time to review it and polish it if need be. He knew that there would be no time later, or tomorrow since the funeral was at 9:00 a.m. He also needed to lay out his clothing for the wake and funeral. He had two dark suits which he knew would work well. There would be no problem for him to still fit into them because he kept himself in good enough shape. His only dilemma was the shirt and tie combination to coordinate with his suit. He finally decided on a white shirt with a subtle tie, as close in color as possible to whichever suit he would wear. He knew that was the safest option and also a very traditional look for the occasion.

After having a quick bowl of cereal with a sliced banana, some yogurt, and coffee, Jordan sat for a few minutes reading what he had constructed for his father's eulogy. He mostly liked what he had written, but with him, every time he read his work, he could find something he thought he should change to improve it. By nature, he was a perfectionist. He often would read and re-read his work right up until his deadline. Like all perfectionists, he knew it was at the 99% level, but he wanted it to be, well, perfect, if perfection existed. So, he tweaked a word here or there, replaced one line with another, and then finally had to pull himself away from it to get on to the other items on his 'to do' list.

First, he needed to check with the restaurant where they were having lunch on Saturday after Thomas's burial. He decided to drive there, rather than call, because it was owned and operated by a close friend of his, who he hadn't seen in a while. On the drive to the restaurant, he had to resist the temptation to pick up his cell phone and call Jackie. Lesson learned, he thought. His car was an older model that didn't have Bluetooth capability. Once at the restaurant he called Jackie to check with her on the menu. They decided on some light fare, but she suggested that Jordan's friend, Kevin, may be able to advise them. Jordan agreed that it was the best way to handle it.

Kevin Kilarney and Jordan had known each other since their high school days. They were teammates on the baseball team and played many other sports together. At times they even double-dated when both were into mini-golf and driving range dates followed by pizza and ice cream. Often when they saw each other now, they reminisced about those good old high school days. After graduation, Jordan went on to college and Kevin went to the Culinary Institute of America in upstate New York.

The road to success for Kevin had many twists and turns, as he liked to tell people. Like most everyone, he started at the bottom, and through hard work and long hours, he was able to advance within the business, always learning something everywhere he worked. He'd say, "sometimes, it's not so much what to do in a certain situation, but what not to do" that was the lesson. After rising to head chef and working at several big-city restaurants, he decided to open his own restaurant in his hometown of Middleboro. As research for his restaurant, he took six months to tour his ancestral Ireland for ideas as to décor, menu, and libations for his venture. While it wasn't an immediate success, it grew steadily with an improved menu, a little advertising, but mostly word-of-mouth referrals. He owned Kilarney's Pub for ten years, and it had become one of the most popular eateries in Middleboro, especially with millennials.

As soon as Kevin saw Jordan, he hugged him and passed along his condolences, "Jordan, I'm so sorry about your dad," he said.

"Thanks, Kev," was Jordan's reply. "He went peacefully at the hospice center. You know that he'd been sick for a while. I guess his body finally ran out of fight."

"How old was your dad?" Kevin asked.

"He was 73, young by today's standards, but he was exposed to some bad stuff while in Vietnam, which likely contributed to his declining health," Jordan offered.

"He was a great guy, always willing to help us with whatever sport we were playing. I learned more about baseball from him than all of my other coaches combined," he told Jordan with a wistful smile.

Kevin was a red-haired, freckled-faced kid as a teenager. As his grandmother liked to brag about him with her heavy Irish brogue, "he had the map of Ireland tattooed on his face." When they were playing ball together, Kevin usually patrolled centerfield while Jordan played left. However, there were times when their coach needed an infielder, so Jordan was sometimes tapped to play either shortstop or second base.

They were almost always together during their free time after school and during summer breaks. Jordan alternately referred to themselves as either, Tom Sawyer and Huck Finn, or Frodo and Sam. Kevin would counter with "more like Mantle and Maris", since both were Yankee fans, but ironically too young to ever have seen those Bronx Bombers in action. It was a friendship that had endured both moving away from Middleboro for some time, Jordan's failed marriage, and two for Kevin; although, he was now married to a wonderful woman, who ran the restaurant so Kevin could concentrate on cooking.

While reminiscing for a few minutes and enjoying some iced tea, Kevin brought up Jordan's column in the morning paper. "That was a great tribute to your dad in your column. I got a chance to read it this morning over breakfast. It was very clever how you wove together the various parts of your dad's life to what was going on in the sports world at that particular time. Also, you rightly pointed out how he had helped not only you, but many others, and not only in sports but life, as well. It was a perfect testimonial and long-overdue recognition to a fine man."

Jordan thanked him, then they got down to the business at hand. Jordan went along with whatever Kevin suggested. He knew Kevin would not steer him wrong, not only because they were long-time friends, but because it was Kevin's reputation on the line. Jordan also knew that it was always best to let the expert in their field make the recommendation. In the end, he was very happy with what Kevin had suggested as a menu, and he knew Jackie would be, too.

Jordan then asked about the cost, "Do you charge a flat fee, or do we pay you based on how many show up? I'm guessing we'll have about 75-100 people for lunch.

"Don't worry about that, Jordan," Kevin replied.

"What do you mean, 'don't worry about that'?" Jordan shot back.

"I've got this. I want to take care of it for you and Jackie, and especially as a thank you and tribute to your dad," was his answer.

"Well, that's very nice of you, and I appreciate the sentiment, but I can't let you do that," Jordan said.

"I insist, good buddy, and, after all, it's my restaurant," Kevin replied with a 'gotcha' smile.

"Kevin, that's too generous, so how about we compromise?" Jordan countered.

"Okay, here's the deal and no argument," Kevin began, then added, "just pay for the wait staff. I'll have five servers working for two hours each at $20 an hour. If I did my math correctly, that comes to $200. Deal?"

Jordan thought for a second, and said, "Okay, and thank you, but I know you're going to lose money, and I don't want that. You're too good of a friend. Please know that I appreciate it."

"Hey, I may get some new customers from the luncheon, so I may come out ahead in the long run, who knows?" Kevin offered as a consolation. "Now, one more thing, please understand that I will not be able to make either the viewing tonight or the funeral tomorrow since I'll be here, so again, I'm very sorry about your dad, and please pass along my sympathies to Jackie," he said, "and I'll see her tomorrow here for lunch to do that in person, as well."

They got up and hugged again, patted each other on the back, and Jordan left. His next stop was one of the local flower shops in town. He was able to meet with the manager. They went over the types of flowers that had been prepared for Thomas's viewing. As far as Jordan was concerned they all looked fine to him. The manager said that they would be taking them to the funeral home within the next hour, so they would get there in plenty of time for the wake. Jordan was fine with all of what he was told.

Jordan's last stop for the day was to get a haircut. He figured even though his hair wasn't quite long enough yet for its next cutting, he should get it trimmed so that he would be neatly groomed for the next two days' events.

Besides, he knew that it would be a nice tribute to his parents, even if they would never know. He stopped by his regular barber and luckily only one guy was ahead of him, so he waited his turn while reading a magazine. When it was Jordan's turn in the chair, his barber, Larry, passed along his condolences, then gave Jordan an especially careful trim. When finished, Larry wouldn't take any payment from Jordan. Jordan thanked him and said, "See you in a few weeks."

About all that was left for Jordan to do was relax for the rest of the day, so he took a long way back home with a stop by the park to see what might be going on and if Nick might still be there. He parked his car up the street from Perk Place and walked back toward the park. As he got closer to the park, he looked in the vicinity of the bench where Nick usually sat, but he didn't see him there. Since it was lunchtime, he decided to grab something to eat at Perk Place.

He entered the coffee shop and immediately noticed that Nick was sitting at one of the tables against the wall with the newspaper and his coffee. Jordan got about halfway to him when Nick looked up over his glasses and noticed Jordan walking toward him. "Jordy, how are you doing? I didn't expect to see you today," he said.

"Well, I got finished with all my errands quickly this morning, so I decided to stop by the park to see if you were on your bench, but when I didn't see you there, I figured I had missed you, so I opted for lunch, and here you are," he said.

"I'm glad you decided to stop by for lunch," he said. "What'll you have? Let me get it for you," Nick said.

"Oh, no!" Jordan replied. "I can get it."

"You have gotten me several coffees already. Let me get lunch for you. Besides, where am I going to spend my money, anyway?" Nick inquired with a smile.

"OK, I'll have a turkey and Swiss cheese on whole wheat with water," he answered.

Nick took out his phone and said, "Watch this."

He typed a few items into his phone and a few minutes later both lunches arrived at their table. "Magic!" Nick declared. "Isn't technology wonderful?" He asked.

"Yeah, when it's working," was Jordan's response.

"Agreed, when it's working," Nick concluded with a nod.

Then Jordan mused, "You decided to stay inside today because of the heat and humidity?"

"Yes, at my age, it's always a good idea not to tempt fate," Nick said. "I know I'm not going to live much longer, but I want it to be as long as it can be if you know what I mean?" Nick asserted, then added, "These conditions are tough on old people like me."

Jordan then light-heartedly interjected, "Don't die on me now, Nick. I'm just getting to know you, and besides, one death a week is enough. So, please plan on hanging around a while, or at least until you tell me about those three amazing games."

"I promise, but you know at my age anything can happen, any time," Nick said matter-of-factly.

"Oh, don't talk like that," Jordan interrupted, then tried changing the subject. "Nick, you never told me your last name."

"It's Marinelli," he answered. "Why?"

"No reason, I just thought it might be good to know," Jordan said.

"Yes, I guess so," Nick agreed, then switched the conversation back to Jordan. "By the way that was a fantastic article of yours in today's paper."

"Glad you enjoyed it," Jordan replied.

"It was interesting how you interwove your dad's tour in Vietnam with what was happening here in the states at the time: the sports world, anti-war protests, and music," Nick said, then added, "I thought you were working on an article about the Astros and cheating."

"I am. That one will run next week. I changed my mind at the last minute, and my editor was good with it," Jordan acknowledged, then switched back to Nick. "You must have fought in World War II."

"I was drafted, served three years in the Army Air Corps, but never left the states. I was lucky," Nick began. "My brother on the other hand was a gunner on a B-24. He was lucky to have survived the war. He got shot down not once, but twice. He spent some time, about seven or eight months, in a POW camp in Germany after being captured. I'm sure he could tell you some interesting stories if he were alive today."

"I would have loved to have interviewed him," Jordan said. Then asked, "What was your military career like, if you don't mind me asking?"

"As I mentioned, I stayed stateside," he began. "I was bounced around the country from one Army base to another for training. I had bombardier training, gunnery training, advanced gunnery training, you name it, I had it. They stationed me from Southern California to

Miami Beach and several places in between: Phoenix, El Paso, and Columbia, South Carolina, to name a few places. There was one time when our whole division, maybe 5000 guys, was lined up waiting to get our orders to deploy. The officer in charge called out one name to stay behind and process all the orders. It was mine. Later, I found out that they noticed I had taken a typing class in high school, so my clerical skills got me out of going overseas. At the time I didn't know how lucky I was."

Jordan was hanging on the edge of his seat and could only utter, "Wow, how fascinating. Bet you were glad that you got to stay behind."

"No, not really," Nick replied. "I was young and didn't have any fear. You know, when you are young you don't think anything will ever happen to you, so I would have gladly gone to fight. Of course, once there and having experienced the enemy shooting at me, I'm sure I would have been scared out of my wits."

They both slowly munched on their sandwiches. Jordan told Nick how good his was and asked Nick, "How's yours?"

"It's very good, also," he replied. "I think they take special care when they know it's my order. You know, they make sure the tomato is not mushy, or the lettuce wilted, and I always get an extra slice or two of meat. I guess a nice tip still goes a long way," he said with a wink.

"Good to know, so when I come in here again, I should say, 'I'm a special friend of Nick's, so please make sure my sandwich is like his'," he said with a laugh.

"I do consider you a special friend, Jordy," Nick replied.

"Well, thank you, Nick," Jordan said. "The feeling is mutual. Now, what can you tell me about those three games that I should know?"

"You will know more on Monday," Nick said with a smile. "Honestly, I have to re-read some material and organize my thoughts. Also, it's a long story, so it may take two or three sessions."

"OK, we'll do it your way, as if I have a choice," Jordan said laughing. "Change of subject: politics, do you like discussing politics?" He asked.

"I don't mind talking politics," came Nick's reply, "just as long as the person I'm talking with respects my point of view. They don't have to accept it, just respect it, and not try to force their philosophy or opinions on me. That said, I'm always interested in different points of view."

"Fair enough," Jordan said. "Let's hear some of your political views."

Nick began, "Well, I consider myself a fiscal conservative and a social liberal. That may sound like a contradiction of terms, but here's what I think about government spending, its function, taxes, and politics in general."

Nick began his soliloquy, "First, let me address the fiscal conservative aspect. Our government spends too much of the taxpayer's money on needless ventures. Congressmen add an awful lot of pork-barrel projects to the budget each year to support their home states or districts. That's been a bad tradition for too long, and it should stop. Also, our foreign aid policy of paying countries to 'like us' has to stop. If they cut out the wasteful spending, then they could reduce taxes and pay down the debt."

Nick continued, "As long as I am on the subject of taxes, I think a flat tax is the only fair tax. The argument against it is that it disproportionately hurts poor people. Well, the argument against a progressive tax is that it disproportionally hurts rich people. But, with a flat tax, everyone pays the same percentage, so it's not only a flat tax but also, a fair tax. The rich still pay more than the poor because they earn more. With that idea should be added the concept of no tax deductions, which are nothing more than loopholes, mostly for the wealthy. That way, no one can complain that someone else is getting some tax consideration that they are not getting. The tax code could be simplified to the point where a fifth-grader could not only understand it, but they could do their parent's taxes. As it is now, not even the IRS understands the tax code. I had a question some years ago and called the IRS. The person I got on the phone couldn't answer my question, and they were the helpline. Eventually, I did get another IRS employee, who did help me, but he had to research the answer for a day. If it's that difficult for the IRS employees to understand the tax code, what chance does the average citizen have?"

"I hear you, Nick," Jordan agreed. "OK, but what about the social liberal part?"

"I believe," Nick said, "that we're all put on this earth to help each other in some way. Some people do it as teachers, some as nurses or doctors, some as policemen or firemen, some as EMTs, some as defenders of the country, and many others as coaches, mentors, or bosses.

The point is, we all need help at some point with some aspect of life. Now, if you can't contribute in one way, then I feel you have a certain responsibility to contribute in another way, and that may be financial, volunteering through charities or churches, or donating blood via the Red Cross."

Nick went on, "There are many people among us who just need a little help from time to time. Not everyone who gets that help stays needy. Most go on to succeed in life. Think of educational grants or scholarships that have helped many poor students get college educations. When they get a job, they pay taxes, which helps other disadvantaged kids get a grant or scholarship. That small initial investment pays huge dividends down the road."

"Of course," Nick continued, "we will always have some people who abuse the system. The bottom line is that the government should be there for the people to provide for their general welfare. That's why we educate children in public schools. That education serves to foster the next generation. One further point – since we provide free education, why not free health care? Did you know that we're the only industrialized nation that does not provide universal health care as a basic human right? Additionally, our health care is more expensive than any other country's health care. We have let those costs get out of control. Almost no one could afford a week's stay in the hospital today without health insurance. Final point: we attack health care at the wrong end of the spectrum. Instead of trying to figure out how to pay for it, why not try to reduce the cost? It shouldn't cost $250,000 for a heart operation."

"They are pretty interesting observations, Nick," Jordan stated. "Where do you see yourself politically?"

"I consider myself an independent, or moderate," Nick began. "I've voted for both Republicans and Democrats, and even some Independents. I try to research all the candidates and make the best decision based on their political positions for all people, not just me."

"What about the most recent elections?" Jordan asked.

Nick replied, "The political pendulum swings back and forth. When it swings too far in one direction, the voting public will correct it. Now, our last two presidential elections were a good example of that. After Obama was elected the second time, the pendulum had moved left, more or less, depending on one's point of view. I don't think there's any argument there. How far left is a matter for debate, but let's say pretty far left for the purpose of this example. Then, 2016 rolls around. We have two flawed candidates for different reasons. No question, Clinton should have won the election on her experience, style, intelligence, or pretty much any metric you want to use. However, she didn't win for a variety of reasons, some self-inflicted, but largely because of a loophole in our electoral process. I'll get to that in a minute. Should it have even been that close? No, never, but it was; possibly because she was painted with the 'liberal' brush, and we had just had a liberal president. That's the backlash factor. It can also be attributed to the backlash from having the first African American president. Some political analysts describe it as the perfect storm that got Trump elected."

"Any other observations?" Jordan asked.

Nick thought for a few seconds, then said, "I mentioned the flawed electoral process. The Electoral College should be abolished by constitutional amendment for two reasons. First, the states with not enough population to warrant the minimum three electoral votes, and there are eight in this category, carry inequitable electoral weight. For example, Wyoming doesn't have the population to warrant three electoral votes. By law, they must have three, as a minimum, one each for both senators and one for their representative. If the same proportional allotment were applied across all states, then California, for example, which now has 55 electoral votes, would get almost 200. The fairest electoral process is one vote per eligible voter. Second, our founding fathers established the Electoral College as a safety net, or check on the people. That is if by some lapse in common sense, or a travesty of justice occurs; we somehow elect an incompetent fool, then the Electoral College could/should correct the mistake. Some would say they had the perfect opportunity to fulfill their responsibility after the 2016 election. It didn't happen, of course, but the point I'm making here is that if the Electoral College isn't going to function as intended, then why keep it?"

"I see you have thought a lot about this," Jordan said. "Anything else?" He asked.

"Yes, we need a viable third party in this country. Right now, like never before in my life, I see that we've become polarized. I don't recall ever seeing so many people taking sides politically. Families are even being divided along political lines, and it's sad. I read that it started in the 1990s with Newt Gringrich and Bill Clinton, and the divisiveness has only escalated from there. It's pretty much ridiculous now. Neither side wants to give an inch. That's where a third party would have a lot of clout. They could be the determining bloc if they played their cards correctly. Preferably, they would be centered and listen to the best ideas coming from the conservatives and liberals/progressives and decide which is best in a given situation. They could be the voice of common sense, or reason instead of extremism."

Nick continued, "One additional thought, then we can move on to another topic if you like. There need to be term limits for all elected officials: senators, representatives, governors, and so on. The founding fathers never envisioned politics as a career. There have been some guys that were older than I am still serving in Congress. Strom Thurmond and Robert Byrd come to mind. It's foolish. Finally, the Supreme Court needs to be term-limited, as well, and less political. I'd say ten years is enough. Forget the lifetime appointment. Well, congratulations, you got my pet peeve rant going."

"Sorry, Nick, I didn't mean to get you upset," Jordan said.

"Oh, I'm not upset. Honestly, I enjoy talking about it, just glad you are interested," he replied. "There's not much I can do about it now. Perhaps I should have put more of my energy into solving those problems years ago instead of working on local folks' issues."

"What do you mean, working on local folks' issues?" Jordan asked.

"Remember what I told you the other day?" Nick inquired. "When I lived up north before moving here, I fixed small problems for people at the behest of my employer. I guess if I were broader-minded, I could have or should have, taken my talents to Washington. I think I could have been a lobbyist with a little training and practice. I'm not saying that I didn't enjoy helping people, because I did, but maybe I missed the big picture, you know, the proverbial forest for the trees."

"I know you were hesitant to tell me about your employer, but what harm is there now? I'm guessing he must be dead by now," Jordan asked indirectly.

"Oh, yes, he died many years ago before I moved down here. So perhaps the only person I'd be incriminating now would be me," he began with a laugh. "My boss was affiliated with the mob, that's the nicest way I can think to say it. He ran a gambling operation, no drugs, no prostitution, just gambling, as far as I knew, anyway. I'll go to my grave believing that, and believing that he had a kind heart for the downtrodden, those poor folks who just needed a break or a little help from time to time. I know for certain that he was extremely charitable. There wasn't one church bazaar or fire company picnic in the entire valley back there that didn't knock on his door for a contribution of some kind all summer long. He would donate a substantial sum to each one, and/or send workers to help them build their stands. In addition, he would personally attend every one. Sometimes there were three or four in a weekend. So, yes, he ran an illegal bookmaking operation in addition to his legitimate businesses, but gambling is a victimless crime. I get a laugh now because many states have lotteries to bilk their citizenry out of their hard-earned money. Do you know what I call lotteries? 'A tax on people who are bad in math.' In addition to the lotteries, the states allow casinos, and of course, tax them. Forty or fifty years ago gambling was illegal, now it's big business. Hypocrites!"

"I never looked at it that way," Jordan said. "Sorry to wind you up, again, Nick."

"You're really pushing my buttons this morning, Jordy," Nick said with a big smile. "Seriously, it's no big deal anymore. The cops in our area knew what was going on. Some of them were my boss's best customers."

"Really?" Jordan asked.

"Sure!" Nick replied. "They were small-time bettors, though. They didn't have a lot of discretionary dough, so they were only betting fins and sawbucks, I mean fives and tens. We called them, Woolworth bettors. You know Woolworth's, don't you?"

"No," came Jordan's reply.

"It was before your time. Woolworth's was a large department store that usually had a lunch counter. It was nicknamed, the five and dime store, presumably because many items only cost a nickel or dime. That was many, many years ago. The best comparison today would be Walmart or Target, but not exactly."

"Back to the gambling operation, if you don't mind. What happened when guys couldn't or wouldn't pay their debts?" Jordan asked.

"That's where Gordon came into the picture," Nick responded. "Now mind you, he was just there as 'friendly persuasion'. Neither my boss nor I ever wanted to hurt anyone. I'd just explain to them in simple terms that there were consequences for actions and bad consequences for bad actions. Gordy was our collection agent."

Jordan was hanging on every word that Nick spoke, having never had the opportunity to get this kind of inside information on quasi mob activity, but he knew his time was rapidly running out for sitting and chatting. He glanced at his watch and knew that he should be moving along. He still wanted to call Jackie to be sure everything was good on her end and to let her know that he had accomplished the chores he told her he would get done.

Jordan began, "Well, Nick, as usual, it's been a delight talking with you. Every time we talk I learn more and more about you," he concluded.

"You only learn what I'm willing to share, Jordy." Nick reminded him. "Someday you'll get the rest of the story, as Paul Harvey used to say. Please tell me you know who Paul Harvey is?" Nick asked.

"No, not really," Jordan said.

"Look him up, Jordy. He was a journalist." Nick replied.

"Okay, I will, but now, I really should get going," Jordan said. "I still have to do a few things, and I don't want to be late to the funeral home."

"Get going, if you aren't five minutes early, then you're late." Nick chided him.

"See you Monday," Jordan said, then departed.

⋙ ⋘

Despite a thunderstorm that provided a downpour during his drive, Jordan made it home in plenty of time to call his sister and check on her. He recalled that the forecast said possible thunderstorms in the afternoon. He was glad they came earlier rather than later when people would be coming to pay their last respects to Thomas.

All was fine with Jackie, except for some problem at Richard's office that could result in him being late to the viewing. She had Richie and Amanda's babysitting covered with Richard's parents. Jordan showered, then ate the take-out dinner that he stopped to get on the way home. It was just a burger and fries, which he quickly microwaved to get semi-warmed up and edible, again. He knew it wasn't the best choice for dinner, but it was something quick, he thought, to satisfy his appetite before the long evening he had ahead.

Since the viewing began at 7:00 p.m., Jordan figured to get there no later than six-thirty. He knew people liked to get there early, especially the elderly who wanted to get in and out as quickly as possible. His drive to the funeral home was easy, but with a heavy heart. It was now finally sinking in with Jordan that he would soon be seeing his father for the first time since Thomas had passed away a few days ago. It was an uncomfortable feeling for him. He remembered the same ill-at-ease feeling going to his mother's viewing two years prior.

Fortunately for Jordan, he also correctly recalled from his mother's viewing, that once the mourners started showing up, he would be fine. Some would be his work colleagues, some would-be friends, some would be family, and some would be Thomas's friends and co-workers.

The good news for him was that there would be people there for him to talk with and pass the time rather than staring at his dad in the casket.

As Jordan had figured the first viewers started arriving twenty minutes before the seven o'clock listed start time. There was nothing the funeral director could do. He had seen it all before, so he graciously greeted them and directed them to Thomas' viewing room. As Jordan had predicted, the old-timers were the first to arrive. Their game plan was to be home before dark, and in some cases, in bed before dark. Jordan would get a private chuckle out of them when they would tell him about eating dinner at four in the afternoon, cleaning up the dishes, watching a couple of hours of television before turning in for the night. He could almost understand that scenario in the winter when it would be dark by five in the afternoon, but during the summer months that would mean going to bed before sunset, and that wasn't something Jordan could wrap his head around. Of course, he thought, 'far be it from me to judge. I may do that, too, when I'm their age.'

About an hour into the viewing, Richard finally showed up. Jackie had called him several times between dinner and his arrival. He went right over to Jackie once he arrived, and Jordan could see them talking quietly in the corner of the room. He suspected something was amiss at Richard's work that had kept him from being able to leave on time. Jordan was holding the fort near his father's casket because there was a steady stream of well-wishers parading through. Ever the polite soul, he was allowing everyone as much time as they wanted with him to talk about his father or reminisce about some good time they had had with Thomas. He thanked each visitor on behalf of himself and his sister, especially when she wasn't there next to him.

At one point the long line of people waiting to see Jackie and Jordan stretched out of the viewing room and down the hallway back toward the foyer. Jordan paused to realize that it was a splendid showing for Thomas and a fine tribute to a wonderful man. He knew that some-how both Thomas and Vivian were smiling.

The last well-wishers were finally through the line and talking with Jordan and Jackie at nine-thirty. That was 30 minutes past the time the funeral home had allotted, but certainly, they weren't stopping anyone from paying their respects. The problem for Jordan and Jackie was that they had been on their feet non-stop for three hours. It was particularly rough on Jackie since she was in high heels. When the last mourner left, they both collapsed into chairs and sat for a few minutes before collecting their belongings and heading for the door.

On the way to their cars, Jordan asked Jackie, "Is everything all right with Richard and his business?"

"He said it was nothing to worry about, just some disgruntled customer," she replied.

"I guess every business has those few annoying cus-tomers from time to time," Jordan said.

"I suppose, but Richard seemed uneasy about it," she observed.

"Perhaps it will all work itself out over the weekend," Jordan offered.

"Let's try to get through the funeral tomorrow," she said, "then he can tackle whatever the problem is on Monday."

"Good plan," said Jordan. He walked her to her car and said "good night, see you in the morning."

They both went straight home since they were exhausted. They knew that they would have to be back on their A-game in the morning at the funeral. Jackie would be doing some scripture readings and Jordan was on tap for his dad's eulogy.

Once home, Jackie asked Richard again if everything was all right at work. He replied in the affirmative, but she could detect something was wrong. She decided to let it lay for the time being since it was late, and she needed to get to bed. Richard had gotten Richie and Amanda from his parents, and they were already in bed by the time Jackie had gotten home. She did a quick look-in on them to be sure they were sleeping, and they were, so she decided not to disturb them by kissing them good night.

During the overnight hours, a cold front had dropped down from the north bringing with it cool, crisp air and a nice breeze. That would be perfect weather conditions for Thomas's burial at Mt. Zion Memorial Gardens which was planned for 11:00 a.m. The funeral was scheduled to start at 9:00 a.m. from the funeral home, then proceed to the church for a one-hour service beginning around nine-thirty.

Jordan was up early, shaved, showered, and dressed by eight with enough time for breakfast between the shower and getting dressed. He wanted to re-read the eulogy one more time just to be sure he didn't miss anything. He accomplished that while eating his cereal and drinking his coffee. He made a few minor editorial changes, but the gist of the homage he was paying to his father remained intact.

On the way out of his house, he saw Agatha and Andy, who waved and said that they would see him at the church. He waved back and said, "See you there, and don't forget lunch afterward at Kilarney's Pub."

His ride to the funeral home took only a few minutes, but he wanted to get there early enough to spend some quiet time with his dad. Once there, he looked Thomas over one last time. He was happy with the dark blue suit, white dress shirt, and neatly knotted light blue, red and white tie. Jordan also wanted to place a few items in Thomas's casket that had been near and dear to him. The first item was a Yankee baseball cap since the Yankees were his and Jordan's favorite team. Next, Jordan placed two pictures inside Thomas's suit jacket. The first was a reprint of Thomas and Vivian's wedding picture. Jordan looked at it for some time thinking how young they were and how far they had come in their married life. The second picture was one of their entire family taken at Thomas and Vivian's 50th-anniversary party. The final item that he laid in the casket was a plastic box with several of Thomas's favorite fishing lures. As he placed them near his right hand, he said, "Dad, now that you're heaven-bound, I know you would want these with you, because I'm sure they have a fishing hole up there better than Jenny Lake."

Around 9:00 a.m. the funeral director gathered Thomas' family and some close friends, who had come to the funeral home, near the casket. There were some prayers offered, then Thomas was loaded into the waiting hearse for the ride to the church.

The funeral ceremony was a traditional one with multiple scripture readings, hymns, and prayers. The casket with Thomas's body had been brought down the center aisle of the church and placed near the front altar. After the ceremony the minister addressed the attendees letting them know that there would be a few words from Jordan, then a procession to the cemetery for the burial, followed by a noon lunch at Kilarney's Pub.

At that point, Jordan made his way to the altar. He had everything he could do to keep his emotions under control and get through the next few minutes. Once at the pulpit he reached inside his suit jacket pocket for his reading glasses and two sheets of paper on which he had written his father's eulogy. He began, "For those of you who do not know me, I am Jordan Marsh, Thomas's son. On behalf of my sister, Jackie, her family, and my Aunt Pat and Uncle Charlie, I would like to thank you for being here this morning. I would also like to thank Reverend Williams for conducting this most beautiful service and his uplifting sermon."

Jordan continued, "While this is undoubtedly a sad time, we must not lose sight of the fact that it's also a celebration of my father's life. Most of you only know my father in one or two aspects of his life, but he was as multi-faceted as a precious gem. To my sister and me, our dad was truly the most wonderful father any kid could have had. The examples of his caring and giving nature are too many to list today, but suffice to say that he frequently did without many things in life so that we could have something special for birthdays and Christmases. Our family vacations during the summers when we were young were always a combination of something fun and something educational. He and my mother were not wealthy people, but Jackie and I never did without anything we truly needed. I came to realize later in life that we didn't get everything we wanted, but we got everything we needed to succeed. I know that there were times after a long, tough day at work when the only thing my dad wanted to do after dinner was to go fishing. However, seeing me sitting on the front steps of our house with my bat, ball, and glove; he would simply tell me that we would play ball as soon as dinner was finished, because my mom had spent time making it, and we owed it to her to eat it while it was warm. The life lessons that he taught us were very consistent and timeless: be respectful of others, help the less fortunate, do a good job, and your fun cannot be at the detriment of others."

From there, Jordan moved to Thomas and Vivian's married life. He explained, "My dad was a husband, married to an exceptionally special person. I know I am biased, but she had to have been to survive the rigors of her overly disciplined upbringing. My mom and dad were married at an early age. My mom's parents opposed it. Not many people know that, but it's true. The day before my dad was about to enter the military, he and my mom gave an ultimatum to my maternal grandparents, accept their marriage, or they were going to elope. At the last minute my grandparents relented, my parents were married in the morning, and my father left for his army induction that afternoon without so much as a honeymoon. My parents were married for more than 50 years with nary a harsh word between them. The irony regarding that part of my father's life is that many years later, he and my mother would spend many summer evenings at my grandparent's home helping them with their everyday chores of yard work, gardening, cleaning, cooking, and laundry. I tell you this not to cast aspersions on my grandparents, but to illustrate the kind, forgiving souls that my parents were, especially my father, who was only a son-in-law to them."

Jordan then moved to his father's military service, "I mentioned that my dad was in the Army. He was drafted when he was 19, just as the Vietnam War was escalating. Unfortunately for him, he was sent there and saw combat. How much or how little, I don't know. He never spoke about it to me, even though I asked him about it a few times. I don't know what he saw or what he had to do there to survive, but I know three things. First, he made it out of there and the Army alive, no small accomplishment. Second, whatever eventually caused his death was attributed to chemical agents that he was exposed to while serving in Vietnam. Finally, and most importantly, he never let any psychological problems that affected many of his comrades, cause him to be anything but a fine, upstanding, hard-working man in our community."

He continued, "That brings me to my dad's work. He began working at the local automobile assembly plant right after he was honorably discharged from the Army. He started at the bottom like so many of us did at our first jobs. Over the years he took classes at the local community college at night through the GI Bill to advance his knowledge in various areas, such as automotive mechanics, business applications, production management, strategic analysis, and quality assurance. Over time he rose to become shift supervisor, then a first-line manager. Before that, he served his fellow production line workers as their shop steward for their local union. He must have done a great job during his 40-plus year career, because last evening at his viewing, there wasn't one of his co-workers who didn't tell me how much they appreciated either working with or for my father. Some of the words they used to describe him were: fair, honest, reliable, trustworthy, hard-working, caring, and conscientious. It did my heart good to hear it, even if I already knew it."

Jordan then moved to Thomas's social life. He continued, "My dad had many other interests and hobbies. As some of you know, he was an avid Yankees fan. As a kid, he grew up listening to the best part of their glory years in the 1950s and early 1960s. He took up fishing as a boy and enjoyed many fun times at Jenny Lake with his buddies. My dad was an exceptional athlete in his youth. He was practically good in baseball, played for the local American Legion Post and semi-pro teams before and after his Army days, and was even scouted by some major league teams. Later in life, he found time to become active in the American Legion and for many years coached their baseball team. As a good friend of mine and a fellow teammate recently told me, 'Your dad taught me more about baseball than all my other baseball coaches combined.' Another fine tribute, he was a coach, mentor, and teacher."

Jordan then finished with, "My dad lived a great life, albeit too short, but who doesn't think that about their loved one no matter how old they are when they pass away? He will surely be missed by his family, and I know he will be missed by others, as well. In the final analysis, isn't that the true measure of a life well-lived?"

Jordan took off his glasses, folded his papers, and put both into his suit jacket pocket before slowly making his way back to his place in the front pew. Pachelbel's *Canon in D* began playing as the pallbearers turned Thomas' casket 180 degrees and guided it down the center aisle toward the waiting hearse just outside the church's front doors. The assembled mourners waited for Jordan, Jackie, and the rest of their family to follow behind Thomas' casket before they departed. As Jordan was walking with his sister he was scanning the people to see how many he recognized. At the back of the church, he noticed two familiar faces that he didn't expect to see. It was Nick and Mary. They were sitting together in the last row. As he approached them, he reached out to shake their hands and also to personally invite them to lunch at Kilarney's.

Mary had come to the church service from work, so she was still dressed in her nurse's scrubs. She explained that she had to go home, shower and change, so she might be a few minutes late, but accepted Jordan's invitation. Nick, also, told Jordan that he would be there. Both told Jordan that the funeral service was beautiful and that the eulogy of his father was wonderful. They felt like they had missed out on knowing a wonderful man.

The ride to the cemetery didn't take long. Only a few people in addition to the immediate family made the trip. Once the hearse arrived and the family assembled graveside, the minister began a short ceremony of prayers. After he concluded the brief prayer service, one by one those assembled, led by Jackie and Jordan, placed a flower on the casket. When the flower laying ritual had concluded, the cemetery workers lowered Thomas' casket into the ground. Jackie then turned to Jordan and said, "Well, I guess it's over. It seems to have gone so fast. I know it was a long haul for Dad, and he suffered quite a bit over the years, but now that it's over, it really seems to have been quick, at least for us, and now we don't have him with us, anymore."

Jordan replied, "I know what you mean. It was difficult seeing him suffering, being in pain, not able to breathe, and just wasting away; but, I'd give anything to have him around for another day just to talk with him. It sounds selfish, doesn't it?"

"No, not selfish. It just means you loved Dad very much and wanted him in your life for a longer time," she said.

"That's a better way to look at it," he concluded. "Well, let's get to Kevin's."

They turned into Kilarney's parking lot a little before noon. Some of the mourners were already there when Jordan and Jackie arrived. Kevin was on hand to greet Jordan, Jackie, and the rest of the Marsh family. He passed along his condolences to Jackie, her husband, aunt, and uncle, made some small talk for about five minutes, then excused himself to attend to his kitchen duties.

Kevin had arranged a fine buffet brunch for the Marsh family and friends. In one area he was serving scrambled eggs, sausage, bacon, ham, French toast, pancakes, and crepes with assorted fruit toppings. In another area, he laid out an assortment of bread and rolls with salad and multiple dressings. In still another area there was carved roast beef, ham, and roasted herb chicken with carrots, peas, and potatoes. All types of drinks were available, as well.

As Jordan would remark later to Kevin, "You outdid yourself, my friend. I guess you decided to change your mind about the menu. This was above and beyond what I expected, and what we talked about yesterday. But, I guess you know what you are doing because everyone here is raving about the food, the presentation, and the service, which reminds me, here is the money for the servers." Jordan then handed him an envelope with ten $20 bills for the wait staff.

Kevin thanked him for the high praise and the gratuity on behalf of his staff and said, "I know they'll appreciate it. They're good folks and good workers. I try to keep them happy. It's hard to find good help, especially in relatively low-wage-paying jobs. I'm sure you understand."

Jordan understood, and said, "Indeed, it's difficult to find good help anywhere, anymore. Your staff is efficient, friendly, and attentive."

Before that exchange with Kevin and while the attendees were enjoying Kevin's culinary delights, Jordan took the opportunity to visit each table. He first stopped at the two tables where his neighbors were, made small talk with them for a few minutes, and took the opportunity to seek out Tom Johnson and quietly whisper in Tom's ear how much he appreciated him fixing his back door earlier in the week. As he was talking with him, he slipped a gift card in Tom's pocket. Tom tried to stop Jordan, but Jordan, again whispering in Tom's ear, said, "It's my way of thanking you. I know you didn't have to do it, but it helped me out, Tom, and I want you to know how much I appreciate it."

Tom was gracious and thanked Jordan, "I was happy to do it, and if you ever need anything electrical, plumbing, carpentry, or mechanical, please call me. Don't pay someone for something I can handle in a few minutes." Jordan said he would, then moved on to another table.

Next, he talked with some of Thomas's work colleagues and friends. They exchanged pleasantries and many told him how wonderful his eulogy was for his dad. They reiterated how much they enjoyed working with Thomas and mentioned how things at work weren't the same after he retired.

From there Jordan worked his way around the room stopping at several more tables of friends, work colleagues, and members of the local American Legion post. He made his last stop at the table with Nick and Mary, who were sitting with a conglomeration of other family and friends. Jordan chatted with everyone else first, then stopped to talk with Mary and Nick afterward. He spent the most time with them thanking them for not only attending the funeral service but also making time to come to the luncheon.

At that point, Jackie, who was also making the rounds, stopped by the same table where Jordan was talking with Mary and Nick. Jordan introduced Jackie to Mary first, then he introduced her to Nick. Nick, ever the gentlemen, pushed back his chair, used his cane to stand, and greeted Jackie, then offered his condolences, "It's my distinct pleasure to meet you, Jackie," he said, then continued, "I'm so sorry about your dad. You have my deepest sympathies. By all accounts, your father was a wonderful man, and your brother is a chip off the old block."

Jackie replied, "Thank you, sir, I appreciated hearing that, but I can give you a few minutes of rebuttal regarding my brother from our younger days." They all broke into laughter.

Jordan smiled and said, "Guilty as charged."

Jackie then noticed that Richard was having a conversation with Amanda, and she could hear him say, "Go to your mother." She excused herself by saying, "I have to put on my mommy hat and see what's going on." When she got back to her table and asked what the matter was, Richard explained that Amanda needed to use the bathroom, and he didn't want her to go there alone. So, Jackie excused herself and took her.

Around one o'clock Kevin's staff cleared the buffet table and placed several pies, cakes, and types of cookies on the table for dessert. Tea and coffee were also served. The diners were more than sated, but no one wanted to miss out on dessert. Kevin let them know that if they could not enjoy their dessert then, he would wrap a dessert for them to go. Many took two.

Before leaving Nick asked Jordan if he was still available to meet on Monday morning. Jordan told him that he wouldn't miss it. Then, it occurred to Jordan, how was Nick getting home. He asked, "Nick, do you need a ride home?"

Nick replied, "No, I have my car."

"Wow," said Jordan. "You still drive?"

"I do," he said with a wily smile, then added, "Apparently, better than you. I've never gotten a ticket."

Jordan burst out laughing, "You are amazingly quick-witted."

Nick made a tip of an imaginary hat as he turned to leave, then looking over his shoulder said, "See you Monday morning, Jordy. Now, get over there and ask Mary for a date before I beat you to it."

Jordan got red-faced, as he quickly looked around to see if anyone, especially Mary, heard Nick. Fortunately, no one was within ear shod, so he was safe and no longer embarrassed. He thought about it for a minute, then decided, why not?

He noticed that Mary was talking with Jackie, so it was natural that he could saunter over there and easily join in the conversation. He began, "Excuse me, ladies, for interrupting. Is there anything I can get for either of you before Kevin kicks us out of here?"

They both laughed, then Mary said, "No, nothing I'm past full. I'm going to have to run for a week to lose the weight I gained here this afternoon. That was some amazingly good food, wasn't it?"

Jackie chimed in, "Kevin's a family friend. I knew he would take special care of us. He knew my father and liked him very much."

"He did an extraordinary job with the food. Everyone at our table was raving about it," said Mary.

"That's nice to hear. I'll pass it along to Kevin and his wife, who runs the restaurant," Jordan said, then added, "I'm guessing he'll get some steady customers now that they have tasted his cuisine."

Mary then asked, "How do you know him?"

Jordan answered, "Kevin and I were best buds in high school. We played sports together, and sometimes we even double-dated. He played on our American Legion team, which my dad coached, so he got to know my dad very well."

"You guys double-dated? What was that like?" Mary asked.

"Oh, the usual stuff for a high school date, mini-golf, movie, driving range, pizza, ice cream, you know, all the stuff kids do and eat when they are young," Jordan replied.

"Yeah, I guess so," Mary concluded.

At that point, Jackie excused herself to see where her family had gone. Once she found them, she attempted to round them up and get them to go home, so she could relax after the emotional morning. Jordan figured this was as good a time as any to ask Mary, but he needed the right segue. He began his inquiry with a broad smile, "You know, Mary, I no longer need Kevin to double-date with me."

Mary bit and answered, "That's good to hear, Jordan."

"If you are still interested in dinner some evening," he continued, "what does your schedule look like next week?"

"Well, first off, I am interested in dinner, and second, my off nights are tomorrow and Monday, but I'm sure I can change nights with someone if another night is better for you," she said.

"You call it," Jordan offered. "I'm flexible."

"How about Monday evening, then? That way, I don't have to ask anyone to change schedules."

"Perfect," answered Jordan. "Now that I'm on a roll, if you're interested, I was thinking of running tomorrow morning at the park."

"I'd love that," Mary said. "I should be available around eight if it works for you."

"Then, after we run, let's do breakfast at our favorite coffee shop and discuss arrangements for Monday evening, you know, where, when, meet there, or I pick you up," Jordan said.

"Sure, good by me," she said.

At that point, Kevin wandered over to Jordan and said, "Jordan, please introduce me to your friend."

Jordan obliged, "Kevin, this is Mary. She was my dad's hospice nurse, but I'm hoping she becomes more than that to me." Then he continued, "Mary, this is Kevin, he owns this pub, is one of my best friends, and don't believe anything he says about anything we may have done during our misspent youth."

All got a laugh out of Jordan's introduction and both Kevin and Mary told each other what a pleasure it was to meet. Mary then added, "I cannot begin to tell you how good the food was."

"Well, don't be a stranger. You are welcome any time. Just mention to the hostess when you arrived that you are a personal friend of mine."

"Thank you, I'll do that," she said. Who knows, you may see us again sooner than you think."

"As I said, anytime," Kevin replied. "But, right now, I must get back to the kitchen. I'm breaking in a new cook, and if I don't watch him closely, a finger may end up in someone's soup. You know I'm kidding, right?" He laughed, then reiterated how nice it was to meet Mary and returned to the kitchen after a wink to Jordan.

Jordan then said, "Well, I guess it's finally over. It seems to have gone so quickly in hindsight, but when we were going through it, it was somehow in slow motion. Does that make sense?" He asked.

Mary replied, "Yes, it does. I recall the same feelings when my mom was dying. It is very weird, somehow surreal. The worst part is not being able to do anything to help your loved ones except keep them as comfortable as you can until they pass. I guess that's why I enjoy my job, so much. The idea that in some small way, we can comfort someone in their final stages of life."

"As I have mentioned, I don't know how you and your colleagues are able to do your jobs day after day, or in your case, night after night," he said.

She smiled, then concluded, "Well, this is getting to be heavy, so it's probably a good idea for me to head home and get some sleep before my shift tonight. I, too, am looking forward to a nice, relaxing run tomorrow and some downtime to chat over breakfast. Until then, be safe, Jordan."

"Thanks, Mary," he said. "I'll see you in the morning."

CHAPTER 7
Come Monday

Jordan's alarm went off at 7:00 a.m. He was in a sound sleep, but he bolted out of bed, hurried to the bathroom to wash up, shave and shower before heading to meet Nick. He wanted to get there early, because of what Nick had mentioned to him about being at least five minutes early, or he'd be considered late. The anticipation of finally learning more about those three games was more than he could stand. He tried to imagine what the backstories, that Nick mentioned, might be. But not knowing the area, teams, players, coaches, or the prevailing climate of the rivalries, Jordan had little on which to base his guesses. About all he knew was that it would be a fun morning.

After washing up and shaving, Jordan decided to dress in a polo shirt and shorts, a little better attire than he might normally wear to a park. He knew Nick always dressed stylishly, so he wanted to fit in with Nick's idea of a well-dressed man. To top off his look, Jordan dug through his hat collection to find one that coordinated well with his outfit. He tried on six or seven before deciding on one to go with his powder blue polo shirt. His shorts were navy blue, knee-length, and pressed, so he knew they went well with his shirt, which was also meticulously pressed.

Jordan was out the door and on the road before seven-thirty. He knew it would take about 30 minutes to get to the park. He had tentatively set an eight o'clock meeting time with Nick, so he knew he should be good on time. He had laid out all of what he anticipated he would need to interview Nick the night before. It was just a matter of grabbing it as he was leaving. His typical interview style was to take notes, but he thought it might be a good idea to record Nick, as well, because he didn't want to ask him to repeat once he got Nick rolling. Besides, if nothing else, he could replay Nick's voice in the future when, alas, there would not be a Nick to talk with and learn from.

As he drove leisurely down the road, he flipped around the radio dial until he found a song he liked. On came Jimmy Buffett's *Come Monday*. Jordan was a longtime Parrothead, so any Buffett tune was appreciated. He figured it was a good omen to hear that song on a Monday while going to see Nick.

The song had another effect on Jordan. It put him in a mellow mood to reflect on his Sunday with Mary. He had met her at the park around eight, and they ran for almost an hour. Both felt in good running shape, but Mary was a bit wired from another difficult night at the hospice center. For her, their run served to burn off some tension and stress. For him, it gave a much-needed boost from the previous two very difficult days. Jordan thought about how well they were getting along, their common interest in running, and wondered what other activities they might enjoy together.

He next recalled with a broad smile that they had spent until noon talking about many items in their lives. She talked more about her son and father, but he knew she was trying not to talk as much as their first meeting. She seemed to want to give Jordan all the opportunity she could to get him to talk about anything he wanted. He did share some stories about his dad and the many good times they had as a family during times of better health for his father.

Jordan then thought about their date later that evening. They had decided to go back to Kevin's restaurant since they knew he would be there and likely stop by their table at some point during the evening. Also, Jordan felt it would be a perfect opportunity to give some business to Kilarney's Pub since Kevin had been so very generous to his family by providing a magnificent buffet luncheon on Saturday. Finally, he knew that the food was the best in town, with the possible exception of his neighbor, Agatha's. Jordan and Mary decided that he would pick her up at five-thirty. Their reservation was not until six-thirty, so Mary had invited Jordan to arrive early, have a drink, and see her home. He couldn't wait, but on the other hand, he didn't want to wish away his morning with Nick. To Jordan, Monday was shaping up to be a double-header sweep for the home team, and he was the home team.

The parking in front of Perk Place was taken so Jordan drove around the block a time or two to find a spot. Eventually, one opened up, and he backed into the parking space with a perfectly executed parallel parking maneuver. After he was in the parking spot he thought about his dad and the many times he had gone over the technique with him when he was learning it some thirty years ago, as a new driver with a learner's permit. Jordan couldn't know it then, but there would be many more times in the ensuing months that he would do something that would fondly remind him of his dad, or a time when he and his father had done something together.

After gathering up his notepad, pen, and recorder, Jordan walked to Perk Place to see if Nick was inside, or on his bench. The weather wasn't too warm, yet, especially at eight o'clock, and not very humid, but he would talk with Nick wherever it best suited him. Jordan didn't notice Nick inside the coffee shop, so he checked the bench and didn't see him there, either. It was still a little early, so Jordan decided to just sit awhile and wait. While he had his head down and was jotting down some questions for Nick, a tap came on his shoulder. It was Nick. Jordan jumped up, and shook his hand, then asked, "How're you doing this morning, Nick?"

"I'm doing well," Nick replied. "It's always a good day when you wake up on this side of the grass."

Jordan smiled and asked, "Where would you like to sit? We can stay here, go inside, or head over there and sit on your bench, you decide. I'm good with whatever suits you."

"If it's all the same with you, Jordy, I'd prefer the bench in the park," he replied. "It's quieter over there, and as I said, no one seems to notice you over there. That's a good thing when you want to have a conversation."

"OK, the park it is," Jordan said. "Now, what would you like to drink or eat?"

"Just a coffee for me now," Nick said. "I'll meet you over there if you don't mind getting it."

"I don't mind, at all," Jordan replied. "The drinks, and anything else you want, are on me."

"That's very nice of you, Jordy," Nick said. "I thank you."

Jordan went inside and ordered both drinks. As he was waiting, he kept looking toward Nick. Something didn't seem right with him. Jordan made a mental note to keep a watchful eye on him.

The ordering process went smoothly, and Jordan was on his way to Nick with both drinks in a few minutes. Once with Nick, he got a chance to look him over in more detail. Jordan had noticed that Nick was moving a bit slower and appeared a bit older than just the week before. He couldn't help to ask, "Nick, are you sure you're all right? You seem to be moving a little slower this morning."

"Thanks for noticing, Jordy. Yes, my leg is bothering me a little. It's an old injury that acts up from time to time. Believe me, it's nothing to worry about. I'm fine," he told Jordan.

"Okay, but if you would rather do this another time, it's alright. Please know that" Jordan tried to assure him.

"Let's get started. We'll see how it goes. Most times when it ails me, it goes away in a few minutes," he intimated.

"Well, you let me know when you have had enough, okay?" Jordan said.

"I will, but honestly, I'd rather do this than sit home and watch television," Nick suggested.

"Well, how would you like to begin," Jordan asked.

"I told you there was background information that would help you understand the reasons I felt these games were so good, the proverbial 'backstories'," Nick started the long-anticipated tale. "So, here we go, stop me for clarification whenever you want. The kids playing in these games all knew each other. They may not have been on a first-name basis, you know, friends, but they knew each other by, shall I say, reputation."

"Reputation?" Jordan asked.

"Not a bad reputation, mind you, most of these guys were good, decent kids. It was a situation where they had played against each other before in basketball and other sports," Nick answered. "So, there was a *history* between and among the teams and the players."

Nick continued, "First of all, there was a great rivalry between the two public schools. Preston and Weston High Schools were separated by a river that ran through the middle of the valley. Most kids stayed on their side of the river for their social activities. It was a brave soul who ventured across the river, especially brave if he wanted to date a girl from the other side of the river. Of course, that happened. I guess it's 'the grass is always greener on the other side' syndrome, and that's part of the story.

Guys, being guys, were more often than not, territorial. They despised it when their athletic rivals came into their territory to date *their* girls. They especially despised it when it was their girlfriend, or ex-girlfriend, as the case was. I call it life imitating art since I think the play, *West Side Story*, had a similar theme. Fortunately, not the same outcome, though. So, you can see the rivalry between the two schools and their very macho athletes was intense."

At that point, Nick stopped and took a sip of his coffee. He remarked, "That's perfect. Thanks, again, for getting it, Jordy. So, that's part of the rivalry. The other school, James Everson Academy wasn't on the same plane as Preston and Weston regarding athletics. For example, they no longer had a football team. They did before the 1970s, but the cost and a smaller enrollment hindered them greatly in competing with the larger public schools. They finally gave up football because they were no longer competitive. They still competed in basketball and baseball, though, and did well for their enrollment size. You might say they punched above their weight class."

"Interesting!" Jordan exclaimed. "Just for clarification, what were the approximate enrollments of the schools?"

"If memory serves me well, Preston was the largest of the three at about 300 graduating seniors a year, while Weston had about 250, and James Everson only about 100. Do the math for the three high school grades, and you can see what a great disadvantage the Jesters had in sports."

"So, how were they able to compete," Jordan asked.

"That's the beauty part of it, Jordy. There were so many good athletes at that time back there, that each school had fierce tryouts to make their teams. Football was huge. The stadiums were packed for every game. Even the traveling team put enough fans in the stands to fill the smaller visitor's side of the field. Sports, in general, were very popular. With that, came the betting, but I'll address that later because it plays an integral part in this story."

Jordan interrupted, "Betting! On high school games?"

"Don't be so naïve, Jordy. If there was money to be made, then someone was going to try to do it. So, yes, of course, there was betting on almost every game. The problem came in when" Nick trailed off, then said, "We'll get to that."

Nick continued, "Back to the rivalries, before the first game in the Rotary Club basketball tournament James Everson had played Weston in baseball a few days prior. It was an exhibition game because the two teams were in different leagues. The game was a good pitcher's duel, played with great respect for each other and sportsmanship. The way it should be with all games. At any rate, two lefties dueled for nine innings each. Normally, their coaches wouldn't let them throw that many innings, but since both were junk ball pitchers, they weren't throwing hard and both were getting outs with only a few pitches per batter. If I recall correctly, the game ended in a 2-2 tie, called because of darkness. The Jesters pitcher was a kid named, Jerry Gamble, while the Weston pitcher was William "Willie" McNeal. My nephew, who played in the basketball tournament, played in that game for Weston and went 2 for 4 with two singles, a walk, and a stolen base. I think he scored both runs. The James Everson pitcher, Gamble, and their first baseman, Donald Bartolo were also on their basketball team.

Nick took another sip of his coffee, which gave Jordan a chance to catch up on his note-taking. Nick then began again, "So, while these guys knew each other and their respective athletic talents, there was no real animosity between their players, mostly because they competed in different leagues. Probably, the same could be said for James Everson and Preston, but perhaps more of a rivalry there because they were both located on the same side of the river, and presumably competed for the affections of the same girls. I don't know too much about that, but I can tell you about the fierce rivalry between Preston and Weston because I saw some of it first hand and heard about the rest from my nephews and nieces, who were all Weston alums, and of course, biased."

Jordan laughed as he was enjoying the story immensely, and by now, Nick was on a roll. Jordan could tell that whatever was ailing Nick before was now only a distant memory. He made a mental note to look up from his note-taking often to be sure that Nick was still doing fine.

Nick then decided to continue with the rivalry theme that he had started. He began again, "In the fall of 1970 Weston Acheson had an undefeated football team. Undefeated, that is, going into their big rivalry game against Preston Acheson on Thanksgiving Day. Preston had a solid team, but because of some losses earlier in the season due to injuries to key players, they were not in contention for the league championship. Weston had clinched the championship before the game due to an upset earlier in the day giving the second-place team from down the valley their second loss. That said, Weston dearly wanted to conclude their season with a win against their archrival and claim the first undefeated season in their school's history. Conversely, Preston wanted nothing more than to spoil Weston's perfect record."

"So, what happened?" Jordan asked.

"Suffice to say, nothing good for Weston. They were beaten from pillar to post. Preston had nothing to lose and everything to gain. They were finally healthy, playing on their home field, and loaded for bear, so to speak. Weston came out flat and never recovered. Perhaps, it could be attributed to their backing into the championship earlier in the day or expecting Preston to lay down since Weston was a heavy favorite. I don't know, but in hindsight, I guess it could have been expected. If you look back on their season, Weston didn't play all that well against teams they should have beaten easily. They got up for the tough games winning a wild shootout in mid-season on the road against the pre-season favorite to win the championship. They even pulled another one out on a final play Hail Mary pass. Somehow, they had won them all until the last one. Then, they were beaten 28-0, and it wasn't that close. To this day it's the biggest upset in their rivalry."

"I'm guessing you were in the stands that day," Jordan asked about Nick's attendance at the game in a roundabout way.

"Yes, we near froze to death," he answered. "It was very cold for late November. Fortunately, about the middle of the fourth quarter, we decided to leave, but by then half the stands were empty - the Weston half, of course. There must have been 15,000 people at that game. It was the largest crowd I can recall for a high school football game. The saddest part was that it wasn't a good game: one-sided, a romp. Weston did all they could to keep it to four scores, though. Preston ran and passed all over them. I don't know the final stats, but I'm sure they were pretty much in favor of Preston by a wide margin. Now, the second saddest part occurred after I left, but I heard all about it. With two minutes to go and the game safely in hand, Preston got the ball near midfield on a punt. Instead of running out the clock against the Weston second team, which was now in the game for some experience; Preston, who still had their first team on the field, went into a two-minute drill and scored on the last play. That caused a lot of bad feelings."

"So, I'm assuming that was the impetus for the intense dislike between the two schools?" Jordan again asked indirectly.

"Definitely," Nick answered. "The next year Weston had the home field advantage and the better team. They didn't let up on the pounding they gave Preston. That game ended up 40-something to 20-something. The rivalry continued on fairly even terms for many years until I left the area. I still check on it, occasionally. Weston has had the better of it, lately."

"So, basketball season came next," Jordan said as a lead-in.

"Yes, it was just starting, and all three schools had good teams," Nick answered. "James Everson was led by a guard named, Ted Bigby. He wasn't tall, only about 5' 8", but he had a good shot and averaged nearly 25 points a game for the season. Their center, Jerry Wall, was about 6' 4" and solid. He was a reliable double-digit scorer. They had one more player of note, their power forward, Donnie Bartolo, who was about 6' 2" and a good rebounder."

Jordan stopped Nick at that point to ask a question. He inquired, "Were they all seniors?"

"No," answered Nick. "Bigby and Wall were juniors. Bartolo was a senior. Most of the rest of their team was comprised of seniors, though. Now before I get to the line-ups for the other teams, I have to tell you about some other aspects."

"Okay," said Jordan. "Shoot, I'm ready."

"First, there was the betting on the games," Nick began. "When I say betting, I'm not talking about the principals from each school betting a beer on the outcome, mind you, I'm talking about big money gambling, hundreds of thousands of dollars. It was nothing for some guys to lay a grand out to win and another grand to cover the point spread. The savvy guys would sometimes take the favorite to win, but also the underdog to cover the spread, thereby winning on both bets, if the 'dog' lost by less than the point spread allowed. They only played that parlay if they figured the point spread was too high. Taking the favorite to win straight up wouldn't get the bettor a big return on his investment, but at least you weren't losing money. Conversely, for the bettor, taking the underdog to win outright was where money could be made if the dog won. Now, the trick for the bookie is to get money on each side of the ledger, that is, some on the favorite and some on the underdog. Of course, that's where the odds come into play. If the odds are 4-1 against the dog, then the bookie wants four times as much money on the favorite. If too much money is on one side of the ledger, then the odds are adjusted to get more money flowing to the underrepresented side." Nick paused again to let Jordan catch up, and asked if he had any questions, so far.

"Yes," Jordan replied, then asked, "How does the bookie make money?"

"Good question," Nick answered. "He makes his money on the 'vigorish, or vig, over-round, margin, juice', whatever you want to call it. Those are terms for the bookie's profit margin. It's the amount of money via percentage basis that's charged to the bettor for the privilege of placing the bet, usually 10%. For example, if you bet $100 with a bookie and you won the $100 bet, then you would only get $190 in return, your original $100 plus the $90 you won after the vigorish is deducted. The bookie makes 10% on every winning bet in this example. Some bookies only take it from the losers, some from the winners, and some from both the winners and losers. You see, they are the ones taking the chance, so they need to get something in return for the chance they are taking. I say taking a chance because, first, it is illegal, and second, they may not get paid if they run a book on credit."

Jordan was fascinated, then asked, "Did you bet on the games?"

Nick replied, "I did, but we'll get to that. Just to conclude this part of the story, let's say it was all very interesting, very analytical, but in the end, everyone had to understand that it was a game with kids playing, and anything could happen, and often did."

Jordan needed a few seconds to catch up with his note-taking, so Nick took another sip of his coffee. He also took the time to look around the park and see what might be going on. It was still early, so not too many people were present, just a few walkers and joggers. Jordan seemed to be happily making notes, not exactly recording what Nick was telling him verbatim, since he was recording it, as well, but making marginal notes about Nick's appearance, facial expressions, and animated movements. The things that a recorder couldn't capture. Finally, Jordan looked up and asked, "What's next?"

Nick began, "Well, it's not anything I know a lot about or have any direct knowledge of, but it needs to be covered to understand the significance of the rivalries. I mentioned previously that some of these young men had romantic interests beyond their traditional boundaries, that is, their side of the river. I best keep this short because I couldn't care less about it, and most of my information was from one of my nieces. Girls back then seemed to know who was dating whom, especially when the jocks were involved."

Nick continued, "At any rate here goes. The starting point guard for Weston Acheson was dating the captain of the Weston cheerleading squad. They were off and on throughout high school. No big news flash there. Well, around the time of the basketball tournament she makes a play for my nephew, who was playing for the YMCA league champs. He didn't reciprocate, but the Weston point guard knew all about it, presumably because she told him. So, he starts dating the captain of the Preston Acheson cheerleading squad, probably out of spite. She had recently broken up with her boyfriend, who just so happened to be the star player for Preston's football team. So, you can see where this is going. Additionally, one of the other players on the YMCA championship team was dating another girl from Preston Acheson, and if memory serves me correctly there may have been some other interschool dating, as well, with James Everson girls dating guys from Preston and maybe even Weston. About all I knew was that it was going to make for bad feelings which possibly could spill out on the basketball court at some point."

Jordan jumped in, "Did they?"

"Just a little here and there," Nick replied with a chuckle. "Boys will be boys."

Jordan laughed, "Yeah, I know, same when I was in school."

Nick then summarized the conversation to that point, "I told you about the rivalries, the betting, but not all of the betting, and the boyfriend/girlfriend aspect, so far. I guess it would be a good time to introduce you to the YMCA league championship team."

"I'm ready," said Jordan.

"Let me start by briefly telling you about these guys in a general sense. First of all, there were ten of them, and they were all good athletes. The starting five were very good athletes, and the two guards were on Weston's

Marine Corps Physical Fitness team. Ironically, I don't think any of them would tell you that basketball was their best sport. I believe seven of them played on the Weston football team that got trounced by Preston on Thanksgiving Day. So, keep that in mind."

"Okay," said Jordan.

Nick continued, "Their starting center was Richard "Ricky" Calvino. He was 5' 11", but jumped like he had springs in his legs. He was their main rebounder and had an unusual technique when he wanted to make a statement about who controlled the boards. He would go up high and grab the ball with a one-hand over-the-top move and come down with his elbows out to the sides. This was meant to intimidate the opposition from coming too close to him under the boards. Sometimes, he even scared his teammates from getting too close. He felt every rebound was his, and if someone from the other team did manage to snag an offensive rebound and try to put it back up, he would smash it back into their face, as a warning. Eventually, he learned that it was better to block the ball toward one of his teammates, so they could run their devastating fast break offense."

Nick then moved to the two forwards. He made sure Jordan was keeping up, then said, "The two starting forwards on the team were Augusto "Augie" Falco and John Paladino, nicknamed "Dino". They were two of our big three scorers. Augie was 5' 10", rather small for a forward, but he was a grinder with the best hands-on the team. He was a receiver on the Weston football team, and I swear, he could catch an aspirin tablet fired from an air rifle in a blizzard. If there was a scramble for a loose ball, my money was on Augie to come up with it. He could shoot, had a strong upper body of a football player, and could rebound when Ricky let him. Dino was 6 feet even and more the pure shooter. He was deadly from the corner and seemed to get his points methodically. He never looked like he was scoring a lot, but by the end of the game, he'd have between 15 and 20 points. He played quarterback for the Weston football team and like his pure shooting in basketball, he was a pure passer.

Nick forged on, "That brings me to the two guards. Danny "Bags" Bagnotti and Paul Marinelli, my nephew. Bags was the shooting guard and could light it up with the best of them. Paul was the point guard who had an innate ability to find the open guy and deliver the ball precisely where his teammates liked it. Danny and Paul were undersized, to say the least. Bags was 5' 10" and Paul was 5' 9". What they lacked in height, they made up for in hustle, speed, and quickness. The starting team was incredibly small, especially to be competing at this level. But, remember, they were all really good athletes that hustled."

Jordan was writing feverishly, somewhat afraid to interrupt, but he did hold up his hand like a kid in the classroom wanting to ask a question. Nick said, "Jordy, if you want to ask me something, just go ahead."

"Well, I didn't want to stop you while you were rolling," he said, but I do have a question. "Were these kids the Italian-American Basketball All-Stars?"

Nick laughed out loud, then replied, "Very observant, they all, except for one, had Italian heritage. The second team had four other very Italian-sounding names, with one WASP surname. You know what WASP states for, White Anglo-Saxon Protestant, although I don't know if he was a WASP. I just knew he wasn't of Italian heritage. His name was James "Jimmy" Shockley. He was the backup center, stood 6' 0" tall, and was very strong. He played linebacker and fullback on the Weston football team. Now, on to the other four guys. The other two forwards were Anthony Simonetti and Ronnie DiGiacomo. Anthony was another football player, also played linebacker and fullback, was short and squat, but a force to be reckoned with if things got rough under the boards. Ronnie was the tallest guy on the team at 6' 1", a district champion sprinter, and the team jokester. Again, these guys were mostly used for rebounding, if Ricky got in foul trouble. The two reserve guards were Timmy Positano and Frank Mezza. Both were on the Weston football team. Frank played defensive back while Timmy was a receiver. Not surprisingly, that team named themselves "The Italian Stallions". It was a clever team name for two reasons. One, 90% of them had Italian heritage, and two, they could run all night, you know, like stallions."

Nick pressed on, "As long as we're talking about team personnel, let me tell you what I know about the Preston Acheson team. Their best player was Kerry O'Boyle. He was one of their forwards. He also played baseball and was widely recruited in both sports, finally settling on the University of Pennsylvania Quakers. He was about 6' 1" and a lefty. The other two main players were Earl Pulaski and Fred Vinovich. Pulaski was about six feet and their center, while Vinovich was about 5' 10" and played the point for Preston. I don't recall much about the others on their team, unfortunately."

"Finally," Nick began, "I'll tell you about the Weston Acheson players. Their starting center was 6' 6" and rail-thin. His name was Jerome Feldman. He was a big weapon for the War Eagles in more ways than size. In most games, the War Eagles' offensive plan was to sink the ball low to him because most teams they played didn't have a big man his size to stop him. Their forwards were two juniors, Doug McIntyre and Jessie Kowalchik. Both played baseball with McIntyre pitching and Kowalchik catching. They made a fine battery. On the basketball court, they were double-digit scorers most games. The most talented player on the War Eagles was Larry Stroebel. He played the shooting guard position and had more moves than a belly dancer with hives. He was beyond fun to watch on a basketball court. He would drive the lane and have no shot when he left his feet, but somehow in mid-air would be able to change direction, or double-pump and get off his shot from an angle no one thought possible. Their point guard was Billy Lafferty, who was also the War Eagles all-star running back."

"Now, you mentioned coaches the other day," Jordan interjected.

"Let's talk a little about them. The Weston Acheson coach was Sylvester Buzinski, as I mentioned to you last week. I told you that he was a very good coach, but a not-so-nice man, a screamer, if you will. You could hear him yelling, 'Feldman' two blocks away every time Jerome did something wrong on the court. I also mentioned that the starting five for the Italian Stallions used to play basketball in his program at the ninth grade and junior varsity levels. The remarkable part is that the War Eagles won their league championship with basically half as good a team as they could have had."

Nick went on, "Now, on to the Paladins from Preston; their coach was a guy named Gino "Guerilla" Giordano. He was called "Guerilla" because he was huge, not just tall, but big all over. He played a few seasons of local pro ball for the Scranton Miners but never made it to the NBA. He knew the game as well as any coach in the league. I recall shaking his hand once, and it was like a bear paw. In direct contrast to Buzinski, Giordano was calm and measured in his coaching style."

"The James Everson Jesters' coach was Patty Lenahan," Nick continued. "Unfortunately, he had no real basketball pedigree. He taught physical education at James Everson, so he was drafted to be their coach. He may have also been their baseball coach. The problem for private schools back then, and probably still today, is that of tight budgets, rising tuition costs, and a crumbling infrastructure. They simply couldn't afford to pay a big-time coach for each sport, so the gym teacher was tapped for the boys' sports programs, and the girls' team, if they had one, usually got the health teacher as their coach."

Jordan jumped in again, "So, did anyone coach the Italian Stallions, or did they just show up and wing it?"

"Boy, you must be a good reporter because you ask the right question at the right time. I was just getting to that," Nick said. "That's how they went undefeated in the YMCA league and won the championship; that is, no coach, they just showed up and played. It wasn't a problem at that level of competition. They rolled through each team frequently scoring 100 points and winning by 30, 40, or even 50 points. But, the tournament level of play was a whole different enchilada. Without a coach, they would be dead on arrival. Even with one, there were no guarantees."

"So, who coached them?" Jordan inquired.

"Here's that part of the background," Nick began. "Paul, my nephew, came to me about two weeks before the first game and asked me to coach them. I guess he thought since I followed sports in general, and the recently concluded high school basketball season in particular, I could help them. I was flattered, of course."

"So, you coached them?" Jordan asked.

"Well, now, wait a minute," Nick continued, "I said he asked me, and I was flattered that he did. But, it's like Clint Eastwood said in *Dirty Harry*, "A man's got to know his limitations". I knew that it would have been a grave injustice to those boys for me to try to coach them because I didn't know the intricacies of the game. I was a fan, not a coach. There's a big difference, and I'm sure you understand that."

"So, what *did* you do?" Jordan queried.

"I got them a coach," Nick said unequivocally.

"How, where, who?" Came Jordan's inquest.

"You've heard the expression, 'I know a guy'?" Nick asked rhetorically. "Well, I knew a guy. Back in the day, he cut his teeth coaching in Philadelphia. It was tough, playground-style basketball, but he knew his X's and O's. When I got to know him, he had moved up to coaching prep ball in the Philly suburbs. He ran a well-organized, highly disciplined, and well-respected program at a private school, a well-financed private boy's school. As long as he won, and he did, his program remained well-financed."

"What was his name? Jordan asked. "Maybe, I've heard of him."

"I wouldn't think so, because it was long before your time. His name was Mike Stonehammer, but his nickname was "the Hammer", mostly because it was the second part of his surname, but also because he could drop the hammer on you, and did if you weren't going to play within his system or by his rules."

"You're right, I've never heard of him," came Jordan's reply.

"It would be unlikely that you would have," Nick said. "He stayed in the Philly area for his entire coaching career and didn't coach above the high school or prep level. Sadly, he passed away while he was much too young, probably before you were born, from a coronary. He had a heart defect that went undetected, something like Pete Maravich had if I'm recalling correctly," Nick mused, then recollected his thoughts, "Let's get back to the topic at hand. I met Mike at a sports banquet around 1965 when he was an up-and-coming basketball coach. I liked him immediately. He was a cool thinker, unflappable, a direct communicator, and just very measured in his response. He was honest, loyal, and appreciated hard work, which on the basketball court meant to hustle."

Jordan noticed that Nick was shifting his sitting posture from side to side now, so he figured Nick may need to move a little. He offered, "Nick, how about we walk over to the coffee shop and get something to eat? I haven't had any breakfast. We've been at this for a while now, so let's take a break. How about it?"

"That's a good idea, Jordy," Nick answered. "There's more I have to tell you about Mike, but for now that'll be enough." He then positioned his cane to use it as a prop to stand. Jordan was quick to assist him by lightly holding his free arm, just in case. Nick responded, "Thank you, Jordy, you're a good kid." Then they both laughed. Once upright, Nick shook his ailing leg and bent his knee and ankle to get some blood flowing to those joints. They proceeded to Perk Place on a slow meandering stroll stopping once so Nick could lean on the sign at the park entrance.

After looking at the park's sign Jordan remarked, "That's an interesting name, Parc de Gisele, I wonder how the park got that name. I know enough French to understand it to mean, "Gisele's Park", but I wonder where the name came from."

"Who knows, you may find out some day. If you do, let me know," Nick replied. "It's a beautiful name, don't you think?"

"Yes, very beautiful," Jordan answered. "It says this park was established in 2000. I can't believe it's been here for almost 20 years, and I'm just finding it."

"Well, better late than never," Nick said. "I'm guessing you were living in New York when it was developed, so that's why you didn't know about it. That, and the fact that it's on the other side of the city from where you live. It does my heart good that you met Mary here, well I guess technically you met her across the street at the hospice center, but you got to enjoy some quality time together here. It's a special place for me. As you know, I come here often. I like to sit on my bench and reminisce, and at 96, I have a lot to reminisce about," he said with a chuckle.

"Glad you mentioned, Mary," Jordan said. "I took your advice and asked her to dinner. We have plans tonight to dine at my friend, Kevin's, place. You know, where we had my dad's funeral luncheon on Saturday."

"That's nice," Nick replied. "I'm sure you'll have a nice time. Please let me know how your date goes, not any intimate stuff, of course, just in general," he said with a smile.

They were at Perk Place now, so Jordan asked Nick, "Would you rather be inside or outside?"

"I'm good with outside," Nick replied, "if you are."

"Outside it is," confirmed Jordan. "Now, what can I get you?"

"How about a bagel? Any kind will do," said Nick.

"I'll get them to re-fill your coffee, as well," Jordan said.

While Jordan was inside ordering, Nick had time to ponder some recent events in his life. On the good side of the ledger, he knew that meeting Jordan was a stroke of good fortune. He had finally met someone who he could trust with his life's story, even if Nick wasn't willing to share all of it immediately. Also, he was happy beyond words to have a younger person to talk with and share his stories and philosophies about life. Nick was also grateful to have lived the life he had. He had survived some tough times in his youth, learned some valuable lessons along the way, was still living independently, and still able to drive himself wherever he wanted, or needed, to go. He knew that was not something to be taken for granted.

On the other hand, Nick knew his time on earth was coming to a close. He understood that on the outside he looked much younger than his 96 years. He still had good eyesight; a full head of hair, albeit white; and most of all, his mind was still sharp. Unfortunately, on the inside, he was an old man with an old man's health issues. His aching leg was the least of his problems.

A year prior during his annual check-up, an irregularity was detected by his doctor. Subsequent scans revealed not only a valve issue that the doctor heard with his stethoscope but an aortic aneurysm. He had discussed it with his general practitioner, who recommended the best cardiac surgeon in the area. Nick made an appointment and more tests were ordered. In the final analysis, the surgeon's conclusion was not to operate on Nick, largely due to his age, but other medical issues contributed to the prognosis. Nick asked for a referral to get a second opinion, which the surgeon was only too happy to oblige. He told Nick that the number one ranked cardiac care facility in the country was the Cleveland Clinic in Ohio. The second-ranked facility was the Mayo Clinic in Rochester, Minnesota. If he didn't want to travel that far, Johns Hopkins Hospital in Baltimore was highly rated, as well.

Nick opted for the Cleveland Clinic. He made all of the arrangements himself: the appointment with one of the top heart surgeons on their staff, the transmission of his records and test results to the surgeon's office, flights to and from Cleveland on the same day, and transportation to and from each airport. After a thorough physical examination, the conclusion was the same, unfortunately for Nick. It was explained to him that he was just too risky a candidate for that surgery because of the location of the aneurysm. The likelihood of him surviving the operation was just too low to take a chance. It was suggested to him, now for the second time, to just enjoy the time he had left. Neither surgeon, nor his general practitioner, could reliably predict when the aneurysm would burst, but they were all clear on the fact that once it did, Nick would die instantly. He was grateful for that, at least.

By now Jordan had returned with Nick's bagel and coffee. "I hope cinnamon raisin is good with you," Jordan said.

"That's fine," said Nick, "and thank you, very much, again."

"No problem," replied Jordan. "I told you, all eats and drinks are on me as a 'thank you' for allowing me the opportunity to hear about your life's experiences."

"You are too kind, young man," Nick countered. He then added, "If I'm boring you at any point, just let me know, and we can move on to another topic."

"You are not boring me in any way, shape, or form," Jordan shot back. "I'm loving this and eating it up with a shovel."

"Okay," Nick said, "let me press on. I was telling you about the Hammer. We have established that I was asked to coach the Stallions but declined because I wasn't qualified to go up against three seasoned coaches, well, two for sure. Therefore, I thought for a while about what to do. Then, it occurred to me to ask Mike. I knew his season was over. His team had just won their third straight prep league title in the northern Philly suburbs, so he was available if he wanted to do it. The best part was that he was better credentialed than any of the three coaches up there, and I figured that he might be looking for a new challenge. He jumped at the opportunity. I knew he couldn't commute back and forth to Philly, since it was a two-hour drive each way. Because he wasn't married at the time, kind of between wives, as he put it, I had him stay with me. We were two bachelors, you know, roomies for two weeks. That was the amount of time available to coach our team into playing shape and play the games. It was a tall order, but I knew if anyone was capable of doing it, the Hammer was."

"How did the players like Mike? Jordan asked.

"Before our first practice, I met with the team. The practice was set up for Saturday morning, April 3rd, twelve days before our first game with the Jesters. I introduced them to Mike and shared Mike's credentials with them. I further let them know that very few people were going to know who Mike was when they saw him, but some would know his name, so keep it 'top secret' that we even had a coach, let alone who he was. That way, we had an excellent chance of being taken for granted, that is, underrated, overlooked. I explained to those ten guys in very clear terms that they had to be committed, or I would walk away, and so would Mike. I further explained to them that without Mike they didn't have a chance. With Mike guiding them, they had a chance, but they had to want it. I asked each of them to sign a pledge that they would hustle at all times; compete for every loose ball; never quit, no matter what the score was or the circumstances were; be team players, and above all, listen to their coach."

"Did they sign?" Jordan asked.

"They all signed," Nick said. "It was just my way of seeing if they were committed to seeing it through. I didn't want to waste my time, and certainly not Mike's time, on a bunch of quitters, and I told them so. The first practice was grueling. It was Mike's way of weeding out anyone who couldn't take it. I watched it from the stands. I felt sorry for our boys, but Mike had to find out if they were serious. I'm happy to report that not one of them buckled after an hour murder session of passing and dribbling drills, running suicide sprints, and one-on-one rebounding scrimmages. After a five-minute break to re-hydrate, the Hammer divided them into two teams for a simulated game, which he ran non-stop for one more hour. When it was all over, they were panting like Iditarod sled dogs. But to their credit, no one complained. Well, at least I never heard it, if they did."

Nick took a break to have a bite of his bagel and a sip of his coffee, so Jordan asked, "What was your role on the team?"

"My role was essentially to function as the general manager. Remember that I mentioned my job in the real world was to facilitate getting things done for a very benevolent boss? Well, I got things done for the team, as well. For example, I got Mike to coach them. I also got them access to the school gym through connections I had with several school board directors. Let's just say, some favors were called in. Finally, I got them uniforms. My boss was only too happy to spring for top-of-the-line basketball shorts, shirts, sweat pants, jackets, socks, and basketball shoes, you know, high-top sneakers, as I called them. He owned a garment factory in the area and had a special run of thirty complete outfits made: ten for each game, three for each player. He didn't care if they got knocked off in the first game. The boys got to keep the three sets. He even had his tailor show up at one of the early practices to measure our players. The color scheme was green, white, and red, like the Italian flag, but he insisted that there be an American flag emboldened above their number on the back of their jerseys and their left sleeve, shoulder level, on their warm-up suit jackets. The team name *Italian Stallions* was on the front of each jersey. They were a little gaudy for my taste, but the boys seemed to like them."

"I'd love to see a picture of those guys dressed in their uniforms," Jordan mentioned.

"I'll look around to see what I have stashed away, or maybe my nephew still has a picture. Remind me again, if I forget," Nick said. "Just to conclude the story on the first practice session, Mike and I discussed what kind of talent we had to work with after we had watched them for two hours. It was pretty obvious to both of us that we had two teams. The first five, the starters, were all good basketball players. The next five guys, our bench strength, were going to be the guys we used to do the heavy lifting. That means, if a game got too rough, we had the guys to settle things down and control the action. They were like the muscle off the bench on a hockey team, think of Dave Schultz coming off the Philadelphia Flyers bench in the 1970s. As it turned out, we would need those guys."

Jordan was feverishly writing, making notes, and jotting down some questions that he wanted to ask but didn't want to interrupt Nick's flow. When Nick stopped to take a sip of coffee, Jordan jumped in with a question. He asked, "So, let me see if I have this straight. I heard about the ten guys on the team. The Hammer was the coach. You functioned as the general manager, the guy who got things done. Was there anyone else?"

"Yes, as a matter-of-fact, there was," Nick said. "Good question, thanks for reminding me. We had two of the guy's classmates function as team managers. Not managers in the sense of game strategy, but more like getting equipment, drinks, basketballs, etc. One other duty that they masterfully fulfilled was that of scout. Both were very interested in sports. Wayne Harden was the sports reporter for the Weston Acheson school newspaper. He followed sports all around the valley and knew each of the teams in the tournament very well. He wasn't an athlete by any stretch of the imagination, but he knew his sports. The other kid, Willie McNeal, I told you a little about already. He was the lefty pitcher on the baseball team, and he, too, knew and followed all sports up and down the valley. He wasn't a basketball player, but he knew who we needed to stop on each of the three opponents."

Jordan inserted a question, "So, what did you have them do?"

"Let's cover that aspect of the background story, now," Nick began. "I gave them $100 in small bills and told them to see if they could get someone in the James Everson and Preston Acheson athletic departments to cough up a tape of one of their games."

"How did that work out?" Jordan inquired.

"We got both tapes, one from each school, and those two kids came back with $50, which of course, I told them to keep. Remember this was almost 50 years ago, and that was a lot of dough back then. So, getting a game film for $25 was a good deal all around. I don't know who they talked to, and I don't care, because those two game films were invaluable to Mike. He studied them for hours at my place each night leading up to the first game. And, here's the kicker. Those boys were smart enough to get the game film from both schools where they played against Weston Acheson, so we had all three teams on two films."

"Wow! What a stroke of luck or genius." Jordan exclaimed.

"A little of each, I guess," Nick offered. "Let's see if I can take you up to the first game, then we can break for today. Is that's okay with you, Jordy?" Nick asked.

"Of course, whatever works for you," Jordan said. By then, they had both finished their breakfast. Jordan had a bagel, as well, like Nick, and both were running low on their coffee, so Jordan offered to get more for each. Nick took him up on his offer. While Jordan was inside and waiting to order, Nick took a few minutes to let his mind wander back to his days after WWII. He recalled getting his honorable discharge and looking for work around the area where he grew up. He thought to himself how fortunate he was to have been seated next to the man, who would become his boss, at a boxing match in Scranton. After talking with Nick for more than two hours and learning that Nick was a veteran looking for work, this soft-spoken middle-aged man, named Sam, offered him a job. Nick was unaware at the time that he was essentially in a job interview, but he didn't care and didn't even know what the job entailed, but he agreed to go to work for Sam, and the rest was history, or as Nick figured *his story.*"

Jordan arrived back at their table with both drinks. Nick thanked him and said, "Now, we move to Sunday, April 4th. Mike decided that he had run the guys pretty hard the day before, so he gave them an easy practice session just having them concentrate on shooting and passing drills. He then went over some basic defensive sets he thought would work well. He knew he didn't have enough time to get too detailed, but at least he wanted our boys to be able to play a hard-nosed man-to-man and a couple of different zone defenses, just in case the need arose. After practicing the defensive sets for an hour he sent five guys to each foul line and had them shoot foul shots. He had Wayne and Willie score the guys. The drill was four sets of 25 shots each, rotating in a new shooter every 25 shots for the first three sets. That was the warm-up. Then, the competition began. Each shooter took two shots, then moved to the back of the line. The next time through he got one shot. Then back to two, then one again, and so forth. The last time through each guy took an extra shot to make 25. Whoever made the most didn't have to run the 10 laps around the perimeter of the gym."

"Do you remember who won?" Asked Jordan.

"It was Dino Paladino," Nick answered. "If you recall, I mentioned he was the best pure shooter on the team. I think he made 23 out of 25, that's 92%. Of course, the starters all made at least 20. The bomb squad, as I nicknamed them, averaged about 14. They weren't as good shooters, but Mike knew why we had those guys, and he knew how to use them.

Jordan inquired, "Why did you nickname them the *bomb squad*?"

"Well, Jordy," Nick began, "who do you call when there's a potentially explosive situation, and you need a bomb defused?"

Jordan smiled and answered, "I see what you mean."

At that point, Nick reached into his pants pocket and took out a small piece of paper. He glanced at it and continued, "I just need to keep the days straight, so I made a few notes. On Monday, the 5th, we had to practice in the evening after track and baseball. We, also, had to use the junior high school gym because the Weston basketball team was using the senior high gym. I had dispatched Wayne and Willie to watch what they were doing. Surprisingly, the report came back that they only ran a few drills, then shot around for about 30 minutes. Mike, on the other hand, ran our boys pretty hard, again. Later, he told me, that he thought our guys were in great shape, and he didn't see the need to push them that hard again. He didn't want to risk any injuries. Instead, he worked with the boys on offensive sets versus man-to-man and zone defenses. After practice, Mike told me that he wanted to run our boys against some real tough competition in a scrimmage game. I asked him what he was thinking. He said that he could get a group of his former players from the Philly area, who were now in junior college to come up to the valley on Saturday morning, but it had to be secretive at a location away from the school, so no one would know what we were doing. I made a call to the athletic director of one of the colleges in Wilkes-Barre. He agreed to let us use their gym on Saturday morning since it was a downtime for the students. Besides, he owed me a favor."

"Was there anyone up there who didn't owe you a favor?" Jordan asked.

"Sure, but people in high places usually don't get there without some help, and I tried to be the guy providing the help," Nick replied. "I never forced them to do anything they didn't want to do, but I never had to ask twice." Nick winked, and Jordan's eyes got as big as silver dollars.

Nick referred to his notes again, then began, "On Tuesday I started checking into the betting line on the first game. As I expected, our team was a huge underdog versus James Everson, and rightfully so, considering most people didn't know what talent we had. Later on, Mike and I along with input from Wayne and Willie started to go over the Jesters' personnel. Willie, Wayne, and I agreed that James Everson had three guys that we needed to concentrate on defending. The rest were just fill-ins that could easily be neutralized. As I mentioned, their three best players were Bigby, Wall, and Bartolo. Both Wall and Bartolo were taller than our tallest guy. Those three accounted for almost 90% of their scoring. I explained to the Hammer that they had had little competition in their league, but did play against both of the other schools during a holiday tournament earlier in the season, and lost to both handily. At that point, we didn't yet have the game tapes, so Mike was left to develop a preliminary defensive scheme. I knew we still had several days before our first game, so I wasn't worried."

Jordan was hanging on Nick's every word but was now interested in the game tapes. He asked, "So, when did the game tapes arrive?"

"We got them both on Friday," Nick answered. "Wayne delivered the first one in the morning, and Willie the other in the afternoon. That was perfect because Mike and I used the weekend to look them over. They weren't the best quality, mind you, but we could see what we needed to see."

"Wow! This is like an espionage drama," Jordan exclaimed, drawing a quizzical look from a lady at a nearby table.

"Hardly," responded Nick. "It was just what needed to be done to get the information we needed to be on the same competitive level as the other three teams. Remember, they all knew each other's tendencies because they had played each other previously. We were at a disadvantage having never played any of the other three teams."

"Yes, but weren't the other three teams at a disadvantage never having played your team?" Jordan instinctively asked.

"To some degree, 'yes'," came Nick's reply. "However, no one seemed to care because they all assumed we were going to lay down, roll over and let them beat us like a rented mule. That's where we had the advantage. Everyone was taking us for granted."

"So, what happened next?" Jordan asked.

"Wednesday, Thursday, and Friday were a blur. I recall Weston playing Preston in baseball at Preston's home field and beating them, 2-0. Doug McIntyre pitched a brilliant two-hit shutout for Weston, and my nephew went three for four with two singles and a double, scored a run, and had a stolen base. The Paladin's pitcher was Earl Pulaski, who also pitched well and was coming off a no-hitter in his previous game. After the game, the War Eagles' manager addressed his team and commented that they had taken the Paladin's star pitcher full circle in two games, you know, a no-hitter the game before to a loss in the next one against the War Eagles. He called it going from 'Cy Young to Sayonara' in less than a week."

Jordan chimed in, "I love that expression!"

"I'm guessing their coach read it somewhere," Nick explained. "It's probably attributed to some pitcher who had a great season, then a bad one and his team got rid of him. So, you go from winning the big award to being sent packing, all in short order."

"I understand it," Jordan said, "and it's so appropriate."

"Anyway, McIntyre played for the War Eagles' basketball team along with their football and baseball teams. Pulaski played football, basketball, and baseball for the Paladins. They were both excellent athletes, but then again, so were many of the kids back then. I think that game was on Wednesday. As soon Augie and Paul got to practice after playing in the baseball game, Mike ran the team through a light conditioning drill, then got into more detail on some offensive sets he had previously taught them. Finally, he gave them a talk that I'm convinced went a long way toward helping our team. He lectured them on team unity. He explained that they needed to be there for one another. There would likely be a game where someone was having an off night, and the others would need to pick up the slack for him. Conversely, there may be a game when one of them had the hot hand, and his teammates needed to feed him the ball set screens for him, and not think of their own glory. He reminded them that there was no 'I' in team, and sometimes you have to sacrifice your glory for the betterment of the team. Fortunately, they seemed to agree. After practice, Mike said to me that he hoped his message had gotten through to everyone. He concluded by saying that he would know more after the Saturday scrimmage."

Nick continued, "Friday was a light workout, just some fundamentals, then a brief shoot-around. It was apparent that the boys wanted to get going to enjoy their Friday evening, likely with dates or just hanging out. I gathered them together before they departed and cautioned them to be careful and not do anything foolish that would jeopardize what we had worked on all week, then reminded them of our scrimmage game in Wilkes-Barre on Saturday morning at ten."

"I'm sensing something came up because of the way you mentioned this," Jordan said.

"Well, about ten o'clock I got a call from one of the local police chiefs. He was a good friend of mine. He told me that he had two of my players in his office. They were brought in for underage drinking. Both were pretty drunk and taking turns running to the bathroom to throw up. He knew the boys, and he knew that I was involved with helping them in the basketball tournament. So, out of courtesy to me, he called me before processing any paperwork. I hustled down to the police station and was surprised to find out that it was two of our starters. Well, long story made short, I talked with the chief and had them released in my custody. He agreed not to process any paperwork, but warned them if they were brought in any time before their 21st birthdays with so much as a parking ticket, he was going to throw the proverbial book at them."

"Which two, if you don't mind me asking?" Jordan inquired.

"I'm happy to say, neither one was my nephew," Nick answered. "Let's just say it was two kids who made a mistake and should have known better, especially with a scrimmage the next morning."

"So, what did you do with them?" Jordan asked with a cringe.

"I took them back to my place to sleep it off," Nick replied, "but first, I sobered them up enough to call their parents to let them know that they were safe and spending the night at a friend's house. I was the friend, you see."

"Not to second guess you, but don't you think you may have done them a disservice?" Jordan asked.

"Perhaps, but they paid for it the next day during the game. They were in no shape to play, but I wanted them to feel some remorse. The Hammer was upset, too, of course. I mentioned to him I thought the best way to handle it was to sit them for a quarter then put them in against the two best guys from Philly. Mike agreed, then pulled them aside before the game on Saturday morning and told them that they were benched for not respecting their teammates, me for all I had done for them, and him who had given his time to coach them. Their heads hung low, but that wasn't the worst of it. Mike put them in the game sometime during the second quarter and had them play the rest of the game without a break. They didn't know what hit them. The two Philly kids ran them to near death."

"Okay, I guess they got the message," Jordan proclaimed.

"I think they did," Nick answered. "No more needed to be said after that. Now on to the real purpose of the Saturday scrimmage. Our guys went into the game thinking they were playing a bunch of other high schoolers. They didn't know that their opponents were junior college players with a high talent level. Naturally, our team was overmatched, but they did well to hang in the game for the most part. Finally, in the fourth quarter, the Philly kids pulled away and won by 13 points. It was our team's first loss. They were used to winning by at least 30 points against some very weak competition."

Jordan jumped in with another question, "What purpose did that serve to overmatch them?"

Nick replied, "There were at least two positive results that Mike and I felt were accomplished. First, our team didn't quit. They fought hard for every ball, boxed out under the boards, and moved well in Mike's offense. Second, Mike and I got to see what the second team could do when the play got physical. Mike had asked his former players to mix it up when our second team was on the court, and they did. Mike recognized that our emerging strength was that we had three (four counting our starting center, Ricky) power guys on our backline that could handle anyone. It wouldn't be with finesse, but with brute force, if need be. They weren't tall, but they were strong, a lot like Wayne Embry years ago, or Wes Unseld later on, or Charles Barkley more recently, to name someone you may be more familiar with."

"I know about Charles Barkley, for sure, and have heard of Unseld," Jordan said, "but I'm not familiar with Wayne Embry." Before Nick could say anything, Jordan continued, "I know, look him up. I will."

"You don't have to," Nick said. "Suffice to say, Embry, Unseld, and Barkley were shorter than most of their contemporaries playing the backline but strong as bulls, and they could rebound with anyone because they knew how to take up space near the basket and box out. Now after the scrimmage I talked with the kids from Philly. I thanked them for making the two-hour drive north and handed each of them an envelope for their expenses. I jokingly told them that they would have gotten nothing if they lost. They laughed, but several of them told me that our team was pretty good, especially for seniors in high school. That was encouraging. So, now to the locker room scene: to a man, our boys were down after tasting their first defeat. Perhaps, it was a good thing to have them realize that they weren't unbeatable. Of course, it could've served to undermine their confidence, as well. After he let them sulk a bit, the Hammer explained to them that the team that had just beaten them was a class above them athletically. He told them that they were all junior college players, and he felt they did very well against them. He told them that the competition level would not be that high in the Rotary tournament, so if the proper effort was put forth, they should do well."

Jordan then asked about the two kids Nick had gotten out of trouble the night before. Nick began, "I asked them to see me after they took their showers, and they did. I explained to them that they could have ruined everything that the team, Mike, and I had been working toward by their foolish actions. They told me that they understood, that they were sorry, and that it wouldn't happen again. I took them at their word, and let it drop. But, of course, it was Saturday night, so anything could happen."

"Did it?" questioned Jordan.

"Fortunately, no," Nick answered. "Well, if anything happened, I didn't hear about it, so I assume nothing bad happened. Now, that's not to say that the guys dating girls from the other side of the river didn't get into a scrape or two, but thankfully, if they did, it didn't amount to anything that I had to get involved with."

Nick continued, "The next day was Sunday, so we gave the boys the day off in hopes that they would take it easy after the tough scrimmage game, perhaps even study, but that was doubtful. We suggested that they try to find some time to shoot some hoops somewhere, just to keep their shooting eyes sharpened. About noon I went over to Louie's Pool Hall to shoot a game or two of billiards and play some cards. I hung around for a couple of hours just waiting to see who might show up. My real reason to be there was to check on the early line of the first game and the odds on all four teams. I was pleased to learn that we were a 10-1 underdog against James Everson, and 20-1 to win it all. Weston Acheson was the favorite at 5-2, followed by Preston Acheson at 5-1 and James Everson at 10-1. Word had not gotten out as to how good we were, nor that the Hammer was coaching us. I decided to put two C-notes on us to win our first game and two more on us to win it all. When I found out that we were 18 point underdogs, I put $500 on us to cover. I knew that bet was a lock. There was no way that we were going to lose by more than 18 points. Our second team could cover that spread. Well, maybe . . . it would just depend if there would be enough of them around at the end to finish the game; you know, if they didn't all foul out."

"So you were betting on the game?" Jordan asked naively.

"Definitely!" Nick asserted.

"How did that work? After all, you worked for a guy who ran a gambling operation as his side business, so to speak," Jordan asked dumbfounded.

"Just because my boss was running the gambling operation, didn't mean I couldn't participate. If I lost a bet, I had to pay up. If I won, I got paid off. Remember, the bookie doesn't care who wins or loses, just as long as he gets the odds correct and equal money on both sides. He's looking for a volume business and skimming off the top."

"Okay, I see," said Jordan. "So, you put $200 on your team to win the first game at long odds, $200 more to win the tournament at even longer odds, and $500 to cover the point spread. How much did you stand to make if you won all your bets?"

"Let's see," Nick began, "$200 at 10-1 is $2000 less the juice, so that's $1800. The bet to cover was even money, so it was $450 after the juice. So, those two bets would profit me by $2250. Now, the bet to win the tournament would return $3600. So, I would be up almost six grand if all went our way, and that was without any bets on the other two games, if we got that far."

"What impresses me more than anything, Nick, is how fast you came up with those numbers," Jordan offered with surprise.

"Numbers, math, arithmetic were always second nature to me, Jordy," Nick stated, then he continued. "I wanted my brother, Joe, to get in on this action. Joe was Paul's father. The problem was that my brother worked for Uncle Sam. He couldn't take the chance, little as it was, to be caught up in illegal gambling. So, I asked him if he wanted me to put a couple of bucks on the game for him. He asked me what I thought. I told him it was a lock for our boys to cover an 18 point spread. Also, I was pretty sure we could win the game, and at 10-1 it was foolish not to take a chance on that, too. Winning the tournament that was another story, so I didn't want to extend him that much for that bet."

"So, what did he decide?" Jordan asked.

"He was pretty conservative with money, but liked to play cards, so he was a bit of a gambler," Nick stated. "Ultimately, we decided on $50 to win at 10-1 and $50 more to cover the spread. He decided on putting up $20 to win the tournament. The worst-case scenario would be that he could lose $120, but I was sure that it would only be $25 if our team lost and covered. If he won the first two, he'd be up nearly $500. So, he bought in, and I placed the bets. I placed the same bets for Mike, unbeknownst to him."

"Interesting," said Jordan. "I can't wait to find out what happened. You weren't kidding about all the back-stories. It almost makes these games anti-climactic."

"I assure you that the games were anything but anti-climactic," Nick said with a smile. "So, now the three days leading up to the first game on Thursday evening were a little on edge for Mike and me, but the boys didn't seem to be bothered by it."

Jordan interjected, "That's good to hear, I mean, that your team was loose."

Nick thought for a second, then said, "Oh, before I tell you about that, I forgot to mention that the Hammer and I looked at the game films most of Saturday and

Sunday afternoons. He made a ton of notes. Mostly, he was concerned with Ted Bigby and Jerry Wall, the James Everson guard and center. He knew that a zone wouldn't work well against Bigby because he could shoot from outside, and he was likely to score over our zone at will. The zone might work well down low to constrain Wall with a double team, though. On Sunday evening he told me he would have to think it through a little more."

Jordan said, "I can see why you liked Mike as your coach. He's very analytical and likes to be well prepared."

"No doubt about it," Nick said. "He was a real asset. More on that later. Monday's practice was the last real strenuous one, but nothing like the previous grueling practices. Again, Mike didn't want to get anyone hurt. He kept the boys a little over an hour, the last 30 minutes were reserved for shooting, some easy one-on-one, and foul shooting. Tuesday's practice was late again due to a track meet and baseball game. Mike had the boys go over a few different defensive sets he was planning on using against James Everson. In particular, Mike explained the full-court press and had them run through it. He explained that we might have to go to it if we fell behind late in the game. After that, Mike explained a variate of that defense he called the zone press. Finally, he told the guys he wanted to start out playing a 1-2-2 defensive zone scheme and varying it with a 2-1-2 zone. He wanted to put high pressure on Bigby with Danny and Paul pushing him farther away from the basket. That way, he felt, he could protect us down low against Wall and Bartolo with either a box around the lane and pressure up top, like a box-and-one defense; or by using our lower three guys on the backline to clog the middle, then hopefully contain Bigby up top with pressure from our guards. Mike was pretty sure we could get turnovers with that approach which would lead to some easy fast-break baskets, because the two fastest guys on the court were Danny and Paul, and once they broke free, no one was going to catch them."

"Well, we're almost to the first game," Jordan observed.

"Yes, just one day to go," Nick said. "By Wednesday word had gotten out that we were better than originally thought and certainly better than the average YMCA champion. The odds had fallen to 5-1, and the line was down to 10 points. The good news was that we had gotten our bets down when the odds were much higher, but better for us, as the case was. Mike took it real easy on our guys and just ran them through a few refreshers offensively. He anticipated James Everson defending us man-to-man, and he planned on countering that with his version of a motion offense always looking for cuts to the basket. It was a knockoff of the Princeton offense of Pete Carril. The idea was to keep moving and wear out the defenders. Mike knew we had the horses, and as the saying goes, 'there are horses for courses'."

Jordan had his phone silenced, but he could feel it incessantly vibrating in his pocket. He had reached into his pocket at least four times to stop it, but by now he figured it might be important, so he excused himself for a second to see who had been calling. When he looked at his screen he could see it was Jackie, and she had called several times throughout the morning. It was almost

11:00 a.m. now, and Jordan's time with Nick was over anyway. Jordan explained to Nick that he had better call his sister to see what was so urgent that she had to keep calling him. He hoped it was nothing problematic with one of the kids. Nick understood and told Jordan, "Please let me know if it's anything serious." Then he hesitated, "Just call me no matter what because I don't want to worry." Nick then collected his belongings and coffee cup before departing.

CHAPTER 8
Secret Lives

A s soon as Jordan left Nick, he quickly called Jackie to find out the reason for her repeated phone calls. When she answered Jordan could tell she had been crying. "Jackie, what's the matter," he asked. "Are the kids okay?"

"The kids are fine, Jordan," she replied. "It's Richard."

"What's the matter with Richard?" Jordan inquired.

"I don't know where to begin," she replied. "He's been arrested."

"Arrested!" Jordan exclaimed.

"Yes, something to do with his work," she said. "The FBI raided his office early this morning, and now they're here looking through our personal papers, computers, and any business and tax documents we have."

"I probably don't have to ask you this," he said, "but do they have a warrant?"

"They certainly do," Jackie confided, "signed by a federal district judge."

"Oh, my God, this sounds serious," Jordan blurted out.

"It is." She said, then asked, "Can you come over now?"

"I'll be right there. Don't tell them anything. Call your lawyer, if you haven't done it already," he urged her.

"I did, someone should be here soon, and I don't know anything to tell them. This is as shocking to me, as I'm sure it is to you."

"I'll be right there," Jordan said, then ended the call.

A million things were now running through Jordan's head as he drove to Jackie and Richard's house. He was trying to be careful not to speed, but he was pushing the allowable margin over the limit. He finally arrived at their upscale community in what seemed like an eternity to get there, but in reality, was only ten minutes. The guard at the gate granted him access once he showed his driver's license, and the guard checked the eligible visitor's list.

Jordan kept running over in his mind Richard's recent behavior. He recalled that Richard was having some work problem during the latter part of the previous week that caused him to be delayed getting to Thomas' bedside at the hospice center. He wondered if that was related to this issue. Also, on his mind was the fact that his retirement portfolio was in Richard's hands, and if there were problems at Richard's office, how would that affect his financial future?

When Jordan pulled up in front of his sister's house he could see a multitude of black SUVs with FBI emblems on their license plates. The agents were attired in dark blue windbreakers with yellow FBI lettering on their backs. Jordan thought, 'This doesn't look good'. At least six agents were moving in and out of the house carrying brown paper bags and boxes with 'Evidence' stenciled on their sides.

He parked across the street, where naturally a crowd had gathered. He thought to himself, 'doesn't anyone work in this neighborhood, and why does this sort of activity always draw a crowd?' He walked toward his sister's house, identified himself to the first agent who looked in his direction and asked to speak with the agent in charge. The agent he spoke with told him to wait outside, and he would get Special Agent Rolfe to speak with him shortly.

Jordan waited outside, as he was directed to do, and shortly thereafter Special Agent Jonathon Rolfe came out to see him. Jordan again identified himself as Jackie's brother, asked if he could see her, and inquired what the search was all about. Rolfe told him that he couldn't let him inside at that time, but Jordan could see his sister outside, and that he would tell her that Jordan had arrived. He also told him that he couldn't discuss any information regarding the case or collection of evidence.

At that point, Jackie came running out of the house and into Jordan's arms. She was crying uncontrollably. Jordan hugged her and tried to calm her, but that was going to take some doing. This wasn't like the old days when he would talk with her after a boy had unceremoniously dumped her, or when she wasn't chosen for a part in her high school play. This was serious, and they both knew it.

Once he got her calmed down enough to talk, he asked, "Has your lawyer arrived yet?"

"No," she said. "He couldn't take my call, but his secretary told me that they would get someone here as soon as they could. They were going to send over one of their junior lawyers. She should be here soon."

"Well, between your background in law and your lawyer's, I'm sure you will be able to find out what's going on," Jordan said.

"I'm guessing from what the warrant said and what I overheard that they are looking for evidence of fraudulent activity on Richard's part regarding his financial dealings and business," Jackie said.

Jordan's heart sank, and not only because he had his financial future tied up with Richard's business, but because of how this situation was going to affect Jackie, Richie and Amanda. He then asked, "Where's Richard? You said that he'd been arrested."

"It's worse than I knew when I called you," she said.

"How so, or do I want to know?" Jordan asked.

"He's in federal custody awaiting a hearing. The FBI arrested him at the airport," Jackie told Jordan.

Jordan excitedly exclaimed, "At the airport! Where was he going?"

"Well, when he left this morning, he told me that he had an overnighter to St. Louis to see a client that had moved there," she began. "I should have known something was up because most of those financial review meetings are conducted via one of those online meeting services, like Zoom, when a client is out of town. At any rate, when they arrested him he was about to board a flight to London with a connection to Djibouti."

"Djibouti? Why there?" Jordan asked.

"No extradition," she said. "And here's the worst part, if you can believe it gets worse, he was leaving with his secretary."

"You're kidding me!" Jordan exclaimed. "Richard was cheating on you? Did you suspect anything?"

"Little things here and there, perhaps, that I should have picked up on in hindsight," she said, "but, he was pretty good at hiding it."

"Well, what are you going to do?" Jordan asked.

"Not sure, but for now he can rot in jail for all I care," she shot back.

"Oh, boy," Jordan said. "This isn't good. How did you find out all of this?"

"Some of the agents were talking while they were searching one of the kids' rooms. I still had the intercom on, so I was able to hear some of their conversation." Jackie continued, "They have been here searching since nine o'clock when I got back from taking the kids to school. That's when I tried calling you."

"I'm sorry that I didn't pick up when you called," Jordan said. "I had my phone on silent. I was interviewing Nick, that old guy I met in the park last week. He and I had planned the meeting for this morning, and we were deep into it. I had no idea how serious this situation was, or I would have cut it short and been right over here."

"Well, you're here now, and thanks for coming," she said. "I just wish that lawyer would get here before they are finished. I'm not sure what rights I have. You know, it's been ten years since I practiced law, and criminal law wasn't my specialty, anyway, so I'm not up on everything as much as I should be. Besides, it's never a good idea to represent yourself."

About 15 minutes later, Jackie's substitute lawyer, Rachel Armstrong, arrived. She asked to see the warrant, read it over, and told Jackie that there was nothing she could do to stop them from searching her home. She talked with the agent in charge, took his business card, told Jackie to stay outside and not to answer any of their questions without her or another of the firm's lawyers being present. Jackie asked her if Richard had contacted her firm. She said he had, and their top criminal lawyer was with him.

Jordan, being out of his element, watched and listened. He knew that he was just there to support his sister and provide any non-legal help he could. He let Jackie and Rachel talk for a few minutes, then watched as the FBI agents concluded their search. Agent Rolfe came over to Jackie before they left and told her that they were finished, for now, but if they needed to return, they would. He cautioned her not to destroy any potential evidence, then in an unusual gesture for a federal agent, he told her how sorry he was for her trouble. Jordan, Jackie, and Rachel were all surprised by Agent Rolfe's comment and looked a bit bewildered as the parade of FBI vehicles departed.

As soon as the last agent left the Cardel property, Rachel knew there wasn't much more she could do, not that she had done a lot, anyway. She, also, told Jackie how sorry she was and suggested she call her office if there were any further FBI activity. She then got into a black BMW 750i with tinted windows and drove back to her office. As she pulled away, Jordan noticed her license plate read 'I SUE U'. Jordan didn't think much of that ostentatious display, so he decided to keep his comments about Rachel to himself.

Jordan then asked Jackie if she needed him to pick up her kids from school. Jackie told him that she would get them. She wanted to keep as much normal as she could. She wasn't yet sure what she was going to tell them, though. Jordan then asked her, "Is there anything I can do for you?"

Jackie replied, "Nothing, just please hang around until my friend, Amy, gets here.

"No problem," he said. "I'll stay as long as you need me."

"I'll be fine. I have to be for the kids. Amy will be here in a few minutes," she said, "then you can go. I'm sure you have things you need to do for work, and I know you have a date tonight with Mary."

Jordan replied, "Don't worry about the date. I can postpone that, and as far as work is concerned, I can work from here. The feds didn't take my computer. Of course, I'd better check, because if they did, that would be twice in less than a week that I lost it," he said with a bit of levity trying to make Jackie smile.

"No, they aren't after you or your computer," she said, then continued, "you are, too, going on your date tonight. What's it been, two years since your last date?" She questioned him.

"Something like that," he replied. "The last one was a horror story. It's the last time I'll ever use one of those dating sites. She was a real beauty, and I don't mean her looks, either. After two dates she was ready to move in. I had to put a stop to that, and it wasn't easy getting rid of her. She was like removing chewing gum from the tread of your running shoe. It was almost like *Fatal Attraction*. Thank God I didn't have a pet bunny."

Finally, that made Jackie laugh. She said, "You always find a way to make me laugh when I need to. You are a good brother. Every sister should have a Jordan for a big brother."

Just then, Jackie's cell phone rang. She looked at the caller ID, and it read 'Granatelli's Funeral Home'. "I better take this, Jordan," she said. "It's Granatelli's."

"Sure, go ahead," he said wondering what they wanted. He could hear a little of the conversation. It seemed to revolve around the payment for their father's wake, funeral, and burial. Jordan knew that Jackie had paid them on Saturday morning before they left for the funeral service, and he suspected she paid them out of Thomas's account.

He heard her say, "I'll check into it and get back to you as soon as I can." She then signed off with a weak and trembling voice.

Jackie was in shock. She crumbled, but Jordan caught her. He tried to get her to move back into the house where it would be more comfortable and out of the neighbors' sight. Once inside, she told Jordan, "Granatelli's book-keeper just told me that our check bounced. I don't understand it. Dad had plenty of money in that account."

Jordan interjected, "Was it the account that you had through Richard's brokerage?"

All of a sudden it dawned on Jackie just how deep the problem with Richard could be. She confessed, "Yes, I paid them from dad's account that Richard managed."

"We're going to have to get a handle on just how bad this is, and quickly," he said.

"I'll call our lawyer's office and see if they can tell me anything," she offered. She knew that Rachel, the lawyer who was just there with them, would not be back at the office yet, so she decided to wait a few minutes to call. She also knew that the legal ramifications could get a bit tricky since the firm was handling Richard's defense. She wasn't sure if they would handle her personal legal needs, as well. Jackie was already thinking that divorce was in her future, but she would reserve judgment on that until she had a chance to talk with Richard and get his side of the story.

Amy Stackhouse was Jackie's best friend among a group of women that played tennis and Mahjongg together, was in the same wine tasting book club, and belonged to the same country club. She figured if any one of them could keep her sudden misfortune a secret, it would be Amy. However, she knew that it would only be a matter of time before everyone in her social circle would find out. She realized that most of those millennial-aged women were as shallow as a parking lot puddle. They lived for gossip about one another. Most of them already had cosmetic procedures to either enlarge their breasts, liposuction their midriff flab, and/or boost their sagging derrieres. They were as artificial as the turf on the Middleboro football field. She also knew that when she fell in social status, she would be cut out of the group like a cancerous tumor, but without the courtesy of anesthesia.

Jackie couldn't let that bother her now. She knew full well that that life was behind her, and she honestly felt that she wouldn't miss it. Her biggest concerns now were how this life detour would affect her kids and how she was going to live if all of her family's finances were in ruins.

Amy arrived at the front door, bolted in without knocking, and ran to Jackie bypassing Jordan like he was a house plant. It didn't bother him, but he worried how much support and comfort this supposed friend would be able to provide for his sister. He knew that ultimately it was Jackie's decision who she confided in and sought comfort from, but he couldn't help being concerned. Finally, Amy noticed Jordan and acknowledged his presence. Jordan went out of his way to be engaging toward Amy and thanked her for coming. He just wondered if her main purpose for being there was to find out as much information from Jackie as she could so she could report back to her witch's coven.

Before Jordan left, he asked if he could have a minute with Jackie in private. He put his arm around her shoulder and cautioned her not to be very forthcoming with any information to Amy. He told her, "You don't know what will happen next. You don't even know for sure what exactly has happened. Therefore, I suggest you keep anything you think you may know to yourself. If you feel the need to talk to someone, I'm always available, no matter what else is going on in my life, and if you need to talk to another woman, Aunt Pat is a great sounding board. She may belong to a different generation, but she's very astute and worldly. She'd be a good listener."

Jackie thanked him for coming and for his advice. She told Jordan that she would keep all of what happened about Richard and his work issue as confidential as possible. She then suggested he concentrate on his work since he likely had a column due. She then told him to have a nice time on his date, and that she thought Mary was going to be excellent company for him. She concluded with, "I hope it works out for you with Mary because you deserve to be happy in life. You're a good man." Then true to her sisterly nature she said, "Of course I want to hear all about it, okay?"

He laughed, then thanked her for the kind words, told her that he would call her later to see how she was doing, but left with a heavy heart. He thought about calling Mary to cancel their date, but he didn't want to begin their relationship on a bad note even though he figured she would understand.

Jordan went home to work on his next column, which was on deadline. He was distracted, to say the least, but being the consummate professional, he plowed through it. He was writing on autopilot, which he hated doing, but with all that was on his mind, he realized that it would be as good as he could do. He struggled to concentrate, but he was able to bang out 800 words in a couple of hours. That left him enough time to check on Jackie before she had to get her kids after school and for him to get ready for his date.

When he called Jackie, Amy was still there, which surprised Jordan. He had figured that she would do a hit-and-run visit when she found out that Jackie wasn't forthcoming with any juicy information. Perhaps, he thought, he wrongly judged Amy. Once Jordan found out that Amy was there, he asked Jackie, "Can you talk without Amy hearing?"

Jackie answered, "Yes." Then moved into another room after excusing herself.

"What's going on? Have you had a chance to contact the lawyer's office? Any more information on Richard?" Jordan rattled off three questions quickly.

"Here's what I found out," she began. "That lawyer, who was here, Rachel, let me know that the FBI arrested Richard because a client brought them enough suspicious evidence that he was running a Ponzi scheme. The FBI must be pretty sure it's solid evidence because they arrested him. Besides, it sure looks like he's guilty because he was arrested at the airport trying to leave the country, and he was indeed leaving with his secretary. I'm not sure if she's involved in his illegal activity, or if it was just romantic. Either way, I can't worry about her. I have enough to worry about on my own."

"Please tell me that you were able to find all of that out without your friend hearing it," Jordan asked indirectly.

"Yes, I took the call in the den and closed the door," she said. "I told Amy it was nothing I could talk about because of what the FBI said. I know that's not quite true, but I don't need it blabbed all over the country club, although they'll find out soon enough because some of them are his clients."

"Yes, I'm sure they will," he suggested. "Nothing you can do about it, but you will soon find out who, if any, are your true friends."

"I guess so, but I'm not counting on any of them, with the possible exception of Amy," she said in a whisper.

"I'm sorry beyond words," Jordan said. "I know you have to get back to Amy, but anything on your finances and dad's?"

"Rachel told me that it looks like Richard had siphoned off almost all of our assets and most of his clients' money, as well, and put it in an off-shore account, which, of course, is untouchable," she said.

"Untouchable, but not lost," Jordan said. "Hopefully, that means Richard can get to it and return it to the rightful account holders."

"That may take a while unless he pleads out for a reduced sentence and promises to make restitution," she said.

"Well, we can only hope, because he has pretty much ruined both of us," Jordan said.

"I know, and I'm sorry Jordan," she said fighting back tears.

"Hey, hold it together. I should not have said that, I'm the one who should be sorry," he said. "Mom and Dad taught us to fight our way through tough times like these, and we will. It may take time, or who knows, they may be able to work some magic up there and fix this mess."

"We'll go with that, for now," she said, "but I'm not hopeful."

"I know you have to go, but what have you decided about seeing Richard?" Jordan inquired.

"He shouldn't hold his breath waiting for me to contact him," she said. "I heard from Rachel that he will be arraigned sometime soon, but they are not expecting him to be given a bail arrangement due to his flight risk. Of course, they could just confiscate his passport. That's up to his lawyer to fight, but even if he does get bail, I'm sure it will be very high, and what's he going to use as collateral? This house is mortgaged to the hilt. He's better off spending his days in jail because he's not coming back here."

"Enough said on that topic, I guess," Jordan sheepishly offered. "I understand where you're coming from, and I don't blame you."

Jackie then concluded the phone call by saying, "Jordan, we will, indeed, get through this together. Now, please put this out of your mind, if you can, at least for tonight, and have a wonderful time with Mary. Remember, you owe me a call later tonight, no matter what time it is. I'm sure I'll be up."

"OK, I'll call when my date is finished," he said. "By the way, do you want me to come over afterward and spend the night?" He offered.

"No," she said, "Go home, I'll be fine."

They agreed to end the call, and that Jordan would check in with her later in the evening. At that point,

Jackie re-emerged and apologize to Amy for taking so long on the phone with Jordan. She told Amy that they were mostly talking about Jordan's date that night, which again was a little white lie, but she didn't want to offer much about the details of her situation. Finally, it was time for Jackie to get Richie and Amanda at school, so she walked Amy out and said "good-bye".

Jordan knew he still had some time before he was supposed to be at Mary's house, so he decided to get ready early, then see if he could track down Nick to talk with him about what had occurred in Jordan's life during the last few hours. He texted Nick before he went into the bathroom to shave and shower. Nick texted back that he was always available to see him, so they decided to meet at the park on Nick's bench.

Fortunately for Jordan, traffic was relatively light, so he made it to the park quickly. Once there, he spotted Nick and noticed that for some unexplained reason, they were both dressed very similarly. Nick had on a different shirt and trousers from when Jordan had seen him in the morning. Jordan thought that was a bit odd, but he didn't question it. He did, however, remark that they were dressed alike. Both had on similar olive green colored polo shirts and khaki slacks. Their shoes were different, though. Nick had on a pair of stylish brown Salvatore Ferragamo cap-toe oxfords while Jordan had on tan Dockers.

Jordan inquired, "I know why I'm all decked out, but what's your story, Nick?"

"You're not the only one with a date, tonight, Jordy," Nick answered.

Jordan was blown away. "You old son of a gun," he said. "All right for you. Where are you going?"

"Oh, I'm kidding you, Jordy. My *date* is quite platonic. I'm meeting a lady friend of mine. It's not a date in the truest sense of the word. We aren't romantically involved, just friends. We're both alone, so we meet here once a week for an early dinner. You know how it is with old people. We eat dinner at four in the afternoon, get the early bird special, go home, and are in bed by eight. I'm joking, again, we're not that bad," he said with a laugh.

"No matter, I think that's great that you get to spend some quality time with someone you enjoy being with," Jordan said.

"I've known Marjorie, that's her name, since I moved down here in the early 1990s. We met at one of those get-togethers for residents at our condo complex. We hit it off immediately as friends, and for whatever reason, it never materialized romantically, which is fine. I think it's because we're too much alike. We talk about everything, well, almost everything. One day you'll find out more about me than even she knows, or for that matter, anyone else knows. But, that'll have to wait, Jordy. Now, what's the reason that you wanted to see me?"

Jordan didn't know how to take what he just heard, but he was wise enough to let it lay rather than press Nick about something he wasn't ready to share. He then began to tell Nick about the events that unfolded after he left him earlier that morning. Nick listened intently without showing much emotion, as Jordan poured his heart out about how sad he felt for his sister. He also mentioned to Nick that he had mixed emotions about his date with Mary because his mind was preoccupied.

Nick formulated his comments carefully. He began, "First off, from what you've told me, your sister is fine at home tonight with her kids. Second, she encouraged you to go on your date with Mary. Third, if you stayed with her, you couldn't do anything to change the circumstances. Fourth, your date with Mary will serve to distract you from your family's unpleasant situation, at least temporarily. Finally, I'm sure Mary is looking forward to seeing you, so why disappoint her? Besides, tomorrow is another day, and sometimes things look better in the morning."

"Thanks for the sage advice," Jordan said. "I guess you are correct. It's just that I feel guilty being on a date when my sister's world is collapsing around her."

"There will be time enough to help her repair the damage," Nick offered. "I know you both have been through a lot lately, but better days are coming."

"I hope you are right, Nick," Jordan said.

"Here's how I look at it, Jordy," Nick began, "life is full of ups and downs. It's usually not as bad as it originally seems when you are going through one of those down periods. Conversely, it's usually not as great as it initially seems when you're at a high point, either. One other thought, your true personality comes to the forefront during times of crisis or adversity. So, what's it going to be, crumble under the strain of it all, or rise and meet the challenge? You're a family, a good one at that. Like it or not, you're the big brother. Your sister needs you now, but you don't have to do it alone, just be there to lead or support, as need be. Together you and Jackie will figure out what to do. Your parents taught you well, so make them proud. I know you will."

Jordan knew that once again he had been given a pep talk that he sorely needed. "Thanks, Nick," he said. "I knew I could count on you to point me in the right direction. You just turned a blue Monday afternoon into a much rosier picture of hope."

Nick replied, "I'm sure I didn't tell you anything that you didn't already know. You just needed to be reminded."

Jordan noticed a well-dressed elderly woman approaching from the coffee house side of the park and correctly assumed it to be Marjorie. He immediately bounded to his feet and offered, "You must be Nick's friend, Marjorie. It's a pleasure to meet you."

"Friend?" She asked. "To this old codger? 'Friend' is too strong a word. After twenty-five years he's barely moved up to acquaintance status." Then she and Nick burst into laughter.

Nick, who by now had risen, said, "See, that's why I let her hang around with me. She's almost as sharp as I am." They both laughed again.

Of course, Marjorie had to have the last word and commented, "You're about as sharp as a bowling ball." By now Jordan had gotten the lay of the land with the two senior citizens. They were more like an old married couple than either one of them knew; and, they obviously enjoyed each other's company very much. Both had a good sense of humor and razor-sharp wit. He knew that they were headed for a fun evening and could easily see why Nick appreciated her company.

"So, where are you going this evening for dinner?" He asked.

Nick spoke up, "I thought we would try your friend's place, Kilarney's Pub. Marjorie has never been there, and I thought she'd enjoy the food."

"That's where Mary and I are going," Jordan said.

"Yeah, I know, but we'll likely be gone before you get there," came Nick's reply. "However, if we're still there, please swing by our table to see us."

"Sure, we'll do that, if you're still there," said Jordan.

Marjorie then took hold of Nick's left arm, since Nick was holding his cane in his right hand and using it to support his bad leg. They then walked arm in arm to Nick's car which was parked just down the street from the hospice center. Jordan watched them for a while and suddenly realized that Nick must live in the Middleboro Senior Living Community. It was a very posh gated community with independent living condos, assisted living apartments, and a nursing care facility. There was a large pond in the center of the complex and walking trails meandering throughout the well-manicured and treed property. Jordan was relieved to learn that Nick would be well cared for if his health deteriorated to the point where he needed help with daily living.

Precisely at five-thirty Jordan pulled up and parked in front of Mary's house. Her neighbor was on his front porch with his sleeveless shirt unbuttoned exposing a rather large belly which Jordan logically assumed was created by consuming too much beer. His assumption was based on the observation of the neighbor holding one beer in his hand and several more sitting on top of a plastic ice chest easily within reach. He appeared to be enjoying a super-sized sandwich between swigs of brew. Mary's neighbor then yelled to Jordan, "Hey, ya visitin' Mary?"

Jordan was taken aback, but politely answered, "Yes, I'm visiting Mary." He was smart enough to keep right on moving toward her front door in the hope of minimizing his conversation with the neighbor.

"Well, she's a nice lady," he continued. "Hope yer a nice guy."

Jordan just waved half-heartedly. He figured the neighbor was probably harmless, but he wasn't there to get into a protracted conversation on what likely would include NASCAR, hunting, fishing, or possibly the WWF. Jordan also noticed a Confederate flag hanging inside the back window of the man's rundown pick-up truck up on blocks in his driveway. He hoped the guy was the exception in Mary's neighborhood rather than the rule.

Fortunately for Jordan, Mary promptly answered the door when Jordan rang the bell. She greeted him cordially, invited him inside, but could hear her neighbor still talking to Jordan. "I see you met my neighbor, Bob," she said with a disgusted sigh.

"Well, I didn't exactly meet him," Jordan began. "He just started talking to me as I was walking up your driveway."

"He's harmless, but he's the type that no one wants to live next to, if you know what I mean?" She offered.

"I know, every neighborhood has one like him. I call them the guy who brings down the property values for everyone else," Jordan said. "Well, I didn't come here to talk about Bob. How are you doing this evening?"

"Pretty good, I guess, better now that you're here," she said.

"That wasn't a ringing endorsement," he concluded. "Is there something you want to talk about?"

"Not now, maybe later," she said. "Let's sit on the back porch since it's a nice evening. I've got some drinks out there and some light hors d'oeuvres."

"Sounds good," Jordan replied. "Shall we invite Bob?" He inquired with a sly grin.

"Only if you want to enjoy his company and not mine," came her quick reply.

"I'll stick with you," he said with a wink. "Besides, you are much better dressed. You look fantastic by the way, although Bob is sporting that much-coveted low cut look."

They both laughed. Mary then asked, "Thank you for the compliment, but how would you like to come home from a long shift and have to see that in the yard next door?"

"Well, look at the bright side," Jordan began, "he has the extra added attraction of being short and bald to go with that beer belly. Kind of reminds me of Paulie from the *Rocky* movies. You can always tell people you live next door to a Burt Young doppelganger."

She let that one go with only an eye roll and motioned Jordan toward her kitchen and out the back door to her screened porch. "This is very nice," Jordan remarked. "Do you use it much?"

"I love it out here," she confided. "The best part is that it's screened, so no bugs. The next best thing is that you-know-who can't see me when I'm out here. I keep my hedge between the yards pretty high."

"How about your neighbor on the other side?" Jordan asked.

"That's Mrs. Richardson. She lives alone." Mary said. "She's sweet, very nice to me. Sometimes I invite her here when I think she is lonely. She must be 80 by now. Not sure how much longer she's going to be able to maintain her house and yard, though."

"That's always a worry when you get too old to stay in your house," he said. "Where do you go? Senior living is expensive."

"It is, for sure, but enough of all that," Mary said, then asked, "What would you like to drink?"

"The iced tea that you have here will be perfect," Jordan replied.

"Please help yourself to the hors d'oeuvres," she suggested. "I have crackers and cheese, some veggies with sour cream and onion dip, and those are scallops wrapped with bacon."

"I think I'll try a little of everything," he said. "It looks like you went to a lot of trouble."

"No trouble, at all, Jordan," she replied, "but I wouldn't have if I didn't think you were worth it. You are a rare good guy, and I have enjoyed our time together, even though it has only been a few short rendezvouses.

"Well, thank you, I appreciate hearing that," Jordan countered. "I hope you know that I, too, have enjoyed the time we've been able to spend together."

Jordan hesitated a bit and Mary could detect something negative was coming. She said, "I sense a 'but' is coming."

"Oh, no, not a 'but' in that sense," he said. "Believe me, I find you very attractive, a ton of fun, clever, witty, and the most caring, giving person I've met in forever."

"Okay, but there was something else you wanted to say," she queried him.

"I was going to say that our date tonight almost didn't happen," he confessed.

"Why? If you don't mind me asking," she inquired.

Jordan then went into his day from the time he left Nick just before noon until he got to Mary's house. He apologized for bringing it up, but he felt it was something he would have to tell her sooner rather than later, and he didn't want her to find out from anyone else. Mary listened with her usual caring nature. After Jordan finished the saga she said, "How's your sister? You know that it would have been fine with me if we had to postpone our date, don't you?"

"Jackie's fine, or should I say, she will be in time," Jordan began. "I knew you would understand if I called to cancel, but honestly I wanted to see you tonight. Does that sound selfish?" He asked.

"I wouldn't say selfish," she said, "I would consider it more of your heart winning out over your head, and you have a wonderful heart. Also, I would consider what Nick told you. There were several reasons why you should have kept our date."

Mary then took her turn to hesitate, and Jordan noticed. He said, "Yeah, what else? I also sense that you have something on your mind."

"I didn't want to bring this up, not tonight, anyway, but it's bothering me, and perhaps if I talk about it, it'll help," she began. "I know we're just beginning our relationship, so perhaps this is breaching some guidelines for first dates."

"True, we're just in the beginning stage of our friendship," Jordan said, "but I'm here for you like you were for me when my father was dying. So, feel free to tell me anything that's bothering you, and I'll be glad to help any way I can."

"Okay, here goes," she started. "Remember the other day when we met in the park? I couldn't stay very long because I had an appointment."

"Yeah, I recall it," he answered. "Why?"

"Well, it was my annual OB-GYN wellness visit, and before you jump to any wrong conclusions, no, I'm not pregnant," she said with a smile.

"Good," Jordan replied, but with a concerned look.

"The doctor told me that there was an irregularity in my left breast. She couldn't say definitely what was there, so she wants me to go for a more detailed mammogram. That's the same breast where my mother's problems began, so as you can imagine, I'm worried."

Jordan immediately got up and spontaneously moved toward Mary and hugged her. He didn't say anything for several seconds, he just held her. She did all she could do to not cry, as she buried her face into his chest. Jordan then said, "Mary, I have to believe that this will be a good outcome for you. That said, no matter what happens, I'll be there for you."

She was barely able to get out, "thank you, Jordan, but this isn't your problem. You have enough to worry about with your own family."

"We will handle whatever comes our way together, alright?" he suggested.

"Alright," she said, this time with a stronger voice. Then she added, "As far as first dates go, this one is starting as a real downer. I guess it can only get better from here, but don't count on it, Buster, the night's young."

He laughed, then said, "I'll help you clean up these glasses and plates, and put away the food and beverages, then we should probably be heading to Kevin's restaurant."

Mary agreed, and they made short work of the clean-up. Jordan took most of the items inside from the porch, and Mary put them away. She then remembered the pie that she had baked earlier in the day and mentioned, "Jordan, please save some room for dessert and coffee, because I would like you to come back and spend some time with me this evening after dinner."

"Of course," he said. "I'd like that very much."

They left via the front door, walked down Mary's driveway where she turned to wave to Bob and wished him a "good evening". Under her breath she told Jordan to keep moving otherwise they could be there for the rest of the evening. He obliged and opened the passenger side door for her and made sure she was inside comfortably before closing it.

They arrived at Kilarney's with time to spare, found a spot a few feet from the front of the restaurant, parked, and went inside where they were instantly greeted by Kevin's wife. She seated them at one of their better tables with a view out the back of the restaurant overlooking their patio dining and the field and trees beyond that. After ordering some drinks and perusing the menu, Mary decided on the entrée garden salad with grilled salmon. Jordan figured it best to eat light, as well, so he went with a starter salad and the fish special. Of course, Kevin sent over several starters on the house, so their plan to not eat too much was evaporating quickly with all the food being sent their way.

Upon arrival, Jordan did a quick check of the restaurant but didn't see Nick and Marjorie anywhere. It didn't surprise him since Nick thought that they would likely be gone by the time Mary and Jordan got there. Later on, Jordan remembered to ask Kevin's wife if Nick had been there. He described Nick to her, but she didn't remember him. That concerned Jordan a little. He decided to check on him but asked Mary first if she minded him sending Nick a text. Mary said she didn't mind and urged Jordan to do it. He simply wrote, 'R U OK? Didn't C U at Kevin's.

At once Nick's reply came back, 'All OK. Thx for checking. C U soon.' Jordan's mind was at peace, but he wondered why Nick and Marjorie didn't make it to Kevin's. He knew it was none of his business to probe, but it also wasn't like Nick to just blow it off. He figured that he would find out when Nick was ready to tell him, or never if that's what Nick decided.

Mary and Jordan finished their entrees and explained to the server that they had other plans for dessert. Kevin was finally able to make it out of the kitchen and to their table before they departed. He thanked them for coming to his restaurant and tried to comp their bill, but Jordan wouldn't hear of it. Jordan thanked Kevin for a delicious dinner and told him that they would be back. Kevin took the time to see them to the door, hugged them both, and watched as they walked to Jordan's car.

As they walked a few feet to Jordan's car, they noticed a large man leaning against the passenger door. The guy had his head down with a hood over it. As they approached, he raised his head. Once he did, Mary's eyes grew wide with surprise and disgust. She said, "What are *you* doing here?"

"Nothing, just hanging out," came the reply.

"Well, do it somewhere else, Dan," she said. "Now, get away from the car so we can leave."

At that point, Jordan asked, "Mary, you know this guy?"

"Yes, Jordan, this is my ex-husband," she said. "He turns up from time to time like the plague."

"Yeah, Jordan, I'm like the plague," he said mocking Mary, "but tonight I'm your worst nightmare." Dan then moved away from the car and took a menacing stance in front of Jordan. Mary tried to get between them, but Jordan stuck out his right arm to prevent her from getting in the middle of what looked to be an unavoidable fight. Jordan being street smart from his days in New York knew enough to not take his eyes off Dan, which was fortuitous. As soon as Jordan had moved Mary behind him, Dan threw a roundhouse right. Jordan reacted instantly and put up his left arm to block Dan's punch. Instinctively, Jordan went on the offensive. He immediately set his feet shoulder-width apart with his left foot slightly in front of his right and countered with two rapid left jabs which split Dan's nose wide open, then followed up with a solid right cross to his jaw. Dan fell to the sidewalk in a heap. The one-sided fight was over, basically before it began. Jordan said, "Stay down, buddy, there's more of the same coming your way if you get up."

Mary was slack-jawed. Kevin came running out of his restaurant since he saw it all unfold from his front window. He said, "I called the police. They'll be right here. I'm guessing this guy didn't know that you could box. Too bad for him. Oh man, Jordan, your hands are still as fast as I remember."

At that point Mary chimed in, "So, you know how to box? Nice work. You must have been giving away 30 pounds, but I have to agree with Kevin. They are some pretty fast hands, but don't get any ideas with me," she said laughing.

The police arrived within seconds, and after getting all the eyewitness accounts of what happened, they arrested Dan, took him to the hospital for stitches and treatment for what appeared to be a broken nose and jaw, then booked him for assault and disorderly conduct. Jordan and Mary were free to go.

At the hospital emergency room, where Dan was being treated in handcuffs, Nick was also there with

Marjorie. She had experienced some chest pain which turned out to be indigestion. Naturally, at her age, a battery of tests was conducted, but fortunately, every test came back negative. It just took some time to get the results, so they were still there when Dan was brought in. Nick walked over to one of the policemen, who he naturally knew, and asked, "So, what's this guy's story, Ron?"

The cop told Nick that the perp got into a fight outside Kilarney's Pub. Nick's ears perked up, "Did you say Kilarney's?"

"Yeah, this guy harassed a nice couple on their way out of the restaurant for no reason other than the woman was his ex-wife," the cop confided to Nick.

"So, what happened to him," Nick asked, as he surveyed Dan's mangled face.

"The girl's boyfriend had some boxing experience, and he flatten him in two seconds from what we were told," said the policeman.

"Please describe this boxer to me," Nick requested.

"Oh, I'd say he was about six feet tall and about 175-180 pounds, a handsome kid with brown hair," Ron replied. "The woman he was with was petite and very pretty, blondish hair."

"Was the guy dressed sort of like me?" Nick asked.

"Yeah, as a matter of fact, he was," the cop answered. "Do you know him, Nick?"

"Was his name Jordan by chance?" Nick asked.

"As a matter of fact, it was," said Ron the cop.

"Well, I do know him, but I didn't know that he knew how to box," Nick said, then he thought to himself, 'I guess everyone has a secret life.'

"Well, it was a good thing that he did," said the cop, "because that jerk over there had him by at least 30 pounds. It's pretty embarrassing when you get beaten up by a smaller guy, especially when you don't even land a punch on the smaller guy."

"I guess so," Nick replied. "Do you mind if I talk with this fellow in private for a few minutes?"

"Be my guest," Ron replied. "We have him hand-cuffed to the bed rail, so he's not going anywhere."

Nick walked over to Marjorie and asked her if she was still feeling okay. She told him that she was. He then asked her if she would mind if he took a few minutes to talk with the injured man. Marjorie said that she would be fine until he got back. Nick then walked the 30 feet to where Dan was lying semi-propped up on an emergency room bed waiting to be seen by a doctor.

Once at Dan's bedside, Nick pulled up a chair, sat down, and began taking the bottom part of his cane apart exposing a blade that only he and Dan could see. He placed it right up against Dan's genitals. He cautioned Dan not to move or make a sound, or he would castrate him with one swipe. Dan neither moved nor said a word. He just listened.

Nick began a very deliberate, measured soliloquy. "I understand you bothered two of my friends tonight. One being your ex-wife, and the other being my very good friend. That can't happen again. Am I clear? Just nod if you understand." Dan nodded, as he was by now sweating profusely. Nick continued, "Just so we are clear, you are never to go near your ex-wife or my very good friend again. If you do, I will have you hurt in ways you cannot possibly imagine. Am I clear? Just nod again if you understand." Dan nodded, since he was afraid to speak, besides his jaw was likely broken, anyway. "Now you may think to yourself that this old man is going to die soon, and you may be right, but there are others I have instructed to take up my work, so don't cross me, if you know what's good for you. I'm giving you a one-time pass today but I could just as easily have you taken away and never heard from again. Am I clear?" Dan nodded. "One more thing, this conversation never happened. Am I clear?" Dan nodded. Then Nick left him with this parting thought, "Just for the record, you're pretty messed up, and you deserved that and more, but I'm telling you what you got tonight will be nothing compared to what will happen to you if you go near Mary or Jordan, again; and for your sake, I hope the doctor is better at fixing you up than you are at fighting."

When he was finished talking with Dan, Nick replaced the bottom part of his cane covering the blade that he had used to threaten Dan, then he leveraged the cane to help himself off the chair. He calmly walked back to Marjorie passing Ron, the policeman, on the way, shaking his hand as he passed. Ron felt something in his palm after the handshake. When he looked surreptitiously into his hand, he saw a $20 bill neatly folded. The cop looked over his shoulder at Nick, who never turned around, but just tipped his cap and kept moving toward Marjorie. He helped her up, and they both left.

In the meantime, Dan just watched the interaction between Nick and the cop, Nick and Marjorie, and tried to get his heart to stop pounding. He didn't know quite what to make of his one-sided conversation with Nick, but he was sure that would be the last time he would bother either Mary or Jordan. Then, almost reflexively, he looked down at his groin and cringed.

Mary and Jordan were back at Mary's house, but neither felt much like dessert. Their ride only took ten minutes, but it seemed longer due to several awkward minutes of silence. Mary had apologized for her ex-husband's behavior. Jordan told her that it wasn't her fault and that she had nothing to apologize for. It didn't make Mary feel any better because she was very embarrassed by Dan's actions and her past relationship with him. Finally, Jordan said with a smile, "Well, as far as unusual first dates go, this one ranks at the top of my list. How about yours?"

Mary smiled, then said, "Not even in my top ten." They both burst out laughing, then she said, "How about a cup of coffee. I have regular and decaf if you are worried about it keeping you awake."

"I'll have whichever you're having," he replied, "and of course, I'll have a small piece of that pie you baked, even if I'm not hungry, but you have to promise to run with me tomorrow morning to work off the calories. What kind did you make?"

"I made an apple pie," she replied. "I got the recipe from my favorite online source, *America's Test Kitchen*. I hope you like it, and yes, of course, I'll gladly run with you in the morning. I guess you have to get your road work in before your next title defense."

They were again both laughing now, and the tension of Jordan's fight with Dan had all but passed. The evening was settling into more of a typical first date. Mary suggested that they take their coffee and pie into her living room where they could watch a movie. Jordan thought that was a good idea. He was ready to sit and relax for a couple of hours before driving home and checking in with Jackie, which he did about ten-thirty. He told her most of the pertinent details of his first date with Mary, leaving out the fisticuffs, but including the long kiss good night.

CHAPTER 9
Chancers and Cheats

The rest of the week was a blur for Jordan. He did meet Mary on Tuesday morning for the run that they had planned and enjoyed breakfast with her afterward. He was also able to see Nick later that morning in the park, but could only spend enough time with him to find out that Marjorie's ailment was the reason they didn't make it to Kilarney's for dinner the prior evening. Of course, Nick brought up Jordan's fight with Dan, but Jordan downplayed it. Nick commented that he was very happy with the outcome and that he was surprised that Jordan's boxing prowess hadn't come up when they were discussing boxing the previous week. Again, Jordan downplayed it, somewhat embarrassed by the brutal nature of the incident. Jordan did confide to Nick that he had taken a few boxing lessons while away at college and worked part-time to earn some extra money as a sparring partner at the local boxing club in his college town. Nick could tell that it was a part of Jordan's life that he wasn't particularly proud of, so he let the discussion drop after adding that he felt there would be no further problems from Dan. Jordan took it to mean that his pugilistic acumen was the reason, and Nick let him think so.

Jordan spent as much time as he had available with Jackie for the rest of the week. When she left her gated community Jordan was with her to help ward off the local press who wanted to interview her to get her side of the story, and of course, to see if they could find out if she was involved in any way, or get a comment about the affair her husband was having with his secretary. Jordan made sure that no one, especially the reporters from his paper, got near her. However, he was astute enough to realize that in Middleboro, a relatively small city, the news would eventually leak out, and when it did, it wouldn't be pleasant for his sister.

Between spending as much time as possible with Jackie and working on his columns Jordan had no time to see Nick and continue hearing his story. Also, he had next to no time to see Mary, which troubled him. He did take the time to text both every day to see how they were doing. He was especially concerned about Mary and how she was handling her possible cancer diagnosis. Fortunately, by Friday some of the demands on Jordan's time had lessened, so he made plans with Mary for another morning run. He was also going with her to her follow-up screening later that morning.

Throughout the week Jackie was able to get more and more information from her lawyer regarding the case against Richard. He was arraigned in federal district court in Richmond and given a two million dollar bail. Unfortunately for him, he was unable to post that amount, since all of his assets were frozen. Therefore, he was remanded to the low security federal correctional institution in Petersburg. As it turned out, Richard was indeed running a Ponzi scheme whereby he was using new customer's investments to show profits in older more established accounts. He not only had taken the money from his family and friends but from several businesses in Middleboro. More than one pension fund had also been defrauded, and much of those funds were now in off-shore bank accounts where the federal government couldn't get them. Jackie and Jordan traveled to Richmond for the hearing, but she was unwilling to see Richard afterward. It would take her some time to be able to talk with him and several weeks for all of the legal matters to unfold.

By Friday morning Jackie's life was beginning to settle into the so-called 'new normal'. She was starting to get used to life without Richard. Being the very organized, efficient person that she was, she was taking care of everything around the house by herself, or with Jordan's help. Knowing that her family's income was now non-existent, she had already canceled her lawn maintenance contract, laid off the housekeeper who came once a week to clean and take care of her laundry. Also, she had sent her resume to several law offices in Middleboro and the surrounding towns. She and Jordan had already mowed her lawn and edged around the trees, driveway, and sidewalk. Fortunately, Jordan had all the equipment necessary to do the work. Further, Jackie had contacted a real estate agent friend to see what their property might be worth.

Jordan, for his part, was very supportive. He made sure that he was there for lunch and dinner every afternoon and evening, often bringing in takeout from one of the local restaurants. He provided a supportive demeanor, making suggestions when he sensed Jackie might need steering in the right direction or validation of the feelings she had at a particular moment. He was also very good with helping her work through the sense of betrayal by Richard, although he was quick to point out that while their respective situations were alike, they were different as well since Kathryn left him for another woman.

During their increased time together Jordan took the opportunity to bounce a few ideas off Jackie concerning Kathryn. They discussed the fact that Jordan wanted no part of Kathryn moving back to Middleboro, but of course, he couldn't tell her that she could not re-locate there. He could, however, tell her that she couldn't move in with him. He just wanted a legitimate reason that didn't sound spiteful. After a considerably long brainstorming session one afternoon, Jackie and Jordan came to a decision that would effectively solve two problems with one masterstroke of genius.

Jordan had mentioned to Jackie that his talks with Nick had allowed him to gain a new perspective on problem-solving. He explained that they needed to lay out all of their options for the problems they were facing. In the end, they decided on a plan that they felt would solve most, if not all, of their collective problems.

Jackie would put her house up for sale as soon as she was legally allowed to do so. She would likely have to split any equity with Richard, but it wouldn't be much after the real estate agent's commission and county sale and transfer tax obligations, not to mention the large mortgage on the property.

Additionally, hanging over both their heads was their father's house and the expenses (property taxes, utilities, and insurance) that went along with that property. Therefore, they decided that they would sell that house, as well, taking the profit from it to have some working capital. Originally, Jordan suggested that Jackie, Richie, and Amanda should move into Thomas' house, but Jackie felt that that option would not be fair to Jordan, since he had an equal share in the house, and she couldn't afford to buy him out, not that he had proposed it. Besides, they ultimately decided that it was a relatively old house with its share of problems and that they could both use the influx of cash from that sale.

That left them with an option that, while not perfect, was certainly workable and in another way was a problem solver for Jordan. They decided that Jackie, Richie, and Amanda would move in with Jordan, at least for the short term, but likely that arrangement would last for the summer months. The beauty of that arrangement was that now there was no room for Kathryn, allowing Jordan a very viable reason for her not to be able to stay with him without him having to outright tell her that he didn't want her moving in, even if it was the last thing he needed now that he was seeing Mary.

Friday morning's run for Mary and Jordan was a fun time despite the looming doctor's appointment and mammogram for Mary. Both were excited about seeing each other again, getting a chance to run together, and having a perfect day in which to jog around the beautiful Parc de Gisele. They agreed to run for one hour or six miles, whichever came first, then stop for a quick breakfast at Perk Place before going back to their homes to clean up before Mary's eleven o'clock appointment. Jordan had arranged the tight schedule to include a quick stop to see Nick if he would be in the park. He would still have time to meet Mary at her doctor's office by eleven.

The run went perfectly. Both were feeling well on a glorious day. They each hit their stride immediately and cruised the six miles in slightly over fifty minutes. Breakfast was a quick bagel and tea for Mary while Jordan enjoyed oatmeal and coffee. Afterward, they hugged goodbye with Mary holding on for an extra few seconds. Jordan, knowing that she was apprehensive about her imminent doctor's appointment and scan, gave her a passionate kiss and then said with a laugh to lighten the mood, "That should hold you until I see you at eleven."

She came back with, "That'll hold me 'til ten, what about the next hour?"

Jordan obliged her with another kiss of equal length and passion. She hugged him again holding on for a long time with her head resting comfortably on his chest. Finally, she disengaged from their hug and said, "As much as I'd like to stay here with you all day, I best be on my way." Then she added, "Jordan, you know that you don't have to go with me to my appointment. I know you have other things on your mind with Jackie and her situation."

"I've got it covered," he said. Then he added, "Now get going and please drive carefully. We don't need any more excitement in our lives."

"No, we don't. I'll be careful, I promise," she replied, then she jogged the few hundred feet to her car.

>>>   <<<

Jordan gathered up the breakfast remnants and deposited them into the trash receptacle before jogging over to see Nick. His prime motivation was to see if Nick was available to meet with him again either over the weekend or early next week. Nick joked with him, "I'm at your disposal." He then inquired, "How's your sister doing?"

"She's doing better," Jordan said. "I think she's beginning to recover from that figurative gut punch, but it'll take time, as I'm sure you know."

"I do know," Nick began. "Everyone has hardships and heartaches that they must overcome in life. Of course, some are worse than others. Now, is there anything I can do for either of you? I hope you know that you can come to me for anything you need and that offer extends to Jackie, as well. I don't want to be presumptuous, but how are you two doing financially?"

Jordan then took a position on the bench next to Nick and began to fill him in on the plan that he and Jackie had come up with. Nick listened without speaking for a few minutes. Once Jordan had finished discussing the plan regarding the sale of both houses and Jackie and her kids moving in with Jordan temporarily, Nick reached out and put his hand on Jordan's shoulder and said, "I'm proud of you, young man. You have passed a graduate-level course in life's problem solving with an A-plus. Just remember, there will be other tests that come your way, but you will learn from each one, and that should help you solve the subsequent ones."

Jordan didn't know what to say initially, but eventually got out, "Thanks, Nick, but honestly you get the credit. You taught me to believe in myself and rely on my parents' teachings, along with a refresher course in problem-solving 101."

"I didn't tell you anything that you didn't already know," Nick said.

"Perhaps, but I want you to know that I appreciate you taking the time to give me some ideas rather than just telling me what to do," Jordan replied.

"Call it a modern-day example of that adage about giving a person a fish and feeding them for a day as opposed to teaching them how to fish and feeding them for a lifetime," Nick offered, "but again your parents get the credit. I just reminded you of a methodology you already knew." Nick then adroitly moved off that subject and said, "Speaking of methodologies, have you been able to come up with any ideas or a plan for your book?"

"Honestly, I haven't had much time to think about it this past week," Jordan began, "but I would like to get back to interviewing you. So, can we start back up tomorrow?"

"Certainly," Nick said. "What time suits you?"

"How about nine, and I'll get the coffee," Jordan stated.

"Sounds good," Nick said. "Now you better get going if you are going to meet Mary for that appointment."

Jordan was dumbfounded, "How do you know about that?"

"I'll let you in on one of my secrets," Nick said. "I can read lips, but I didn't have to be a lip reader to know that I saw two people in love with those two long kisses."

Jordan turned a slight shade of red but managed to skip over the comment about the kissing, then replied, "Nick, that must be thirty yards from here to the coffee shop."

"What can I say, I still have perfect long-range vision," Nick confided, "and my hearing is still good, as well."

"The more I find out about you, the more I realize that you're a guy no one should get on the wrong side of," Jordan said.

"I'm just a harmless old man, Jordy," Nick contended, then he laughed a laugh that told Jordan not to believe it.

Nick and Jordan said their goodbyes and reaffirmed that they would see each other in the morning. Jordan jogged to his car and hustled home to shower and get ready to meet Mary. He had enough time but wanted to be five minutes early (by Nick's standard), so as not to be late.

Mary was outside the Middleboro Women's Clinic waiting for Jordan when he arrived, but Jordan was early, as well. She explained that her anxiety made her get there as early as possible in the hope of getting the test and results sooner rather than later. Jordan understood and walked her inside opening the door for her, then quickly finding two empty chairs in the waiting room while Mary checked in at the reception desk. After seeing the receptionist, Mary sat next to Jordan and began filling out the requisite paperwork, which was the same information that she had filled out the previous week. While waiting, Mary told Jordan that her doctor was someone she had worked with many years ago when she was employed as a registered nurse at the Middleboro Medical Center. She also mentioned to him that Doctor Lauren Sapperstein was top in her field, and if worse came to worst, Dr. Sapperstein would be doing her surgery.

Jordan cautioned her, "Let's not jump to any conclusions. Let's think positively."

"Okay, but I'm trying to think ahead," she replied, "and I did say 'if'," she reminded him.

Jordan knew enough not to escalate the debate any further, so he just offered, "You're right. We'll handle whatever comes along."

At that point, a staff member called Mary's name. She rose from her chair to go for her test, and as she did, Jordan reached out for her hand, squeezed it, and whispered, "Good luck."

She smiled at him, then disappeared behind the door that led to the examination and scanning areas. The women's clinic was a full-service operation offering a variety of tests and examinations under one roof. Mary had explained to Jordan that she would have an answer when she left there that day since they had a radiologist on staff to read her scan.

For his part, Jordan sat in the waiting room fidgeting for the forty-five minutes it took for Mary to re-emerge. He was almost as nervous as Mary and recalled a saying that his father had used to describe himself when Jordan and Jackie were born. He'd say "I was as nervous as a long-tailed cat in a room full of rocking chairs".

When Mary opened the door and came back into the waiting room she and Jordan locked eyes. Jordan could tell immediately that Mary had gotten a good report because she was beaming with a beautiful smile and flashed him a 'thumbs-up' sign. He immediately got up and met her with a big hug. The rest of the women in the waiting room didn't know what to make of it. Some probably thought Mary was pregnant because she looked younger than her mid-40s.

Mary checked out quickly, and they both went for a long lunch where they could talk, and Mary could relay to Jordan what the doctor and radiologist had told her. In the final analysis, she was given several important pieces of information. First, the scans today are so good that they often pick up abnormalities that weren't seen previously. Second, not all of those abnormalities are problematic. Third, and most important to Mary, no tumor was present, but she was to continue with her annual screenings, and of course, if she detected any change, or felt any lumps, then she should contact Dr. Sapperstein immediately.

Jordan made it back to Jackie's house in plenty of time to finish a column he had originally started the day before. He was on deadline, so he knew he could work on it while Jackie got her kids from school. Once the article was complete, Jordan began working on dinner. He and Jackie had decided to grill some burgers, which were easy for Jordan to get started since he had made them for himself many times at his home. While they were cooking on the grill, he started chopping lettuce for a salad. Jackie had made potato salad the night before, so that would fill out the menu.

When they got home, Amanda and Richie ran through the house to find Jordan. They competed to tell him all that had happened at school that day. Amanda would start by telling him something that had happened in Mrs. Rutherford's class, and when she stopped to take a breath, Richie would jump in to tell Jordan what had happened on the playground at recess. The tag team discourse made Jordan wonder if he and Jackie had done that to their parents thirty-five years before.

Jackie finally put an end to the one-upmanship of elementary school Friday highlights by suggesting that Amanda and Richie needed to change out of their school clothes before dinner, which was almost ready. They quickly returned, attired in their play clothes, and were at the dinner table as the food arrived. Since the kids loved hamburgers and potato salad, they made short work of those culinary delights and even ate enough of their salad to make Jackie happy. Jordan had promised to play ball with Richie after dinner, so Jackie suggested that she would take care of the clean-up while the boys went out to play. Amanda wasn't interested in ball playing, so she plinked away on her piano. As she did, Jackie wondered how Amanda would adapt to not being able to have her piano after they moved into Jordan's house.

Jordan hung around for an hour or so after the kids went to bed so he and Jackie could have some adult time in case she wanted to talk about anything. She told him that she had called their Aunt Pat earlier in the day to let her know about her situation, and of course, Aunt Pat felt awful for Jackie. Jackie then told Jordan that she had heard from her friend, Amy, a couple of times since Monday, but none of her other so-called friends. Jordan was neither surprised, nor amused. Finally, she got around to asking about Mary. Jordan gave her the information that Mary had shared with him. Jackie was happy for both, especially Mary. Without much more to talk about, Jordan figured it was time to go home and draft the reply letter to Kathryn that he had been putting off for more than a week. He said 'good night' to Jackie and explained that the rest of his evening would be spent on the letter. She understood and hugged him.

The much anticipated day when Jordan would hear the details of Nick's favorite games had finally arrived. He had gotten to the park early with his recorder and note pad after a quick stop at Perk Place to pick up two coffees and a couple of bagels just in case Nick was hungry. Right at five to nine, Nick strolled up to Jordan, who was already sitting on Nick's bench. Jordan jumped to his feet when Nick arrived and said, "Top o' the morn to you, Nick."

"Tis a beautiful day," Nick replied with his best imitation of an Irish accent causing both to laugh.

After they got settled on the bench and indulged in the coffee and bagels, Jordan began. "So, we were to the first game, Thursday."

Nick picked right up and began, "The game was scheduled for seven o'clock, but had to be pushed back a few minutes due to both teams needing some extra time to get to the James Everson gym since most of the guys on both teams had a baseball game or track practice. The gym was at capacity with standing room everywhere spectators could fit without affecting play. Of course, there was still room for the Jesters' cheerleaders, who entertained at the breaks and halftime."

"Did that cause any problem for your team," Jordan inquired.

"The delayed start or the cheerleaders?" Nick asked.

"The delayed start," Jordan reiterated.

"No problem, except it cut short the Hammer's pre-game instructions," Nick replied. "He had five minutes to let our boys know that he wanted them to start the game in a 1-2-2 zone defense with high pressure on Bigby, their star guard. When we had the ball, he wanted to run the motion offense that they had practiced. He reminded the boys to play hard and to not take the Jesters for granted."

Nick continued, "Both teams had their pre-game warm-ups cut a little short. Instead of the usual fifteen minutes to run lay-up drills and shoot around, they only had five minutes. It should not have been a big deal for either team, because these guys were very loose and ready. If anything it may have helped conserve their energy since most of them were coming from another game or practice."

Jordan was getting antsy with all the build-up and preliminaries, but he kept his question short, "So, how did the game start?"

Nick began, "Ricky Calvino easily out-jumped the taller Jerry Wall. We had a play set-up off the jump ball where Ricky tapped it to Dino. Paul had no responsibility on the tap other than to take off for our basket. Dino got the ball and flipped it to Bags who hit Paul in stride for an easy lay-up. That was as easy as it would be all night."

"Why? What happened?" Jordan quizzed Nick.

"Well, I won't go into a play-by-play, mainly because I don't recall that much detail. What I do recall is that the first quarter ended at 14-all, and by the half, we were behind by four, 30-26. We were getting beat down low by Bartolo and Wall. Our zone had too many holes. The Hammer made substitutions and switched defenses. First, to a 1-1-3 zone, then a 2-3 zone, then man-to-man; but nothing was working near the basket. The only bright spot was that Paul was absolutely embarrassing their all-star guard, Bigby. He had picked Bigby's pocket for three steals and blocked two of his shots. He, also, had him in foul trouble with three by the half. The best part was that Paul had 16 points and was holding us in the game."

"Wow! How was that possible?" Jordan asked.

"I found out after the game from Willie that Ted Bigby liked his alcohol, mostly beer," Nick began. "Since the Jester basketball season had concluded three weeks prior, Bigby had gained a few pounds. So, his usual quickness and jump shot were gone, or at the very least, they had taken the night off. At any rate, Paul was blowing past him like Bigby's feet were in wet cement, and when Paul took his jump shot, Bigby couldn't elevate to defend it. Paulie even posted him up a time or two and scored with a fade-away jumper the likes of which would have made Earl "the Pearl" Monroe smile."

"So, didn't the Jesters coach make an adjustment?" Jordan asked.

"He did at the half," Nick replied. "Starting the third quarter, he put the other guard on Paul, but it didn't matter. He couldn't stay with Paul, either."

"Okay, so your team is four down at the half," Jordan said as a lead-in to a question. "What did the Hammer tell them in the locker room?"

"He told them that they were in good shape and not to worry." Nick relayed to Jordan. "The Hammer told me later that he said that to keep them from tanking. He knew that the only thing holding them in the game was Paul's play. The motion offense wasn't working because the Jesters' defense was sagging down low instead of playing an aggressive man-to-man, as he expected. They were effectively stopping us on the baseline. So, he modified it by having our best shooters fake to the basket and pop back outside for open jump shots."

"Did that strategy work?" Jordan asked.

"In a word, 'no'," Nick answered. "It was just a bad shooting night for our boys."

"So, your team lost the game!" Jordan said horrified.

"I didn't say that," Nick answered, "but I don't want to give away the second half, just yet."

"Sorry, please continue," Jordan said.

"We played from behind the entire second half," Nick got underway. "I believe we were still behind by four, or maybe it was even five or six, after three quarters. Our big three scorers were putting up enough bricks to build a school. It was just one of those off nights, I guess. Mike had made several substitutions throughout the first three quarters trying to get someone on the backline to stop Wall and Bartolo, but all the backline subs (DiGiacomo, Simonetti, and Shockley) were able to accomplish was to foul and put their big guys on the free-throw line."

"This isn't sounding too good for your team," Jordan interjected.

"No, not good at all," Nick affirmed. "Honestly, I thought our guys were going to be dead on arrival at the final buzzer. They were hustling, but their shots weren't falling, except for Paul's."

"So, what did the Hammer do," Jordan asked.

"With about four minutes to go," Nick said, "Mike called a timeout and told them that it was time to feed Paul on every offensive possession. He switched Bags to the point and Paul to shooting guard and instructed our guys to look for opportunities to set screens for Paul around the foul line."

"Did that work?" Jordan inquired.

"Mostly," Nick answered. "The best part was that they started to overplay and double team Paul. So, the uncovered guy was getting an open look and fortunately, two or three of those open shots fell. Ricky even got a tip-in over Wall and Bartolo. We had battled back to within two points, 50-48, with less than a minute to play, and we had the ball. Mike called a play that had our shooter running a huge circle route off a double screen and ending up with an open look just to the right of the foul line. Paul was the shooter and hit the shot to tie the game with less than forty seconds to go."

"This is getting exciting. I wish I was there to witness it firsthand," Jordan said. "So what happened next?"

"They brought the ball up, and we picked them up defensively at mid-court." Nick began. "Unfortunately, there was another defensive lapse down low, and Bartolo scored an easy lay-up with about twenty seconds left. So, again we're down two. We hurried the ball up the court, and Paul again scores off a give-and-go high screen set by Ricky. He hit a short left-handed jump hook over the outstretched arm of Wall. The Jesters called their last timeout to set up their offensive strategy, which I assume was to hold the ball for the last shot. Hit it and win it. Miss it and go into overtime."

"You are killing me, Nick, what happened?" Jordan asked excitedly.

"Here's where a great coach earns his paycheck," Nick began. "During the timeout, he told our boys that if the Jesters lined up a certain way, the ball was going to Bigby, then to Wall down low off a Bartolo screen. Mike had remembered them running it when we viewed the tape."

"So?" Jordan asked.

"Their in-bound play was exactly as the Hammer described," Nick said. "They got the ball into Bigby, who foolishly tried a bounce pass to Wall, just where Mike said it would go. Bags got a hand on the bounce pass and Augie came up with the ball after a wild scramble where at least three players had a chance at it. Mike's edict of 'always hustle and fight for every loose ball' paid huge dividends. Augie passed it quickly to Paul who forced the ball to midcourt, then called timeout at Mike's urging. There were three seconds left."

"So, now, you guys got the last shot?" Jordan inquired.

"We did, and Mike had a brilliant play to run, of course," Nick said proudly. "He wanted Paul to take the last shot because he was our hot shooter, but Mike knew that he would be well guarded and probably doubled teamed. So, Mike had Paul put the ball in-bounds right in front of our bench. He knew that would eliminate any double team because James Everson couldn't afford to leave anyone unguarded. What he diagramed was the other four guys lined up along our side of the lane. Two were going to screen for the decoy shooter, which was Dino. He was going to get the inbound pass. The fourth player, Ricky, came to the sideline to set a back screen on the guy guarding Paul on the in-bound pass. Paul for his part would fake a toss into the backcourt, then bounce pass the ball into Dino on his left. By then Ricky would be screening for Paul, who would run to his favorite spot just to the left of the foul line."

"Did it work?" Jordan asked too eager to wait.

"Perfectly!" Nick asserted. "Dino hit Paul on his spot, and Paul drilled the sixteen-footer without even hitting the rim, nothing but net, as the saying goes, and by the way, the buzzer went off just as the ball was going through the net."

"So, your team pulled it out, 54-52," Jordan said pumping his fist in the air. "Just out of curiosity, how many points did your nephew have?"

"Thirty-two," Nick answered proudly. "He was hotter than a three-dollar pistol that night."

"Did the boys celebrate after the game?" Jordan asked.

"If they did, it was without Mike and me knowing about it," Nick answered. "Mike talked with them briefly after the game and told them that he was very proud of them because they didn't quit and hustled all game. He explained that they got away with an ugly win since they hadn't played their best. However, he told them that he knew they were a better team than what they had shown that night. Mike also knew a few other things that he shared only with me. First, we likely had a much tougher game coming on Friday night at the Preston Acheson gym. Second, the two other coaches were in the stands scouting us. Mike figured that could work to our advantage because of how poorly we played. He told me that would probably make the other two teams over-confident. Third, since the Paladins had two big guys like James Everson, we had to figure a way to neutralize them. Finally, his job wasn't to beat our boys down for their poor overall performance but to build them up and emphasize what they did well. I commented that the Weston Acheson coach was the brow beater, and that was the reason Mike had the horses he had, our Italian Stallions, playing for him."

"So, you cleaned up on that game with the betting," Jordan offered.

"I did, and my brother did, as well," Nick said. I even had some bets down for Mike, so he made out well, also. I didn't tell him about any of the betting. I didn't want it to affect his coaching. Now, that said, the betting was only a sidelight, not the main reason for wanting to win. We had a bunch of guys who were out to prove a point, which was a team comprised of not necessarily basketball players, but great athletes, could walk onto three very good opponents' home courts and beat them at their own game."

"Fantastic," said Jordan. "People love an underdog story."

"Well, we were, and we weren't," Nick offered, "if you know what I mean. After all, our guys were great athletes and not bad basketball players. It was a situation where no one knew it. Let me correct that, no one except the players on the other teams. They knew what they were up against playing our guys."

Jordan then checked his watch and asked Nick, "How are you doing? Do you want to continue, or stop for the day?"

"I'm good to go on for a while longer, Jordy," came Nick's reply, "but let's take a break so I can use the restroom."

"Good idea," said Jordan. "While you're in there, I'll get us re-fills."

They took a break for a few minutes and walked to the coffee shop. They chatted about the weather being so nice, but Jordan noticed that Nick was moving slower than normal. Jordan asked if Nick was all right, and he replied that his leg was a bit stiff from sitting, so Jordan let it pass.

Jordan got the coffee re-fills, then waited for Nick to re-emerge from the restroom. They took a slow walk back to Nick's favorite bench in the park.

Once back at the bench, Nick started anew, "So, our team barely beat the Jesters. I'm guessing they were a little tight, you know, nervous, plus our big three scorers all shot poorly. However, in the end, they were able to pull it out. Now, on to Friday and Preston Acheson."

Nick continued, "As soon as our last player left the locker room Thursday night, Mike and I took a few minutes to discuss our next opponent. He recalled from viewing the game tape that they were much more physical, liked to play an aggressive man-to-man, and were almost as athletic as we were. He told me that he would have to think about how we should play them. We decided to sleep on it, and I told Mike that I would meet him back at my place since I had a stop to make on the way home."

"Where did you have to go?" Jordan inquired.

"I needed to stop by Louie's Pool Hall to see what the early line was on the next game," Nick answered. "As it turned out, our poor showing against James Everson had us an overwhelming underdog at 12-1 to win and 15 point underdogs. After watching our guys against James Everson I was no longer sure we could stay within 15 points against The Little Sisters of the Poor wheelchair basketball team let alone a good team like the Preston Paladins. But, since I was up a couple of grand, I went ahead and bet $500 to win and $500 more to beat the spread. I bet $50 and $100 to win and beat the spread for Joe and the Hammer, as well.

"Okay, I'm ready," Jordan said, "What happened in that game?"

"Well, a lot, to say the least," Nick started out saying. "But, before I get into the game itself, there was one more bit of information I need to tell you. Around four that afternoon, and just before Mike and I were ready to leave my house to get something to eat before going to the Preston gym, I got a call from Sal at Louie's Pool Hall. He asked me to stop by before the game. I told Mike to go on ahead to Mama's Italian Kitchen, and I'd meet him there."

"So, what was that all about?" Jordan asked.

"Sal told me that one of our player's father had put down a sizeable bet on Preston to win. So, now I had to figure out if the kid knew about it, and if so, what to do."

"That's a tough call," Jordan said. "Did you tell Mike?"

"I had to," Nick said. "I couldn't let the Hammer go into the game not knowing that one of his players could potentially sabotage our chance of winning."

"So, what did Mike do?" Jordan asked.

"We decided to wait and watch," Nick replied. "Since we weren't sure that the kid was in on it, we didn't feel it prudent to make any accusations. It could just have been that the father saw our lousy game the night before and figured we were going to lose against Preston, and quite honestly, I was just as skeptical."

"Do you want to tell me which player?" Jordan inquired.

"I'd rather not, but it wasn't one of the starters, so that cuts the suspect list in half," Nick answered. "On to the game against Preston, which had its own set of problems."

"Like what?" Asked Jordan.

"Well, as the game unfolded both Mike and I could detect an obvious bias in the officiating," Nick began, "and it wasn't in our favor. By the end of the first quarter, all five of our starters had two fouls. Preston wasn't whistled for one, and our boys were getting banged around a lot. Mike tried talking to the referees, asking them what was going on, because it was obvious that the fix was in, but they warned him to sit down or they would give him a technical foul. The only good news was that our big three scorers, Augie, Dino, and Bags were out of their previous night's funk and were shooting the ball much better."

Jordan then asked, "You mean to tell me that your team incurred ten fouls to none for Preston while they were fouling you?"

"Yes, it was getting pretty ugly and our fans were howling, throwing objects on the court in protest after each terrible call. The charade continued through the second quarter and by the half we were down by six, something like 32-26. Mike talked with our boys at the half about a change in strategy. He proposed that we start the second half the same way we did against Mike's former players from Philly in the scrimmage game, except now we were to contest every shot with unrestrained physicality. They were all for it. So, the bomb squad took the floor to start the second half and dished out a large scoop of beatdown on the Paladin starters. Mike figured that if the officials were going to call fouls against us, then those fouls were going to be real, and they were going to hurt. In the first three minutes of the third quarter, two Preston players were on the bench with ice packs and another was on his way to the hospital for stitches. The fiasco came to a head when two Paladin players went onto Jimmy Shockley's back after he grabbed a rebound. Jimmy flipped them over his head and onto the floor. Ronnie and Anthony just stood over them hoping they would start something. Frank and Timmy squared off against the guys guarding them. At that point, the referees jumped in, called time-out, and asked to meet with both coaches."

"Are you kidding me?" Jordan asked.

"No," Nick replied. "It was very unfortunate to have had to come to that, but we had no choice. For his part, Mike calmly explained that the punishment would keep coming until the officiating was fair. The Preston coach, Giordano, put up a mild rebuttal, but he knew what was happening. To his credit, I found out later that he wasn't in on the 'fix', which was good for him if you know what I mean, and by now, I think you do."

"I'm beginning to learn," Jordan offered, "that there's much more to your past than I may want to know."

"You'll find out, Jordy," Nick said, "all of what you need to know about me in time. I'm guessing that you have already figured out one thing about me, and that's I don't like cheating, lying, bad behavior, or anything that isn't fair. But, for now, back to the game. After the break, we had two new referees and the officiating was the way it should have been from the start. The unfortunate situation for us was that we were now behind by 14 points with about a quarter and a half to go."

"Did the Hammer have any rabbits he could pull out of his hat?" Jordan asked.

Nick paused for a second, then started, "He put our starters back into the game and changed our defense to allow it to flow more easily into our offense."

"How'd he do that?" Jordan inquired.

"He decided to go with the full-court press alternating that defense with a zone press," Nick said. "That way, he hoped to pick up some easy baskets off some steals. It worked reasonably well, but we did surrender a couple of baskets when their team made some good ball movement. Remember, they had an all-star forward named, Kerry O'Boyle. Well, he could do it all and was, for the most part, hurting us with his scoring. His favorite play was to come across the top of the key from their offensive right side to his left, because he was a lefty, and pop a fifteen footer from the foul line area. I'm telling you that because it factors into the end of the game."

"How so?" Asked Jordan.

"Well, fast forward to the last few minutes," Nick said. "Once the officials started calling the game fairly, we began chipping away at the 14 point deficit. It was no easy road. Our big guys did well limiting them to one shot because our rebounding was great. I think Ricky ended up with 22 boards. With about two minutes to go our team had it down to four points after consecutive baskets by Dino and Bags from the corner and the right-wing, respectively. That's when the Preston coach, Giordano, pulled the ball outside and tried to run out the clock.

"Oh, he was going to use the same ploy that was used against him by the Weston coach in the championship game," Jordan recalled.

"Very good," Nick said. "You remembered that. Yes, that was his intention. But obviously, the Hammer wasn't going to let him run out the clock. We attacked their delay game by overplaying their guards. Eventually, a pass went astray, and we converted it into an easy layup. When Preston brought the ball into their offensive court, we countered with double teams wherever the ball went and got another steal, which again led to an easy lay-up to tie the game at 58-all with about 15 seconds to go."

Jordan was as excited listening to Nick's re-enactment as Nick was in telling it. Jordan then guessed, "I'm assuming it was Kerry O'Boyle time?"

"Yes, but you're getting ahead of yourself," Nick cautioned. "Giordano called a timeout as soon as the Paladins got the ball into their offensive end. That left 12 seconds on the clock. Mike figured that O'Boyle was going to get the ball in his favorite spot around the top of the key, and so did everybody else in the gym. He hadn't missed that shot all night and probably had at least 25 points. So, the Hammer had Danny pressure their inbounds pass and Dino play O'Boyle straight up man-on-man. The ball went into their point guard, Vinovich, who killed some clock before firing a pass to the cutting O'Boyle right where we thought he'd get it. The difference this time was that Mike had Paul sag down from his outside responsibility, and when O'Boyle turned to shoot, Paul came up behind him and put his hand right on top of the ball for as clean and beautiful a block from the backside as you have ever seen. Paul then rolled the ball off O'Boyle's hand and started down the court to our basket. Vinovich was back on defense, but now it was two on one with Danny Bags filling the left side. Paul took it hard to the basket, and as Vinovich went up to block his lay-up, Paul made a perfect behind-the-back pass to

Danny, who laid the ball in off the glass with one second on the clock. Preston tried a desperation full-court pass, but Ricky out jumped Pulaski and O'Boyle, with one of his patented swooping overhand grabs. He then cradled the ball into his mid-section until the horn sounded ending the game."

"Unbelievable!" Jordan exclaimed. "The Stallions not only beat the Paladins, but they had to beat the referees, too. I'm guessing they would've won handily if the game was officiated honestly from the beginning."

"No one knows that for sure," Nick speculated, "but all things being the same, yes, probably. Now, you mentioned the referees. Obviously, they were in on some sort of a fix, and I wasn't going to let that slide."

"So, what did you do?" Jordan asked hesitantly.

"I didn't confront them directly." Nick started out saying. "Remember, at that time, I had Gordy working for me, so if I wanted, I could have, well, you know."

"Yes, I think I do know," Jordan acknowledged, "but I'm guessing you handled it another way."

"I did," Nick said. "Over the weekend I did some investigating. First, I heard from my bookie, Sal. The rumor on the street was two Preston Acheson school board directors wanted a rematch with Weston Acheson, so they put the fix in with the referees. Second, on Monday I met with the PIAA district commissioner. He was the overseer of scholastic sports in the area. He confirmed the rumor, and that made my blood boil; but honestly, I half expected it. Here's what went down. During that timeout after the near brawl, the commissioner met with the two referees. They were so scared that they gave up the whole plan. As it turned out, two Preston school board directors paid the refs $200 each upfront to fix the game. If Preston won, they would each get another $300, presumably from the winnings off their bets. The commissioner immediately replaced them with two substitute referees to finished the game. They happened to be there with the commissioner as spectators."

Jordan interrupted, "Excuse me, Nick, was this the rule or the exception there?"

"Thankfully, the exception," Nick replied, "but it happened more than it should have, especially in prior years."

"Sorry for the interruption," Jordan said. "What happened next?"

"I asked the commissioner to make sure those two referees never got another game above the elementary school level," Nick said. "I knew they weren't the source of the problem, just pawns, so I decided to go easy on them, but I made them *donate* their ill-gotten gains."

"That was kind," Jordan acknowledged, "but, what about the two school directors?"

"I gave them a choice," Nick replied. "They could either resign their positions immediately and never run for political office again, or I'd have Gordon pay them a visit."

"What did they choose, as if I don't know?" Jordan asked half-jokingly.

"They resigned, of course," Nick answered. "Now, don't think badly of me. I did take the time to make it a teachable moment. I explained to them that by trying to fix the game, they were taking the rightful victory away from ten very hard-working young men. That was consideration number one. Secondly, others had bets on the game that they would have lost instead of winning, and it was wrong to cheat them. So, for their punishment, they had to see Sal the first of each month for one year and pay him $100 each. If they missed the first of the month, then it was 10% juice per day. I told them it was to square things with my boss. Honestly, he didn't need the money. We kept it in an account that we called the 'widows and orphans' fund. There were several contributors to that fund over the years, and we used it to help many needy people."

"That's fantastic," offered Jordan. "Any more info on that Friday game?"

Nick thought for a few seconds, then answered, "Yes, our top three scorers had much better nights than the previous game. Dino poured in 17 points, Bags got 16 and Augie had 15. Ricky and Paul had 6 each. I mentioned that Ricky had a ton of rebounds, more than any three other guys. For his part, Paul handed out 12 assists and had four steals. So, as you can tell, it was a team firing on all cylinders. Honestly, I believe we would have won by double digits if the referees hadn't put us in such a hole. One more thought, our basketball-playing footballers very much enjoyed some payback for the beating Preston gave them on Thanksgiving."

"Well, that was some game." Jordan conceded. "But, I have one more question: what about the kid whose father bet against your team?"

"I don't think he knew," came Nick's reply. "The Hammer put him in the game to start the second half, and he was dishing out as much punishment as every other guy on the bomb squad, so I'm guessing he wasn't aware of his father's bet. I would have hated to have had to confront him about it if there was a problem, but I would have."

"I'm sure you would have," Jordan said. "By the way, how are you feeling? Did you want to call it a day? We can continue another time, whenever you want, Nick."

"That's probably a good idea," Nick confessed. "But, before you go, if you don't mind me asking, what's happening with your brother-in-law? I only know what I read in the newspapers."

"I don't mind," Jordan began. "He's in jail in Petersburg, some minimum-security federal prison. I hear the feds want him to plead guilty to a host of charges and make restitution in return for a reduced sentence."

"What's the maximum he can get?" Nick asked.

"Not sure, but I'm guessing hundreds of years if the sentences run consecutively rather than concurrently," Jordan said. "Often a judge gives the offender concurrent sentencing if they plead out. Then, if he makes parole, he could be out before he's very old. Again, I'm not sure, but it doesn't seem fair to me."

"No, not fair to anyone who lost money," Nick answered, then reiterated his lament, "I don't like a cheat, liar, crook, fraud, or anyone who isn't honest. I call them 'chancers and cheats', you know, from that movie, *Leap Year*, with Amy Adams. There's more to the quote, something about backstabbing snakes, but I left that part out because I don't recall it exactly."

Jordan said he knew the movie and like it, but decided to let the rest of Nick's comments drop. He asked if the next morning was free for Nick to continue with the details of the last game. Nick said that he had something to do, but could see Jordan on Monday morning. They agreed on Monday at nine at Nick's bench.

CHAPTER 10
Boys to Men

Nick's alarm clock rang at 7:00 a.m. He liked to take a few minutes to clear his head by sitting on the edge of the bed before standing. He grabbed his walker, which he kept alongside the bed for nighttime trips to the bathroom. At his age and with a gimpy leg he knew the walker was a good idea. Once he felt alert, he hoisted himself out of bed and proceeded to the bathroom pushing his walker. He shaved, brushed his teeth, took a shower and washed his hair, dried off, applied deodorant, dried and combed his hair, then splashed on some cologne; just like he had done for most of his adult life. In his walk-in closet, he selected a crisp, freshly dry cleaned white shirt, red and blue striped tie, light gray slacks, and navy blue sport coat with American flag lapel pin. He was dressing to conduct business.

On most Sunday mornings Nick would attend nine o'clock mass at Saint Benedictine's just down the street from where he lived, but on this Sunday he was on a mission. He had made arrangements to be picked up by Tony DePalma, a policeman he knew who usually patrolled in and around Parc de Gisele. Tony was to pick up Nick at eight o'clock, so Nick had plenty of time to get ready for their trip. Nick figured the trip they were making was about a three-hour drive, so he and Tony would take time to stop for a nice breakfast somewhere along the way, then stop again for lunch on the return trip. It would just depend on how heavy the traffic was. Nick knew that an early start would improve their odds of making it to their destination without much, if any, delay. The return trip might be another story. Fortunately, it was another beautiful day so their 140-mile trip would be driven in good weather.

Nick met Tony soon after Nick arrived in Middleboro. Tony was a rookie police officer on the Middleboro force. They became instant friends, despite their vast age difference, largely because they were like-minded: fair, honest, protectors of the less fortunate or needy, and benevolent. It didn't hurt that they both had Italian ancestry. However, what made Nick take an interest in Tony was that Tony, like Nick had observed in Jordan, had that old-fashioned respect for his elders, even at the young age of 20.

Nick's family originated from the Italian region of Calabria. His mother and father were born and raised in Maida. They met there when both were young school-aged children. Nick's father, Paolo, was an orphan, having been the offspring of a wealthy landowner and servant girl on his plantation. Since the plantation owner disavowed any knowledge of, or responsibility for, his son, Paolo was put in an orphanage. Eventually, he came to live with the Senetta family, but when Paolo came of age, he decided to make his way in the world with a name all his own, and he chose Marinelli. In time he asked his childhood sweetheart's father for permission to marry Emanuela, which the father granted. Paolo and Emanuela immigrated to America in 1908 after they were married in Italy. Paolo came first, found a job working in the mines, then sent for Emanuela, who by then already had one son.

Tony was a third-generation Italian American. His family hailed from a variety of Italian ancestral regions, but mostly Abruzzo, Tuscany, and Sicily. He liked to tell people who would ask, that he wasn't Italian but rather Italian-American. Then add with a smile that he didn't have purple feet, presumably because he wasn't stomping grapes like a true Italian might do to make wine.

Nick and Tony met from time to time for dinner or a trip like the one they were taking that day. To pass the time and sharpen their debating skills they would get into friendly disagreements about who knew more about a certain subject, be it sports, politics, or the best Italian restaurant in the area. Nick would invariably end up calling Tony 'chooch', which roughly translated meant a stupid person or meathead, but Nick always meant it more to mean 'jackass', as in a stubborn mule. Tony would often egg on Nick to get him to call Tony a chooch, then laugh uncontrollably for ten seconds when he succeeded. Conversely, when Nick wanted to have some fun with Tony he would morph into a half-baked combination of Italian and English, mostly gibberish, and would conclude with the Italian word 'capiche' meaning 'do you understand'. Tony would answer with 'Si', whether he understood or not.

Tony arrived at the front door of Nick's condo building just before 8:00 a.m. in the large black sedan that Nick had rented the afternoon before. As instructed by Nick, Tony was dressed in the size 52, custom fit, three-piece, black pinstriped Armani suit that Nick had purchased for him for occasions such as these. Tony was also attired in an open-collared white dress shirt, showing a gold chain with an Italian horn dangling from it and snuggly fitting around his muscular neck. To top off his outfit Nick had him in wrap-around Ray-Ban sunglasses, a black fedora, and a gold pinkie ring. Tony looked more Mafioso than Luca Brasi, the *Godfather's* strong man.

The very imposing duo hit the road precisely at eight, taking several state and county roads before eventually getting on I-95 South. Nick had asked Tony to keep close to the speed limit to eliminate any unwanted police attention. This was to be as secretive a mission as Nick could make it. He was sure the person they were going to see would not know either of them, and if for some reason he did, he would be instructed in no uncertain terms, that the meeting never took place.

After an hour on the road, Nick suggested stopping for breakfast. Tony was only too happy to oblige. They took a 30-minute break when they saw a convenient diner. Tony mowed down the super deluxe breakfast of scrambled eggs, hash browns, sausage, pancakes, juice, and coffee. At six feet four and 260 pounds it just about filled his stomach. Nick enjoyed half a waffle and two sips of coffee. They were back on the road after a bathroom stop and made their destination just after eleven.

The entrance to the Federal Correctional Complex at Petersburg was less than imposing. Being a minimum-security institution it didn't harbor hardened criminals, just the white-collar variety. Nick had researched the visiting hours and knew that on Sundays they were liberal with visitors. He and Tony were allowed admittance largely because of a letter Nick produced signed by a federal judge granting him access.

Their visit with Richard Cardel wasn't going to take very long, and it would be very direct, but Nick wasn't sure if Richard would agree to meet with him. He figured he could entice him, if necessary, by asking the guard to relay that Nick had a message for Richard from his wife. Fortunately, Nick didn't have to use that tactic, because after nearly a week in custody with no visitors, except his lawyer briefly, Richard would have met with Darth Vader, Hannibal Lecter, or Lucifer, the devil himself.

Once Nick and Tony were admitted into the open visitor area, and Richard was brought to them, Nick and Richard sat at a cafeteria-styled table while Tony stood menacingly behind Nick, as he was taught to do many years ago for these type meetings. Nick began the conversation, "I'm sure you don't know me, do you?"

Richard replied sarcastically, "No, I don't. Should I?"

Nick bristled a bit and said, "I'd change my tune right now if I were you."

"Why?" Richard snapped, then asked, "What are you and your goon going to do, kill me?"

"It's not my first choice," Nick answered sternly, "but it's still on my list."

"Yeah, how can you get to me in here?" Richard asked.

As Tony slowly positioned himself between Nick and the guard blocking his line-of-sight to the table, Nick put his cane on the table and began unscrewing the bottom portion. He only exposed enough of the blade to make sure Richard saw it. Then, he said, "If they got to Kennedy, what makes you think you're safe in here?"

The blood drained from Richard's face. He looked up at Tony, then back at Nick, and contritely asked, "Who are you, and what do you want?"

"My name isn't important. Consider me a friend of the people that you swindled," Nick answered.

Richard gulped, then said, "Sorry about that."

"Sorry that you got caught, or sorry that you did it?" Came Nick's next question.

"Sorry that I did it," Richard replied.

"Well, Mr. Cardel, sorry doesn't feed the bulldog," Nick stated tersely. "In layman's terms that means sorry isn't enough."

"I suppose not," Richard admitted. "But, what can I do now?" He asked.

"There are a lot of things you *can* do," Nick began, "but, here's what you're *going* to do. Tomorrow morning you are going to tell your lawyer that you want to take the best deal he can make for you with the federal prosecutor. Don't ask how I know, but the federal judge will sign off on it."

"Is that all?" Richard asked.

"No, not by a long shot," Nick replied. "Next, you are going to make restitution, or as much restitution as you can with the money that's still available. I hear that you have it stashed in a foreign account to which only you have access. Correct?" Nick asked.

"Uh, yeah, that's true," Richard answered.

"Well, you're going to release it back to the feds so they can get it back to the people from which you stole it, as soon as it's legal to do so. That should get you some brownie points with the federal prosecutor and likely will help with your sentencing."

"Is that all?" Richard asked.

"I'll tell you when I'm finished," Nick said in a cross tone, and as he did, Tony puffed up his chest and took a step closer to the table. "What percentage of the money is still in the off-shore account? An estimate is fine."

"Almost all of it," Richard offered.

"I asked for a percentage," Nick reminded him, again in a very cross tone.

"Uh, I'd say probably 99%. I didn't spend much," Richard said with a weak voice.

"That's good to hear, and good for you, too," Nick said, "because whatever funds you are short in returning to your investors, you are going to make up to them over time with interest from your future earnings. Am I clear?" Nick asked.

"Yes, very clear," Richard replied. "But, it may take the rest of my life, if I ever get out of prison."

"It will take time," Nick stated, "and you will have lots of time to think about how you are going to re-pay that swindled money while you are in prison. You're a CFP, so maybe you can put that knowledge to some good use, and for your sake, I hope the stock market continues to do well. I know all of this sounds harsh, and it is, but, remember, there are consequences for actions, and bad consequences follow bad actions. To put it another way, you made your bed, now you have to lie in it, and unfortunately for you, your bed is now a prison cot, not the nice comfy California King you had at home."

Richard just bowed his head, his chin almost touching his chest. He didn't say anything. Nick then continued, "As far as your marriage is concerned, I cannot tell you what to do there. That's up to you and Jackie. However, you are not to give her any trouble regarding the sale of your house; custody of the children; divorce, if she wants it; or anything else she may determine is best for her and the kids. Am I clear?"

Richard nodded as if he were Dan in the emergency room when Nick posed that question to him several times. Nick then concluded with, "Are there any questions?"

Richard replied that there were not. Nick then asked, "Is there anything you need?"

Richard was dumbfounded and caught off guard by Nick's question, but he finally mumbled out, "Could you please pass along to Jackie how very sorry I am for the pain and suffering that I have put her and the kids through."

"That's going to be a little tricky, but I'll do that for you," Nick said. "However, you need to do it, also, when you have the opportunity. I believe you to be sincere, but if you are not, it won't be good for you; either in here or on the outside, when you get out. Oh, and don't think for a minute that once I'm dead, all this goes away. There will be others coming behind me to take up my work." Nick concluded the brief get-together as he often did with the reminder to Richard that the meeting never happened. He then reached inside his jacket pocket and pulled out an envelope. He slid it across the table to Richard.

Richard asked, "What's this?"

Nick replied, "It's my investment in you, so to speak. I'm giving you a few hundred bucks because in here you'll need it to procure some items that you'll need, possibly even protection. It's not much, but it'll help you get by for a while. Learn to work with people, learn to barter. It's a skill that will serve you well while you are incarcerated. It helped me." Nick then got up from the table with the use of his cane, which by now he had re-assembled, and said, "Good luck, young man. I sincerely hope that you listen to me, and I hope you can turn your life around, because you still have lots of it left, if you are smart."

In less than ten minutes Nick's conference with Richard was over, and he and Tony were traveling back home. About 30 minutes into the trip Tony decided to ask Nick about his business. It was something that he had never done before, but now his curiosity had gotten the best of him. He began, "Nick, I know you to be the most giving person that I've ever met."

Nick interrupted, "I detect a 'but' coming."

"Yeah, well, I know it's none of my business, but I'm curious," he said. "Why do you do what you do? I mean, we take this long trip for a ten-minute meeting with this con man thief, and now another long trip back home, for what? Don't get me wrong, I appreciate very much what you pay me for driving and being your wingman, but why, Nick? No offense, you're an old man, and this can't be good for you. Besides, you don't get anything out of it. Between what you're paying me and what you left him, you must be out nearly a grand, and that's not even considering the car rental and dining. That's just today, and of course, we've done this sort of thing many times over the years."

Nick waited a few seconds to formulate his answer, then replied, "You're correct, ultimately it's not your business to know why I do what I do, but I've known you for almost thirty years, and of course, I love you like family, so I'll share my philosophy with you since you asked. It boils down to this. Sometimes, sacrifice on your part is required for the good of someone else. In the case today, many people back in Middleboro have suffered a great financial hardship because one man did the wrong thing, but why? For the love of money. It reminds me of that old saying, 'Money is the root of all evil'. Well, that's not entirely true. The love of money is the root of all evil. This guy, that we met with today, loved money so much that he was willing to risk everything, his wife, kids, friends, business, etc., for it. Now, it's okay to have money, and even lots of it, if you're willing to earn it the right way. But, when you steal it from hard-working, good people, that's when I have a problem with your methods. So, I'm willing to sacrifice a little of my time and a few dollars to try to help many people get their investments back."

"Well, I guess I see your point, Nick," Tony said, "but couldn't you just help people by donating your time and money to charity?"

"I do, Tony," was Nick's reply. "However, this way I also try to correct a societal wrong that cannot always be corrected in your line of work, capiche?"

"Yeah, I think so," admitted Tony.

"It's like this," Nick began to explain, "I'm not saying that we don't need the police, because we do. However, there are limits, and there should be, regarding what you can do and how much justice the legal system can exact. My way, there are fewer limits. Believe me, I don't relish doing what I sometimes do, but at times, it's necessary to get the desired outcome quicker, and that outcome always benefits someone other than me."

The rest of their trip was easy with less than the normal amount of Sunday traffic. Nick had Tony stop for lunch and once again, Tony ate his fill. They found a quiet Italian restaurant in Alexandria where the pasta, garlic bread, and vino were some of the best either had ever enjoyed. On the trip home Tony had all he could do to stay awake after the big midday meal, but Nick kept him alert by singing along loudly with the Italian songs he had brought on CD.

Jordan arrived early at the park on Monday morning. He figured that he was just too excited to sleep much past 6:30, so instead of lying in his bed, he got up, washed, dressed, ate a small breakfast, had some coffee, read some of the paper, then made some notes before driving to see Nick. While on the way he was thinking of other topics that he could engage Nick in discussion after the details of the championship basketball game were learned. When he couldn't come up with any off the top of his head, he decided to wait and see what might arise, knowing that sometimes spontaneous ideas were better than pre-determined ones.

Like clockwork, Nick arrived at five minutes to nine. Jordan knew he could set his watch by Nick and jokingly said, "If you aren't five minutes early, you're already late." Nick laughed and Jordan handed him a perfect temperature cup of coffee. "How was your Sunday, Nick?" Jordan asked.

"Oh, the usual," Nick replied in a noncommittal fashion. "I just had something to do. Sorry, we couldn't meet yesterday."

"No problem, Nick," Jordan said. "It gave me time to see Mary. We took a long drive to the western part of the state, did some hiking, had lunch, then drove home. It was a beautiful day for being with someone you, well, enjoy being with."

"You were going to say 'love', weren't you?" Nick began. "It's okay to say it if you mean it."

"Well, I think I'm falling in love with Mary," was Jordan's stumbling reply.

"I read a beautiful and very appropriate quote about love," Nick offered. "You know how I like numbers, math, and statistics, well, this quote combines both. It's by Mignon McLaughlin and goes like this, 'In the arithmetic of love, one plus one equals everything, and two minus one equals nothing'."

Jordan thought about that for a few seconds, then offered, "I'm guessing that could sum it up for my parents. When they were together, they were everything to each other, but once my mom died, my dad was just waiting to die and join her. He gave up on living. It was like he had nothing to live for, anymore."

"I can certainly understand that sentiment, Jordy," Nick said. "But, I think it's much more difficult when you are older and your mate dies than when you are younger. Because when you're younger, you have your whole life ahead of you, and you do yourself a great disservice by not trying to live it to the fullest. That's not to say that you don't miss that special loved one, but you have to push through it and get on with living."

"Sounds like there have been some romantic relationships in your past, Nick, that didn't work out quite as you may have wanted," Jordan mused.

"One or two, Jordy," Nick hinted, "but you'll have to wait to learn about them another time."

"Whatever you say, Nick," was Jordan's reply. "I'm all ears when you want to talk about them. But, we're not here to discuss love lives, present or past, so please begin telling me about the championship game."

Nick began, "Well, first off, it was at the Weston Acheson gym, which was the home court for both teams. So, our team finally had a home game even though they were listed as 'Visitors' on the scoreboard."

"How about the officiating?" Jordan asked.

"Thankfully, it was a fair game," Nick said. "I don't think I mentioned to you that in the previous night's game, the Preston Paladins shot 27 fouls, and we shot only four all game. So, you can see how one-sided the officiating was before the commissioner made the change."

"That's ridiculous," Jordan offered. "I can see why your team was so upset and had to take matters into their own hands."

"In the end, I was just glad it all worked out," Nick said. "The better team won despite an unfortunate effort to change the outcome. Now, on to the championship game. As I've mentioned, the players all knew each other very well, since they had played against one another since 8th grade. We were able to get some video of their games for Mike to watch. He was impressed with their shooting guard, Larry Stroebel. Mike knew that he was going to be a handful to stop, so his game plan was to limit Stroebel to his normal amount of points, but lock down the other four starters. It was what the Celtics used to do against the old Philadelphia Warriors. They knew they couldn't stop Wilt Chamberlain, so they gave him his points, but they concentrated on stopping the other four guys. Hence, they won the vast majority of games. Mike knew that the theory had been proven. Now, it was time to execute it."

"I'm ready," Jordan said.

"To review," Nick began, "the Weston Acheson War Eagles' starting five were: Jerome Feldman at center, the two forwards were Doug McIntyre and Jessie Kowalchik, the point guard was Billy Lafferty, and I already mentioned their shooting guard, Larry Stroebel. If my memory is correct, they only lost three games all year: one against a non-conference team highly rated in eastern Pennsylvania early in the season; one to Preston Acheson on their court, which some contend was another bad officiating job; and the last one in the district championship game. They were 20-3 going into the tournament and correctly seeded as the favorite."

"What did the Hammer tell the Stallions in the locker room before the game?" Jordan asked.

"He began by telling them that he was exceptionally proud of them for winning the first two games and getting to the championship, especially because of the adversity they had to overcome in both. He then explained that the job wasn't done, and there was another game to play and win. He told them that he knew why many of them didn't play for their high school basketball team. He didn't want to comment on that directly, but he told them that this was their opportunity to send a message. If they played well and were able to win the game, it would show everyone just how great a team Weston Acheson could have had by combining the best parts of both teams. Mike finalized his pre-game comments by telling the team that he wanted to start the game defensively in a straight-up man-to-man with Ricky on Feldman, Dino on Kowalchik, Augie on McIntyre, Danny on Stroebel, and Paul on Lafferty."

"What was his plan offensively?" Jordan asked.

"Well, wait for a second," Nick replied, "the Hammer, also, explained that he wanted to pressure Feldman with a body on him at all times, so he was going to rotate in Jimmy Shockley and Ronnie DiGiacomo to make him work and force him away from the basket. Mike wasn't concerned if they fouled Feldman because he wasn't a good foul shooter. Offensively, Mike wanted to return to the motion offense because he expected the War Eagles to play their aggressive man-to-man defense, and he knew it to be susceptible to backdoor cuts. He just needed to draw Feldman away from the basket."

"Anything else," Jordan asked, "before we get into what happened during the game?"

"Yes, Mike confided in me," Nick started out saying, "that he figured the key match-up was going to be our point guard against their point guard."

"That would be your nephew, Paul," Jordan interrupted, "against Lafferty, right?"

"Correct!" Nick exclaimed. "The Hammer's thinking was Feldman would outscore Ricky, but Ricky and our bench strength at center would hold their own on the boards. Stroebel was going to be a handful for Danny Bags, but Bags would get his points, just not as many as Stroebel was likely to get. Where we had an advantage was at the two forward positions, Augie going against McIntyre was a clear win for us and more so when it came to Johnnie against Kowalchik. So, that left the point guard match-up. It was just going to be a matter of who had the better game. On paper, it looked like advantage Lafferty, but sometimes those analytics aren't worth the paper they're written on."

"All right, the preliminaries are over," Jordan blurted out, "now onto the main event."

"Nice boxing analogy, champ," Nick said with a large smile. "Just for the record, since you brought boxing up, what was the combo you threw at Dan to KO him?"

Jordan hesitated for a second, then reluctantly said, "I blocked his roundhouse right with my left arm, then fired two quick left jabs to his nose, followed by a right cross flush on the jaw. He went down, thankfully, because if that didn't do it, I was out of punching power."

"It did the trick," Nick said, "I saw the damage for myself."

Jordan quickly changed the subject back to the game by asking, "I forgot to ask about the betting on the last game. How did the odds change, if any?"

"Glad you asked," Nick said. "The odds dropped to 4-1 with us naturally still the underdog, and the spread was reduced to eight points. I put a few hundred on us to win and cover for each my brother, Mike, and me. After the first two games, we were up a pile of dough, so I wanted to protect most of those winnings. I knew not to bet so much that it would cut significantly into our winnings if we lost and also failed to cover. There's an adage that I learned a long time ago, and it applies to investing, as well as gambling. It goes something like this, 'pigs get fat and hogs get slaughtered'. There's a subtle distinction there: 'don't be greedy, when you have enough, be satisfied'. As long as I'm philosophizing, here's another adage that applies to the Hammer, 'the difference between knowledge and wisdom is this: knowledge is being book-smart, while wisdom is the ability to apply that knowledge optimally for the situation at hand. Mike knew the game, but he also knew how to apply his knowledge and teach his players."

"Got it, Nick," Jordan said, "this is like a student being in a one-on-one class with a professor."

"Hardly," said Nick, "but I'm flattered, nonetheless. Now on to the game. Mike designed a play off the opening tip whereby we could grab a quick lead. He had watched the films of the War Eagles and knew they liked to tap it back toward their opponents' basket where they had two guys lined up side-by-side around the mid-court circle. Well, he instructed Ricky not to jump, but to reverse pivot around Feldman once the ball was in the air and grab the tip. Once Ricky outjumped the two War Eagle players, Mike wanted him to pass the ball to Danny, who would force it up the court and draw coverage from their back defender. Paul would release and go for the basket and get an alley-oop pass for an easy lay-up."

"Did it work?" Jordan asked.

"Perfectly," Nick exclaimed, "and the topper was that Paul got fouled on the play by the trailing Lafferty. He made the foul shot, so we were up, 3-0, after only a few seconds. Mike had our boys pick them up with full-court pressure immediately. He knew that despite playing the previous two nights, we were in better shape physically than they were. Mike also knew that if he made the War Eagles work to get the ball up the court and into position to run their offense, it would pay dividends later in the game."

"How did that part of the game plan fair out?" Jordan was quick to ask.

"Well, Jordy" Nick began, "you're once again getting ahead of yourself, but suffice to say that Mike's game plan was spot on. That doesn't mean that it was a cakewalk or even a win for us, because the Weston Acheson War Eagles were the league champions, and they had five good players plus bench strength. They weren't going to roll over for us, because they had an enormous amount of pride, as well."

"So, the game was another good one, wasn't it?" Jordan interjected.

"In a word, 'yes'," Nick answered. "From there the game unfolded pretty much as Mike had expected. Stroebel was doing his thing for the War Eagles. He was driving and putting in twisting, off-balance shots just as he had done all season. We were pushing Feldman as far away from the basket as we could, but he was getting his points. For our part, Bags, Augie, and Dino were lighting it up. Ricky, Ronnie, and Jimmy were rotating in every few minutes and controlling our defensive board with their superior strength."

"How was your nephew, Paul, doing against Lafferty?" Jordan asked.

"Pretty well," Nick said. "Paul was holding his own and doing all he could to harass Lafferty all over the court. He picked his pocket for one steal and deflected two other passes that resulted in turnovers. Paul was even ahead slightly in scoring at the end of the first quarter which contributed to the Stallions being up 18-16 at the break."

"So, let's hear about the second quarter," Jordan eagerly suggested.

"Well," Nick began, "the second quarter jump ball wasn't going to be like the opening tip, so Mike went to plan B. He let Ricky at 5' 11" try to outjump the 6' 6" Feldman."

"Yeah, what happened?" Jordan inquired.

"Ricky was so pumped," Nick said, "I thought he was going to hit his head on the ceiling. Well, not really, but you get the picture. He outjumped Feldman, and we controlled the tip, which brought an awful howl from the War Eagles' coach. He screamed 'Feldman' so loud, I thought he was going to blow the windows out of the gym."

"I'll bet that served to unnerve Feldman," Jordan said.

"I think it did," Nick said. "After that, he seemed to be looking to see where Ricky was when he got the ball because the last thing he wanted was to be blocked by a guy seven inches shorter. He was now intimidated."

"So, that factored into the rest of the game? Jordan asked indirectly.

"It did," Nick said. "Here's how. Feldman was so upset that Ricky outjumped him that he became obsessed with trying to block one of Ricky's shots. Mike sensed this and had Ricky play the high post, and our boys had free run along the baseline. The backdoor cuts were there, and when the War Eagles would sag to stop that tactic, Danny, John, and Augie hit their jumpers. By the half, we were ahead 36-32, so it was still close because Stroebel had about half their points."

"What did Mike tell them at the half?" Jordan asked.

Nick replied, "He explained that our game plan was working well and that he thought we were in much better shape than they were. He implored our boys to keep up the pressure defensively because he knew it was taking its toll on them, and eventually, they would lose their legs, and then their will to win."

"What were the third quarter highlights," Jordan asked.

"Well, at the outset, Feldman and Ricky got into an elbow jousting match before the opening tip, so the referee tossed them both out of the circle. We put Augie in there against McIntyre and controlled the tip. On our first possession of the second half, Mike had set up a play where Ricky came out high bringing Feldman with him. Dino set a back screen on Stroebel freeing up Danny for a back door cut and two quick points off another alley-oop pass from Paulie. It worked like a charm, so we were up by six and were able to maintain that lead throughout the third quarter. It was 56-50 after three periods, so again, we weren't home free, yet."

"Did the War Eagles make a run at your team in the fourth quarter?" Jordan asked.

"You must've seen my notes," Nick said jokingly. "They did, indeed, but not against our first team. Mike cleared the bench when we went up by ten with four minutes to play. However, the War Eagles' starters were just too good for our second team. In less than two minutes our lead was down to two."

Jordan couldn't contain himself and blurted out, "Oh, please don't tell me that your team lost."

"Here's what happened," Nick began with a sly grin, "Mike called timeout and put the first team back on the court. During the timeout, he told them to run the play that they had used against James Everson at the end of the game. It worked again with Paulie hitting the 16-footer and getting fouled by Lafferty on the play. That fouled out Lafferty, by the way. Paulie converted the foul shot, so we were up by five. Mike, also, wanted our guys to play the zone press defense after any made shot, because we had not shown it to them, yet. It worked to perfection and not just because their point guard had fouled out. The War Eagles struggled to get the ball up the court. Our boys got two steals and parlayed them into quick points. With a little over a minute to go, we were back up by ten, so Mike called off the dogs and re-substituted the second team. Our starters got a standing ovation when they left the court. We lost some of the lead, but not the game. The final was 71-66."

"Why did Mike play it so close?" Jordan inquired. "I mean he had the War Eagles on the ropes and could have put them away, but he took a chance of losing the lead when he put in the second team."

"I asked him the same question after the game," Nick said. "Honestly, I was getting worried, myself. Here's what he told me. First, he wanted the second team to get into the game because they had worked just as hard as the first team in preparation for the tournament. Second, he knew that he could put our first team back on the court, if need be, to finish off the War Eagles. He explained to me that his coaching experience told him that he knew our team was still firing on all cylinders at the end of the game, but the other team was gassed, finished. Of course, they were still better than our second team, but at that stage of the game, they weren't going to touch our starters. Third, and finally, Mike was trying not to run up the score, call it coaching courtesy, but he knew our boys were just dying to pile it on, you know, to prove a point about which team was better, and they didn't want there to be any room for debate."

Jordan morphed into his journalist mode, "So, what happened after the game?"

Nick started in a low tone, then ramped up his voice, "I was very proud to see the sportsmanship that our guys exhibited after the game. Led by our team captain, Dino, they lined up and shook the hands of each War Eagles player and all their coaches. They refrained from any jubilant celebration until they got into the locker room to not hurt their opponents' feelings. They conducted themselves in this manner after winning the previous two games, as well; although, I'm not sure why they were so nice after the rob job they got against the Preston Paladins."

Nick continued, "Mike asked Willie and Wayne to secure the basketball at the end of the game while he went to shake hands with Syl Buzinski. In the locker room after the game, Mike had everyone involved with the team sign it. That included the ten players, Wayne, Willie, Mike and me. The players all signed their names with their numbers. Before everyone signed the ball, Mike neatly wrote the scores of the three tournament games, and above that 1971 Rotary Club Basketball Champions: The Italian Stallions. Since I was personal friends with the principal, school superintendent, and every school board member, it wasn't going to be a problem having the ball put into the school's trophy case at the main entrance. I'm sure it galled Syl Buzinski every time he walked by that trophy case, but it served as a reminder to him just how good a team he could have had, had he just reined in his volatile coaching style and not alienated so many fine players."

Jordan was smiling broadly after listening to Nick's account. He was very happy that Nick had taken the time to tell the story his way and in the detail he felt was needed to give the three games their due. Jordan also realized that Nick and Mike gave those ten kids a lifelong memory, but mostly it was Nick's foresight to get Mike to coach them that won the championship. Jordan still had some questions. First was the final betting outcome, and second, he wanted to know what became of the ten guys who stunned the local basketball scene back in 1971 in Nick's old stomping grounds.

Nick answered the first inquiry by letting Jordan know that he could have put a kid through four years of college in the 1970s with what he had won betting on those three games. He didn't specify the exact amount, but he confided it was more than $10,000. He also mentioned that his brother, Joe, made a bundle, as well, and so did Mike, although Mike didn't know it at the time.

Before Mike drove back to Philadelphia on Monday morning, Nick handed him an envelope with $5000 in it. The winnings from the bets he placed for Mike and Joe didn't account for all of the money Nick gave each of them. Mike didn't open his envelope then, but he knew what it was, and he wasn't surprised, knowing Nick's benevolence. What surprised him later was the amount of cash in the envelope along with a hand-written note to Mike which essentially conveyed Nick's gratitude for taking the time to coach and mentor some very deserving young men.

After Nick finished with the details regarding Mike's well-earned reward, he told Jordan of a heart-warming story about his brother, Joe. Joe's wife, Maria, had a sister, Francesca, whose son was very ill with Hodgkin's disease. Paul's cousin, Allan, was ten at the time. Joe knew that Francesca and her husband, Dom, weren't able to pay all of the medical bills that came with a child fighting a major illness, even though they had health insurance. Joe didn't initially tell Maria that he was betting on Paul's games via Nick, but when he came home with the $5000 in cash, he explained how he obtained the money. Joe offered it to Maria and suggested that they drive to Francesca and Dom's the next weekend and give them the $5000 to help with Allan's medical bills. At the time Allan was in dire need of a very expensive experimental medication that the insurance wouldn't cover. The money from Joe and Maria enabled Allan to get the medication, and because of it, Allan lived another five years before finally succumbing to the disease.

Jordan's jaw was agape listening to Nick's story. For once, he couldn't speak to ask a question. Nick then told Jordan the rest of the story. He finished it by saying, "Fast forward to 2009. Francesca passed away with no heirs except her sister, Maria, since Francesca's husband had pre-deceased her several years prior. In the 33 years between her son's death and hers, Francesca had worked as a county employee at the local courthouse. While working there, she became friends with an elderly gentleman, who advised her in the art of investing. By the time Francesca passed away she had a stock and bond portfolio north of $500,000, and her wealth exceeded $600,000."

Jordan blurted out, "Are you kidding me?"

"Absolutely not," Nick answered. "I was told all of that by my sister-in-law, Maria. Now, you may ask, why do I tell you this feel-good tale? Because I believe it's not only a fabulously heart-warming account, but it's also an excellent example of one good deed being repaid one hundred times over, many years later, without the slightest initial expectation."

Nick then articulated to Jordan what he knew about the events in the lives of the Stallion players after graduation. He began by saying that his information was neither complete nor accurate beyond the time he left the area, nor what he had been told by either his niece or nephew.

He explained that Anthony Simonetti worked in law enforcement and ultimately became a federal protective officer after selling the family business he inherited. One of his hobbies was weightlifting, which led him to compete in and win a few local meets. He eventually settled in the area after retirement enjoying the good life with his wife, kids, and grandkids.

Timmy Posatano graduated from La Salle University with a degree in accounting. He had a successful career for a large business firm in Philadelphia. After college, he married a girl from Preston Acheson and still lives in the Philly suburbs.

Frank Mezza was a good athlete who played Division III football at one of the local colleges. He later coached football at Weston Acheson as an assistant. He eventually took over his family's trucking business, which he still runs very successfully today.

Jimmy Shockley went on to Temple University on a football scholarship and played linebacker and fullback.

He graduated with a degree in business development and rose to executive vice president for one of the largest businesses in South Jersey. He still lives outside of Philadelphia.

Ron DiGiacomo graduated with a political science degree from a local college. He went into politics, first at the local level, then was elected to the state legislature. There were always rumors circulating about him and his female staff members, which wasn't surprising since he never married and fashioned himself as a ladies' man. He eventually ended up on the governor's staff as Internal Affairs Coordinator. Nick commented, "You can't make this stuff up."

Nick then began telling about the starting five of the Stallions. He recalled that John Paladino was a top student, class officer, and National Honor Society member. He went to the Air Force Academy and became a fighter pilot, where his call sign became "Dino", naturally. Word had it that John flew several sorties during the First Gulf War and was a full bird colonel when he retired. He stepped into a job with Boeing after his Air Force retirement and now lives in Colorado.

Augie Falco graduated from Syracuse where he played football and earned a teaching degree. He volunteered his time over the years coaching football at Weston Acheson as an assistant. After teaching for 40 years he retired and still lives in the area.

Ricky Calvino went into finance after college. He worked for a time on Wall Street. After 9/11 he moved his business back to the area to enjoy the quiet, peaceful life that he missed while being in New York. He retired and lives there today.

Danny Bagnotti was another kid who attended one of the local colleges. He graduated with a degree in business administration and went on to run his family's real estate business. Danny, Jimmy, Paul, and some of their classmates hook up at class reunions for a round or two of golf.

Nick told Jordan that he had already given him a lot of information regarding his nephew's athletic attributes, but not anything regarding his career pursuits. Paul, like his father, Joe, worked for the government after his college graduation. Paul's degree in mathematics allowed him to become a data analyst for the Army.

Nick then said, "About the only items left to tell you about are the newspaper report on the games and the celebratory party."

"I'm all ears," offered Jordan.

Nick began, "For some reason, the only local newspaper to cover those games was *The Sunday Gazette.* That was probably because the four teams were located in their readership's area. The *Gazette* was a weekly publication covering the region's political, social, sports, and general news. At that time they had a young sports reporter named Ernie Alderman who was interning at the *Gazette* while going to college. He wasn't much older than the players he was covering. At any rate, he wrote a seminal article about the tournament lavishing great accolades on the Stallions for their three upset victories. I'm guessing you can find it online with some digging. I think you will enjoy reading his account to supplement what I've told you. It's another source without my biased perspective."

Jordan laughed, said he would check it out, and then asked about the championship party.

"I had a cabin on a couple of acres bordering a lake not too far from the school," Nick stated. "After the game, I invited the players, their families, their girl-friends, and of course, Willie, Wayne, and Mike, up there for a fun-filled celebration on Sunday afternoon. I hired a local restaurant to cater a picnic, you know, cook hot dogs, hamburgers, Italian sausage, corn, baked beans, and all the rest of the food you might expect at a pic-nic to include a big cake from an Italian bakery with the words '1971 Rotary Club Basketball Champions' written on it. The icing was red, green, and white, of course. Fortunately, it turned out to be a decent day, because April in Northeastern PA can be unpredictable. Everyone had a grand time re-living the games. The guys ended up playing a touch football game that showcased their athletic abilities. Mike marveled at their speed and agility. He mentioned to me that he could see why they were football champions but wondered how they lost to Preston Acheson. Before the party broke up around five the Hammer called his team together for a private talk and told them that he had witnessed a transformation of a bunch of boys to a team of men; he wished them well; and told them that they had provided him with the crowning jewel of his coaching career. He shook each of their hands, and as he hugged them good-bye, he whis-pered something into each young man's ear. There were more than a few teary eyes."

CHAPTER 11
The Bell Tolls for Thee

Nick and Jordan met regularly over the next several months, except for two weeks in early June when they both were on vacation. When they met, it was either at Nick's bench when the weather permitted or inside Perk Place when it was either too warm or raining.

During those meetings, they discussed a variety of topics including politics, climate change, race relations, the Vietnam War, sports, and current events. Nick would often begin their conversations with a question to Jordan regarding what he thought of a certain topical news story; such as, one of the mass shootings in El Paso or New Zealand, or Hurricane Dorian hitting the Bahamas, or the wildfires in the Amazon rainforest, or the college admissions bribery scandal, or the problems with the Boeing 737 Max, or the redacted Mueller report, or the United States Women Soccer team winning their fourth World Cup.

Nick was interested in Jordan's opinion on these news stories for two reasons. First, he wanted to see what a Gen Xer thought, and how Jordan's view might differ from someone Nick's age. Second, he was interested in hearing if Jordan had any additional information on a story that he may have been able to obtain from his colleagues in the newsroom.

Jordan used those opportunities to probe Nick for more information about his past or to find out more about his family. Nick was clever about only divulging enough information to keep Jordan's interest. For example, he explained that he had moved to Middleboro after he retired because he was looking for a nice retirement community with managed care for seniors. He also gave Jordan more information about his family in Pennsylvania and where most of them now lived because many had relocated out of the area for better employment opportunities.

Jordan was always cognizant of Nick's age, even though Nick looked much younger than his 96 years. Therefore, he would try to limit the duration of the meetings to two hours or less, but often when he sensed Nick was getting tired, he would cut them shorter.

Occasionally, Nick would invite Jordan back to his condo for lunch after a morning get-together. Those were the special days because he knew Nick was feeling well. Additionally, Nick always ordered lunch from one of the better restaurants in town and had it delivered. An extra treat for Jordan was when Nick would invite Marjorie to join them. When Marjorie was dining with them, Jordan would just sit back and enjoy the banter, and it was usually lively. Nick would always have some Big Band Era jazz and swing music from the 1940s playing in the background. It wasn't Jordan's favorite musical genre, but he enjoyed it because Marjorie and Nick did.

At least once a week Nick would ask Jordan the status of the case against his brother-in-law, Richard. Jordan would update Nick on the details as they were unfolding. Finally, after a couple of months, Jordan was able to let Nick know that the federal prosecutor and Richard's lawyer had reached a deal whereby Richard would be sentenced to ten years confinement in a minimum-security federal facility. Nick knew that those ten years would likely translate to less than seven with time off for good behavior and petitions for early release or parole. Also, Richard had to make restitution as a condition of the plea bargain. He released the funds that he had stolen and secured in the off-shore account to the feds for repayment to the investors. Jordan mentioned to Nick that he figured to recover almost all of the funds that were stolen from him by Richard, which made both very happy.

Nick was also concerned about Jordan's sister. He made a point of always asking Jordan how Jackie and her kids were doing, and if they needed anything. Jordan kept Nick informed when her house went on the real estate market, and when it sold. Nick wasn't surprised that it sold within days of being put on the market and over the asking price because it was in the most desirable neighborhood in Middleboro. Jordan talked with Nick about having three more people in his house, and how that was working out. Nick listened and was supportive, explaining that it was only temporary. As usual, Nick was right. Within six weeks Jackie had accepted a position at one of the local law firms. One month later, Jackie had found a condo and moved out of Jordan's house.

She, Richie, and Amanda were acclimating to their new lifestyle.

Thomas's house was eventually put on the real estate market, as well. However, it needed some work to enhance its curb appeal. Jordan and Jackie decided to hire Tom Johnson to do the few repairs that it needed, and Tom completed them in his usual expert fashion. Also, he put a fresh coat of paint on all of the shutters, front door, and window trim. Had Thomas been healthy, these were the jobs that he would easily have accomplished. When the house sold, Jackie and Jordan were sad that the family homestead was gone but happy that a young family would have the opportunity to build a life together in the house where they had grown up and enjoyed many great times. They used the proceeds from that sale to get their respective financial affairs back in order. In addition, they had worked out an arrangement with Granatelli's to make installment payments on Thomas' funeral bill until his house sold, then they made a lump sum final payment.

The summer had come and gone with no additional contact from Kathryn. In the first few weeks after Jordan had written his reply to Kathryn letting her know all of what had happened in his and his family's life, and that there was no room for her at his house, Jordan dreaded picking up his mail and answering his phone. Fortunately for him, no news was good news. He surmised that she must have decided to stay in New York and continue teaching since she would be on her own if she came back to Middleboro. As far as Veronica was concerned, Jordan neither cared nor was interested as to how Kathryn and Veronica's relationship either worked out or didn't.

On a better note for Jordan, his relationship with Mary was progressing splendidly. They were meeting several times a week in the mornings to run together since both were planning on running a marathon in the fall. They had run some 5K charity races during the summer as part of their marathon training. One, in particular, benefitted the Mercy Hospice Center. Both Mary and Jordan ran the race and helped with race preparation and sponsorships. On Mary's days off they spent time together taking day trips, hiking, biking, shopping or just enjoying each other's company. On her non-work evenings, they dined together, sometimes eating at one of the area's restaurants and taking in a movie, or sometimes Mary would make dinner at her house. Both were now enjoying life more than they had in years.

Work for Jordan was also progressing well. Along with writing his daily column, he was expanding his horizons by working on a series of articles that he was readily selling to magazines and other newspapers. His weekly syndicated column continued to be very popular with his readership. Additionally, he was organizing his ideas regarding the long-planned book that he now finally figured was ready for writing. The meetings with Nick had become an interesting source of philosophical ideas and a vast database of first-person historical accounts that Jordan tapped time and again for thoughts on life lessons, problem-solving, relationships, politics, history, and of course, sports.

Sadly for Jordan, those meetings with Nick ended a couple of weeks after Labor Day. Jordan got a call one afternoon from Marjorie that Nick was found slumped over at his kitchen table reading the sports page which was opened to Jordan's column. It was a column about a young boy who had been taken to Yankee Stadium when he was 11 years old by his uncle to see Babe Ruth. Jordan's article didn't mention Nick by name, but it told the story of that young boy eventually becoming an elderly gentleman that the writer had met in the park one spring day 85 years later. It mentioned that the elderly gentleman had become a life-long Yankees fan because of the kind act of his uncle, who was essentially functioning as the boy's surrogate father because the boy's biological father had died when he was only four.

Two weeks later on a Saturday morning in late September, Mary and Jordan along with Nick's family, Marjorie, Tony, every prominent local official, and what seemed to Jordan to be half the population of Middleboro attended a memorial service on the grounds of Saint Benedictine's under a large tent. The church officials had been asked by Nick several years before to organize and officiate his memorial service, which they were paid very handsomely to do. Nick had every detail planned to include the biblical passages, music, flowers, and after ceremony party. He wanted everyone to have one last good time on him, and they did. What he didn't want, but it was out of his control after his death, was a litany of speakers extolling his virtues. They lined up by the dozens to speak, but in the end, Saint Benedictine's pastor, Monsignor Finnegan, decided to limit the tributes to six.

During the memorial service, Jordan listened intently to the series of speakers who took the pulpit to eulogize Nick. First was Tony DePalma, the cop that had known Nick since he relocated to Middleboro. He spoke about Nick's generosity to the policemen in particular and the police department in general. He cited several examples of Nick's charitable works that only he knew, such as the anonymous purchase of protective vests for the department's officers; but, he never mentioned any of their persuasive off-duty meetings with nefarious characters. Next was Marjorie, his friend for most of his life in Middleboro. She had several anecdotes about her relationship with Nick that resulted in uproarious laughter from the congregation. The next three speakers were local city officials (the mayor, the president of the city council, and the city planner) who also spoke of Nick's unyielding generosity. They mentioned how he was always first in line to contribute to or drum up support for, any civic project, church function, city festival, golf tournament, or other charitable endeavors. To a person they all spoke of Nick's kind heart; caring nature; his desire to make Middleboro a better place to live for everyone; his abhorrence for liars, cheaters, bullies, con men, and the like; and his desire to help people who sometimes just needed a point in the right direction, even if it only required a bit of wisdom or advice.

After thirty minutes of eulogies and tributes, the final speaker made his way to the pulpit. He began by saying,

"Thank you all for being here today. I have to say, this is a wonderful tribute to Nick."

Jordan was trying to figure out who this speaker was because he more or less knew who the previous five speakers were and their association with Nick, but he couldn't place this fellow, who appeared to be about Jordan's age and spoke with a slight accent. Mary, who was sitting next to Jordan quietly asked, "Do you know who this guy is?"

Jordan just shook his head back and forth slightly and whispered, "No, I have no clue."

The speaker continued, "I realize that no one here knows me, so let me introduce myself. My name is Nicolas Bergeron." He paused for a few seconds, took a deep breath, and then said, "I'm Nick's grandson." There was an audible gasp among those assembled.

Jordan turned to Mary and said, "That old son of a gun. He never mentioned a word of this to me. I wonder if he even knew he had offspring."

Nicolas pressed on, "I know this revelation comes as a shock to you. Please know that I'm not here to tarnish my grandfather's image in any way. He asked me to speak at his memorial service a few months ago. Now, here's the rest of the story that no one knew, including my grandfather, until six months ago. About a year ago I took an ancestry test. I did it mostly on a whim, but also because my father was an orphan who grew up in France, and I hoped in some way to find out more about my lineage and his. To make a long story short because you very fine people have been here a long time, I got a match to someone in Connecticut. The results came back as a distant relative, and I don't mean that because I was in France, and they were in America." That caused a nervous laugh from those in attendance.

After the respectful laughter subsided, Nicolas continued, "It took some months of back and forth communications, some emails and some phone calls; and ultimately additional genetic testing before we were able to ascertain that my father's father, my grandfather, was Nick Marinelli. My father was born in April 1945 in a concentration camp just as World War II was ending in Europe. Unfortunately, my father's mother, my grandmother, died in childbirth, largely because the Nazis were on the verge of losing the war, and they weren't interested in providing medical care for a French detainee. My father was born prematurely and barely survived, largely because of the care and kindness of other detained French women in camp. Before she died, my grandmother made it known to the other women that she wanted her baby named Nicolas. After the war ended, my father was put in an orphanage and raised by French nuns. My grandmother's parents had been arrested for harboring Nick after he was shot down in June 1944. Nick had lived with them and hid from the Germans for a few months while he convalesced from a leg wound, which some of you know bothered him from time to time, resulting in him using his cane. During that time my grandmother and Nick fell in love and my father was conceived."

Nicolas paused for a moment, then began anew. "On a very sad note, both of my great grandparents, Henri and Marie, were executed by the Nazis, and their house and barn burned to the ground because they were suspected of harboring Nick. After the war ended, Nick was assigned to help rebuild a village in Germany. While there Nick made several trips back to France to look for my grandmother. Eventually, he found my great grand-parents' farm but was dismayed by the razed buildings with no sign of life there. He told me how much that saddened him and that he continued to look for them until he found out that they were all dead, which was true. What he didn't know was that my grandmother had become pregnant with his child, my father, and that she had given birth in a concentration camp in Germany, because no one had any records of that. So, until six months ago, Nick was unaware he had a son or family."

At that point, Mary glanced over to Jordan, who by now had tears running down his cheeks. He took out his handkerchief and wiped away the tears. He wasn't embarrassed by his display of emotion because as he looked around at the other attendees he noticed that there wasn't a dry eye anywhere.

Nicolas continued telling his story, "My father was raised by the nuns in that orphanage until he became of age to venture out on his own. He chose the last name Bergeron since he didn't know his mother's or father's surname. My father is still alive but couldn't make the trip here due to a health issue. Fortunately, he and Nick were able to meet this past June in Normandy as part of the 75th-anniversary commemoration of D-Day. They were able to spend several days together, and Nick got to meet his entire family which consists of my mother and father; my wife, me, and our two children; my two sisters, their husbands, and their five collective children.

It was quite a family reunion, to say the least, with lots of hugging, kissing, and crying, not to mention the wine, cheese, and bread." That again brought polite laughter from the congregation.

Nicolas concluded his remarks by paraphrasing John Donne's quote regarding death. "Because we are all part of mankind, any person's death is a loss to all of us. From looking out over this large gathering, who all knew and loved my grandfather, I think that is particularly appropriate. Don't ask for whom the bell tolls, because it tolls for thee. We have all lost a great person in our lives."

As Nicolas descended from the pulpit and took his seat in the front row, there was a momentary silence where the only sounds were that of weeping. Then, after what seemed to be an eternity, the final hymn began. The mourners had been invited to a luncheon on the other side of the church under another large tent immediately following the conclusion of the service, and most of them joined in the celebration of Nick's life.

Jordan and Mary saw that Nicolas was besieged by dozens of people offering their condolences. Therefore, they decided to seek him out later at the luncheon. On their walk around the church grounds to the luncheon tent, Mary asked Jordan, "How much of that story did you know?"

"None of it," Jordan replied, "but I'm sure going to try to get more details from Nicolas when I get a chance to speak with him."

"This is certainly going to add another aspect to your book," she offered.

"Yes, it will," Jordan conceded, "and it may require me to re-organize my material. But first, I need to find out more information from his family. That is, Nick's Pennsylvania family, especially his nephew, Paul."

Once at the luncheon tent, Jordan began asking some of the church officials to point out Nick's family, if they could. After several unsuccessful inquiries, Monsignor Finnegan was able to locate Paul Marinelli among the crowd. Jordan politely excused himself and made a bee-line for Paul with Mary at his side.

The luncheon tent measured 120 feet square and had been set up with dozens of circular dining tables each seating as many as 12 people. Several buffet-style tables with many varieties of brunch foods and drinks were lining the perimeter. All of the dining tables had white linen tablecloths to the ground with a centerpiece of mixed flowers. One of Nick's last requests for his service was for the table where his family sat to have some typical French flowers, such as purple lilies and red poppies. This perplexed the planners because they always assumed he had Italian ancestry, which he did, of course, but now they knew why the traditional French flowers were requested.

Fortunately for Jordan and Mary when they arrived at Paul's table, there were two empty chairs next to Paul. Jordan introduced himself and Mary to Paul and the rest of his family that were present, passed along his deepest and most sincere condolences, then asked if they minded if he and Mary joined them for a few minutes. They were very gracious and extended the invitation to join them. After all the introductions were complete, Mary excused herself and went to get something to eat for Jordan and herself while Jordan began a conversation with Paul.

He told Paul how he had met Nick, and that he and Nick had become very close friends over the last four months. He explained his fascination with Nick and Nick's mysterious life. He further stated that he was interviewing Nick for a writing project that he was working on and explained that he hoped for it to become a book at some point. Paul was intrigued, but not sure why Jordan was sharing that information with him. He let Jordan continue. Eventually, Jordan got around to telling Paul that Nick had shared the story about the 1971 Rotary Basketball Tournament that Paul's team won, and then asking if he could interview him sometime about those games to get his, a player's, perspective.

With a furrowed brow and quizzical look, Paul asked, "What Rotary Basketball Tournament? I don't know what you're talking about. My Uncle Nick must've been pulling your leg."

Jordan's face lost all of its color. He knew that Nick was a storyteller, but he couldn't imagine that he had spun a deceptive web about three mythical games over several interview sessions just to have someone to talk with. Jordan couldn't even formulate a question he was so taken aback.

Paul could see the horror on Jordan's face, then asked, "So, in brief, what did Uncle Nick tell you about these imaginary games?"

Jordan didn't quite know where to begin, but eventually got out, "Well, there were four teams, your YMCA championship team; a private school team, James

Everson Academy; and two public school teams Weston Acheson and Preston Acheson. There were three games with the fourth-seeded team playing at the third-seeded team's court on the first night of the tournament. The winner played at the second-seeded team's home court on the second night, and that winner played at the top-seeded team's court on the final night."

"Well, so far, that's pretty far-fetched, but this sounds like a story Uncle Nick might concoct, please go on," Paul chimed in.

"Your uncle told me that your team ran the table," Jordan began, "won all three games, and that you won the first game pretty much single-handedly."

"Yeah, and he probably told you I had 32 points," Paul said.

"He did!" Jordan exclaimed practically coming out of his seat.

At that point, Paul couldn't keep up the charade, smiled, and said, "Sorry, Jordan, I couldn't resist having some fun. Sure, what do you want to know about those games?"

Jordan immediately felt relieved, then asked, "How long are you going to be in town? Maybe we can meet for an hour or so."

"Well, we're planning on leaving tomorrow morning to drive home, but I can push it back an hour," Paul said, then continued. "I figure I owe you that much since I probably almost gave you a heart attack just now."

"You really had me going," Jordan declared. "You name the time, tell me where you are staying, and I'll pick you up and show you where your uncle and I would talk.

We can even grab a bite to eat at a little coffee shop that's right there. I think you'll like it, and breakfast is on me."

"You don't have to do that," Paul said. "We're staying at the Springhill Suites on Madison. How about eight o'clock. Is that too early?"

"Not at all," Jordan replied. "I'll see you then."

By that time Mary had arrived with two plates full of food. She and Jordan dined with the Marinelli's, conversed about their respective lives, occupations, and of course Nick. Jordan even got up the nerve to ask about Nicolas and how all of that transpired. Paul explained that it was pretty much as Nicolas had outlined in his tribute to Nick. One of Paul's cousins in New England was contacted by Nicolas several months ago about being a possible relative through DNA testing. Some communication had taken place and more DNA testing to narrow the field. Then Paul said, "Once we realized that the only Marinelli to be in Europe around that time was Uncle Nick, we had a winner."

"That's an interesting way to put it," Jordan said.

"Well, you know what I mean," Paul said. "I think it's only right that Uncle Nick found out before he passed away. I think it answered a lot of lingering questions for him."

"I'm sure it did," answered Jordan. "By the way, when I was talking with Nick, he told me that he never left the states during his military service and that his brother, presumably your father, was the one shot down and captured."

"Don't feel too bad about him not sharing all of his life's story with you." Paul began. "Uncle Nick didn't share that much with any of us, either. I think he was trying to deflect any fame, glory, or maybe pity, away from himself. I did find out that he got a Purple Heart because of his war wound, you know, his leg injury. He got hit by a piece of shrapnel when his bomber was shot down, the second time. I overheard him tell my father one day that he figured his leg was broken, but he splinted it and just kept walking west toward France after he parachuted out of his burning plane. I can't imagine how much it must've hurt when he hit the ground."

"I think your Uncle Nick was a lot tougher guy than perhaps either of us knows," was Jordan's response. Jordan then saw Nicolas and asked Paul if he would introduce him. Paul agreed and made the introductions. Jordan and Mary both offered their condolences. He then asked if Nicolas had a few minutes to talk. Jordan was interested in finding out from Nicolas if there was any more information about Nick that he learned while Nick was visiting with them in France. Nicolas explained that Nick had told them about his war experiences, how scared he was during combat, being shot down, how hospitable Henri and Marie (Nicolas' maternal great grandparents) were, about being captured by the Nazis, his eight months in the POW camp in Germany, being rescued by British forces in May 1945, and his failed attempts at finding Nicolas' grandmother.

Nicolas then told Jordan about Nick's meeting with his newfound family in Normandy in June. He explained that Nick was immediately accepted by them and that Nick very much appreciated seeing Normandy at ground level rather than from overhead in a bomber. Jordan asked about Nicolas' father's medical condition and found out that it was the same one that took Nick's life. The advantage for Nicolas' father was that he was still young enough to withstand the operation, but also his aneurysm was located in a much more easily accessible area of the heart.

By then Jordan realized that he had taken up enough of Nicolas' time, thanked him for the opportunity to speak with him, and told him that he did a wonderful job with his talk about Nick. As a parting gesture, Nicolas invited Jordan and Mary to be his guest if they ever got to Paris. Jordan and Nicolas exchanged contact information before Nicolas bid Mary and Jordan 'Au revoir'.

Jordan arrived at Paul's hotel at 7:55 a.m., and Paul was outside waiting. As he got into Jordan's car, he said, "I see my uncle indoctrinated you into being five minutes early, otherwise you're late."

"You, as well," Jordan replied. Then, they both laughed.

On the short drive to Perk Place Jordan was able to tell Paul about the park, Nick's bench, and the many enjoyable times they had there. Paul shared with Jordan that Nick functioned as a surrogate grandfather to him and Nick's other nieces and nephews since they never had a grandfather. Paul also mentioned that Nick frequently slipped them a few bucks to enjoy some of the childhood luxuries they wanted, or money to go on a date. He further mentioned that Nick even umpired Little

League games when no umpires could make it. Those stories just reinforced Nick's benevolent nature in Jordan's mind.

Because it was Sunday morning the traffic was light, and there was ample street parking right in front of Perk Place. They quickly ordered breakfast and coffee, then got right to talking about the games that Jordan wanted a player's perspective.

Paul started by telling Jordan that his team was so naïve that they thought they could just show up, and they'd breeze to three easy victories. It took a couple of sessions with Mike and the drubbing at the hands of the junior college players from Philly to put them in the right frame of mind.

Jordan interrupted to ask, "So, after the hard practices did you figure your team was in the best shape of any of the four teams?"

"Honestly, we were never out of shape. We all were playing some sport all the time. Augie and I were playing baseball. The rest of the guys were running track or doing field events. Danny and I had just competed in the Marine Corps Physical Fitness Challenge with four other guys from our school. Speaking for myself, I was in the best shape of my life, and I'd guess, so were all of our guys. That's not to say that the other teams were sitting around eating pizza and drinking soda or beer, but I doubt they were as fit as we were."

"Tell me about your first game, and please don't be modest," Jordan said.

"Here's the deal about that game," Paul began. "I wasn't supposed to be a shooter. I was our fifth-leading scorer. My job was to play defense and run our offense for Bags, Augie, and Dino to score. Ricky was our rebounder and defender around the basket. That night our top three scorers were all shooting poorly. That's incredibly unusual, but it happened. I recall feeling good that night, and immediately knew the guy guarding me couldn't keep up. I was beating him off the dribble and shooting over him. Fortunately, everything I tossed up that night went in."

"Your defender was an all-star guard named Ted Bigby," Jordan reminded him.

"Yeah, a sad story there. I heard his alcoholism progressed, and he died before he reached 40. To be fair, he was a great player when he was in shape and sober, but that night he was definitely slow, and as you know, if you lose a step on the court, you've lost your game."

"Well, I appreciate your humility, and since you don't seem to want to talk too much about your game that night, we can move on," Jordan said.

"Sorry, what else do you want to know?" Paul began. "I don't remember specifics, but I recall Mike setting me up for the last shot, and I swished it, but you have to remember, it was still a team effort. Yes, I had the hot hand that night, but my teammates recognized it and kept feeding me. Without them getting me the ball in good spots and setting screens, I would not have scored like I did, and we would likely have lost. So, our team did what it had to do to squeak one out."

Jordan then asked about the Preston Acheson game. He inquired, "What did you think of the officiating in that game?"

"None of us knew the full story, but we knew that we were being robbed," Paul started out saying, then continued. "It had been a problem for our varsity team there when they played the Paladins during the regular season. I found out years later from my uncle what happened. It's a shame that they couldn't let us just play the game fairly. That night our big three were back on their games and playing well. I think we could've beaten them by ten or more if the refs had called it fairly from the beginning."

"What about the last play when you stripped Kerry O'Boyle?" Jordan asked.

"Uncle Nick remembered that, huh?" Paul said. "Mike knew that play was coming off their in-bound pass. So, he had us looking for it. I sagged down on Kerry from behind and got ready to put my hand on the top of the ball. When he released his right hand, his guide hand, I rolled the ball off his left hand just as he was shooting his jumper. As soon as I got control of the ball I raced toward our basket. I knew their point guard would be back on defense, so I was going to go up strong and at least draw a foul. At the last second, I saw Danny filling the other lane, so I went up for the lay-up, then flipped him the ball behind my back. He laid it in with a second to spare. I thought our side of the gym was going to crash down the stands. They were jumping up and down like a bunch of kids on a trampoline, and the explosion of noise was deafening."

"Wow, some kind of ending," Jordan said. "What about the beginning of the second half and your second team's physical statement."

"That wasn't the way we wanted to play," Paul stated unequivocally. "However, Mike had to do something to let the referees and the Paladins know that we weren't going to take a beating and lose. He told us 'We may lose this game, but we are *not* going to be beaten up physically.' He further said, 'It's up to you guys, you can rollover, or dig deep and show them who's the tougher team.' So, the bomb squad started the second half and didn't care about scoring. They were instructed to dish out as much punishment as possible without swinging their fists unless of course, someone threw the first punch. I was very happy to be on the bench watching it rather than be on the court because I was the smallest guy on either team."

"You said that wasn't the way you wanted to play," Jordan followed up.

"Of course not, we were there to play basketball as it was properly meant to be played. But, the Paladins were hacking us all over the court because they were allowed to, and we were the ones getting called for all the fouls. So, Mike decided if that's the way they wanted it, then that's the way they were going to get it. I think one of their players ended up with some stitches in his lip and two others had to have ice applied to their face after a couple of particularly brutal fouls. Elbows were flying everywhere. It came close to becoming a full-scale brawl. But, again, they had it coming. Hey, if you can't take it, then don't dish it out."

"Good enough," Jordan said. "The final game . . . what are your recollections?"

Paul started by saying, "We knew them really well, and they knew us. We figured we were better than they were athletically, but they may have had a slight edge from a basketball perspective. So, our athleticism was going to have to carry us, and obviously, it did. Credit goes to the Hammer. He had it figured right from the start. We wore them out. By the middle of the third quarter, we knew we had it."

"But it got close late in the game because Mike cleared your bench," Jordan reminded Paul.

"It did, but Mike wanted everyone to play," Paul said. "We were toying with them at that point. We finally put them away for good with about two minutes to go."

"Do you recall your team's final point totals?" Jordan inquired.

Paul thought for a second or two, then offered, "If memory serves me well, Ricky and I had about eight or nine points each. Ricky had at least a dozen rebounds, and I had several assists. Bags, Augie, and Dino had between 16 and 18 points each. The other guys had the rest. Interestingly, our point total was 71, the same as our graduating year. That's how I remember it."

"What about their coach," Jordan asked.

"Not a nice man, but a good coach, except for the screaming," Paul offered. "He knew his basketball, but he had a bad habit of embarrassing his players in front of the fans. It's alright to yell and holler at them during practice when no one is around, but don't do it during a game when everyone can see it. It's just bad form. He could have had Ricky, Dino, Danny, and Augie on that team."

"Not you?" Jordan asked.

"I doubt I would have made the team," Paul said, "or, if I did, it would have been as the last guy on the second team, or maybe third team, if they carried that many guys. I was just not as good as the rest of those guys. What I brought to the court were hustle and scrappiness. So, if we had Lafferty, Stroebel, Danny, Dino, Augie, and the others, our team would have been loaded, maybe overloaded."

Jordan thought for a second, then said, "This never came up when I was talking with your uncle but did the Rotary Club officials give out a Most Valuable Player award after the tournament since those types of tournaments usually do?"

"They did," Paul began, "however, in 1971 they announced that they couldn't come up with one player who stood out, so they awarded it to us as a team award. That was sort of redundant since we won the tournament championship trophy, but it was fair, I think since we played as a team. In the locker room after the game, the players agreed unanimously to award it to Nick as a memento of our appreciation."

"He never mentioned it, but then again in hindsight, that sounds just like Nick, doesn't it?" Jordan mused, then asked, "Who *was* the best player in the tournament in your opinion?"

"Probably, Larry Stroebel, but Kerry O'Boyle was great, also." Paul replied, then followed up with, "Unfortunately for them, neither was going to get the MVP trophy since their team only played one game and didn't win the championship."

"I know we've used up most of our allotted time," Jordan began. "I just want to tell you how much I appreciate you meeting me this morning and delaying your trip home."

"It was my pleasure, Jordan," Paul said. "Those were good days for our guys. I see some of them at our reunions, and we reminisce a little about those games. I even golf with some of them on occasion. So, again, fun times for all of us."

Jordan drove Paul back to his hotel, and Paul and his family left shortly thereafter for their drive home. Paul was elated that Jordan had the interest in those games and also the initiative to seek out a player's perspective. They exchanged contact information, and Paul asked Jordan to please keep him in mind if he needed anything further from him. Paul then requested a copy of whatever came out of his research and interviews with his Uncle Nick, which Jordan said he would gladly provide.

CHAPTER 12
Nick's Gift to Jordan

On the Monday after Nick's memorial service Jordan received a registered letter from Nick's lawyer requesting Jordan's presence at his office on Friday, October 5th at ten o'clock. Jordan was naturally curious, so he called to see what it concerned. The lawyer's office would only tell him that it was Nick's wish that Jordan was present at the reading of Nick's will. Jordan told the secretary that he would attend.

Jordan arrived at the lawyer's office at 9:45 a.m. and was escorted to a small conference room. He wasn't sure why he was asked to be there, but figured, if nothing else, it could be part of his book. Already in the conference room when Jordan arrived was Paul Marinelli. They shook hands and again joked about being early. In Paul's hand was a manila folder, which he handed to Jordan and said, "I think you may be interested in this. My uncle wanted it, but after our conversation last week, I suspect he wanted it for you."

Jordan opened the folder and broke into a huge grin. Inside was a picture of the Italian Stallions in their red, green, and white uniforms. They were in two rows with the taller guys standing behind the shorter guys, who were kneeling in front of them on one knee. The guys in the back row were holding small trophies while the kneeling players had their trophies on the floor in front of them. Jordan noticed that many of the guys had pencil-drawn Fu Manchu mustaches (except Anthony Simonetti who grew his own), and asked Paul what that was all about. Paul laughed and told him that it was the idea of the team jokester, Ronnie DiGiacomo. Jordan also noticed the length of the shorts the guys were wearing, and they both laughed. Also in the folder was the newspaper article on the tournament which greatly interested Jordan since he was unable to find it via any archived newspaper search. He likened it to the publication having gone out of business before the process of archiving had begun.

Eventually, Nicolas Bergeron, Tony DePalma, Nick's friend, Marjorie, and Monsignor Finnegan arrived. They made small talk until the lawyer entered and commenced with the reading of Nick's will.

Nick's lawyer began with the formalities and explained that Nick was of sound mind and body when he had recently modified his will. He went over a few other details explaining that at Nick's stipulation all of his financial holdings were to be liquidated, thereby leaving only cash to his heirs. He continued by reading the legalese of the will, and when he finished, there were only happy people in the room.

For the most part, Nick had left percentages of his wealth to each of his heirs, and that wealth was substantial, but not disclosed at the reading. The lawyer explained that each heir would receive a check or direct deposit, if that was their preference, once the liquidation was completed. Additionally, there were a few personal items that he left to certain people. His record collection went to Marjorie, and his cane along with his old style golf hat collection went to his son.

The lawyer then read the following. "My son, Nicolas Bergeron, is bequeathed 40%." He was represented by his son, also named Nicolas Bergeron. "The living Marinelli nieces and nephews are to divide 40% evenly." They were eight in all, and they were represented by Paul Marinelli. All of Nick's brothers and sisters had pre-deceased him. "Saint Benedictine's is to receive 10% with the stipulation that it be used to build a shelter for unwed mothers and an orphanage." Monsignor Finnegan smiled broadly. "Tony DePalma and Marjorie McNulty are to receive 5% each."

At first, Jordan wondered why he was even asked to be there since he figured that he wouldn't be included in Nick's will. Then the lawyer took a gift-wrapped box from under the conference table and asked Jordan to come forward. He gave it to Jordan and explained that Nick wanted Jordan to have the contents. At that point, the lawyer concluded the meeting and told those assembled that they were free to stay and converse if they liked. Jordan made a point to see each of the others before everyone left and told each how happy he was for them to be remembered by Nick in his will.

On the way out of the lawyer's office, Jordan decided to stop by Perk Place for his favorite brew before returning home to see what Nick's surprise gift was. Perk Place was mostly on the way, and he was now in the mood for his favorite drink. Although his heart was still heavy with sorrow at Nick's passing, he consoled himself with the realization that Nick would somehow try to cheer him up, even after he was no longer able to be there in person for him. The card on the gift simply read, "To Jordy, OPEN IN PRIVATE! All my best, Nick".

Jordan's present was beautifully wrapped and appeared to be about the size of a box of computer paper. It wasn't overly heavy, but not light, either. The wrapping paper was scotch plaid with dark red, white, blue, and green colors running throughout in a tartan Stewart design. The ribbon around the box and bow were an amazing shade of green. Jordan thought, 'This is perfectly wrapped, probably by Nick himself, who was as *perfectly wrapped* a human being as anyone I have ever known – how appropriate', he thought, 'and green being my favorite color, I'll bet he somehow knew that, too'.

On his way home Jordan was particularly careful not to make any sudden stops. He didn't know what might be in the box, but he was taking no chances with it tumbling off the passenger's seat. Jordan even considered strapping it in securely with the seat belt and shoulder harass, but he figured if the contents were fragile, Nick's note would have told him so. He knew that Nick didn't miss a trick, and he wouldn't mess up his perfect record with his last expression of benevolence.

The drive was easy, so he was able to get home quickly, since it was the middle of the day with little traffic. As he pulled into his driveway, he hoped to not see any of his neighbors since he wanted to get right to the contents of the box. Fortunately, Agatha and Andy weren't in their front yard, so Jordan quickly slipped into his house undetected.

By now Jordan felt like a kid at Christmas. He knew that he could be setting himself up for disappointment, but somehow he felt that whatever was in the box would be something truly special, because, of course, it was from Nick. He placed the box on his kitchen table and carefully removed the ribbon and bow without destroying them. The wrapping paper was another story. At first, he tried to neatly tear it open along the taped edges, but after 15 seconds his patience ran out, and he just ripped it open.

The box itself was fairly sturdy. As it turned out, it was indeed a computer paper box with a lid that was lightly taped for ease of wrapping. Jordan slit the tape with an ever-handy kitchen knife, then gently removed the lid, not knowing what to expect. He was sure nothing was going to pop out at him, but the contents could be almost anything from sports memorabilia to a stack of old newspapers to Nick's collection of Scottish golf hats, although those went to his son.

Once he looked inside, Jordan noticed green bubble wrap around the contents, though still unseen, and therefore still unknown. He tried to lift the entire contents out of the box but soon realized that it was a snug fit, and he was working at a bad angle. He re-positioned the box on the floor and put one foot on each side to hold it down while he pulled the contents out and placed them on the table. The bubble wrap was neatly and securely protecting whatever was within its confines. Of course, it was neatly taped, as well, so Jordan once again had to use his kitchen knife to gently and carefully slit the tape.

The unwrapping process required Jordan's patience and diligence. He didn't want to ruin, in any way, what Nick had so carefully sought to preserve. As Jordan began unwrapping, he noticed a hand-written letter at the top of the stack of what appeared to be some old books. He picked up the letter and began to read it. It said:

Dear Jordy,

By now you know that I have passed away. Don't be sad, young man. I have lived a very long and great life. One of my few regrets is that I did not get to meet you until my last year on earth. You are truly one of the good souls on this sometimes crazy planet. Keep doing the things that your parents taught you. They raised a great son.

Regarding the contents of this box, I have entrusted in you my life's story by way of this journal in two volumes. Once you read through them, you will realize that I was not always completely honest with you concerning my endeavors, my experiences, my employment, and my escapades. Sorry for that, but sometimes it's better this way, at least it was for me. I never really liked talking about myself, so I felt more comfortable telling you about certain parts of my life while walking in other people's shoes, so to speak. Ironic for someone who hated liars, isn't it?

At any rate, I wanted you to have my journal. I started writing in it at an early age and continued throughout my life with only periodic gaps which you will see and easily understand why. As you have undoubtedly figured out, yes, writing is one more trait that we have in common, along with our favorite color being green.

Speaking of 'green', I left you some of that underneath the journals. If you decide to work your magic and write your book, perhaps some of what you read in my journal, and what I've told you can assist in making an interesting story. On the other hand, if you do not feel it is worth your time, or the material is just not that interesting, and you would rather not pursue it, then that's OK, too. After all, I will never know. By the way, the $15,000 is not taxable since it is right at the federal tax limit for gift giving this year. You may need it to publish your book, or just use it for something fun for you and Mary.

Well, my friend, as the saying goes, parting is such sweet sorrow. I know your life has sometimes been difficult, but remember our true personality and character is defined by how we handle adversary. You will be fine. Give it some time, after all, it is a great healer. Good luck with your book and thank you for making our short time together so very enjoyable.

All my best,
Nick

Jordan put down Nick's touching letter on the table beside the two volumes of his journal. He was fighting back tears but didn't want to get any on Nick's letter. He then carefully picked up the first volume of Nick's life work. The cover was badly worn. It looked to have been through a war, so to speak, and Jordan would soon find out how prophetic that observation was.

Volume one had a brown cover with badly faded gold inlay around the four sides. He gently opened the cover so as not to damage it in any way. Inside the front cover was Nick's name neatly printed in black ink. Below that was a note that read, "If found, please return to the last address, no questions asked, substantial reward." That was followed by a series of addresses. All but the last address (Nick's current one before he died) had been crossed out. Jordan thought, "Nick, you shrewd dude, you tried to cover all your bases all of the time, didn't you?"

Turning to page one of Nick's journal, Jordan noticed that the first date was in 1929. He figured that Nick was only six years old at the time, and of course, the writing was pretty much that of a six-year-old. In part, it mentioned getting a diary for his birthday from his Aunt Bonnie and Uncle Al. Not much else was of interest, just items that would be important to a six-year-old, such as, school matters, baseball, and a pretty girl he liked. At that point, Jordan flipped to the back of the first volume to see what years it covered. The last entry was late in 1969 and mentioned something about it being a turbulent decade. He decided not to get too involved in reading what appeared to be full weekend's worth of very interesting prose, so he put down volume one and again gently opened volume two, which was in much better shape, roughly the same size, but had a blue cover.

Jordan decided to call them the brown book and the blue book. What surprised him was that neither was green.

As expected, it began in early 1970. He had some entries about his work and getting to know some people he had become acquainted with through a mutual friend. Jordan then leafed through to the part of Nick's journal when they met. What he read made him emotional, yet again.

Tuesday, 15 May 2019: Nice young fellow, Jordan Marsh, holds the door for me while I'm leaving Perk Place. Later, he stops to chat for a few seconds after he meets Mary Starling for breakfast at Perk Place. Saw disturbing sight: two teenagers make a filthy gesture toward Jordan's friend, Mary, after she reprimands them. Called Big Tony, who takes care of it.

Jordan mused aloud, "So, Nick, indeed, knew Mary's name before I even met her, or they were even introduced? That old son of a gun knew everything that was going on around him. 'Big Tony' is Tony DePalma. He was the cop I saw that day talking to those two boys, and it was Nick who called him to get on those ill-mannered kids."

Wednesday, 16 May 2019: Jordy, as I have nicknamed him, stops to talk with me while I sit in the park. Brings me my favorite drink from Perk Place. Spends some of his time with me despite having had his father pass away the previous evening. I knew he was a good kid the moment I saw him. We make plans to meet again soon. I decide to let him interview me for his project. Later: Jordy stops by again in the early afternoon to talk. He is struggling with a few issues. Called the police chief to get his bogus ticket squashed and asked him to find Jordy's computer that had been stolen earlier in the day. Chief Galetti assures me he will personally take care of it. Jordy's ex-wife issue is a problem I've decided to leave for him to solve. Gave him a few ideas. Hope it helps.

Jordan smiled and thought, 'Well, that explains why the cop showed up at my door with my computer and an apology for the traffic ticket. I'm not sure what connections Nick had around here, but he was a man who could get things done, or get people to get them done.'

At that point, Jordan put down the journal and looked at the rest of the contents of the box. Underneath a thin piece of cardboard, he found 15 packs of $20 bills. Jordan quickly figured that each stack of twenties must contain $1000, so each bundle must have fifty $20 bills. Jordan noticed that they were all crisp, freshly printed twenties with consecutive serial numbers as he thumbed through them. For a brief moment Jordan thought perhaps they were all counterfeit bills, then what would he do? He held one up to the light and could see the thin thread of ribbon running through it, so he was greatly relieved that they were real.

Jordan wasn't sure what to do with the money, so he put it all back in the box and carried the box to the closet in his bedroom, where he put it on the floor in the corner. He figured to deal with it at some point, but not now since he still had a column to write for his paper's next edition.

※》 ※《

When Jordan finally got back to Nick's journal, he decided to read through it chronologically and make some notes about the more important and more interesting passages. He saw the notation in 1934 about being taken to Yankee Stadium by his Uncle Al and seeing Babe Ruth hit a home run. There were several entries about how difficult his mother and family had it in the 1930s during the Great Depression with no father and very limited income. His family's main source of food was from their garden, so taking care of it was of paramount importance. Jordan felt bad reading those passages. He knew he could not have changed any of those circumstances, and that everyone else was pretty much in the same situation during that time, but it didn't make him feel any better.

The next passage of interest was in 1940, and Jordan would soon learn that what Nick mentioned in his cover letter was true. He had concealed parts of his story in other people's identities.

Saturday, August 16, 1940: Mom passed away this afternoon around 4:30. Father O'Hanlon gave her last rights, heard her confession, and gave her communion. Afterward, he called me aside and told me that Mom told him that Martha and James forced her to sign a new will leaving them as the only heirs.

Monday, September 8, 1940: Sue, Joe, and I challenge mom's will in court citing undue influence by Martha and James regarding her second will. We lost the court case, even after Father O'Hanlon testifies on our behalf explaining that mom told him that Martha and James forced her to sign the second will.

All of a sudden Jordan realized the story that Nick told him about his friend being cheated out of an inheritance by a second will and coerced signature was actually about Nick and his family. He quickly scanned ahead to see if there were other entries relating to the will, the court proceedings, or any dealings with his siblings. He found one more.

Wednesday, October 8, 1940: After discussing with Sue and Joe, we decided not to pursue any further legal action against Martha and James. No good will come from their inheritance, anyway, not that it was much. Lessons learned: (1) Never trust anyone completely when money is involved; (2) Forgive, but don't forget; and (3) Don't let the bad behavior of someone else make you become someone you don't want to be.

Jordan smiled and thought, 'That's just like Nick to make it a teachable moment for his siblings and to not hold any ill feelings against his brother and sister, even if he had good reason to do so.'

The next interesting part dealt with World War II. Jordan began reading and learned that what Nicolas and Paul had told him about Nick's war experience was true. Now, he would learn it from Nick's first-person account.

Wednesday, October 14, 1942: Draft notice arrives in the mail today. Must report by end of the year.

Jordan read through several entries between late 1942 and early 1944 mostly relating to basic training, advanced training, gunnery training, and the many bases where the training was conducted. He noticed that Nick made mention of the many different women that he knew in each town where he was stationed. Of particular note were Margaret in San Diego, Betty in Tucson, Leana in Miami Beach, and Judy in Denver, but there were many others and sometimes multiple listings from one place. Jordan concluded that Nick was quite a ladies' man in his younger days and wouldn't be surprised if there was another offspring or two that he never knew. He also mused, 'at least this part of what he told me was true.'

Thursday, June 1, 1944: Flying B-24 Liberators out of RAF Horsham St. Faith (USAAF designated Station 123) Norfolk, England. Had our first bombing mission today over Germany. Gunnery training was nothing like actual aerial combat. Very different when the Luftwaffe is shooting back at you. Was so scared I thought I would die of fright. Used up nearly all my ammo on way to the target. Will have to learn to conserve ammo. Still shaking from the experience. Other crew members tell me it gets better if you live long enough. We made it back to base without any causalities, but I don't know how. Our plane is all shot up. Now I know why the B-24 is called the 'Flying Coffin'.

Jordan was glad to finally get the truth from Nick, even if it was after he was dead. He recalled that Nick said he never left the states while serving in WWII, but that his brother was a gunner on a B-24. Once again, Jordan thought, Nick had chosen to tell his story while giving the limelight to someone else. Jordan was mesmerized and could not read on fast enough.

Friday, June 2, 1944: Not as lucky today. German fighters were all over us on route to the target, then we took heavy flak on the bombing run. Not sure if our bombs hit their mark. Bombardier has an impossible job holding sight on target with aircraft bouncing and shaking. One engine knocked out on way to the target, then two more on way back. Lost two crew, both were gunners like me (Hank Greenblatt and Benny Lemongello). Good guys, nice guys, to be sure. Captain Barnes had to ditch in Channel. The rescue boat fished us out quickly, thankfully, as the water was very cold. God was watching over me today. Only 23 missions to go! Heading into town for some R&R. Later: Met Annie at the pub. The guys and I spent most of the night with her and her friends. Fascinated by her English accent, wavy brown hair, and blue eyes.

Saturday, June 3, 1944: Flew two missions today. Rumor has it that something big is up. No one knows anything for sure, but the scuttlebutt is that it must be big for us to be running double missions. Some talk about Allied land invasion on the French coast. God help those guys going ashore if that is what it is. Not sure where we were, somewhere over France, but we dropped a lot of ordnance today, which looked to be gunnery emplacements. Hope we hit our targets. Got my first kill today (Messerschmitt), but overall, only light resistance. Sorry for him, but better him than me, or any of my crewmates.

Sunday, June 4, 1944: For some reason, we get the day off. Mostly hung around the base. Did laundry, rested, relaxed, read Stars and Stripes. Heading into town later. Have concluded that English grub is bland and their beer (ale) too warm to enjoy. Later: Saw Annie and her friends again tonight. Danced and enjoyed each other's company until curfew.

Jordan noticed that the next entry in Nick's journal was dated August 1945. He knew why there were no entries between June 1944 and August 1945, but he wanted to read Nick's own words as to what happened.

Monday, August 13, 1945: Finally made it back to Horsham. Could not believe my journal was being kept for me along with my other personal items. Lots of writing to catch up on. Unfortunately, some dates will be approximated and details sketchy. Will do my best to resurrect the last 14 months . . . here goes!

Monday, June 5, 1944: Shot down somewhere over western Germany. Later find out that the big push with bombing missions was to soften up German positions in advance of the Allied Invasion. Not sure if anyone else survived the explosion when our plane was hit, but I think what saved me was being a tail gunner that day. I parachuted at the last second to minimize being a target while hanging in the air defenseless. The plane went down in a fireball in a field. After landing, I secured my chute and hid it under some brush so the Germans would not find it. Was injured by shrapnel in the explosion. Tied off my leg wound with my handkerchief and splinted my leg with two sticks. Scared worse than when Messerschmitts were attacking us, and we were flying through all that flak. Somehow managed to hide out until night, then walked (limped) west, I think, for miles trying to make it to France. Tried to find something to eat and a place to sleep. No luck with food, but slept in a barn I found after walking for miles.

Tuesday, June 6, 1944: Later, I find out this is D-Day and not a good day for the guys trying to make a beachhead at Normandy. For me, though, it's a good day. I'm rescued by a French farmer and his family. They feed me, even though they have little food to spare, doctor my wound, and hide me in their basement from the Germans, who are now looking for me and any other fliers who were shot down.

Wednesday, June 7, 1944: We get reports that the Allies have landed at Normandy and are pushing inland against heavy resistance. My hosts, Henri, Marie, and their daughter, Gisele are very kind to me. They know a little English, and I know no French, but somehow we manage to communicate.

Several days later: Henri lets me know that there is a French Underground that can help me get back to my lines. It takes a while to understand, but I figure it out. He doesn't know when he'll be able to contact them since there are many German patrols. So, we decide to wait. My wound is healed, but I suspect my leg may have been broken. I cannot just sit around and not help Henri, so he dresses me like a French farmer, and I help him work in the field and tend to the cattle. I learn a little about farming.

Sometime in early July: Gisele, who is 19, and I are becoming friendly. She knows more English than her parents, and I'm teaching her more and more each day. She's also teaching me French, although her English is progressing much better than my French.

Later in July 1944: I've been a guest of Henri and his family for about six weeks. My apprenticeship in farming is going well, but my friendship with Gisele is going even better. I don't want to ruin this sanctuary, but we both have romantic feelings for one another. I consider trying to talk to Henri about it but fear that he will ask me to leave. My leg has healed thanks to Marie's doctoring.

Early in August 1944: Our romantic feelings for each other overwhelm us late one night. I had been staying in the barn with fairly comfortable arrangements. Occasionally, Gisele would sneak out there after her parents had gone to sleep. Until now, we had just kissed and cuddled, but this night we made love. She stayed most of the night, then just before dawn went back to her bedroom.

Later in August 1944: Our love affair was now getting to the dangerous stage. Gisele was coming out to the barn every night. I knew it would be just a matter of time until either Henri or Marie suspected something, or God forbid, caught us.

Near the end of August 1944: Unbeknown to me, Gisele tells her parents that we're in love and that she wants to marry me. Henri gets very mad. He accuses me of seducing his daughter and sullying her reputation, or at least that's what I can make of it through his combination of French and English. The bottom line is that I have to leave. He would never turn me over to the Germans since he hated them, but now he was going to contact the French Underground to get me back to my lines. Later, I find out that the Allies have retaken Paris.

Early in September 1944: Two members of the French Underground show up to take me on a march north. Gisele and I have not been allowed to see each other alone since she talked with her parents about us getting married. I have just a few minutes to gather my belongings, say goodbye to Gisele, and thank Henri and Marie for their help and hospitality. Gisele cries and runs into the house. Also, I apologize for any inappropriate behavior on my part. Henri wasn't very accepting of my apology, but I think Marie understood that it was just two young people during wartime that were caught up in the moment and the passion.

A day later in September 1944: While moving at night, we run into a German patrol. I'm captured and sent to a POW camp. I never find out what happened to the two French Underground guys, although I'm guessing they were interrogated, then shot. War's hell . . .

The next day, still early September 1944: I arrive at Stalag 11B, near Fallingbostel, Germany. My interrogation is scary. The Germans want to know when I was shot down, where I was staying, who helped me, how I was able to evade capture. I gave them my name, rank, and serial number, only. They tried to coax me with special items like cigarettes, chocolate, warm clothing, and a hot shower. I told them I didn't smoke or like chocolate, and my clothes were fine. Later during interrogation, their frustration with me only answering with name, rank and serial number earned me several slaps. Nothing I couldn't take, of course. Eventually, they gave up on me, mostly because another prisoner had arrived. I got five days in the cooler for my non-cooperation.

Mid-September 1944 to early April 1945: Each day as a Kreigie (short for kreigefangenen, which means prisoner of war in German) is pretty much the same. We were rousted up early to stand outside no matter the weather for roll call. Our barracks guard, Sgt. Johann Schmitt, was pretty good to us. I think he knew the war wasn't going well for the Germans, and by early 1945 he was trying to be as kind as he could without arousing suspicion from his superiors. Smitty, as we called him, tried to alert us to any surprise inspections. We had a few prisoners who tried to escape from time to time, but it was pretty much futile. The Germans checked all vehicles leaving camp. They had dogs patrolling and sniffing around all the time. The guard towers were so well placed that there were no areas to get through the wire without being seen, and besides, we had no means to cut the wire anyway. Tunneling was out of the question since we had no tools to dig with unless you used your fork or spoon. We knew that the Allies were making great progress, and we just needed to stay alive until they liberated us. Our rations were meager, so the Red Cross packages kept us not only alive but kept our morale up. Over time I learned to barter for the items I needed or the ones my barracks mates needed. In short order, I was looked upon as the best scrounger in camp.

Since I didn't smoke, I could use my cigarette ration for other items, like soap or chocolate. We knew Smitty liked chocolate, so he could be bribed for other much sought-after items, like paper and pencils to write home, an extra ration of bread, a clean towel, or a sharp razor. By the end of my confinement, I had honed my skills as a scrounger to the point that I needed a supply locker and an assistant to handle all the supplies.

Monday, April 16, 1945: The British Second Army marches in and liberates us. Never so happy to see those guys in my life. Most of the Germans guarding us "escaped" the night before. We could hear the artillery in the distance and knew our guys would be there to rescue us soon. I consider myself lucky to have had to only endure about seven months in a POW camp. Some of our guys were there for a couple of years and didn't look too healthy.

Late April 1945: I get medical exam: wound and broken leg are healed, and I'm cleared to return to combat, but fortunately the war in Europe is all but over.

Monday, May 7, 1945: Germany surrenders effectively ending WWII in Europe.

Late May 1945: Assigned to help with clean-up of a village and pull out of Allied forces somewhere in Germany. Easy work, good food, and locals are glad for the help.

Early June to mid-August 1945: Whenever I get time off, I commandeer a jeep and drive into France. I'm not sure where to look, but I try to find Gisele and her family. Finally, in early August I find what I remember to be their farm. Their house and barn are burned to the ground, and no one is there. It's abandoned. I drive around for hours trying to find anyone who may know what happened to them, but no luck. I return to base resigned to the fact that I'll never know. Finally, on my last trip before heading back to England, I find out that Henri, Marie, and Gisele are all dead. This is the worst day of my life.

Tuesday, August 14, 1945: Back at Horsham. Go into town to see if I can find Annie. After asking around for a couple of hours, I find someone who knows her and gives me her address. I go to her flat and find her married and pregnant. She introduces me to her husband, Nigel Pennypacker. Nice enough fellow. She asks me what happened that I stopped coming around. I tell her my story, except the part about Gisele. She invites me to stay for dinner, but I lie and say I have to get back to base. I'm a bit heartbroken, but pragmatic, I know it was unrealistic to think that Annie would wait around for me after knowing me for only a few days and then not seeing me for 14 months. Life must go on . . .

Jordan decided to take a break from reading. He felt very badly for Nick being heartbroken. In short order, he had lost two women that he cared deeply for, especially Gisele.

Friday, April 19, 1946: Happy Birthday to me! Just back in the states. Heading to Scranton to take in the fights with Joe and some of the old gang. Later: I get seated next to a guy named Sam. We talk for hours about the war, boxing, and my future. He offers me a job working for him. Don't know what he does, but it's a job.

Wednesday, May 22, 1946: Sam sends me to Harrisburg to see our state representative. I just have to deliver a package. Easy drive down and back. So far, easy job.

Jordan read through several more such entries from 1946 to the early 1950s about Nick meeting various local and state officials, elected representatives, judges, and several business leaders. Most entries didn't detail any information about the meetings except that a package or envelope was delivered. He skimmed through much of the entries in the 1950s about the Korean War, Truman, and Eisenhower, and the Yankees being in almost every World Series, but nothing much about Nick's personal life. There were a few entries about work and doing some jobs for his boss. He mentioned filling in as a driver for his boss's bus company, a truck driver for some of his boss's dress factories, and running a pool hall, but nothing that would explain how Nick might have amassed any significant wealth.

The entries in the 1960s were similar, but Jordan, being the sharp journalist and researcher that he was, could detect a change in the level of significance of Nick's work responsibilities. It seemed that Nick had moved up from Sam's gopher to Sam's assistant and right-hand man. Subtly, and over time, the entries divulged that Nick was taking a more prominent role in the decision-making process involving Sam's business ventures. He was no longer the errand boy, but was now working side-by-side with Sam, much like an understudy, not only learning from Sam at his elbow, but making minor decisions as to what businesses to invest in, or not. By the late 1960s, Nick was running all of Sam's dress factories in the area. He was making weekly trips to New York's garment district and deciding what contracts to sign and which ones to pass on. Jordan was also able to determine that around that same time, Gordon entered the picture as Nick's assistant, friendly persuader, and body man (guard).

By the mid-1970s Sam was in his early eighties and was pretty much retired. He had passed operational control of his business empire to Nick. Jordan learned from

Nick's journal entries that Sam had no heirs, and when he passed away in 1978, Sam left everything to Nick; lock, stock, and barrel. So, now Jordan knew how Nick came to be so wealthy, but he didn't know, nor would ever find out, just how wealthy.

Jordan next wanted to see what Nick had written about the basketball games, so he went to that section of Nick's journal and carefully read what he had already heard Nick tell him personally. As it turned out, it was the same narrative, so Jordan surmised that the journal was where Nick went to make some notes for their talks in the park. He did find the entry for his birthday to be particularly interesting.

Monday, April 19, 1971: Called PIAA district commissioner, Wendell Hopkins, about the game on Friday night. He asked for a lunch meeting since he didn't want to discuss anything on the phone at his office. Immediately, I suspected that what I heard from Sal was true. During lunch he told me that the Preston people wanted another shot at Weston, so they tried to "engineer" a certain outcome. The refs were in on the "fix". I thanked him for his time and candor; and explained that our meeting never happened (he understood). He asked what I might do. I told him the less he knew the better (he understood). I asked him for a favor: the two refs need to be removed from doing any more games above the level of youth rec or elementary school basketball. He understood that I would handle the rest. Later: my brothers, sisters, nieces, and nephews meet at Pilleggio's for my birthday. Life is good!

Jordan again skimmed the next several pages and found where Nick mentioned Sam's death in 1978 and

Nick's subsequent inheritance of the business. He also found the entries associated with Gordon's passing in the early 1990s and when Nick decided to retire and move to Middleboro around the same time. The last significant entry was his disappointment that none of his family wanted to run the business empire that he had helped create and expand. Jordan learned that Nick's many business enterprises were sold off one by one, and the proceeds well invested.

After taking a break for lunch Jordan pressed on with his reading. He came upon some additional significant revelations.

Tuesday, October 19, 1999: Finally able to convince the last city council member to vote for the creation of a new park. Needed it to be unanimous. Not sure why it has taken five years to get this done, but it was worth it. Signed over the deed for the land to the City of Middleboro this afternoon. (Legally sold it for $1.) Very sorry to have ruined some political careers along the way, just can't understand why they would oppose it. I feel the park will benefit the people, first and foremost, and also, the city in many ways. Eventually, I see businesses springing up all around it. Time will tell. Hope I live to see it. Two contingencies: (1) It can never be linked to me in any way, and (2) It must be named 'Parc de Gisele'. I'll miss her every day, forever.

Jordan had suspected the park's name for some time. He felt very bad for Nick that he had lived 75 years without the love of his life, and only knew her for a few short months. He now understood why Nick sat on his bench for hours in the park that he had created as a tribute to Gisele.

Wednesday, September 19, 2018: Dr. Raul Vishnavi gives me the bad news about an aortic aneurysm. Will seek additional opinions. It's a sad realization to know that you're a ticking time bomb, but it makes you enjoy every day you have left to the fullest.

Jordan had known the cause of Nick's death, but he didn't know how long Nick was carrying that news around with him. He marveled that Nick never wore it on his sleeve and was always happy to see him and spend his precious last days with him.

Friday, April 19, 2019: The happiest and saddest day of my life . . . my 96th birthday. Today I find out that I have a son that I never knew about, until today. Ironically, today is his 74th birthday, and his name is Nicolas. I'm stunned, to say the least, but very happy to find this out before I die and never know. The sad part is that his mother, my love, Gisele, died right after he was born. I would have given my life for her to have lived and raised Nicolas, but alas, it wasn't to be.

Jordan read on and found the entries of Nick's trip to France to meet his family and the moving commemoration of the 75th anniversary of D-Day. Nick didn't dwell on it but remarked that after seeing what his allied brothers had to face when they landed on the beaches of Normandy, he was extremely proud of them and very thankful that he wasn't called upon to storm the beach.

He also mentioned the manicured cemeteries and moving ceremonies attended by his brothers-in-arms.

Other entries detailed the very emotional experience it had been for him to meet his son and his long-lost family. Nick wrote how he delicately explained the love affair between Gisele and himself and how he wished things to have been different. He knew they all understood, and he wrote that they conveyed their sympathies to him for losing Gisele before they had a chance to make a life together.

The last significant entry that Jordan found related to Nick and Tony's meeting with Richard at the Petersburg Federal Prison. Jordan was surprised to learn that they drove down and back on a Sunday to explain to Richard what Nick wanted him to do to correct the problem he created for the hard-working people of Middleboro by stealing their money. It further explained the anonymous note that his sister, Jackie, had received in the mail explaining how sorry Richard was for the pain and suffering he caused her and their children. Jordan knew that Jackie accepted Richard's apology, but she could never trust him again, and ultimately, that led her to file for divorce.

One month after the meeting in the lawyer's office where Nick's will was read and his wishes for his assets were made known, Jordan and Mary were in the park finishing a training session for their upcoming marathon. They had just completed one of their long runs and were now going to Perk Place for something to eat. Since it was a beautiful day, they decided to enjoy outside dining and sat at the same table where they had had their first breakfast together.

As usual, while they were sitting and eating their breakfast, Jordan took the opportunity to survey the park. In the distance, he could see what appeared to be a circle of kids with two combatants in the middle. He watched for a few seconds, then saw a police car pull up. Out came two policemen. One was particularly huge. Jordan immediately recognized Tony DePalma.

Jordan excused himself and started to trot over there to see if he could be of any assistance. As he got to the other side of the street, he noticed an elderly gentleman sitting on Nick's bench. What threw him was that the guy was wearing a hat just like the one Nick typically wore. Jordan couldn't resist. He walked up to the man, and when he got close enough to see his face, Jordan's knees buckled, and he screamed, "Nick!"

Mary, who was watching Jordan, could see and hear what had just transpired. She gathered up their belongings and cleaned up their table before sprinting across the street and up to Jordan. When she got there, she too was shocked to see a younger Nick look-a-like. Jordan regained his composure and said, "Excuse me, sir, but you look exactly like a friend of mine who passed away a few weeks ago."

The man on the bench replied with a very heavy French accent, "That would be my father, Nick Marinelli. I'm his son, Nicolas Bergeron. It's a pleasure to make your acquaintance." He stood up, tipped his hat to Mary, took her hand and kissed it, then shook Jordan's hand.

By that time Tony and his partner had broken up the fight, and Tony was heading in their direction. Once he arrived, he greeted both Mary and Jordan, and said, "I see you've met Nick's son, Nicolas." He then thanked Nicolas for calling him and giving him a heads-up on the fight in the usually tranquil Parc de Gisele.

Jordan asked Nicolas if he and Mary could have a few minutes of his time. Nicolas agreed, of course. During the subsequent conversation, Nicolas revealed that he had just arrived in Middleboro because he wanted to see where his father lived, and he wanted to meet some of his father's friends. Fortunately, Nick's condo hadn't been sold yet, so Nicolas was able to spend as much time as he liked there. He further explained that he would eventually make it to Pennsylvania to visit the rest of his relatives at a family reunion and that Tony had agreed to make the trip with him.

Jordan and Mary talked with Nicolas for over an hour. They eventually let him get back to his peaceful park gazing, but not before inviting him to dinner that evening and their wedding on the Friday after Thanksgiving. Their honeymoon would be a river cruise on the Seine to include Paris, Normandy, the French countryside, and a visit with the Bergerons.

The End

CPSIA information can be obtained
at www.ICGtesting.com
Printed in the USA
LVHW022230150721
692785LV00011B/1063